**"Katie, go back in**

A car suddenly careened up onto the sidewalk. would plow right into them. Brayden drew his gun and fired into the windshield, but the car didn't slow. He spun to the side and fell, rolling several times before he smacked into the brick side of the store.

Brayden scrambled to his feet. The car was empty now, front end mashed from the impact...and Katie was gone. "Call the local police," he yelled at Charlie.

Ella sprinted to the fenced alley between the shop and the building next to it, barking for all she was worth. The K-9 must be following Katie. He took off in pursuit. As he, too, rounded the corner, he saw Ella chasing them, Katie a few steps ahead of the man who had taken her. She turned to look back, eyes huge with fear. As she did so, she stumbled and went down.

"Stop! Alaska State Trooper!" Brayden yelled.

*USA TODAY* Bestselling Author

# Dana Mentink

## and

*New York Times* Bestselling Author

# Shirlee McCoy

# Arctic Rescue

2 Thrilling Stories

*Yukon Justice* and *Blizzard Showdown*

LOVE INSPIRED SUSPENSE
INSPIRATIONAL ROMANCE

Special thanks and acknowledgment are given to
Dana Mentink and Shirlee McCoy for their contribution
to the Alaska K-9 Unit miniseries.

# LOVE INSPIRED®

## INSPIRATIONAL ROMANCE

Recycling programs
for this product may
not exist in your area.

ISBN-13: 978-1-335-47599-2

Arctic Rescue

Copyright © 2024 by Harlequin Enterprises ULC

Yukon Justice
First published in 2021. This edition published in 2024.
Copyright © 2021 by Harlequin Enterprises ULC

Blizzard Showdown
First published in 2021. This edition published in 2024.
Copyright © 2021 by Harlequin Enterprises ULC

For questions and comments about the quality of this book, please contact us
at CustomerService@Harlequin.com.

Love Inspired
22 Adelaide St. West, 41st Floor
Toronto, Ontario M5H 4E3, Canada
www.LoveInspired.com

**Printed in U.S.A.**

# CONTENTS

**Dana Mentink** is a nationally bestselling author. She has been honored to win two Carol Awards, a HOLT Medallion and an RT Reviewers' Choice Best Book Award. She's authored more than thirty novels to date for Love Inspired Suspense and Harlequin Heartwarming. Dana loves feedback from her readers. Contact her at danamentink.com.

Visit the Author Profile page at
LoveInspired.com for more titles.

# YUKON JUSTICE

Dana Mentink

What shall we then say to these things?
If God be for us, who can be against us?
—*Romans* 8:31

To those first responders and their families.
Thank you for being the hands and feet of Jesus.

# ONE

The young reindeer nuzzled Katie Kapowski's palm with velvet lips, pawing the ground uneasily as nighttime settled around them. The animal was too thin, with an Alaskan winter closing in.

"It's okay, Sweetie. We'll get your mama back." Anger at Uncle Terrence burned in her stomach. The baby reindeer was suffering since Terrence had stolen his mother, Lulu, from the Family K Reindeer Ranch. At least the rest of the small herd had kept a close eye on Sweetie. Reindeer, above all else, were a family-oriented species. People should be so devoted.

Katie felt her own quiver of uncertainty at her return to the ranch. The job she'd left behind for a week pulled at her, assistant to Alaska K-9 Unit Colonel Lorenza Gallo and the group of elite state troopers along with their highly trained dogs. How hard she'd worked to get there. She was accustomed to the sleek Anchorage office, her multiple computer screens and a constant bustle of activity. But now she'd exchanged her stylish slacks and low heels for jeans and grimy work boots, auburn hair caught in a hurried ponytail. No professional polish required on a ranch near Palmer, Alaska, a town of barely seven thousand people, thirty-seven miles from the K-9 unit headquarters.

Goose bumps prickled along her neck. She whirled around. Nothing was there, only a twig borne by the autumn wind. The ranch was a broad sweep of flat pasture that lost itself into the neighbor's forested property to the west. The Frontier River defined the eastern property line. Isolated and wild. The quiet made her jumpy. The older animals shifted, intricate antlers highlighted by the setting sun. Reindeer were the only members of the deer species where the females sported antlers as well as the males. "Girl power," she whispered to a nearby female. "Wear those antlers proudly."

Katie stroked the baby reindeer's wiry fur in an effort to soothe them both. Was the animal also hearing noises? Or perhaps he was uneasy about the recent abduction. Three of the precious rescued animals had been stolen over the last few months. The Alaska K-9 team had recovered one, but Thunder, the male, and Sweetie's mom, Lulu, were still missing. Katie's worry grew every day that they were not found.

Why steal reindeer to get back at Aunt Addie? It was still so hard to believe the culprit was her own uncle. Katie hadn't even known of Terrence's existence until the K-9 team found DNA that proved the perpetrator was a relative. Aunt Addie had no choice then but to come clean about her estranged brother. Still, stealing reindeer to punish his sister for some perceived slight?

Could someone really be so juvenile? None of it made any sense to Katie.

*Oh, Aunt Addie. Why couldn't you have told me sooner?* she thought. Things with her aunt hadn't exactly gone smoothly since Katie's temporary return. Her aunt was still the same surly, stubborn woman who'd raised her from the age of ten, even less likely to filter her comments now that she was approaching sixty. Tact and finesse were unknown concepts in Addie's world.

"No one tells me how to run my ranch," she'd said. "I'm not changing a single thing, even if my brother has turned up to harass me. He's a cruel-hearted louse. Always has been."

Addie was doubly stressed with Terrence bent on not only ruining the ranch but also sabotaging the annual Christmas Fair looming in two months. So, yes, Katie knew her aunt had good reason to be short-tempered. But it didn't help that her outbursts had caused both her regular ranch hands to quit. Blaze was no loss, since he'd been stealing petty cash, but Gary had been a steady worker who'd endured one tongue-lashing too many from Addie. Now, with virtually no help, two hundred and fifty acres of Alaskan wilderness and a herd of twenty-three rescued reindeer to tend to, things were getting downright desperate.

Which meant, whether her aunt wanted to admit it or not, she needed Katie's help. Perhaps she could set a few things in order during her week away from the office without a major blowup with Aunt Addie.

A leaf scuffled over the top of her muddy boots, startling her. Her sideways movement subsequently alarmed Sweetie, who edged back to the comfort of his reindeer sisters.

*Relax, Katie*, she told herself. Addie was back at the main house. Law enforcement drove by on regular checks of the property, including Trooper Brayden Ford. An image of him popped into her mind along with the ever-present tension. Ridiculous. It didn't matter now that he'd almost cost her a position with the Alaska K-9 Unit in their Anchorage office. And, certainly, he must know she had not meant to humiliate him when she told him the truth about his girlfriend Jamie, though it proved mortifying. Water under the proverbial bridge, right? Still, she wished it was anyone but him patrolling her aunt's ranch at the moment.

Her eyes drifted upward. The October moon hung low in the inky sky and she sighed appreciatively as she breathed in the cold, scented with the musk of the animals gathered in the pasture pen and the meager remnants of the willow leaves they'd finished devouring. The lighter fur of their chests glimmered against the darkness. So quiet here, so peaceful, except for the ever-present drone of the mosquitoes. Nights like these made it hard to imagine why anybody, even Addie's disgruntled brother, would want to harm the ranch.

Why such covetousness over a place that existed purely to care for rescued reindeer? The ranch barely covered expenses, let alone made a profit. Not exactly a money factory. She said a quiet good-night to the animals. The gate squealed as she closed and secured the holding pen.

Something snapped in the distance. She tensed.

If Terrence was still bent on ruining the Family K, maybe he wasn't deterred by the trooper's attention. But the noise could have been anything, a rock tumbling from the bank into the Frontier River, a moose foraging for a snack, an elk, a bear... It was certainly *not* her uncle. She would spot him coming from way off since there was no cover to speak of.

Her phone pinged with an incoming call. Startled, she thumbed it on. "Hello?"

"It's really dark out here." The voice was a deep baritone.

She swatted a mosquito trying to settle on her windbreaker. "Very." Picturing Brayden and his big Newfoundland dog, Ella, made her sag with relief. She was grateful he had not witnessed her panicky behavior. It probably made her seem even more like a kid than the freckles splashed across her nose. And she certainly didn't want to give him any more reason to think her less than competent.

"Finishing up my security check," he said. "Everything's okay except Ella ate the bologna sandwich I was saving for dinner."

She could not restrain a smile. Ella, his highly trained underwater search-and-rescue canine, was a menace to all unsecured food items. She was grateful that Brayden and the other K-9 team members had been trying to help unearth the ranch saboteur. They had plenty on their hands already, including hunting down the murderous groom and best man who had framed the would-be bride, Violet James, who was currently in hiding to protect her unborn baby. With such an important case to tend to, she was doubly grateful that Brayden was checking up occasionally. Still, it would be easier if it was another officer, *any* other officer. Maybe she wouldn't feel so hesitant around someone else. There was just too much distrust between them. Still, though, the man needed a meal, and as Katie's mother used to say, "Anyone in my vicinity won't leave hungry unless they want to."

"Sorry about your dinner, Brayden. If you come by the main house, I'll fix you a peanut butter and jelly sandwich."

He sighed. "I guess I can't hope for bologna from a vegetarian."

"No, but I can offer some amazing tofu if you'd rather, with garlic and spices. You won't even miss the meat." She could not resist the gibe.

"I'll stick with the PB and J."

She was about to respond when several of the reindeer twitched, then bolted to the far side of the pen to huddle together. All of them were stiff with anxiety, ears pricked. They'd heard something she hadn't. But how could she explain it to Brayden without sounding like a scared kid? Bad enough she was twenty-four to his thirty-two and the one who had thrown the spotlight on his fickle girlfriend. It was *not* the time to add paranoia to that list. She must have remained silent for a beat too long.

"What's wrong, Katie?" he asked, suddenly stone-cold serious.

"I'm not sure. I'm near the pasture pen. I thought I heard something..." But there was nothing in the moonlight except the sprawling flatland, stubbled with wild grasses and the occasional clump of fireweed. "It's quiet now. It must have been my imagination."

He was all business now. "I'm driving down the river access road. I'll meet you at the gate."

"But there's probably no reason to—" Her sentence was cut short by distant shouting, followed by a shrill scream.

"The dock," she blurted into the phone. "It's Aunt Addie!"

"I'm on my way."

She kept the connection active, racing out of the pasture gate and securing the complicated latch system behind her with shaking fingers. Addie had been working on her computer in the main house not a half hour ago. Yet the scream had originated from the dock that jutted over the Frontier River. Had her aunt been out for a walk and fallen? Or was it something more sinister?

Katie's feet pounded as she charged across the grass and over the dirt access road, avoiding the mud as best she could. No sign of Brayden's vehicle yet. Another scream.

She shouted into the phone, "Addie's in trouble, Brayden. Help!"

Not waiting for an answer, she raced on. Grit from the road ground under the soles of her mud boots. The dock finally came into sight. She caught her aunt's silhouette, the sheen of her silvered brown hair glinting in the gloom. One slender arm was outstretched as if she was trying to ward off a blow, but there wasn't anyone else there, as far as Katie could see. She thought she heard a pop over the roar of the water. *A gunshot?* Addie jerked as if she'd been struck and toppled backward off the dock.

Instinct overrode all other inputs. Heedless of anything except saving her aunt, Katie made it to the edge in three strides and dived in feetfirst. She had grown up on the ranch since her parents were killed. She knew every inch of the place, especially the riverbed. This offshoot of the Frontier River that branched and meandered shallowly in most places was deep near the dock.

And *frigid* with snowmelt from the surrounding Chugach Mountains no matter what the season.

On impact, the freezing water stripped her of breath and turned her muscles into knots as she sank. The heavy boots she'd been wearing immediately filled with water and became anchors that dragged her toward the bottom. Why hadn't she thought to shake them off before she'd jumped in?

Gasping in shock, she fought off momentary paralysis. She freed her feet from the boots, kicked hard and propelled herself to the surface. Dashing the water from her eyes, she turned in a tight circle. There was no sign of her aunt anywhere. Nor was there anyone else. Had she imagined the gunshot? Panic roiled through her. Addie was tough as nails but she was small-framed, like Katie, and had been recovering from bronchitis, which had sapped her normal energy. The river could suck her away and snuff out her life in a matter of moments.

"Aunt Addie!" she shouted, treading water. Her arms were already numb and she was beginning to lose feeling in her legs. Flying insects danced across the choppy surface as the dark eddies of water rolled and curled over themselves. She felt a presence on the dock. Hope sparked inside her… It must be Brayden and Ella. She opened her mouth to call out to them until she realized her grave mistake.

It wasn't Brayden. A figure stepped clear of the shadows for the first time. She recognized the body type, long and lean, the slightly bowlegged stance so like her aunt's.

Her long-lost uncle, Terrence Kapowski.

Then her brain registered the other fact. He was holding a gun.

The sound she'd heard had indeed been a bullet, aimed at her aunt.

"Uncle Terrence," she yelled. "I'm Katie, your niece. Please…" Her request trailed off.

Terrence's expression was blank in the eerie light, but his steady grip on the pistol did not waver.

It was dreamlike, her uncle standing there against the pewter sky, the gun pointed at her, a small and deadly circle of gray. She saw more of the family resemblance visible in the determined line of his jaw, the narrow chin so like her aunt's.

So like her own.

"Uncle Terrence," she shouted again.

He cocked his head as if the sound of his name confused him. "You think you're going to get it?"

"Get what?" she asked, teeth chattering.

"The ranch. You can't have it. Not Addie, not you. I'm their only son."

"No one wants to take anything from you," she tried telling him.

"And no one will." He took a step closer. "I'll see you both dead first."

Her brain could still hardly process the facts. Terrence had been trying to kill Addie, who was now lost in the water, perhaps already dead.

Now he meant to do the same to her.

She watched helplessly as he took aim, ready for the kill.

Brayden was out of the vehicle and running for the dock. Ella lumbered after him, black fur blending with the gloom as the last remnants of sunlight surrendered. There was a man on the dock whom he recognized from the photos. Terrence Kapowski. Terrence immediately sprinted for the bushes.

"State trooper," Brayden shouted. "Stop or I'll shoot." The man skidded down the bank, vanishing into the darkness. Ella barked furiously, her deep woof echoing across the water.

*"Brayden!"* The scream was barely audible over Ella's racket and the sound of the rushing water.

He raced to the edge of the dock. Frantically he scanned the river for any sign of Katie or Addie. "Katie," he thundered. "Where are you?"

Katie's head bobbed up to the surface, her face a pale glimmer in the tumult. "My aunt's been shot."

Again he scanned behind him, under the dock, along the bank. Had Terrence found a hiding place, waiting to unleash more gunfire? Control the shooter or get the women out of the water? Muttering a prayer that he was making the right choice, he stripped off his gun belt and cell phone. Ella was already dancing in eagerness on the edge of the dock.

"Find," he told her. She would normally do her job from the bank or the deck of a boat, but nothing about this was normal. Addie, he prayed, was still alive. If she was, Ella would find her. The K-9 charged off the edge of the dock, cannonballing into the river. Brayden followed suit.

The cold slammed into him as he hit the surface feet-first. He swam immediately to Katie.

"I'm okay," she said, waving him off. "We have to find Addie."

But she was shuddering with cold, her lips dark, which meant the onset of hypothermia could be moments away. He grasped her forearm. "Get out of the water. Ella will locate Addie."

She ignored him. "I know this river. It will carry her toward the far bank. She's unconscious. We don't have time." She pulled away and swam farther out.

"Katie," he started.

"I have to find her." Katie's tone was laced with panic.

A splash from several feet away jerked their attention. He exhaled in relief. Ella had indeed found Addie. "Good girl, El. Bring her to shore."

Wasted breath. Ella knew what to do. She always did.

Katie started toward her aunt, but Brayden stopped her. "Trust the dog. We need to get you out right away."

Addie was floating on her back, eyes closed. Ella

grabbed her by her shirt collar and began towing her toward the bank. Addie's weight was no match for the muscular Newfie. The dog's webbed paws cleaved the water effortlessly. He turned his attention back to Katie, but her eyes were riveted to her aunt. Before he could offer any assistance, she was swimming hard toward shore.

He followed suit, scanning for any sign that Terrence might still be lying in wait. He'd radioed for an ambulance and his fellow troopers as soon as he'd heard the first gunshot. Two were close by—they'd already be en route along with the local cops—but it would take a good thirty minutes for anyone else to get there from their Anchorage base. The ambulance would arrive much sooner, he hoped.

Brayden slogged out of the water at the graveled portion of the bank where Ella had deposited Addie and begun to lick her face. Katie dropped to her knees and put her cheek next to her aunt's mouth.

The look she turned on Brayden made his stomach drop.

"She's not breathing," Katie whispered.

"Ella, watch," he said. The big dog shook the water from her thick coat and sat up, nose twitching as she sampled the air. She was not an attack dog, but if Terrence tried to get close again, Brayden felt confident she would alert him with a bark. It was that same bark that proved maddening at three in the morning, but now he was grateful for it.

Katie had already started rescue breathing, thanks to the training Colonel Gallo insisted every member of the department receive. He took over. "Try to find the bullet wound and stop the bleeding."

After a quick exam, Katie stripped off her jacket and pressed it to her aunt's shoulder.

He clasped his hands together and began to administer compressions, alternating with respirations.

After several cycles, they stopped to assess. Addie remained cold and lifeless.

"Come on, come on," he whispered. "Breathe."

Were they going to lose her? Katie's distraught expression told him she was entertaining the same horrible thought.

He started in on another round of CPR.

But Addie's chest remained still as the Alaskan night.

"Aunt Addie," Katie entreated. "Please don't leave me."

He added his silent plea to hers as he launched into more compressions.

# TWO

Brayden's arms flexed in regular motion as he kept up the compressions for another series. Water poured from Addie's mouth until her lungs cleared.

Katie's limbs were rubber and she was trembling badly as she sought a pulse. "I'm not sure. I'm shaking too much."

Brayden checked Addie's neck. The seconds rolled by in torturous slow motion. "I got it," he said. "A heartbeat."

With a flutter of hope, Katie put her cheek to her aunt's lips. "She's breathing."

They watched and monitored with painful attention while she maintained the pressure on her aunt's bullet wound. Brayden left just long enough to retrieve a pair of blankets from his vehicle, one to put over Addie and another that he draped over Katie's shoulders. They huddled there shivering, eyes fixed on the woman, until the ambulance arrived and a cop directed the medics to take over.

Katie noticed two other officers who arrived on scene. Troopers Poppy Walsh and Helena Maddox quickly listened to Brayden's rundown, their two dogs tense with anticipation. Ella greeted her canine coworkers with an enthusiastic tail wag.

"We'll see if we can track Terrence," Poppy said, snapping a long leash on her Irish wolfhound. "I'll check the riverbank."

Brayden spoke through chattering teeth. "Not alone."

Helena flashed a smile. "Nope. Luna and I have her back." Helena patted the sleek Norwegian elkhound sitting obediently at her side.

"So I don't need to tell you to exercise extreme caution?" he said.

"Affirmative," Helena retorted in a sassy tone. "You don't."

"There's a section of the bank where the water runs shallow," Katie said. "It forms sort of a cave. There are a couple places like that where he could be hiding. Please... I know Brayden doesn't have to say it, but I do. Be careful. My uncle..." It almost hurt to call him that. "He would have murdered us."

Both women nodded. "Take care of your aunt," Poppy told her. "We'll report if we find anything." She glanced at the horizon. "There's a storm rolling in, so we'd better be quick."

Katie watched Addie being eased onto a stretcher and loaded into the ambulance. The adrenaline was beginning to pass, leaving her in a daze. It was unreal, what had just happened. *Sickening.* Her kin, her family member, had tried to kill her. She went dizzy with the shock of it.

Brayden took her hand. "Let's get you into the car.

We'll stop at the house and you can put on some dry clothes before I drive you to the hospital."

The hospital. Of course that was where they would be going next. Because Addie had been shot. Would she die? Through a haze, she saw Ella stand and shake water from her voluminous coat. On impulse, she knelt and cradled the dog's enormous head in her hands. "Thank you, Ella, for rescuing my aunt."

The K-9 licked at a strand of Katie's sodden hair.

She turned to Brayden. "And thank you, too."

Brayden shrugged. "Ella did the real work. She loves any excuse to get in the water. Come on now."

He opened the rear door of his SUV for Ella and the front for Katie. Then he handed her his coat to throw around her since the blanket was soggy, an Alaska State Trooper emblem emblazoned on the front. "D-don't you need it?" she asked.

"I'll change into a dry uniform at the house." He cranked up the heat. "Besides, I'm very rough and tough and manly and all that. My blood is naturally warm," he managed through chattering teeth.

Amazingly, she felt her mouth curl into a smile, and a tiny laugh escaped—a giggle, of all things. "Of course. I should have realized that."

Quiet settled between them as he drove. The blackness of the night seemed to swallow everything until they pulled up the graveled drive of the house. Hurriedly, she raced to the guest room and threw on another set of clothes, a windbreaker and tennis shoes. She found Brayden emerging from the downstairs bathroom in a dry uniform.

"Ready?"

Was she? She swallowed the panic and nodded.

Back on the road, she wondered what they would find at the hospital. She relived the pop of the gunshot, her aunt's scream, the weapon aimed at her forehead. It came back to her like a sledgehammer blow. Aunt Addie had been *shot* and might not survive. In one moment, Katie's life might be stripped of the woman who had taken her in after the death of her parents. That had been completely unexpected, too. One moment they were alive and the next they were gone. If Aunt Addie died, Katie would be all alone in the world.

Without warning, she was sobbing, tears running in rivulets down her cheeks. Gulping in deep breaths, she tried to stem the tide, but she could do nothing but wrap her arms around herself and cry, wishing the darkness would swallow her up.

She felt the car slowing, and the next thing she knew, Brayden had pulled off the road and stopped. He went around to the passenger side and opened the door, unbuckling her seat belt and pulling her into his arms. His skin was warm now, his spare clothes smelling of a recent laundering.

She detested being like this in front of him. It was humiliating to be so out of control, yet she simply could not stop. Choking gasps escaped her and she cried, "I don't want to lose her like my parents." The words bubbled out in a rush of misery. The old wound had torn open again, unleashing fresh agony.

Brayden hugged her close and pressed his cheek to the top of her head. "It's going to be okay." And to her

surprise, he said a gentle prayer, asking God to inter-
cede for Addie and for Katie's own peace and protection. Her anxiety diminished and soon she was able to
breathe regularly. She pressed her face against his broad
chest, delaying the inevitable rush of embarrassment
that was sure to follow. Just for a moment, she allowed
herself to accept the comfort he offered, the relief from
her terror of the "what-ifs."

He moved her to arm's length. His green gaze peered
at her so intently, her face flushed hot. Here she was,
crying like an overwrought child all over Brayden Ford.
And hadn't he voted during her oral board examination
to "not hire" her because he found her too young, too
inexperienced for this line of work, too...*emotional*, as
she'd accidentally seen on the note sheet? If Lorenza
Gallo hadn't overridden his no vote, she would never
have gotten the job.

She straightened and swiped at her eyes with the back
of her hand. "I'm sorry. How embarrassing."

He didn't smile. "Not embarrassing. *Human.* You're
afraid for your aunt. You've just been through something awful."

She cleared her throat and tried to push the sodden
hair away that had escaped the ponytail, but her fingers
wouldn't cooperate.

Gently, he reached out and smoothed the strand for
her, tucking it behind her ear.

"There," he said. "Picture-perfect."

*Perfect.* That was a good one. She hiccuped, looked
away, fiddled with her jacket. "I'm okay now. Can we
keep going?"

"Of course," he said, guiding her back to the vehicle, where Ella still snoozed in the back seat.

Cheeks still burning, she tried to explain. "My parents were killed in a wreck when I was ten, along with my unborn brother. I came to live with Addie on the Family K, which I am sure was not what either one of us wanted." The words would not stop spilling out. "She was strict, brusque and no-nonsense, and it took me such a long time to get used to it. My mom was the exact opposite, warm and charming. She made me little notes in my lunch bag and drew faces on my bananas." She swallowed hard at the memory.

Surprisingly, he looked genuinely interested. "So Aunt Addie had big shoes to fill?"

Katie sighed. "Addie never signed up to be my mother, or anyone else's, but she sacrificed for me, did the best she could. I remember she helped me finish a fourth-grade project about reindeer. There was a parent-night presentation and I had no one to bring, of course. My aunt not only came, but she trailered a reindeer to the school parking lot for a sort of show-and-tell. The kids were wowed." She felt tears threaten again. "When I think that she might not make it…"

He reached over and squeezed her hand. "One thing I've learned in this business, Katie, is that nothing is over until God says it is."

That surprised her. "Anyway, thank you." She tugged at her necklace, trying to still her nerves. Twisting the enameled pendant always calmed her and she was relieved it hadn't come loose in the river.

"I recognize that flower," he said, pointing to her pendant. "I've seen it before."

"It's a forget-me-not, a Christmas gift from my mother. I never take it off."

"Alaska state flower, right?"

"Right."

"I earned a wilderness merit badge in Scouts, you know," he said with mock pride. "I know my way around wildflowers."

His cheeky grin lightened her spirit, as she figured he'd intended to do. She'd not seen this side of him and probably never would again. Extreme circumstances and all that, the same reason she was babbling her life story.

When they pulled into the parking lot, Brayden's phone rang. He answered. After a moment, he fell silent, listening intently before he thanked the caller. He disconnected.

She didn't have to ask if it was good news or bad. His frown said it all.

"Terrence got away," he said. "Storm's coming in tonight, so they'll work the area tomorrow after it has passed to see if they missed anything."

"Maybe he's gone. He might have decided to leave town." The words rang false even to her own ears.

*"I'll see you both dead first."*

Remembering his angry expression when he'd pulled the trigger, she knew he wasn't going anywhere until he got what he came for.

Brayden tapped his pencil on the notepad in front of him in the briefing room of the Anchorage-based K-9 team headquarters. He hadn't realized his fingers had been working on a project of their own until Hunter Mc-Cord nudged him in the ribs, his smile impish. "Stick with your day job."

"What?"

Hunter pointed. "You'll never make it as an artist. I did better drawings in preschool."

"Funny." He hadn't realized he'd been doodling a picture of a flower, and he noted with a start that it was a forget-me-not. Why was the state flower of Alaska on his mind?

Hunter fixed him with a blue-eyed stare. "Thinking about someone?"

"No," he said hurriedly. Hunter, above all people, should know Brayden wasn't seeing anyone since Jamie had shredded his heart. Hunter's own cop father had been killed by a shady girlfriend, and it had helped Brayden to know that he wasn't the only one blinded by love, or what he thought was love.

He remembered Katie's tentative smile. *"It's a for-get-me-not, a Christmas gift from my mother. I never take it off."* Funny. That constant twiddling, the nervous pacing, had given him the impression during that oral board interview eight months before that Katie was not sure of herself. But he'd been right then, to "not recommend" her during that interview, hadn't he? Others were more qualified, more seasoned in police procedure. His skin went clammy at the memory of what had happened three months after that...how she'd told him what he didn't want to hear about Jamie.

*"Is this your way of getting back at me for not rec-*

*ommending your hire?"* he'd demanded. *"You'd make stuff up about my girlfriend?"*

He still remembered the scarlet flush that instantly colored her face. Maybe it was the same hue that colored his when he realized later that she'd been telling him the truth.

"The doctors are confident that Addie Kapowski will recover."

He snapped back in time to hear his boss, Colonel Lorenza Gallo, finish with, "Katie is taking on the running of the ranch until her aunt can return."

Trooper Sean West grinned suddenly. "Plenty of reindeer in Nome, if Katie wants to add to the herd. They prefer the road to the tundra when it snows, and man, can they block the highway."

There was a ripple of laughter.

Lorenza continued. "I granted her request to extend her time off to an official leave of absence. I know we're stretched thin right now, so I'm making some private arrangements to ensure her safety. But I want to assign one of you as full-time point person on the Terrence Kapowski case." The colonel's silver coiffure was perfect, her posture tall and erect as she stared at him. "Brayden, that's you."

He blinked. "Me? I don't think…"

"Poppy and Maya are knee-deep in finding the Seavers."

The Seavers were a survivalist family proving hard to locate. Their team tech guru, Eli Partridge, was committed to finding them, particularly since it was his dying godmother's last wish. Brayden himself had found a trace of the off-grid family's presence in a cabin in the Chugach State Park, but the trail had ended there.

"And Gabriel's got a lead on Violet James," Lorenza added. "Time's getting short since she is approaching her due date. We've got people working multiple assignments and you're already on the Kapowski case since you and Ella were on scene last night. So, yes, I'm assigning you." Her eyebrow arched. "Unless you have some sort of compelling reason to refuse?"

*Compelling reason?* Only that he could hardly bear to look Katie in the face, and she no doubt felt the same. And the fact that she was as close to his boss as a granddaughter. Sighing, he scrubbed a hand across his jaw. And he was sure there were plenty other great reasons to stay far away from Katie that he could not bring to mind at the moment. "No, ma'am," he heard himself say. "I have no reason to refuse."

The colonel smiled a cat-in-the-cream grin. "That's what I thought. We can smooth out the details later." She turned to Gabriel, whose Saint Bernard sprawled at his feet. "Report on Wells and Dennis?"

Everyone perked up. Lance Wells and Jared Dennis were wanted in the murder of a tour guide and the attempted murder of bride-to-be Violet James, the pregnant woman who was now in hiding. The stakes were high and the thought of having Wells so close to Violet made everyone's pulse beat faster.

"Nothing new. Last sighting was in Anchorage, as you know," Gabriel said. "Worrying, since Violet was spotted here, too."

"Probably going for prenatal care, but we haven't been able to nail down where yet," Helena interjected.

Gabriel's mouth tightened. "We need to get Violet home safe and sound by Thanksgiving."

"I second that, since my darling fiancée has it in her heart for Violet to be her maid of honor at our Christmas wedding." Hunter smiled. "What's a wedding without your best friend?"

They did a round-robin sharing and discussed next steps. Brayden felt both frustrated and bewildered that he was now assigned full-time to the Terrence Kapowski case. Was he being diverted from the main action? Or especially trusted with someone who meant the world to the colonel? When the meeting wrapped, he slugged down a cup of coffee, which he managed to drip on his shirt before he popped into Lorenza's office.

She glanced at him over the top of her reading glasses. "You're wearing your coffee."

"Er, yes, Colonel. Sorry. Um, I wondered what you meant by private arrangements to protect Katie."

"I would have been disappointed if you hadn't come to ask, but before I get to that, let's just clear the air here. You don't want to work with Katie because she found out you didn't recommend her for the job. What's more, she tried to warn you about the woman you were dating, whom you ultimately wound up arresting, leaving you ashamed and humiliated."

He choked and felt his whole body go warm. "Uh, well, thanks for laying all that out so succinctly. I think those are two pretty compelling reasons why—"

"Not relevant,"

"It seems pretty relevant to me," he said hotly.

She put down her notebook. Her old husky, Denali, snored softly in the corner. Retired from duty, he was a fixture in the office building. The colonel's face softened. "I love Katie like the family I never had. She wouldn't ask for help and that's why I'm determined to give it to her. Until her aunt returns to full strength, she needs us." She paused. "She needs *you*."

"But..."

"Remember when you first got Ella and she couldn't walk down the street without jumping in every puddle from here to Nome? We got advice from various experts that we should wash her out and start you with another dog."

He nodded.

"You didn't do that, did you? You doled out treats and positive praise and worked with her until she got through it. Remember?"

"Yes." He couldn't figure where the colonel was going with this.

"I want someone around Katie who's like that— determined, dedicated, averse to failure..."

He opened his mouth to remind her any of the squad would fit the bill.

"And gentle," she added. "With a touch of the goofball."

*A touch of the goofball?* For the life of him, Brayden did not know what to say. Should he feel flattered? Put upon? Worried about messing things up? "I...uh..."

Lorenza looked as though she'd set the universe right. "Details are that I hired two private security guards to patrol the ranch on a daily basis." She held up a hand. "The money comes from my own pocket, of course. The property is too remote and too big for you to handle round the clock, plus you have other duties. The security guys will wait to hear from you. Figured you'd want to plan their routes personally."

He hesitated. But what was he supposed to do now? Pretend like his rocky past with Katie didn't matter?

"Did you want to say something, Trooper Ford?"

Did he? What excuse could he come up with to get out of this assignment? But the colonel was already looking at her paperwork again. "Addie will be in the hospital for a few days. She'll have protection there. If I know Katie, she'll be heading to the ranch as soon as possible. Do what's necessary to keep her safe."

He closed his mouth. "Yes, ma'am," he said, leaving the office and shutting the door behind him.

Ella sat on her haunches waiting for him in the hallway. Her eyebrows twitched as she regarded him, before a soft sigh ruffled her lips. "Do you think I'm a goofball, El?"

She swiped a wide pink tongue around her fleshy mouth and shook herself.

"You owe me, by the way," he said, bending to massage her neck. "The colonel doesn't know you still jump in puddles sometimes, and we're not even going to tell her about the case of the disappearing doughnuts from the staff room." Plans formed in his mind as he sauntered back with Ella through the office, heading for his SUV. *Check the security of the house, locks, windows, install motion detector lights. Design the most efficient routes for the security team...* He was so lost in thought, he almost bumped into Helena and Poppy.

"What's up?"

"We went back today to the riverbank when the storm let up," Helena said. "We found something."

A tickle of dread flickered in his stomach. "What?"

"A dry suit, some empty cans and a waterproof sleeping bag in one of the caves Katie told us about," Poppy told him gravely. "Terrence has been staying there, using it as a base of operations, I would imagine, analyzing the ranch layout. He might return when things simmer down, to finish what he started."

To murder Addie and Katie.

And right then, he knew the colonel had been right in giving him the assignment, because every muscle in his body snapped to attention. Brayden would not let anything divert him. He was a trooper, first and foremost, and he would do his job, no matter who the protectee was. "He's not going anywhere but to jail. Come on, El. We've got to see a lady about a reindeer."

# THREE

Katie's feet ached from pacing the hospital floors the night before. Now she was in her Anchorage apartment packing what she would need for her stay at the Family K, watering her plants and emptying the fridge of anything that would spoil.

These tasks did not quite keep her mind off the previous night's horror. Thinking about Aunt Addie lying lifeless on the dock made her go clammy all over. Brayden had sat awkwardly next to Katie at the hospital until the doctors assured her that the bullet had only penetrated the soft tissue of Addie's shoulder without impacting any major organs. Barring complications, her aunt was likely to recover fully, but it would be a long time before she was back to 100 percent.

He'd escorted Katie to her apartment, and she knew the local cops and some K-9 team members had driven by every hour or so to check that she was safely tucked away for the night.

Picturing Brayden and Ella circling her apartment made her feel simultaneously safe and skittish. He'd been so kind when she'd broken down, but her mortification rose every time she thought about snuggling up on his wide chest.

*You know how he views you.* And she wasn't anything like the tall, manicured, *reckless* woman he'd dated before. Looking back, she shouldn't have told him what she'd accidentally discovered about Jamie. But they were a family, Lorenza always said of her team, and what harmed one of them, harmed *all* of them. That "help" had backfired in a monumental way. She swallowed down a lump in her throat. Best not to think about it.

After pulling on a denim jacket and twisting her hair back into a clip, she waved at the local cop who had been parked outside her door since before dawn. At least it was not Brayden. The glorious morning made the horrifying incident with Terrence seem almost unreal, but the memory of it made her flesh crawl. Nothing was going to keep her from her aunt, even a murderous uncle.

Jaw set, she drove her Jeep to the hospital. All of her angst disappeared into a cloud of joy when the nurse told her Addie was awake and could have a visitor. Maybe she could allow herself to believe that Addie really was going to be all right. She nodded to the security guard stationed at her aunt's door.

Addie was pale and wan and looked so much older than she had the previous day. Deep lines grooved her forehead. An IV was attached to her arm and her wounded shoulder was heavily bandaged. She appeared to be sleeping.

"Good morning," Katie said softly.

Addie's eyes opened halfway. "Katie?"

She nodded.

Her aunt seemed relieved, the confusion clearing. "How are the babies?"

The *babies*…her reindeer. "They're fine. They were fed before… I mean…before Terrence showed up. The police drove by last night to check and everything was secure."

Addie shifted as if in pain. "I was stupid to go out to the dock, but it's always been my thinking place and I felt restless. I never dreamed I could be hurt on the Family K."

Katie hesitated for a few moments. "Can you tell me any more about Uncle Terrence?"

Addie flinched. "Don't call him that! He doesn't deserve to be your uncle."

Sensing her aunt had more to say, Katie stayed quiet.

"Terrence left home at eighteen, couldn't stand my parents' rules. He was always stubborn, hankering for an argument. I tried to find him when our parents passed. He didn't come for the funerals, though I posted notices in the paper thinking he'd see it. I did the same thing when your mother and father were killed." She scowled. "Why did I even try? After all, why would I expect him to care about our sister when he hadn't even shown his respect to our parents? *Stupid.* I never thought my brother, my own flesh and blood, would try to kill me." Addie paused. "And you. He would have murdered you, too."

Katie patted her arm. "Don't spend time thinking about that. You need to focus on healing."

Addie licked her dry lips, her gaze roving over Katie's face. "I wasn't a good aunt, was I? And I sure wasn't a great substitute mom, either."

Katie had never heard such talk from Addie. "You did your best. That's…"

Addie's jaw clenched. "Katie, I should have told you about Terrence, but I thought he'd vanished out of my life. I figured maybe he was dead. Good riddance since he was always a selfish, entitled jerk." She took a breath. "I saw his face there on the dock before he shot me, the way he spoke. He won't go away. He'll never quit. The best thing for you is to leave here, go somewhere safe where he won't find you." Her fingers squeezed Katie's arm so tight it hurt.

Katie kept her voice calm and controlled. "There would be no one to run the ranch if I left. I'll stay."

"I can't ask you to do that."

"You're not asking," Katie said.

Addie's face crumpled. Was it tears she saw in her aunt's eyes? Even at the funeral for Katie's parents Addie had not cried, just stood there as if she was carved from stone. "No. You have your own life to live. We'll have to find homes for the animals somehow. I'll sell the property when I can find a buyer." One crystal tear slid down her weathered cheek.

The Family K had been the hub of her aunt's world ever since Katie had known her. The only thing that made her smile was the reindeer. Katie had realized that, accepted it shortly after she'd come to live with Addie as a child. They'd tended the ranch together and that was how they connected. That single tear coursing down Addie's cheek washed away any misgivings in Katie's heart. In that moment she realized how much she loved her gruff, surly, single-minded aunt Addie. She'd never understood why God took her parents and her unborn brother in that crash, but she knew He'd not left her alone. Addie was right, she hadn't been much of a stand-in mom, but she'd done what she could, offered what she had, and Katie would do the same.

She cleared her throat. "Listen to me. You are not going to lose the ranch. I'm taking up the reins until you're better. It's my decision. I took time off from work. It's all arranged."

Addie pursed her lips as if she was struggling to keep from crying. "But…"

"It's settled," Katie insisted.

"Thank you," Addie breathed. Her aunt had never sounded so vulnerable before. "That means everything to me."

"You're welcome," she said, giving the other woman's hand a squeeze.

A shadow crossed over Addie's features. "But it's not safe. Terrence will find you, *hurt* you…"

"No, he won't."

Katie whirled to see Brayden standing in the doorway. Ella sat quietly at his side. "I'm not going to let your niece get hurt, ma'am. I've been assigned to make sure that doesn't happen."

*Assigned?* "But you've got other cases to work on," Katie protested. "What about—?"

"This one has risen to the top of the list," he said, cutting her off.

"So you'll look out for her?" Addie murmured, sagging in relief.

"Yes, ma'am. And we're going to arrest Terrence, too."

Katie looked at him, unsure what to say.

"I am glad you are feeling better, Ms. Kapowski. I'd smuggle you in some home-cooked food, but I've been told I am the worst cook in Alaska unless you want something grilled. That I can do." He turned his attention to her. "Katie, I'll be waiting in the hallway for you. Consider me your shadow." He did not smile as he turned away and marched out.

Her mouth went dry. "A shadow. Just what I need."

Addie's look went suddenly mischievous. "A very handsome shadow with a sense of humor. You two could…"

"No, we *couldn't*," Katie hurried to say, annoyed that she could feel a blush creeping up her neck. "We aren't compatible."

"How do you know until you try?"

Before Katie could set Addie straight, the woman launched into a set of directions. "The only way we're going to stay afloat is to hold that Christmas Fair. The planning meeting is on Friday. Everyone's already been invited. How can I leave that all up to you? I haven't even made the agenda yet."

"I won't tell you to relax, because I know you're not going to, so I'll just remind you that I'm very organized and I've been to the Christmas Fair every year since I was ten years old. I can do it, Aunt Addie. I'm sure the agenda hasn't changed much."

"But…" She winced in pain as she struggled to sit up higher.

"You've got a new phone since your other was damaged," Katie said firmly. "We'll have constant contact. I will call you if I need any clarification. You can text me if you think of anything that I might need to know. And you'll probably be home in a few days anyway, so you can take over the meeting."

A nurse came in. "I need to check vitals now, please."

Katie kissed the older woman's cheek. Addie gripped her arm, fingers rigid with intensity. "Be careful," her aunt whispered.

"I will." She forced a bright smile. "I've got a shadow, remember?" About that shadow… She'd be careful about the active threats, but extra vigilance would be necessary to keep her cool in front of Brayden Ford. She'd persevered in spite of him in the past and she would continue to do so now. Temporary partners. Settling on that descriptor put her on steady ground.

True to his word, Brayden drove behind Katie from the hospital back to the Family K. She tried to ignore his presence as she ticked off the massive to-do list in her mind. The reindeer needed to be cared for and fed, the agenda for the Christmas Fair meeting would have to be generated, the house cleaned and snacks prepared. She'd need to recruit help since Addie's two ranch hands were gone. Hopefully with a little sweet-talking she could persuade a local to help her with all that. And she had just the person in mind.

Her thoughts strayed to the two missing animals… Aunt Addie's "babies." Thunder, the big male, and Lulu.

Had Terrence stashed them somewhere to harass his sister? Killed the animals out of spite? The thought pained her as she pulled from Brighton Road onto the dirt access trail, temporarily bypassing the main house on her way to the pasture. Though she was hungry and her feet hurt, nothing could come before the care of the remaining reindeer.

She hurried to the pen, intending to examine them visually before opening the small holding area and freeing them into the vast pasture. Later, she would make sure they had an ample supply of alfalfa and willow leaves, but for the present, they were content to meander the sprawling property, nosing around. They were natural foragers, and their antlers enabled them to fork up lichen from under the Alaskan snows when winter blanketed the landscape. Until then, they'd eat leaves or grasses if available. There they were, outlined against a crystal-blue sky. What a sight. There was nothing more beautiful than a group of reindeer standing in pristine white snow, breathing puffs into the air.

Katie realized she considered the animals as her babies, too. The thought both pained and comforted her. Brayden and Ella joined her at the fence. Ella's nose twitched, but she did not seem excited to be so close to the reindeer. After all, there was no water at hand for her to splash in. "All present and accounted for?" Brayden said.

"Yes. Happy and healthy, as far as I can tell."

"What makes a reindeer happy?" he asked, helping to ease back the heavy gate.

The question surprised her. She pondered a moment.

"They're like people, I guess. They need shelter, food and each other."

"Social."

"Very." She looked at the animals filing out.

"What's that clicking noise?"

"Their hooves," she explained. "They have an ankle tendon that rubs over the bone when they walk. It makes a clicking sound, which helps them find each other in snowy conditions. That's where the song comes from about the reindeer up on the house top…click, click, click."

"Wow. I did not know that. Handy to have your own tracking device. Keeping the family together, right?"

"Only a few of them are related, but they've become a family anyway." She chewed her lip, thinking about the missing members of the herd.

"We'll find them," Brayden said quietly, as if he'd read her mind.

Was she that transparent with her thoughts? "I hope so. If they were hurt, it would devastate my aunt."

"And you, too."

She felt his eyes on her and she ducked her chin. "Yes, me, too. I called a man from Palmer, on the way over. His name is Quinn and he's out of work right now, so he was happy to be offered a job."

"I know him. Good guy," Brayden said. "He's got two kids and one on the way, so that's a win for everyone. Plus, he's former army, so he knows how to handle himself. He'll be a good roomie 'cause he doesn't mind dogs."

"Roomie?"

Brayden nodded. "Sure. Ella and I are sacking out in the bunkhouse. I'm your shadow, remember?"

The bunkhouse? Brayden would actually be staying on the property 24/7? Well, of course he would. She resisted an eye roll. "Right." She swallowed. "I'll, uh, make sure it's ready for you both."

"Don't lift a finger. It's fine however it is. I back-packed through New Mexico one summer a few years ago, and believe me, I learned how to be grateful for any kind of shelter that doesn't involve sleeping on the ground, especially where there are fire ants. You ever sleep on a fire-ant nest? Talk about a rude awakening."

He was chatty. Nervously so? She got some sort of satisfaction out of knowing that he wasn't exactly indifferent to her presence. She noticed him glancing over the terrain, out toward the dock. He was looking for signs of Terrence. Swallowing hard, she refocused on the business. "I've got to get their immunizations done. And I'd better get started on the phone calls about the Christmas Fair planning meeting."

"Can I ask a favor first?"

He needed a favor? From *her*? "Of course."

"I missed breakfast, and not to be pushy, but you did offer a peanut butter and jelly sandwich. I can fix it myself. Okay if I do that before you launch into the ranch agenda?" He added gently, "And I want to check over the main house real quick."

To make sure Uncle Terrence wasn't lying in wait?

A murderous uncle possibly lurking in the house and Brayden helping himself to the kitchen? She forced a light tone to match his. "Absolutely."

\* \* \*

Brayden figured the isolation of the Family K was both a danger and an asset. The open terrain would make it easy to spot an approaching vehicle, yet the riverbank and the surrounding forest provided excellent concealment. It would be tricky to patrol all of it, but he'd instructed the private security people to report in, and he felt better knowing Quinn would be on the premises, as well.

"So what do you think, Ella?" he called into the back seat. He'd rolled the window down so she could get her share of interesting smells. She happily slobbered on the glass as she took in the surroundings. Best police protocol was to have a K-9 crated in the back seat, but at one hundred and fifteen pounds, Ella did not fit comfortably into any cage. She was a completely relaxed dog unless she was around the water or Brayden became upset for some reason. Her fine qualities made up for the occasional food-snatching incident. The term "gentle giant" really did capture Ella's essence.

As they drove to the main house, he analyzed Katie's reaction to his announcement that he was going to occupy the bunkhouse. She was surprised, yes, but clearly not pleased. No wonder. He remembered the feel of her in his arms, fragile and strong at the same time. Why did the memory refuse to leave his mind? On the heels of that recollection, another flooded in.

*She needs us. She needs you*, the colonel had said.

He was used to being needed on a professional level, wasn't he? This was no different. *You're on assignment, that's all.* But why him…with her? Yes, all the other officers were busy, but surely someone could have switched roles. His ego began to chatter. Was he being shuttled aside? Had he missed out on the bridal-party investigation for this smaller protection duty? Yet, somehow, it didn't feel in any way like a small thing to be safeguarding Katie Kapowski. And if he failed... The colonel would bring in someone else, which would be a blot on his career, yes, but failure meant that Katie would suffer. A nasty scene from his past scrolled through his mind.

A hesitant Katie. *"Jamie's using you."*

*"What?"*

*"She was talking to some friends in the coffee shop. She said it was fun dating a good-looking cop, but that you were..."* She cleared her throat. *"...too old and straitlaced for a long-term relationship."*

Shock and embarrassment had flooded through him, quickly concealed behind anger. *"You must have misunderstood."*

*"No, I didn't. I'm sorry."*

*"Sorry? I don't think so. You're telling me this, why? To get back at me for your interview?"*

She'd flushed, turned on her heel, and that was it.

Things had gone from bad to worse after that with Jamie and he eventually realized Katie was telling him the truth, but he still figured he'd been right about her motive in revealing it to him. He'd hurt her, she believed, and she'd retaliated. The score was even. But it sure didn't feel like they were competing anymore, did it? Frankly, he wasn't sure what he felt except the strong desire to get the job done and leave the ranch as soon as possible.

They passed the small storage sheds and he added that to his tasks for the day. They would all need to be checked and secured. Mulling over the tactical aspects of the ranch security put him back on professional footing. Trooper stuff... That he could do. His boss was counting on him.

Katie hauled a small bag out of her car and headed for the front door while he freed Ella from the back seat. Brayden noted that the old building was clearly in need of some TLC. The cedar siding was warped in some places, and staining on the steep roof indicated some leakage might have occurred. Such was the nature of buildings in Alaska. Harsh weather contributed to never-ending repair needs. He doubted the ranch brought in much of a profit. It was truly a labor of love for Addie and now for Katie.

And there he was, staring at her again. Her hair shone almost coppery in the morning sunlight, her stride determined as she approached the front door. He was mentally admonishing himself for daydreaming when it hit him. *The door.* The old levered handle was turned down just slightly, as if the locking mechanism hadn't completely caught. Something was preventing it from shutting properly.

He bolted forward, shouting, "Katie, don't!" Ella barked at Brayden's frantic tone.

With her fingers still on the handle, Katie half turned. He grabbed her wrist and pulled her backward. As he did so, the door swung open. There was a tremendous crash. Something fell, scattering debris everywhere.

"Stay here with Ella," he commanded. Katie's eyes were wide as Brayden pushed through the door. The closed drapes left it gloomy, but there was enough light to make out the booby trap. A can of nails wedged above the door, waiting to fall when it was pushed open. It was heavy enough that it might have fractured her skull if he hadn't pulled her back in time.

He stood there, vision adjusting to the dim light, half crouched, listening.

Only one question remained.

Was Katie's murderous uncle hiding somewhere in the house, waiting to see if his booby trap worked? Gripping his revolver, Brayden eased step by step into the house.

Terrence wasn't going to vanish this time.

That was a promise.

# FOUR

Ella pressed close to Katie's side. They waited together, Katie's heart slamming against her ribs. She was alternately terrified and furious. This was her aunt's home, the only place where she'd felt secure after her parents died. The ranch was the sanctuary where Addie had helped her put the pieces of herself back together, and now it had been violated.

Good old Uncle Terrence? Had to be. Thinking about him possibly lying in wait for Brayden made her body ice over. Ella was agitated as well, whining slightly, gaze riveted on the open door. Minutes passed. Should she call for backup? Her thoughts branched in all directions, like lightning forking the tundra.

Footsteps made them both go tense. If it was Terrence, what would she do? Scream and run? Throw rocks or whatever else she could find at him? Stomach flipping, she waited. Brayden appeared in the doorway, holstering his weapon and carefully stepping around the debris. "Nobody inside."

She let out a breath she hadn't known she was holding. Gone, and still at large.

Brayden beckoned her. "Come inside through the garage. I've got Gabriel coming to help check for prints and photograph, and the security guard is driving the perimeter, but I don't think we'll find much. Terrence obviously set this all up and took off. If anything, he's watching from a distance."

All those trees on the neighboring property. She shivered.

Dutifully, Ella and Katie circled around to the garage so the booby-trap evidence could be photographed and prints taken. She noticed how Brayden waited until she was settled in a kitchen chair.

His brow furrowed as he clicked off his phone. In a few moments a man in a security outfit joined them. He was almost as tall as Brayden, but rail thin with a shining bald head.

"I'm Phil," he said, shaking Katie's hand. "Alex is my counterpart. I'm sorry about what happened. No sign of anyone on the main roads. Maybe he crawled up from the riverbank again?"

Brayden scowled. "I'll get a team on that. When Alex gets here for his shift, I'll fill him in. I'm going to install a camera on the house, but for now, let's increase the patrols around the riverbank and the forested area next to the north and south pens."

"Yes, sir," Phil said. "I'll start on that right now."

When the security officer left, Brayden started to prowl the kitchen. "I'll make you tea," he said.

"Thank you, but I'm okay, really."

Her words didn't seem to make a dent. "Tea is what people drink in times of crises, I'm pretty sure. I don't care for the stuff myself, but I recall after my parents split my mother must have felt cups of tea would make it all okay since she fixed it every time my sisters and I stayed with her. My folks had joint custody." He rooted around in the cupboard, knocking over a box of pancake mix.

He appeared filled with intense energy. Her hands were shaking, and her pulse was still rocketing. Patrols of the property? Hiding places along the riverbank? A forest full of places for Terrence to conceal himself?

It was almost too crazy to believe.

He was on to the next cupboard. "Where do you keep the tea bags?"

"Brayden?"

His voice was muffled by the cupboard. "Am I getting warm?"

"Brayden," she said again, a bit louder this time.

Now he looked at her. She pointed to a carousel in the corner that held individual pods. "We're coffee drinkers, not tea. And we have a machine, but I appreciate you working so hard at it."

He quirked a smile. "Ah. Well, then. Care for a cup of coffee?"

"If you'll have one." Had she sounded coy? She desperately hoped not. Talking to Brayden was chore enough. She'd never think about flirting. She was trying to conjure a follow-up comment when he sighed.

"I have never passed up a cup of coffee yet." He poured in water and busied himself with the procedure until he produced two steaming mugfuls.

"Gabriel's nearby, so he'll be here in a few." Brayden

added two spoonfuls of sugar and a packet of dried creamer to his drink. She wondered how he kept such a narrow waist if he doctored his coffee on a regular basis.

Katie let the warmth of the mug seep into her palms. She cleared her throat and said, "If you hadn't noticed the door was not shut properly, I'd be next to Aunt Addie in the hospital with a fractured skull or worse." A polite thank-you was all she'd meant, but the words made her eyes brim. "Why does Terrence hate me so much? We'd never even met before he held me at gunpoint."

"Because he doesn't know you. If he did, I can't see how he wouldn't like you."

His eyes were a mesmerizing iridescent green, and she found herself caught by the color and his sentiment. Brayden was being kind. That was all.

"You hated me," she said softly. "For telling you about Jamie."

His cheeks went red and he sank down at the table. "*Hate* is a strong word." His eyes found hers. "Why did you tell me about her, anyway? The truth."

Now it was her turn to shift in the chair. "I wasn't going to, but something changed my mind."

"What?"

Katie shrugged, withdrawing into her shell. "Not important."

He paused, perhaps to see if she would answer after all. "Anyway, you were right…about Jamie. I didn't believe you, but it wasn't long before it all came out. I was an idiot not to suspect. She wanted to talk about my job all the time, but not much of anything else. And she made excuses to bring her friends by to see me when

I was on duty, but I lost my allure when I was dressed in civvies. Plus, she got a good laugh out of my choice of movies and music and such. I guess I was probably the source of a lot of humor for her and her friends."

"I'm sorry."

His face grew pained. "Too bad we couldn't have ended things amicably, but that was out the window when I arrested her. She didn't take it well."

Katie tried to look surprised, but the gossip had spread like lightning throughout the force. She kept quiet and let him say it.

"She was driving under the influence with a car full of her young friends."

*Young friends.* One of the reasons he'd advised against hiring Katie. Too young and inexperienced. That opinion probably hadn't changed. The conversation was becoming *way* too personal. "Thank you for the coffee." She sipped from her mug. "Maybe your mom was on to something. Could be it doesn't matter that it's coffee or tea. Drinking something warm is medicinal."

"Mom always tried to fix everything. The divorce was the one thing she couldn't fix."

"How old were you?" she asked.

"Twelve."

"That's a hard age to have your family split up."

He sighed. "They both loved me, I know that, but I always got the feeling when I was pinballed between them that Dad took me out of duty, not the desire to spend time with me. Not ideal. Made me realize that a broken marriage is worse than no marriage at all."

A muscle ticked in his jaw. "Maybe that's why lately I don't seek out relationships, that and the Jamie fiasco."

"We all have our reasons."

He arched a brow. "You, too? I wondered why you and John didn't stick."

Of course he knew about her brief relationship with local attorney John Fitzgerald. Now her face was positively crimson, she was sure. "He is a good man, but we wanted different things."

"Like what?" He grimaced. "Wait. Nosy, right?"

"He's on the fast track to marriage."

"And you don't want that?" he murmured.

"Not right now."

"What *do* you want, Katie?"

She looked him in the eye when she answered. "I want to be good at my job, to prove that I can stand on my own."

"Not one for letting others hold your hand. I noticed that. To be honest, I thought it was standoffishness at first. But I get it now. You're independent."

The words floated out before she could bite them back. "I'm afraid not to be." *Afraid?* What was she doing blabbering on to Brayden Ford about her fears?

"Because your family died when you were a child?" His voice was soft.

How had he put his finger squarely on it? "Everyone I relied on was gone in a minute. Aunt Addie took me in and taught me to take care of myself."

"Does that mean someone else can't take care of you, too?"

How had she gotten into this conversation? Too much.

She'd shared too much. Now all she could do was offer a tight smile. "Doesn't seem like we should go too deeply into my psyche right now."

"Of course, right. Sorry to pry." He fiddled with his mug and spilled some liquid on the table. Mopping it up with a paper towel, he shot a look of chagrin at her. "I am beginning to understand why the colonel thinks I am a goofball."

Katie laughed. "It's a term of endearment, probably. She knows you are a great trooper."

He cocked his head. "I'm not so sure. Figured if she did, she'd want me on the Violet James case…" He broke off abruptly.

"Instead of babysitting me?"

His cheeks went dusky. "No. I didn't mean that."

She pulled her eyes away. He had meant it and now she understood. Lorenza had assigned him to her case when he would much prefer being in on the manhunt for the two men who had committed murder and framed Violet James for it. Why wouldn't he? The entire team had been on fire to close the case, especially Hunter McCord, who'd promised to rescue his fiancée's best friend. "More incentive for you to catch my uncle, right? Close the case and get back to the manhunt."

"That came out wrong. Big surprise. I'm glad to be here at the Family K. Really, Katie." He placed a hand over hers. Her brain demanded that she pull away immediately, but her heart relished the feel of his strong fingers on hers. "I don't look at this as babysitting. You are… I mean, I've had great respect for you since you came aboard."

In spite of his reluctance. At least he *had* come to value her work. His touch was warm and encouraging. Talking with Brayden was like tending an untamed reindeer. Sometimes smooth and easy, but most of the time tense and strained. "It's okay," she said, finding the strength to pull away. "You don't have to explain anything. Hopefully, you'll arrest Terrence soon and this mess will all be over."

Then Brayden could return to his heart's desire, catching the murderer who was waiting to ambush Violet.

Brayden started to speak again when Gabriel Runyon entered through the garage door with a camera and his Saint Bernard, Bear, by his side. Gabriel was a tall man, as tall as Brayden, but Bear stood nearly to his waist. The K-9 greeted Ella with a tail wag as Gabriel joined them.

"Hey, Katie. We miss you at the office. No one knows where anything is, and we forgot everything we ever learned about the Wi-Fi. That and the colonel is irritable without you."

"I miss you all, too." *And my job. Especially now that things are getting so awkward with a reluctant babysitter around.* Maybe she had made a mistake taking on the Family K, but how could she turn her back on it?

Gabriel listened to the details of the most recent incident from Brayden.

"He's getting pretty brazen, isn't he?" The two men exchanged a knowing look. She didn't need to have a badge to decipher it. Terrence was becoming a loose cannon, heedless of the risk of capture. Armed and very dangerous, their look said.

"All right. I'll photograph the scene," Gabriel said. "Figured out the point of entry?"

"Window jimmied in the back. I'm going to get some alarms installed today."

Gabriel readied his camera.

"What's the word on the James case?" Brayden asked.

"Helena figures she's been coming to Anchorage to visit a clinic, but we are still checking. The docs are pretty close-lipped about their patients, and she undoubtedly used a fake name, so it's slow going." Gabriel blew out a breath. "Where has she been holing up the rest of the time? That's the big question. And how can a very pregnant woman be so hard to find?"

Katie tried not to listen in, but she'd been part of the whole investigation since April, when the murder of tour guide Cal Brooks occurred and Violet had been framed for it. That was the main case Brayden should be working on—a pregnant woman at risk of being killed, vulnerable and alone.

*Vulnerable and alone.* Those words struck a chord in her own heart. She fought back against them, willing away the feeling of helplessness she'd felt in the back seat of her parents' wrecked car so long ago, silent except for the sound of her own crying and the drip of gasoline on the snow.

*You're not alone*, Katie reminded herself. She had the security guards and Aunt Addie coming home soon, and Quinn would arrive to start work any moment now. Let Brayden install his cameras and whatever else he decided they needed to keep Terrence away, and then she'd prove to him she didn't need a babysitter.

He could go back to his life and she to hers.

Case closed.

Brayden got a broom and helped Katie sweep up the nails after Gabriel left. He detected a coolness in her, probably after he'd stuck his foot in his mouth earlier. There was truth in his dumb remark—he did miss being out of the loop on the James case—but he did not see his current detail as babysitting. As a matter of fact, he discovered the more time he spent around Katie, the more he enjoyed it. There was something about her, something genuine and intelligent and strong. Her life had imploded at age ten, his at twelve. Though she didn't want to share much with him, he understood they had more in common than he'd realized.

That line of thinking was unprofessional and unsafe, he scolded himself. When Katie left him in search of Addie's address book, he breathed easier. Now he could focus on installing the window alarms and cameras he'd asked Phil to bring. Then once that was done, he would have to mentally prepare himself for the next big challenge…the Christmas Fair planning event the next day. He'd tried to talk her into postponing, but that hadn't gone well. And he honestly didn't blame her. The ranch was on the brink of going under. That much was clear. Katie was working on getting him a list of the attendees and their car license numbers and models, which he would pass on to Phil and Alex.

Ella turned her massive head as a motorcycle approached.

Quinn, the local man Katie had hired, got off, jammed his helmet on his handlebar and limped over. Brayden got down off the stepladder and shook his hand.

"Nice to see you again," Brayden said. "You okay? That knee looks painful."

Quinn grimaced and scrubbed a hand over his fuzzy beard. "Wish I had a better story to tell. Tripped on the sidewalk and landed on the knee I already injured in the service. I can't work as a painter until I can do ladders again." He lowered his voice. "I…didn't want to tell the boss in case she'd think I can't do the work."

"Too late," Katie said from the doorway. "Cat's out of the bag."

Quinn looked at his feet. "Aw, sorry about that, Miss Kapowski. I should have been up-front about the knee, but I really need the job. Rent's due at the end of the month."

"You can call me Katie, and it's okay. I know you'll be all right with the reindeer. They don't need much wrestling anyway, except during hoof trimming, and that's been done recently."

Relief spread across his features. "I appreciate it, more than you know. Wife and kids are visiting Grandma for a couple of weeks, so I can stay the nights, easy. I'll do whatever you need done without complaint. I really appreciate the work."

"And I appreciate your help, too," Katie said. "Go ahead and get settled in the bunkhouse, and we can talk after. There's no kitchen, but I can cook well enough to keep you all alive. Sorry, I don't cook meat, though."

Quinn laughed. "I'll lay in a supply of beef jerky."

"You'll have to keep it safe from a meat-eating machine," Brayden advised, pointing to Ella. "I've seen this stalwart officer of the law swipe a kid's hot dog without the slightest show of remorse."

"Yes, sir. I'll keep a sharp lookout," Quinn said.

"Okay. Let me know if either of you needs anything." Katie headed back to the main house.

Brayden watched until she made it inside, locked the door and waved. It was quite an inconvenience to keep the door locked, he was sure, but she'd uttered no complaint. He walked Quinn to the wood-sided bunkhouse. "I might as well see it, too, since we're roomies."

The inside was a simple cabin setup. Two small bedrooms, each with a single bed, and one bathroom no bigger than a closet. The bedrooms had windows, but in the primary living area Brayden was sorry to find there were no windows that looked directly out on the main house, only a small one set up high in the wall to improve lighting. The bunkhouse was built for functionality, not aesthetics.

Ella padded to one of the open bedroom doors, waddled on in and heaved herself up on the bed. Brayden and Quinn watched in surprise.

Quinn chuckled. "Uh… So I'm guessing that's gonna be your room."

"Looks that way. I'll bring her cushion in from the car and try to explain to her once again that she's a dog."

Quinn tossed his duffel on the other bed. "Good

enough for me. With three kids, I'll take any kind of quiet I can get."

"Well, this kind of quiet is likely going to be broken by dog snoring."

"Better than kid noise, trust me." He hesitated. "Been hearing things in town. About Terrence."

"I'll fill you in on the ways he's been terrorizing the ranch. But what have you heard?"

"That he shot Addie and maybe stole those reindeer that went missing. Fact or gossip?"

"Fact on the shooting. Only theory on the reindeer for now, but pretty likely." Brayden told him about the booby trap.

"Can't think of a reason anyone would do that kind of thing, except for one." Quinn's mouth tightened. "Hatred, pure and simple."

Brayden exhaled. "Yeah. That's why I'm here along with two security guards and now you. Consider yourself deputized to help in any way if Katie's safety is in danger, but don't put yourself at risk."

"Think he's given up?"

Brayden didn't hesitate. "Nope."

They dropped their bags in their respective rooms and looked at diagrams of the ranch property. Brayden pointed out the places he felt were most vulnerable. "No way to secure the entire riverbank, and the dock is out of camera range of the main house. Wi-Fi here is terrible."

They studied and discussed until Katie rejoined them, frowning. "I found the list of attendees for tomorrow. You're not going to like it."

He arched an eyebrow. "Let's have it. How many?"

"Fourteen." She stopped his reply with an out-stretched palm. "I know you think we should cancel."

"Not cancel, *postpone*. Until Terrence is in custody."

"There is no telling how long that will take. We can't delay the planning meeting any longer or we run into conflicts with Thanksgiving and Christmas. We're already down to the wire. It's now or never." He saw her anguish, though she kept her expression sedate.

"Maybe there's another way," Brayden said. "We can brainstorm."

"If there was a way to keep this ranch afloat without the fair, don't you think we would have tried it?" Her eyes flashed fire.

He should have figured she'd blow through any pie-in-the-sky "it's gonna be all right" sentiments. She might have made a fine cop, he thought, admiringly.

"We are completely dependent on donations and we never know how many mouths we'll need to feed," she said. "Last spring we rescued two babies whose mother died of disease and a full-grown male from a foreclosed ranch and he had to have surgery for an ulcer. The bills never stop. Neither can the Christmas Fair."

Her chin was tipped upward, mouth set into a firm line. He wondered at that moment what it would be like to kiss those determined lips. *Whoa, fella. Let's try to keep some sort of control on your ridiculous imagination.* The experience with Jamie should have taught him that. "Understood," he said, shooing the thought away. "What's the itinerary?"

"We'll meet in the house at ten tomorrow morning. After the meeting, Addie usually shows everyone the animals and gives a family history of the herd so the volunteers can share with visitors when the time comes. We provide bag lunches and people sit at the picnic tables outside to plan their individual parts of the fair."

"Such as…?"

She ticked off the items on her fingers. "The barbecue area, sleigh rides, reindeer meet and greet, snowshoeing lessons, pictures with a reindeer…"

"Man. This sounds like the best event in town. All right. Fourteen people it is. We'll keep the house secure and I'll see if I can recruit some help to monitor the tour and picnic."

"Great," she said.

"And you," he said with a smile, "will have the undivided attention of a large black dog and one clumsy state trooper."

Her cheeks took on a fetching shade of pink and she looked away.

Quinn shifted. "Would Terrence actually target the visitors?"

"I would have said no a few days ago, but boobytrapping the house and shooting Addie are pretty brazen. His primary target is…"

"Me," Katie said.

Her expression was calm and courageous, but he didn't miss the quick ripple of fear that passed across her face.

*He won't get near you*, Brayden promised silently. "If he shows, we'll arrest him. Since I can't talk you out of postponing…"

"I won't do anything risky," Katie said, "but I have to

make sure this ranch succeeds and we find the missing animals." Her voice hitched. "Lulu came to us pregnant. She had her baby in June, so he's four months old now. His name is Sweetie. He's not thriving since his mother's been taken. They normally nurse for six months, so we've been supplementing with bottles, but it's not optimal and he's underweight. I don't want to think about him going into the winter months without his mother. We just have to get her back soon."

He saw from the way Quinn did not meet Katie's eye that he did not believe the animals were still alive. And despite his own fears, Brayden truly wished he could share Katie's hopefulness about a good outcome. For her sake *and* the animals that she and Addie loved so dearly. Those reindeer were a tight family and that was a rare thing in this world. He knew that much from painful experience. Katie wasn't in a hurry to marry into a human family, but she was sure enough tight with her antlered one.

"All right. Cameras are up. Next order of the day is to search the storage units and secure them. You and I will have the keys, Quinn, no one else."

"Roger that," the other man said. "I might as well go with you now and see where everything is that I'm going to need."

Katie walked off the porch first. Avoiding him or focused on her to-do list?

He paused a moment to take in the sweep of vast acreage, the solitude broken by the wind and the tumbling waves of the nearby Frontier River. He wasn't deluding himself. All the security measures he could put into place were only inconveniences to a resourceful relative who knew the ranch.

A man fueled by hatred.

And hatred was a powerful force indeed.

# FIVE

Katie toyed with her necklace, groaning as she perused the shopping list dictated by her aunt Addie early that morning. "Fourteen people can eat a lot."

"Especially carnivores," Brayden said mischievously. They'd decided to take her Jeep to the grocery store in town since his car was filled with too much equipment and dog gear to fit the necessary supplies.

She couldn't help it. Babysitter or not, she was glad for his company. Sometimes it seemed as if there was no awkwardness or age gap between them and that they were meeting for the first time instead of sharing an uncomfortable past.

They drove along the main street. Most of the storefronts hadn't changed much over the years. "I used to come here with Aunt Addie for the Friday Fling Farmers' Market." She recalled the white tents that would line the street in the summer months. "My favorite was the honey. Sweetest I ever tasted. Addie isn't a great cook, so I learned how to make biscuits for us. That was sort of our treat, homemade biscuits with Friday Fling honey." She bit her lip.

"Thinking about Addie?"

She nodded. "She's gruff and ornery, but deep down she is made of gold."

Brayden's look was sympathetic. "She'll be all right. Home before you know it. Doctors are optimistic about her recovery, right?"

"Yes. She's stubborn, though, and I don't see her convalescing like she'd supposed to at the Family K. I'm more concerned with having her come home when Terrence is still bent on destroying the ranch."

He squeezed her lower forearm. The gesture surprised her and somehow felt natural at the same time. Confusing.

"One good thing about his recklessness. He's going to slip up. They always do. We'll get him. You can take that to the bank."

Her cheeks went warm at his earnest tone. Almost as if he cared personally. No, it was just the job. He said he shied away from relationships as much as she did, probably more so after Jamie. What a shame, she thought. Brayden Ford would be a wonderful spouse for someone. Maybe down the road he'd find his soul mate. She wondered why the thought gave her a pang.

She noted he checked the rearview mirror from time to time. He was also carrying his weapon and a badge clipped to his waist, though he wore jeans and a soft T-shirt that brought out the jade in his eyes. He was not off duty on this errand, probably never would be around her.

Jamie had been fortunate to have a man like Brayden courting her, even if she couldn't see that.

She got out and he took up position at her elbow. Ella lumbered along, too, nose quivering. The dog's state trooper vest was a free pass to go anywhere with Brayden, but she knew he'd need to keep an eagle eye on his canine around the food items. She enjoyed the feel of Brayden's strong arm against her shoulder, the clean, spicy fragrance of his soap.

He ushered her into the store, and they walked to the deli counter. Brayden struck up a friendly chat with the butcher before he turned to Katie.

Charlie the butcher measured out the meats and wrapped them. His lips pursed under his full mustache. "I heard about what happened to Addie."

Katie's smile dimmed. "Yes. Thankfully my prayers were answered and she's going to be okay."

"She's a tough customer. Knows what she wants and gets it."

Was that criticism? Katie knew her aunt's faults, but she wasn't about to let some stranger add his two cents. She stiffened. "I love my aunt. She's been great to me."

"No offense meant." He chuckled. "Don't get me wrong. I like her a lot. Have for ages. As a matter of fact, I'm on the fair planning committee this year."

"Oh, of course. I recognize your name now from the planning meeting list."

He nodded. "I've been trying to get her to let me take her out to dinner. She's my kind of person—no-nonsense, takes care of her business and doesn't ask for handouts. Love a strong woman like Addie. That's why I was planning to call and tell you."

"Tell us what?" Brayden said.

He scanned the empty aisle and leaned forward, voice low. "I think I saw him."

"Who?"

"Terrence."

She could feel the tension emanating off Brayden like electrical waves as he responded. "When and where?"

"Yesterday. Cops came around a few weeks ago and showed us pictures of him, and I'm almost positive the same guy came into our store. I told the owner that it was him shopping real early in the morning, right after we opened, but he says I'm seeing things. The guy was bearded, wearing glasses, but you can fake those things, huh?"

Terrence had been in this store? Goose bumps erupted along her arms.

Brayden was listening attentively. "What made you think it was him?"

"The demeanor mostly, I guess. Everyone is friendly around here, good at small talk, except for Addie, maybe." He grinned. "Anyhow, this guy didn't want to shoot the breeze. Came in, got what he wanted, headed for the checkout."

"Do you have an in-store camera?" Brayden asked.

"Uh-huh. Cheapie one, super old, but it works. I'll get the key and tell the manager."

Katie felt dazed as she followed Brayden and Charlie to a cramped workroom where Charlie shoved an old-fashioned videotape into the slot. The picture came to life, grainy and gray as a time clock ticked away at the bottom right corner. At 6:35 a.m., a man walked into view. He was indeed bearded, with glasses, and he seemed to hunch over as he disappeared down an aisle. When he came into view again carrying a hand basket, Brayden stopped the video and took pictures with his phone.

"What do you think, Katie? You're the only one who's seen him close-up except for your aunt. Is it Terrence?"

She continued to watch the tape as it started up again. The man was careful to keep his face down, paying with a ten-dollar bill fished from his pocket. He gathered his bag and strolled away from the counter, but she'd seen enough. The profile, chin tucked to his chest, prominent ears, grizzled brows.

"That's him," she whispered.

"Did you see what vehicle he drove? Which direction he took when he left?"

"I'm sorry." Charlie sighed. "I had a shipment coming in, so I had to get back to the deli counter. That's why I haven't had a moment to call you, either."

Brayden rewound the tape and they watched it again. She was not sure what he was looking for until he froze on the spot where the man put his basket on the counter for the cashier to scan.

Bread.

Peanut butter.

Carrots.

And one more item that made the breath congeal in her lungs.

Several rolls of duct tape.

Outside, Brayden hurried to open the passenger door for Katie, but Ella had stopped dead in front of him and he almost took a header over her. Her nose quivered as she sampled the air. Suddenly she started to bark, her hoarse vocalizations deafening.

"Katie, go back in the..." he started.

But a car suddenly careened into view, driving right up onto the sidewalk. Terrence was behind the wheel. In a matter of moments, he would plow right into them. Brayden drew his gun and fired into the windshield, but the car didn't slow. It grazed a newspaper machine, which was knocked from its bolts and launched right at him. He spun to the side and fell, rolling several times before he smacked into the brick facade of the store.

Charlie came out at a gallop. "What's going on?"

Brayden was scrambling to his feet. Terrence's car was empty now, front end smashed from the impact with the newspaper machine, engine still revving... And Katie was gone. "Call the local police," he yelled at Charlie.

Ella sprinted to the fenced alley between the shop and the building next to it, barking for all she was worth. She had to be following Katie. He took off in pursuit. Ella's barking echoed and bounced along the narrow walls. As he, too, rounded the corner, he saw the dog chasing after Terrence, Katie a few steps ahead of him. She turned to look back, eyes huge with fear. As she did so, she stumbled and went down.

Ella barked, skidding to an ungainly stop as Terrence closed in on Katie. The dog was confused, unsure what to do.

"Stop! Alaska state trooper!" Brayden yelled. He didn't have a clean shot. Ella was in between them and

Katie just behind Terrence. There was no way he could risk a bullet hitting either one of them.

Ella broke off from barking at Terrence and decided to make a run for Katie. As the mountain of a dog raced toward him, Terrence leaped up, grabbed the top of the fence and heaved himself over. Brayden holstered his weapon and did the same. He clawed his way up and dropped on the other side, yanking out his gun again.

A startled maintenance worker stood immobilized, holding a trash bag. He stabbed a forefinger at the alley, which exited onto the street. "Guy ran that way."

Brayden started in again, sprinting for all he was worth. Arriving at the street, panting, he looked both ways, just in time to see Terrence hopping into a departing bus. He yelled and tried to wave down the driver, but the vehicle was already pulling away. Frustration burning like wildfire through him, he phoned in to the local cops to shadow the bus route. But Terrence wouldn't be on it, he thought with a sinking heart. As soon as he was out of sight, he'd pull the stop cord and demand to get off.

He ran back to find Katie limping from the alley, Ella glued to her side. As fast as possible, he urged her back to the safety of the Jeep, which had escaped damage. Inside, he called the colonel as they sped away from town. Then, as they drove, he briefed the local PD about the sequence of events that had just transpired.

His pulse was still thudding intensely five minutes later. The wide streets were quiet save for the occasional car. Couples on errands, ranchers who offered friendly waves as they rolled along. He was still on the lookout, expecting to see Terrence at any moment, and he knew Katie was, too, but there was no sign of him. He'd vanished, like smoke.

Brayden shot a look in the rearview at Ella. "You know, for an underwater search-and-rescue dog, you really saved the day. Extra treats for you, big girl."

Katie still said nothing.

He wanted to take her hand, but she was rigid with tension. "Your knee okay?"

"Just scraped."

"We'll get him," he said.

"Do you really believe that?"

Brayden knew she was too smart for false reassurances, but still he offered her a smile. "It's a matter of time before we bring him down. That's the honest truth. Don't worry." He almost rolled his eyes at his own platitude. *Don't worry* had to be the most useless phrase in the English language. When had that sage advice ever made someone stop fretting? The woman had almost been flattened moments ago or abducted. Terrible possibilities rolled through his mind.

She seemed to read his mind. "So it's nothing to worry about that Terrence was in the store buying duct tape?"

Katie was sharp. He should have known she wouldn't have missed that detail. He cleared his throat. "The bigger problem for me is how he knew we were going to be shopping just then."

"He's got a source? Some helpful shopkeeper whom he's paying?" Katie shrugged, a casual gesture that did not ease the tension in the line of her shoulders. "If Terrence wants my aunt to give him the ranch, maybe he's decided to kidnap me to force her to comply. He might have hoped he'd knock me out with the bucket of nails and come back to get me. When that didn't work, he decided to snatch me outside the store."

"I'm not sure he's thinking that clearly. His acts have been reckless, thus far."

The morning sunshine caught her hair and set it aglow. He wanted to reach out and comb his fingers through it. To soothe her after everything she'd just been through...

"Or maybe he wants to punish my aunt by taking me away from her."

He tugged gently at a copper strand. It was soft satin, as he'd imagined. "Hey there. We're going to keep you safe, Ella and I. Don't let your fears carry you away." His teasing gesture did not produce any effect. "Tell me what else."

She stared out the windshield. "I was worrying that there might be another motive brewing in Terrence's mind. He probably knows that I am next in line to own the ranch, since my aunt has no children. Maybe he wants to try to force me to change the will after he kills Addie."

He took her hand. Though his tone was Mr. Cool, his gut was vibrating like a plucked wire. What if Ella hadn't been there to bark a warning as Terrence careened toward Katie? "Let's not get ahead of ourselves. We have no hard evidence about what Terrence is planning, only supposition."

When she didn't pull away from his grasp, he allowed

himself to savor the closeness. Her skin was warm, like the woman herself.

*I'll take care of you*, his heart whispered. The startling thought caused him to let go. She was his boss's assistant, he reminded himself. Much *younger* assistant. He'd wanted to take care of Jamie, too, and instead he'd turned out looking about as dim as Alaska in December. Katie had no doubt enjoyed telling him about his girlfriend's betrayal, though she didn't admit it.

"The carrots," Katie said, pulling him from his self-recrimination.

*"What?"*

"The carrots Terrence was buying at the store. Addie said Terrence never showed any interest in the reindeer, so he wouldn't know."

"Know what?"

"It's a misconception that reindeer eat carrots, probably due to the whole Santa business. The truth is, reindeer have no front incisors on the top, so it's hard for them to eat, much less digest, carrots. We don't feed them to our reindeer. When we allow guests to offer food, it's willow leaves or lichen."

"What do the carrots in Terrence's basket tell you?"

She began to twist her necklace around one finger. "That he's bought into the misconception. He was buying that big bunch of carrots to feed the reindeer he stole."

"Could be he was just buying them to eat himself."

She eyed him. "Would you? A bachelor who is buying bread and peanut butter, would you really buy a bulk bag of carrots that you'd have to peel yourself to eat or cook?"

"No."

"That was Terrence," she said. "I know it. And he has our reindeer. They have to be close. Where could he be keeping them?"

"I'll alert the team and have them search."

Her brows were drawn into a V. "The reindeer won't stay healthy. He doesn't know how to care for them."

Brayden saw she was starting to breathe fast. He took her hand again. "They are strong animals. Big, too. He can't keep them hidden for long."

She blinked. "He's done a pretty good job of it so far."

He considered his next comment. It probably wasn't appropriate for him to share his spiritual thoughts in the present circumstance. When he'd tried with Jamie, she'd started calling him Preacher. Katie was his job, his duty, and they were professional colleagues, nothing more, but he felt compelled to share anyway. "You know what my mom used to say? God is for us, even when we're losing, so keep your eyes up, not down."

Katie's glance was puzzled. "Like Romans?"

He grinned. "Yes. You know your Bible. She was speaking about Romans 8:31. I've seen a lot of things, *bad* things, during my time in law enforcement. When I was a rookie, it would eat me up sometimes. I'd ask my mom, so if God is for us, why are things so bleak in this world? She said, God walks us through the struggles, and He's promised us the win. Eyes up, not down."

To his surprise, he saw tears well in Katie's eyes.

She detached herself from him to pull a tissue from her pocket.

*Foot in mouth again, Ford?* "I'm sorry," he said. "I didn't mean to make you cry."

"They are happy tears, believe it or not."

He'd never really understood the concept of happy tears, but he was glad he hadn't added to her sadness. Ella shoved her head in from the back seat and licked the side of Katie's neck, which set her to giggling. When her giggles subsided, she continued.

"After my parents died in the wreck, I was crippled by fear. Living out in the middle of nowhere on a ranch didn't help, I guess. I wouldn't sleep with the lights off and I didn't want to go to school. Aunt Addie finally walked into my bedroom late one night and opened the Bible. She took a highlighter and underlined Romans 8:31. She said in her typical grumpy way, 'Katie, are you gonna believe Him or not? He's smarter than you and He promised. All you gotta do is believe Him.'" She laughed. "There were not warm, fuzzy pep talks from Aunt Addie."

"She's a to-the-point lady," Brayden said.

"True. Funny thing is, I made my choice and somehow God got me out of bed every day and back into life. It wasn't smooth or pretty sometimes, mind you. The kids in my school weren't welcoming. I guess I seemed weird, having no parents, dressing in the ranch clothes Addie sewed, caring more about the bugs and plants than academics. I learned how to play by myself." He thought she might cry again, but instead she turned a smile on him, the sweetest smile he'd ever seen, a smile that made his heart thump. "Your mother and my aunt gave us the same verse. How's that for amazing?" she said.

*Amazing.* Definitely. He didn't know why he was over-the-moon grateful that he'd shared the memory. A God thing, as his mom used to say. Too bad he didn't let more of those God things out of his mouth. Might be less room for his foot.

She nodded. "Eyes up, not down. I like the way your mom put it."

"Me, too."

Judging by her more relaxed demeanor, her spirits were lighter by the time they arrived at the ranch. So were his.

At the ranch, he checked with Alex, Phil and Quinn, none of whom had a theory on how Terrence had known they'd be at the store. Then he went into the living room with Ella and joined the scheduled Zoom meeting to report in.

Lorenza's normally serious face grew downright grave as she listened. "He's getting too close."

"I agree." Brayden outlined the safety precautions he'd taken on the ranch. "But I could use help trying to canvass the area. There's too much wilderness where Terrence could have hidden those reindeer for me to search by myself. And that might be the key to finding him. If Katie's theory is right, he's not feeding them well, but at least we can assume he hasn't killed them. Yet."

Maya Rodriquez unmuted her microphone and spoke up, pausing for a moment when her Malinois, Sarge, poked his nose at the screen. She flipped her dark braid over her shoulder. "Sarge and I will see what we can find. He couldn't have taken them too far out of Palmer if he's in town buying supplies for them."

Brayden nodded. "He's holed up somewhere, likely a place with a fenced field or a corral."

Maya nodded. "We're on it."

Brayden thanked her. "And an extra person tomorrow for the Christmas Fair meeting wouldn't hurt, either. We've got fourteen people coming, and I'm concerned about the forested property and the riverbed. Both weak points for security."

"I can do it," Gabriel said. "I—"

"One moment," the colonel said, looking at her phone. "I just got a text from Poppy."

Brayden took a breath. Poppy and her wolfhound had been combing the wild acres of Chugach, searching for any sign of Cole Seaver, Eli's godmother's missing son. Brayden had met Bettina Seaver at a police family gathering several years prior. He'd liked her intense blue eyes and the impish smile she reserved for her godson Eli. Eli explained how pained she was when her son became more and more enamored with the wilderness until he cut all ties with his old life and simply disappeared. Rumor was he lived in a remote off-the-grid homestead with a wife and child.

Bettina was struggling with stage four cancer, and Eli wanted to grant her wish for a reunion with her son before she passed. How would that feel, he wondered, to have someone you loved with your whole being removed from your life without a word? It had been hard enough on him to have his father walk out when he was twelve.

*"Why did Dad leave?"* he'd asked his mother again and again.

"He got tired of it all," she'd snapped one time in exasperation at his repeated question.

Tired of him? He'd wondered if he'd gotten better grades, been the star on the baseball team, shared his father's interest in ham radios… The adult in him realized he wasn't to blame for his father's departure, but some part of him deep down worried that maybe he just wasn't enough. Jamie must have thought so.

*Too old…too straitlaced.*

He flashed briefly on Katie. Did she feel that way, too? He was eight years older. Was he also too one-note, too bland outside his trooper identity to warrant interest? And why did he wonder about that, anyway?

*Pay attention.* He held his breath while waiting for Lorenza to share the text. Had Cole Seaver been found?

"Poppy says she encountered a teenage male, declined to give his name, but he claims to know the Seaver family."

"Finally," Brayden said, resisting the urge to whoop with excitement. "Where?"

The colonel continued. "Kid's cagey. He didn't want to give up their whereabouts. He promised to pass on Poppy's contact info and tell them she needs to talk to them."

Brayden's shoulders sagged. "Is this kid even telling the truth in the first place? And if he is, will he really deliver the message?"

"And will Cole Seaver actually contact us?" Hunter McCord put in. "He walked out of his mother's life years ago, and he might not be willing to do an about-face."

"If we can talk to Cole, explain things…" Maya said. "I can't believe he would turn his back on his dying mother."

Lorenza put her phone away. "All we can do is make contact. The rest is up to him."

"We're looking for a wilderness family, stolen reindeer, a fugitive uncle, and we've still got a murderous groom and his target out there somewhere." Helena Maddox blew out a frustrated breath.

The stakes had gotten so high so fast they were all striving to keep up. As much as he wanted to help Poppy search for Cole and Gabriel locate Violet James, he knew his focus had to stay on Katie and the Family K. Had he really resisted the assignment only a few days ago? Now her safety was all he could think about.

They ended the meeting and Brayden listened to Katie's kitchen clatter. She'd started to hum something, a tune he didn't know. Her quirks surprised him. Quiet, serious, no-nonsense, but she seemed to be singing something about frogs in a watermelon patch. Ella's tale wagged as she listened. When the dog lumbered into the kitchen to check things out, Katie put down a water bowl for her.

"Don't…" he started. *Too late.* Ella dived her paws into that bowl and scrabbled for all she was worth until the water was splattered everywhere and Ella was satisfied.

Katie laughed, a belly chuckle that made him smile, too. "Sorry."

"I should have warned you about her level of enthusiasm for water. I'll get some paper towels and dry that up," he said.

After another chuckle, she went back to her frog-and-watermelon song.

If she could still laugh while her murderous uncle was at large, then he would allow himself the pleasure of being near her.

It was an assignment, and he wouldn't forget it, but how could he resist?

# SIX

Katie slammed her alarm off and sat up groggy the next morning. She came to full alertness with a gasp. Six thirty? She'd meant to be in the kitchen by six. Frightening dreams she could not quite recall had roused her on and off during the night. Once she'd actually gone to the window, searching the dark acres for signs of Terrence. Instead, she'd seen Brayden and Ella returning from a drive around the property.

He hadn't noticed her at the window, as he gave his beloved dog a good belly scratch. Ella rewarded him by standing on her hind legs, which put her golf-ball-sized nose about even with his face. She imagined Brayden's smile and it made butterflies take flight in her stomach. At least she'd been able to sleep for a few hours after that. Their temporary arrangement was awkward, but it did ease her spirit to have him close by.

A quick face wash, ponytail, clean jeans and a shirt, and she was hurrying down the stairs, surprised to find Brayden already in the kitchen. He was wrapped in her Reindeer Roundup apron, a leftover from a long-ago fundraiser. The comical cartoon reindeer dancing in tutus across the pink fabric looked completely out of place on the big man spreading mustard and mayo onto sliced bread.

He waved a rubber-gloved hand at her and pointed to the coffee machine. "Heard you coming and brewed you a cup. I did not break anything while doing so, I might add, so that's a win."

"You don't have to make the sandwiches," she said.

He pulled a look of mock offense. "I am the meat master, as we discussed. I figured I'd get a head start. You were on brownie duty yesterday."

She pulled the foil-wrapped tray from the counter. "I sure was. Thirty-six chocolate peanut butter cup brownies."

He became overly focused wiping at a spot on his reindeer apron. A contrite look revealed delicate crow's-feet around his eyes. Surprisingly attractive. "Er, actually, it's closer to thirty-five. I got up early, as I mentioned, and there was the quality-control issue to consider. Um, might even be thirty-four left because I take my job assignments seriously."

The sheepish look made her laugh. "I understand completely. How is the quality, by the way?"

"I would give it a two thumbs-up if my thumbs weren't already busy making sandwiches."

"Glad to hear it." Unaccustomed pleasure bubbled in her spirit. He liked the brownies. Embarrassed by her own silliness, she got to work. She laid out brown paper bags and tucked the sandwiches inside as Brayden finished them, along with a bag of chips, an apple and a brownie. Pitchers of iced water and lemonade would be prepared closer to the noon hour and placed outside on the long weathered picnic benches. Eyeing the dark wall of clouds that was rolling in with the promise of a storm, she mentally figured on ushering everyone inside if the rain came before the food was finished. Compared with the other complications, a storm was a mere trifle. Alaskans could handle inclement weather without the slightest concern.

Her phone rang with a familiar number, Addie calling on the new cell they'd gotten her. Fortunately, her number hadn't changed.

"Hi, Aunt Addie. How are you feeling?" Addie probably hadn't slept well, either, she realized, as the older woman's worries came spilling out. Katie listened patiently and reassured her that all the details of the upcoming meeting were taken care of. It required a good twenty minutes of calming before her aunt could be persuaded that she should hang up. Brayden was done with sandwich construction by the time she ended the call.

He inquired with a raised eyebrow. "I take it Aunt Addie isn't comfortable with delegating?"

"That's an understatement. She's particularly worried about Sweetie. Addie got his mom, Lulu, from a family in town who had to move away and couldn't keep her. She wasn't in the greatest health, since they didn't know much about raising a reindeer. I was visiting the Family K when Lulu delivered Sweetie." The moment was embedded in her soul. She realized she'd gone quiet only when Brayden touched her shoulder.

"A powerful memory?"

"Yes. He was so small and clumsy when he was born,

smaller than any other reindeer baby I'd ever seen. Lulu cleaned and nuzzled him. Then she got up and walked away a few feet and lay down again. Sweetie tried and tried to get up. He took one step toward her and collapsed. I wanted so badly for Lulu to go to Sweetie and help him, but she didn't. Instead, she got up and walked away a few more steps and lay down again. It took him another fifteen minutes before he managed to master his legs enough to get to her, and then they both lay down for a good nursing."

"Nothing like a mother's love."

"No, there isn't." She touched a finger to the smooth pendant. "I don't remember everything, but I know Mom was ecstatic to be pregnant with my brother. I gathered they thought she could not have any more children."

A fountain of grief burst out for the tiny brother she'd never had a chance to meet. Katie had never talked about it with anyone, even Addie. She could not tell Brayden about the crayon pictures she'd taped all over a corner of the room she would have shared with him, or about the piggy-bank coins she'd been collecting to buy a two-seater kayak that they would paddle together someday on their grand adventures.

Brayden leaned his cheek on the top of her head. Just for a moment, she wondered what it would be like to share everything with him, the faults and fears and fumblings. But she didn't trust anyone that much, especially Brayden Ford. She clung to him for another second, struggling to catch her breath before she detached herself.

"What am I doing? Crying onto your reindeer apron? Dunno where that came from," she said, sniffling.

"I don't mind."

"I was talking about Addie's phone call," she blurted. "Anyway, she's worried about Sweetie and she won't take my word that he's okay. Not surprising. When he was born, he was so small that we wanted to keep a round-the-clock watch over him. I volunteered to take a shift, but she insisted on staying there all night. I think she was worried I might doze off and miss something critical."

There was still a soft and thoughtful gleam in Brayden's eyes, but he did not press. "I have an aunt like that, too, only her area of focus is senior dogs. This hospital stay must be getting on Aunt Addie's very last nerve."

"Yes, and I fear the nurses are getting the brunt of it. The good news is she might be allowed to come home next week."

"Ah. That is good news."

There was a shade of calculation in his tone. She realized the comment had set his mental wheels turning. With Addie's return, there would be two targets instead of one.

*Targets.* He was focused on his protective details. And why shouldn't he? It was his assignment, after all. The embrace was just part of that protectiveness, nothing more. It was a good reminder to herself that though Brayden was certainly not the hard-nosed person she'd thought him to be, baring her personal drama with him was ridiculous and risky. She was a job to him, just like

Addie. What was more, solving the Terrence case would be a way to prove himself to the boss and maybe give him a career boost.

Determined to keep her head in business mode, she finished the bagged lunches and put them in the fridge. On the porch, she tugged on a pair of boots. Brayden followed her to the pen, where Quinn was already taking care of tossing hay to the herd. He handed her an enormous glass bottle of milk. "Care to do the honors?"

She nodded gratefully. The truth was, she dreaded giving up her nursing duties for Sweetie. Could be she was more like Addie than she cared to admit. *A mother's love*... It was hard enough seeing the young reindeer wandering around and bawling for his mother. Somehow, feeding him that bottle was an unspoken promise she'd made to Lulu and, in some odd way, made her feel connected to her own mother.

*We'll find you and I will do everything I can for your baby until you come home.*

Sweetie noticed the bottle and approached with a mixture of longing and concern. She crouched down, having learned by trial and error that it made the animal more comfortable.

"Here, baby," she crooned. "Mama would want you to drink up your milk." She needed to wait only a moment more before Sweetie's hunger overcame his hesitation and he latched on to the bottle. His vigorous sucking made loud smacking noises that left her chuckling.

"Biggest baby I ever did see," Brayden said.

"Not really. Most reindeer babies are weaned by six

months, so he needs two months more of bottles before he's ready to completely give up milk for greens." She ran a hand over Sweetie's ribs while he sucked up the last swallow. His sides were warm, his winter double coat coming in nicely. The thick underfur was an excellent cold-weather protection and the longer hollow hairs on top would allow him to swim with ease. She enjoyed the surprised reactions she got from visitors when they were told that reindeer could float like corks and seemed to enjoy their swimming. In the wet months, the small lake on their property was an entertaining spot to watch the reindeer swim.

"He's a blue-ribbon eater," Brayden remarked, watching Sweetie guzzle his milk. He'd stayed outside the fence, arms resting on the wood planks.

"He wasn't at first. It took me ages to get him to accept the bottle. He's still too thin."

"But coming along," Quinn said, handing her a towel to wipe the milk drops from her fingers. "When I first came out here to show my girls your new addition, he was spindly as all get-out. You've fattened him up some."

Sweetie detached from the empty bottle and skittered away. Ella took notice now and meandered over to him, sticking her muzzle through the wood posts. Brayden laughed. "Would you look at that?"

The dog extended a slobbery tongue through the fence to swab all the milk drops from Sweetie's face. They all laughed, the mingled sound floating away in the pristine air. Ella finished and Sweetie darted off to follow the adults from the pen into the pasture.

Quinn cleared his throat. "Uh, now that you're finished, I was thinking you might want to know what I found in town."

Brayden opened the pen to let Katie out and they all stood together. A cold pit of worry formed in Katie's stomach.

"What is it?" Brayden prompted.

"I was gassing up my truck last night and I saw this." He pulled a neatly folded paper from his pocket. He held it tight against the buffeting wind. "Tacked to the 'for sale' board they got at the station. I always look there since I like tools and I can't afford new ones. Anyway…"

He unfolded the paper and handed it to her, with a look of trepidation.

Katie read aloud. "'Reindeer, female. Lame. Penned at Yukon Trail Road juncture. Asking $200.'" The picture was blurry, but still her fingers went cold.

"Is it Lulu?" Brayden asked, his big, broad shoulder warm against hers as they studied the paper.

"I don't know. It might be. I can't see the antlers well and her head is down." She fought to keep calm. "There's only one reason you sell a lame reindeer."

"For the meat," Brayden said.

She nodded. All of their reindeer were rescues. Addie had vowed none of them would ever be slaughtered. "Sales of reindeer meat soar around the holidays. What if this is Terrence trying to make some money? Or…"

"Or lure you to a spot where he can hurt you." Brayden's expression was grim as he took the poster from her.

"Yukon Trail Road is about an hour and thirty minutes from here," Quinn told them. "There isn't anything there that I know of except some old farmhouses."

Brayden was texting a message. "I'll run the phone number and the address. Do you have a picture of Lulu?"

She pulled one up on her phone and texted it to him. "We have to go right away, to see if it's her."

He held up a palm. "As soon as I can do some research, but you're not going anywhere near that reindeer until we check the situation out thoroughly."

She huffed out a breath. He was right, but she didn't enjoy being given commands.

"I'll go," Quinn said. "I can get there and back by the time the meeting starts."

Katie tried to put all her gratitude into her smile. "Thank you very much, Quinn, but I don't want you hurt, either. And I need your help today. We may have to move everything inside if the storm comes in early." A car puttered along Brighton loop onto the gravel road. Brayden checked it against the notes in his phone.

"The guests have started to arrive," he said. "Ready or not, here we go."

Katie stood straighter. Though everything in her wanted to hop into her Jeep and speed right to the spot where her missing reindeer might possibly be, she had promised Aunt Addie she would take care of the Christmas Fair planning day, and she would not turn her back on those duties.

Still, as she saw Brayden putting the phone to his ear, she wondered what he would find. A trap? Her missing animal? Or Terrence Kapowski himself?

\* \* \*

Gabriel gratefully accepted the bag lunch Brayden offered him at the noon hour. The Saint Bernard sitting at his feet nosed hopefully at the scent. "Katie wanted to make sure you got it while you're out and about on the property."

"Very thoughtful. I'm obliged," he said, unwrapping and taking a huge bite. "And starved since I skipped breakfast to get over here." He cocked a mischievous eyebrow. "Katie said you made the sandwiches yourself and that you are a vision of loveliness in your pink reindeer apron. If only she had texted a picture for me to share with the team."

He rolled his eyes. He knew his buddy would be sure to spread that fun fact all over headquarters. "I'll make a point to thank her for sharing that with you. Anything in the woods?"

"Not that Bear or I could find, except some old tire tracks. I took pictures. Nothing to be gleaned except that it's probably the way Terrence stole the reindeer and got them off the property without being spotted. Could be he was also watching the results of his booby-trapping from there if he's got real high-powered binoculars." He paused to take another bite of his sandwich. "Good thing you messed up that plan. Still, it's a lot of ground to cover. And anyone can access the woods if they have a mind to and get out without being seen. What did you run down from the reindeer-for-sale poster?"

"Number belongs to a Hank Egland, age seventy-five, unmarried. Moved to the Palmer area a couple of years ago. No criminal record. He's got a property with a couple of acres. Scoped it out on Google Earth. It's a bit of a mess, but there is a pen there."

"Large enough for Katie's missing reindeer?" Gabriel queried.

"Probably. This Hank guy could be helping Terrence out by posting the ad. Or it could be unrelated. I'll check it out as soon as I can." Brayden observed the blanket of clouds rolling across the sky and wiped away the first drops of rain. "Have a feeling we're about to lose the weather window."

"I'll help you escort everyone to the main house if it gets worse. When we're clear here, how about I pay Mr. Egland and his reindeer a visit? I can get a picture and text it to you for Katie to identify."

Brayden blew out a relieved breath. "That would be fantastic. I wanted to check it out, but I can't leave her."

Gabriel's lips curled. "Can't...and don't want to, huh?"

He jerked a look at his friend. "What do you mean by that?"

Gabriel continued to eat his sandwich. "That you and Katie look good together, that's all."

"I'm eight years older than she is."

"So what?"

He gaped. "And she's practically the colonel's kin."

"The colonel has a discerning eye for quality individuals," Gabriel countered.

"And I don't think she's forgotten that I didn't recommend her for the job."

"Old history. Things change. People move on."

"This is... I mean, I don't..." Brayden stopped and tried again. "There's nothing between us."

His teammate arched a brow. "Because she isn't interested or because you are a dork?"

"Neither. Do I have to remind you that the last time I had a girlfriend things went just swimmingly?"

Gabriel winced. "You do win the 'worst relationship ending' prize for having to arrest your girlfriend."

"Yeah, a girlfriend Katie warned me about and I accused her of trying to get back at me."

"Was she? Trying to get back at you?"

Brayden thought it over. "No, now that I've gotten to know her better, I don't think she told me about Jamie to humiliate me."

"There you go, then." His friend grinned. "Stop trying to find reasons it wouldn't work."

"Are you, the world's most confirmed bachelor, trying to advise me on relationships?"

"You're family material. I'm not. Plus, you're a little dense, so I figure you need the help."

Brayden was indeed family material and that was another confirming factor, since Katie said she wasn't interested in marriage and which was why she'd broken up with John.

"Well?" Gabriel said. "I'm not hearing anything sensible coming out of your mouth."

He was too flustered to manage a retort before Gabriel socked him on the shoulder.

"All right, all right. I've rattled you enough, I can see. It would be fun to harass you some more, but work before pleasure. Gonna take a look along the river. See you later."

Brayden watched the other man go. Why exactly were

Gabriel's comments unnerving? Could his friend detect the attraction he felt toward Katie? *Was* it attraction? Fondness? A growing respect? Something deeper? Whatever it was, he was pretty sure it was only one-sided.

*You and Katie look good together.*

Looks could be deceiving, he told himself as he headed off on another security check.

# SEVEN

The rain held off until late afternoon, when Katie shuttled everyone into the large front room of the old house. The sofas were worn and saggy, but with the addition of folding chairs, there was plenty of seating. The wood fire she'd set did a decent job of warming the room. Cups of hot tea and coffee were offered and Brayden helped out with the brewing of it, taking extra pains, she thought, not to spill any. Aunt Addie would have been satisfied with how the early part of the meeting had gone. Not exactly a well-oiled machine since she'd forgotten to make copies of the planning packets, but enough to get the job done. Everyone had been given the tour and updated on changes to the herd.

The twelve ladies and two men sat chatting in their smaller team groups. They opened various boxes and unloaded flyers and craft supplies to check their inventory. The volunteers who could not attend the meeting had made sure their materials were ready for the planning session. Charlie, the mustached butcher from town, was present. Katie was particularly pleased to see

him, since she'd learned of his pursuit of her cantan-
kerous aunt. Maybe she could slip in a good word for
him when she debriefed Addie. Charlie was a decent
guy, it seemed, and maybe God meant for her aunt to
have a companion in her later life. Why not? Charlie
just might be good-natured enough to balance Addie's
harsher tendencies. He gave Katie a thumbs-up.

"I can speak for the sledding team," Charlie said.
"We are A-OK and ready to roll."

The committee chairs reported on their progress
until a fidgety blonde whose stick-on name tag read
"Shirlene" cleared her throat. "I feel like there is an
elephant in the room that needs to be addressed and it
looks like that's up to me."

Katie sat up straighter in the card chair. "What sort
of elephant?"

"The fact that your uncle is terrorizing this place.
He almost killed Addie, if anyone doesn't know that
already."

In this small Alaskan town, Katie had no doubt that
everyone knew about the shooting almost as soon as
it happened. Shirlene's gray eyes were intense, her
lips tight. Brayden looked up from petting Ella as the
woman continued.

"I see you have police protection and security, which
is why I felt safe to come today, but how long can they
stay here? What if Terrence isn't caught by the time of
the Christmas Fair? It's only five weeks away."

Brayden spoke up. "We're actively investigating,
ma'am. We'll get him."

"But you haven't yet, no offense. He's stolen animals, shot Addie without penalty so far. He's out there somewhere, maybe watching us through binoculars right now." Shirlene rubbed her palms on her knees. "I don't want to be bringing this up, but someone has to. I am wondering if it's wise to have a Christmas Fair this year."

Katie felt as if all her self-control was evaporating. She could not let her aunt down.

"Let's… Let's take a break for a few minutes. Everyone, please have some food." She picked up a small box from the table next to the front door. It was marked Christmas Fair Supplies. She'd overlooked it in her attention to all the other details.

How could she salvage the situation? What could she say to assuage them? Mechanically, she reached for the box cutter in the drawer to open the package.

*Think, Katie. Aunt Addie is depending on you.*

Could they postpone the fair? Turn it into a spring event? She chewed her lip. How could they reassure the participants that Terrence would be caught when he continued to terrorize her at every turn?

*Lord, help me figure this out, before it's too late for the ranch…and for me.*

She readied the cutter to press it into the box.

Brayden wished he could think of something to say. The meeting was sinking like a rock in the pond and it was all due to the fact that he hadn't been able to catch Terrence, or even slow him down. What could he say to reassure them?

Ella cocked her head from under the food table where she'd parked herself to catch any fallen scraps.

Katie was visibly nervous, shoulders stiff with tension, fidgeting with the edges of a box. He was desperate to comfort her and salvage things, but his brain felt slow and clumsy.

Ella whined. Picking up on Katie's anxiety? Unusual for the big Newfie. Ella was many things, but she was not particularly interested in the humans and their social dramas.

Katie readied the cutter to slice open the tape.

Now Ella was on all four paws, nose twitching, staring straight at Katie.

The cutter plunged deeper into the box.

Brayden caught Ella's low whine, and then he was in action, throwing himself at her.

"Katie, don't open that!"

He reached her and knocked her away just as the cutter slid home. The box somersaulted through the air, landing next to the curtains. As it hit the hardwood, there was a loud bang. The package disintegrated, shooting pieces of metal in all directions. One jagged slice buried itself into the floor near Ella's feet.

The fair planners screamed and raced for the safety of the kitchen.

He scooped Katie up and delivered her there, too, Ella at his heels.

"Everyone stay here until I come and get you," he commanded.

Once he was assured that they would do as he'd asked, Brayden eased back into the living room to examine the package bomb. He'd never seen one before, but this one was obviously intended to wound with flying shrapnel. Judging by the shards sticking into the small table and littered on the floor, it would have done its deadly job, maiming or killing Katie or anyone else close by.

He returned to the kitchen.

"Did anyone see how the package got into the house?" he demanded.

Shirlene raised a shaky hand. "It was me. I... I saw it lying by the mailbox at the property gate. I figured one of the volunteers had dropped it off for the meeting, so I brought it in." Tears gathered in her eyes and streaked her mascara. "I didn't think... I'm so sorry."

Katie gently gripped the other woman's forearms. "Don't be. This wasn't your fault...and...and you're right. We shouldn't be having any meetings until Terrence is caught. The Christmas Fair is postponed until that happens."

Shirlene grimaced. "Believe me, I don't want to add to your worry. None of us do. A bunch of us have been supporting Addie and this place for years. So it's terrible for me to have to say this, Katie, but it's just not safe with Terrence on the loose."

Katie answered with a silent nod.

Brayden spoke up. "If we catch him, you'll change your minds?"

Shirlene's head bobbed reluctantly. "Of course."

A woman named Barb spoke softly. "Katie, honey, word's already gotten out about Terrence. The fair might not bring in the income you need anyway."

Katie looked as though she might cry. The wobble in her chin made him feel desperate.

Charlie spoke up. "Well, I am not going to quit on you. I will be here to help, Terrence or no Terrence."

His words seemed to lend her some composure. She gulped in a breath and stood. "I understand how you all feel, and I am so very sorry for what happened here today."

"Terrence will be caught," Brayden said. "It's a priority of the Alaska K-9 Unit. That's why I'm here."

On the way out the door, Shirlene hugged Katie. "I really am sorry to bug out on you. It's not fair, but it must be faced."

"I understand. I really do."

Shirlene left.

*Not fair?* Well, that was the understatement of the century. A man who didn't get what he felt he was due could destroy everything Aunt Addie and Katie had worked so hard for.

Not fair by a long shot.

Well, it wasn't going to end that way, not if he had a breath left in his body.

It took another hour to debrief the local police bomb squad and fill Lorenza in.

When Katie went upstairs, he sat in the dark shadows of the porch with Ella, listening to the rain pounding on the roof. Putting the Christmas Fair on hold would be a hard blow for the ranch, but injury or worse to Katie was his main priority. He felt the responsibility for that resting squarely on his shoulders. Terrence had to be captured. Quickly.

He stroked the dog. "Do I need to add bomb detection to your list of job skills?" He'd already given her a pile of dog treats and let her frolic in the water running from the downspout. The dog was probably a better trooper than he was.

He glanced again at his phone, waiting for a message from Gabriel. The for-sale ad Quinn had brought to their attention might provide some answers. His mind drifted back to Katie and her quiet resolve, the way she'd handled the meeting. Impressive, pure and simple.

She was not the same woman he thought he knew, the young, flighty person he had not believed ready to manage a job with the Alaska State Troopers.

*And she'd been wise enough to warn you about Jamie.* Maybe *courageous* more aptly described it. They didn't have a great rapport before that, and she'd stuck her neck out to try to give him a heads-up. Instead of being appreciative, he'd not believed a word of it. Instead of thanks, he'd given her anger.

The buzz on his phone interrupted his thoughts. It was a call from Gabriel. Brayden answered.

"Hank checks out okay," Gabriel said. "No connection to Terrence. Here's a picture of his reindeer to show Katie to ease her mind, but it's an older female he's had for a while. I'm no expert, but he says it's fifteen years old and I believe him. The critter's pretty rickety." Gabriel paused. "He's hoping to find someone to take it, or he's going to put it down before he moves in with his son in Anchorage."

Brayden became aware then that Katie was standing

there, wrapped in an oversize sweatshirt and pants. He gestured her closer.

"Thanks, Gabriel. Appreciate it."

He clicked off and showed her the photo.

"I heard what you said." Katie looked at the screen, her shoulders sagging. "That's not Lulu for sure. Gabriel's right. She's much older." She frowned. "Poor baby. She needs her hooves trimmed and some vitamin support. She might be developing IKC. It's an eye condition that needs treatment."

He was happy when she settled into the chair opposite, arms wrapped around herself. She looked so young, younger than Jamie even. *This* isn't *Jamie*, he reminded himself, but the lingering unease drifted across his memory. He'd made a fool of himself about his former girlfriend, and she'd completely manipulated him. How could he have been so gullible? He cleared his throat and got to his feet.

"I'd better get Ella settled in at the bunkhouse before I check in with Alex. He's doing the night shift."

She nodded distractedly.

"Lock the door behind me, okay?"

"Yes." Still he knew her mind was far away.

"I…" He wanted to tell her how sorry he was for ever thinking she lacked the skills to work for the department, but when she looked at him with those soulful eyes, he forgot how to string words together. "Uh, I… Good night."

And then he was out the door, lashed by a curtain of chilling rain. Ella began to romp in clownish circles as she did anytime she was around moisture, trying to capture the droplets in her mouth.

"Stay out of that," he yelled. "I just got you dried off from the downspout." Too late. She'd located a bread-loaf-sized puddle. The massive dog was doing her able best to compact herself into that tiny pool. Her contortions were impressive. If it wasn't going to mean a lengthy drying-off session, he would have laughed.

"Ella, come here," he commanded.

She didn't, of course. He was ratcheting up to his "I mean business" tone when Katie called from the doorway. He left Ella to her merriment and hurried back to Katie.

Her brows were quirked in worry as she stepped back enough to allow him, dripping, into the foyer.

"I don't want to bother you," she said.

"No bother. What's on your mind?"

She hesitated. "I have to take her."

*"Her?"*

"The reindeer. I can't let Hank put her down. No one is going to buy her in that condition. With proper care, she could live out her life peacefully here, with the herd." She bit her lower lip. "I know what you're thinking. It's not smart. We have limited funds and the ranch is in jeopardy. And that after that package bomb, the absolute last thing we need is an elderly animal to add to the herd."

"Actually," he said slowly, "I was thinking—"

"It's impractical, bad business, a flighty decision based on emotion, not logic."

He saw that lush lower lip tremble and it sent his

stomach fluttering in sympathy. "I was thinking," he repeated, "that I'll call Hank right now and arrange it. I'll buy her for you, for the ranch. My treat."

"You don't need to do that."

"A gift. My pleasure."

She put a knuckle to her mouth and he saw the shimmer of moisture in her eyes. "Thank you," she whispered. "For not saying it was a dumb idea."

"No thanks necessary, ma'am. You want to help prevent this animal from suffering and death. There's nothing dumb about it. I'm sure if I ask nicely, Hank will drive over and deliver it here. Quinn and I can unload her."

Katie smiled. "Do you know how to get a reindeer out of a trailer?"

That stopped him. "Uh, no, but I can coax a hundred-pound dog in and out of the back seat of my car, so how different could it be?"

"About two hundred pounds different. I can help unload her." She held up a palm to stop his comment. "I promise I will wait patiently behind the gate, all safe and sound."

He hesitated, thinking it through. The thought of her being there, seeing her face when he rode in with the poor animal, made a note trill inside his heart. He blinked and scrubbed a hand over his damp hair to steady himself. "I'll make the call right now."

He had his answer in a matter of moments.

"Hank's real eager to off-load the animal," he told her. "He'll have her here at first light, and he's even throwing in the trailer as a bonus."

"That's fantastic."

And then she reached out and hugged him, a friendly squeeze, then a quick kiss on the cheek that sent his pulse skittering. How could any woman's lips be so incredibly soft?

"Thank you, Brayden. I understand this isn't practical, but now I can sleep tonight, knowing that sweet girl will not be put down."

"Aw, well, you know, you're welcome," he said gruffly. "It's the least I could do after such a rotten afternoon. So, uh, I'll try to get my dog out of the water now. See you in the morning."

She nodded and closed the door.

As he eyed Ella's unfettered rejoicing, he felt an unexpected rush of something vaguely similar.

Katie had a moment of relief from the terror of her life. And he'd helped. It shouldn't be a reason for the odd feeling in his heart, but nevertheless, it was.

"Come on, Ella. I need some sleep."

The soggy dog finally pulled herself from the water and followed Brayden back to the bunkhouse, both of their steps light.

# EIGHT

Katie was ready by sunup. She hoped a harness, blanket and a handful of green leafy treats would be enough to coax the old reindeer out of the trailer and into a pen. It might not be an easy task if the animal hadn't been transported for a while. Quinn would set up a comfortable stall near the other animals, but separate until it was clear she would not spread any diseases to the herd. Hank had told Brayden the animal's name was Tulip.

*All right, Tulip. This is going to be your forever home, in spite of Terrence.*

Trying very hard not to think about the package that had exploded in the living room only hours before, she went to brew the coffee. She was finished with her first cup when Brayden joined her. He squinted, bleary-eyed.

"How can you look so chipper this early?" he said.

"Because we're bringing home a bouncing baby reindeer."

He drank from the coffee cup she handed him. "Not exactly a baby."

"But a new addition, nonetheless. Are you ready?

Gabriel texted me they'll be at the front gate soon." She paused. "Hold on." If she hadn't been in a state of excitement, she might not have had the courage to reach up and smooth down the section of his hair that stood up at the temple. Her fingers brushed his jaw and she felt an electric spark. Quickly, she pulled her hand away. "There. All set."

"Thank you. Ella, stay with Katie, okay?"

Katie settled Ella into her Jeep and drove to the dock entrance, stopping well behind the fencing, as Brayden specified. She waved to Alex, who parked his vehicle next to hers as extra security. Brayden left to meet Hank at the ranch entrance at the end of the frontage road that paralleled the river. With the animal in tow, he'd drive the trailer to the dock gate and they'd cut through the pasture to the penned area where the new reindeer would be quarantined.

She sat with the windows rolled down, listening to the sound of the rushing water. It seemed like a lifetime ago since Ella had pulled her aunt out of those treacherous waves. The thought of Terrence being out there somewhere, waiting for another chance to strike, made her temples pound. The drive to the front of the property was several miles, so she couldn't see Brayden until he drove up, the ranch pickup now towing Hank's small trailer. Katie reached out and ran her fingers through Ella's dense fur, waiting.

"He's almost here," she whispered.

When Brayden got close enough, she could see him grinning as he guided the truck and trailer. It warmed her heart again to consider how he'd helped make this rescue a reality, a gift she would always remember. At times, it felt as if he had as much love for the Family K and its inhabitants as she did.

In a blink, everything changed. A shot rang out from the shrubs at the other side of the river. The first bullet hit something metallic. She was not sure what. The second must have exploded the truck's tire, because it skidded out of control.

She could hear Alex shouting into the radio, *"Shots fired!"*

Her body felt numb with terror, immobilized.

In a matter of moments, Gabriel's trooper vehicle flew onto the frontage road, siren wailing.

Alex yelled at her, "Get down."

She scrunched below the dashboard, encouraging Ella to do the same, until the shooting stopped and Gabriel's siren faded into the distance as hc pursued the perpetrator. Desperate to see what had happened to Brayden, she risked a look. Horrified, she found that the truck had flipped on its side and was sliding down into the Frontier River, towing the animal trailer behind it.

Had Brayden gotten out?

Alex clicked off his radio. "Gabriel's chasing Terrence down the access road. Terrence is on a motorcycle."

If Terrence was speeding away from the destruction he'd just caused, then he wasn't close enough to be a threat anymore.

And Brayden needed help.

She flung open the door and she and Ella raced through the gate and straight to the edge of the water.

\* \* \*

Brayden tried to regain his equilibrium, but his senses were spinning. The truck was nose down in the river, filling rapidly through the shattered front window. And the trailer had toppled, too. As far as he could tell, he hadn't been shot, unless the adrenaline and the shock were camouflaging the pain.

*Get out. Get to Katie.* He reached for his seat belt and released it. Water rushed in, pushing against him. He shoved at the door, but found it jammed. Three vicious smacks with his shoulder did no good. He wasn't getting out that way.

He began trying to smash out the rest of the front glass, but the pressure of the water prevented it. Stopping for a moment, he reconsidered. Waves were splashing at his chest now, numbing him quickly. He searched around for something else to use to break the glass.

Katie appeared out of nowhere, wading through the water toward the truck.

"No, Katie." She could be shot at any moment, swept away by the rushing water.

She stayed, searching for a way to get him out.

He bashed again at the windshield with his boot. This time, it gave.

Katie worked from the other side, climbing up on the front fender and kicking for all she was worth. Ella bobbed next to her, paddling in frantic circles. When water began to swamp his nostrils, the glass finally gave way. He swam out, clutching at Katie's wrist, plunging through the turbulence with her. Ella stayed right next to them, ready to intervene if they couldn't make it. They struggled on until the three of them were on the muddy bank.

"You shouldn't have…" he gasped.

"Gabriel is pursuing Terrence, and they're off the property," she said when she could get a breath in. "I had to help you." Then her eyes went huge with fear. He followed her gaze to the trailer that was taking on water. The old reindeer would be dead within minutes.

"Get to Alex. I'll help her."

"I can help," she insisted.

"Katie, I'm not moving until you get to safety."

Reluctantly, she moved a few steps up the squishy bank.

Slogging through the water, he reached the back end and released the trailer door. The frantic animal surged out into the water, knocking him aside. He heard Katie cry out. What could he do? Reindeer were great swimmers, but this one was old and obviously feeble. She was sucked out into the current. Valiantly, the reindeer tried to keep herself afloat, but within moments only her nostrils and gnarled old antlers were visible.

Katie's face was dead pale, hands pressed to her mouth.

Ella acted before he even realized what was happening. She leaped back into the water with a splash and paddled straight to the struggling reindeer. Grabbing the bridle in her mouth, she began to swim toward shore. It was an enormous effort until the reindeer stopped struggling and allowed Ella to lead her back to land.

Katie broke away from Alex, grabbed the bridle and

helped her out. Ella shook herself mightily, none the worse for wear.

"Get them all away from here," Brayden shouted to Alex and Quinn, who had appeared at a run.

Quinn took the animal from Katie, and Alex led her to his car. Her expression as she looked out the window at him was both worried and wondrous. He raised a hand halfway to show her, to *tell* her somehow, that he appreciated her help. That he was grateful to the Lord to be alive, and that he was blessed that she had not been hurt.

Her hand went to the glass, pressed there for a moment as if in answer before Alex whisked her away.

Then he bent to his dog, water dripping off them both.

"Ella," he said. "You are the best trooper in the state of Alaska."

Goose bumps prickled her skin as Alex drove them toward the main house. Part of her brain was struggling to keep up. He'd known… Terrence had known when Brayden would be driving along the river. How? "Alex, did you tell anyone about our plans?"

The security guard shot her an offended look in the rearview. "No, ma'am. I did not," he said as they pulled up the drive.

She moved to get out, but he stopped her.

"Brayden said to wait. He wants to check the house cameras."

Katie was shivering in spite of the roaring car heater, and she was anxious to grab dry clothes and help Quinn get the reindeer settled in. Surely Terrence couldn't be wreaking havoc at the house when he'd just been chased off the property. Then again, he seemed to be everywhere.

She saw Brayden arrive on foot and run up to the porch with Ella.

He was soaking wet, and she saw his shoulders slump.

She waited until she could not stand it anymore. Rolling down the window, she called out, "Brayden, what is it?"

Slowly, he walked over and turned the cell screen around so she could see.

"I'm sorry, Katie," he said.

He felt the sting of failure as he showed her the photo taken from the camera at the main house. The grainy image revealed Terrence on the porch, as he plunged a knife through the wood of the front door fifteen minutes before he'd taken cover in the trees and shot the tires of the ranch truck. He'd known Brayden couldn't be checking the camera and meeting Hank at the same time. Then he'd jogged off, heading for the direction of the riverbank, ready to kill him or Katie if Brayden hadn't insisted she stay well back from the dock.

It galled him, leaving every nerve in his body sizzling with anger. He left Katie in Alex's vehicle and strode to the front door again, taking pictures with his phone. As he stood there, he heard Katie approach. She was not content to sit in the truck, shielded from the truth, and he didn't have the energy to argue with her.

She came close enough to see it for herself, the knife cleaving the wood, pinning a note there.

*Get off my ranch.*

He imagined the rest of the threat was probably clear to Katie as it was to him.

*...or I'll kill you.*

She didn't say anything. He watched her absorb it all. Her profile was troubled, but with a resolve in the tilt of her chin. It hit him that five months before he'd been involved with Jamie, concerned about which restaurants to take her to, sights they could see, events she might enjoy that would be worth telling her friends about. So much of their relationship seemed to have been focused on entertainment. It all seemed so frivolous and unimportant now as he took in the woman in front of him.

Katie was passionate about things that mattered—her family, her animals. The standoffishness he'd sensed was self-protection concealing an exceptionally tender heart. Brayden wondered at the realization until he brought his brain back to heel and asked Katie to stay on the porch.

He sent a text to Alex. I've got this. Take another loop around the property and report back.

On it, Alex confirmed, then drove off as Quinn approached at a jog.

"Got her in the isolation pen. So far, she looks a little shocky, but Doc Jake should be here any minute." He eyed the knife. "You two, uh, okay?"

"Yeah. Give me a minute to check the house."

Quinn nodded. He understood and took up position next to Katie.

Brayden took Ella inside, more for her nose than any-thing else, though it was clear that Terrence had left. The situation could have been tragic. He wasn't going to make any more careless errors like the one he'd made in allowing Katie to be too close to the dock entrance.

He cleared the house, room by room, as a precaution, but the camera footage was sufficient. Terrence had not entered. *This time.* He let Katie in. Quinn brought him a set of dry clothes from the bunkhouse and a towel to dry Ella. Brayden stewed on everything that had trans-pired as Katie changed her clothes, all business as she emerged, beelining for the front door.

"Where are you going?" He shook his head. "Never mind. I know. I'll go with you."

She nodded. "I saw Dr. Jake's van pull up. I want to be there for her exam. Quinn's coming, too."

"Katie…" he started, reaching for her. "Thank you. For helping me get out of the truck."

She smiled. "You're welcome. Ella would never have forgiven me if I let you drown."

Her spirit and resilience astonished him. "I can't fig-ure out how he's tracking our every move. That wasn't a spontaneous act. He knew I was driving to get the reindeer and when."

"Do you think Hank tipped off Terrence?"

Exactly the problem he'd been wrestling with. "I trust Gabriel's assessment that there was no connection between the two, but it's possible he missed something. Or there's some other way Terrence is anticipating our moves."

"My aunt said he wouldn't stop." Her self-possession

gave way to fear that she couldn't completely hide. She sighed, a sound so long and filled with despair that he could not resist pulling her into a hug. He held her to his chest, reveling in her closeness, wondering at his own craving to be near her, to make her world better. But he *hadn't*. Clearing his throat, he released her.

"As I said, I never should have let you wait for me near the dock."

Her chin went up. "I'm a grown woman, Brayden. You don't 'let' me do anything. I chose to go because I didn't believe there was any threat, either, so you can't take all the blame."

He wished he could let himself off the hook as easily as she did. "I'm the trooper and that's my duty here, to keep you safe. The colonel entrusted me to handle this case."

Something shuttered in Katie's face. "I will try not to get in the way of your duty, Brayden. I know how much your job means to you."

And then she was out the door, leaving him with his mouth open, trying to figure out how he'd once again said the wrong thing.

Terrence had somehow outsmarted him, knowing their comings and goings. Teeth gritted, he decided that he was going to solve that mystery if it took him the rest of the day and night. It was his sworn duty to protect Katie, and he was going to do his job. No homicidal maniac was going to stop him.

# NINE

Brayden patrolled every square inch of the property himself, in addition to sending Phil out on another set of patrols to back up Alex. As much as he'd dreaded telling the K-9 team what had happened, he'd reported in and now some of his fellow troopers were on their way to help scour the property. Brayden had already coned off the road and photographed the submerged truck and trailer in which he and Tulip had almost drowned.

His foul mood grew darker as the day wore on. And by late afternoon, he returned tired and hungry to his starting point, the Frontier River gate that led out to the dock. He let himself through, hoping standing at that vantage point, alone with his thoughts, would reset his peace of mind.

When the cold wind started to freeze him an inch at a time, he climbed below where the pilings were buried in the riverbank. The shallow area was rocky and there was enough exposed surface that he could stay out of the water. Nothing unusual on the massive wood posts.

"No swimming," he firmly told Ella, who was staring with a familiar excitement at the rippling water.

She flopped dejectedly onto the wet bank and gave him the "you are a crotchety old man" stare. He guessed he was, too. His back ached from driving the property, and the knee injury he'd gotten on a drunk-and-disorderly call back in the day before he became a K-9 handler throbbed. If he wasn't a good trooper, then what was left in his life? No wife, kids, no hobbies even, unless dog grooming and planting vegetables that died a slow death counted. He shut off the self-pity faucet. He was an Alaska State Trooper, and a good one, too. He wasn't about to bungle things now.

And why was this case, this *duty*, so very personal to him all of a sudden? He wasn't sure Katie felt much more than neutral toward him, and he'd felt no real rapport with her, either…until he'd landed on this out-of-the-way ranch. Then something changed. Was it her? Or him?

He looked down to find Ella slowly commando crawling toward the water.

"Stop right there," he called. She flapped her ears and returned to him. Figuring he could dissuade her for only so long, they trudged up to the dock again, over the wooden boards where she sat heavily at his feet. From here, there was an excellent view of the main building. You could even see the bunkhouse and a glimpse of the storage units. Terrence was familiar with the riverbank, but even he could not remain there 24/7 to track their comings and goings without being seen. Unless…

He examined the warped wood that formed the narrow platform. The individual boards were badly weathered by Alaska's unforgiving winters, sticking up at the edges like a series of snaggly teeth. They were secured to the pilings that jutted up every few feet or so.

Ella found a sunlit section of board and sprawled out to bask. Small solace since she'd been prohibited from enjoying the water. Over the top of her fuzzy head, he saw something that made his gut go tight. Hustling close to the piling, he inspected the tiny item, no bigger than his thumb, connected to a small battery and fixed in place with wire. It had been hidden by a broken bit of board that had once been nailed there.

A camera, he figured. The picture wouldn't be very clear, but it would provide Terrence with enough of an image to see vehicles coming and going from the property and who was in the front seat. It probably fed to his cell phone, similar to Brayden's security cameras. The information wouldn't have helped, though, unless the man was camping out in the woods in time to act on it, and they'd already checked that. No sign of him in the woods or the riverbank.

With a pen pulled from his pocket, he disconnected the battery from the camera. Soon the power would be drained and Terrence would not receive any more info from his spy gadget. He photographed the camera, too, summoned Ella and drove back to the ranch.

Ella was with Dr. Jake and Quinn across the field at the isolation pen, and he would have joined them, but two Alaska K-9 cars rolled onto the property, parking at the main house. One was Gabriel and Bear and the other... He pulled in a breath. The other belonged to Colonel Lorenza Gallo herself. That surprised him, but it shouldn't have. She loved Katie, and after the last report he'd given, she must have decided to pay him a personal visit.

His sense of cold intensified as he got out and greeted them. "Terrence had a camera on the property," he said, showing them the picture on his cell phone. "Can we get Helena out here with Luna to check for any others?" Though Luna was only casually trained in electronics detection, she would be able to sniff out any hidden gizmos much more efficiently than he ever could.

"I figured that might work, too," Gabriel murmured. "She's already on her way. Should be here soon."

Lorenza frowned and fixed Brayden with a hard look. "Let's get right down to it. Why did you let Katie wait for you at the dock entrance?"

Why *had* he? Because he'd believed it was safe and he'd wanted to grant her heart's desire to help with Tulip's transition. What a colossal misstep on his part. He blew out a breath. "No excuses. I messed up."

"Yes, you did," she concurred.

Gabriel shot him a sympathetic look as the colonel continued.

"I'm going to push her to leave, get her into a safe house. We've got officers who can cover that duty."

*Other* officers, she meant. Not him. "I think she might not be amenable to leaving."

"You are correct—she won't," Katie said, joining them. He'd not been aware of her approach. "Hi, Colonel. How are you? I miss you and Denali."

She smiled. "Hi, Katie. We miss you at the office, too. I know Denali misses all the treats you used to sneak him. The office temp we got to fill in is almost up to speed, but he's not got your knack for keeping us all organized, that's for sure. You've had quite a time here, I understand."

Katie cocked her head. "Both the truck and the trailer are a wreck, but I am in one piece and so is Brayden. Our newest reindeer will survive, too, if we're fortunate."

The colonel smiled. "I'm relieved to hear it."

"And I want to clear the air," Katie said. "I wanted to help with the reindeer's arrival. It was *my* decision to be there, so you shouldn't blame him."

"He's wearing the badge, not you," she snapped. "He's paid to make better decisions than that."

Brayden's face went molten. He felt the same level of humiliation he'd experienced finding out from Katie the truth about his girlfriend. Now here she was, defending him to his boss, no less.

Without looking directly at her, Brayden rested his hands on his hips and spoke up. "The colonel is right, Katie. You should go to a safe house."

"I'm not leaving," she said firmly.

Lorenza took on a more severe look. "Now is not the time to be stubborn. I know you're worried about the Family K. We can hire someone to help Quinn. Other people can take care of reindeer besides you." Her expression softened. "You are not the reindeer whisperer."

"Yes, I am," she said. "Didn't you know? I thought I had that on my résumé." She laughed. "It could be why Brayden here didn't think I was good law enforcement support material."

Now he was thoroughly flummoxed. That laughter. It told him she really had forgiven him for his "nonrecommend" on her oral boards. It released a knot inside him he'd carried for a long time.

He kept his gaze away from her in case he might be tempted to relish the delight of that smile.

*Get yourself sorted out, Ford. You're not a teenager.*

But he felt like one, hardly able to keep his gaze off her. He stood up straighter, refocusing, reminding himself where his focus should be.

"Fortunately," Gallo said, "the department hired you anyway, in spite of any negatives from your interview. Which were supposed to remain confidential, by the way."

Brayden could only wish they had.

"That aside, it's not safe for you to stay here anymore. If Terrence can shoot tires out and get to the front door in spite of a cop, cameras and two security guards, we can't secure the ranch. Too wide open and too many access points."

Katie gave her an apologetic look. "I appreciate your concern," she said. "But there's something you should know." She wiggled her phone. "The hospital called and Aunt Addie is being released first thing Monday morning. I'm not just being stubborn by staying." Any mischievousness was gone, leaving Katie serious as the grave. "I have to take care of her because she has no one else. I don't have a choice. She didn't turn her back on me when I had no one, and I'm not going to turn my back on her, either."

"We can arrange for her to visit the ranch occasionally, for both of you to…" Gabriel started.

"You've met my aunt, right?" Katie said.

He nodded.

"All of you have?"

Lorenza and Brayden added their affirmatives.

"Do any of you think there's the slightest chance you'll convince her to go stay in a safe house?"

There was dead silence.

"Yep," Katie said. "Me, neither. She can't turn away from these animals and I can't turn away from her, so it looks like you troopers are going to have to catch Terrence so we can all get back to business as usual. If you can do it soon, maybe we can save this sad-sack ranch after all."

Her phone buzzed with a text. "That's Doc Jake. I need to go talk to him. Let yourselves into the house if you want to have a meeting. I'll be back soon." She jogged away.

Lorenza stared after her. "Such a determined young woman."

*Like someone else I know,* Brayden thought. It was clear that the colonel admired Katie for her strength. Something in her expression made him think she'd not for a moment believed Katie would agree to go to a safe house.

They sat inside and Brayden took a seat facing the window where he could barely make out Katie's bright green shirt, Quinn by her side, as they talked to the veterinarian.

Far out of rifle range, he assured himself. Alex's security vehicle was making a pass up the dirt access road. He would shorten Phil's and Alex's routes and increase the frequency. Call Phil to brief him and rethink the night sweeps.

He needed to make some changes to ensure her safety. Would Katie allow him to bunk on a sofa in the main house? It didn't feel right not being able to personally secure the main house during the night. Better to have his ears and Ella's close in case...

"Brayden? Are you still with us?"

He looked up to find the colonel staring at him. "Yes, ma'am. Sorry. What did you say?"

Gabriel was doing his best to hide a smile. He was probably enjoying the fact that it was Brayden on the receiving end of the colonel's ire instead of himself. "I was explaining that Anchorage PD called this morning. They said they have footage of a woman matching Violet James's description at an ATM."

"An ATM?" Brayden said in surprise. "I didn't think she had a wallet with her, or that she'd dare use it." Violet was the orphaned daughter of a late Alaskan oil baron, so she had money, if she could access it. So far, she hadn't, to his knowledge.

"We haven't had any activity on her bank accounts," Gabriel confirmed, "but I'll check again." He glanced out the window.

Helena Maddox climbed out of her car, long hair pulled into a brown twist. The eager Norwegian elkhound pranced along next to her. The dog was a whiz at tracking people, but Helena had been enhancing her abilities by cross-training in their spare time.

"Hey," she said, as Gabriel let her in. "Sorry to be the bearer of bad news, but Anchorage says the woman they spotted isn't Violet. Same height and coloring, but she's not our gal."

Gabriel groaned. "Violet is another strong woman with grit. How she's managing to remain a fugitive when she's due to have a baby in a month is completely beyond me."

"Me, too," Helena said, "but she's doing a great job of it."

"Time's getting short." Gallo's mouth set in a thin line. "The longer we don't find her, the greater the likelihood Lance will. She'll be easy prey with a newborn."

"Ariel is about beside herself. She's going to be crushed that this latest sighting isn't Violet," Helena said.

Ariel Potter, fiancée of Hunter McCord, had more reason than all of them to want to solve the case. They'd both been at the wedding-party guided tour in the Chugach when the murder had occurred, and Ariel had been pushed off a cliff. She woke up to find Violet on the run, accused of the murder of the tour guide. She'd defended her friend's innocence staunchly from the get-go. Brayden figured Ariel must have a dose of guilt over the whole thing, too, since she'd been there when Violet's fiancé had committed murder and tried to frame Violet. Not Ariel's fault, of course, but guilt was a hard thing to shake. Didn't he know it?

"I've been training Luna on the electronics sniffing, but no guarantees," Helena said. "She's not an expert yet, so I'm not sure she can spot more of Terrence's spy gear if there is any."

"She's our best choice right now along with good old-fashioned boots on the ground." Lorenza got to her feet and they all followed suit.

Brayden handed Helena the battery. "I'll show you the camera so Luna can get a good sniff."

"I've got to go," the colonel said. The officers walked with her back to her vehicle. "I am going to the hospital to try to talk some sense into Addie. It will be like rolling a boulder uphill, but I'll give it a shot anyway." She gave the three of them a pointed look. "I want to know what you all accomplish here today. Give me a rundown on any new security procedures, whatever the dogs find, et cetera. I'll expect a *full report* before the close of business today."

"Yes, ma'am." The emphasis on the last part made it clear the colonel's state of mind. She wanted dotted *i*'s and crossed *t*'s. No need to remind him. He wasn't going to make another mistake.

His career depended on it.

His gaze found Katie across the pastureland.

And something much more precious than his badge hung in the balance.

# TEN

Katie sat cross-legged on an old ratty blanket watching Tulip through the wire enclosure, talking softly to the animal every so often. The reindeer still appeared dazed, but she'd stopped shivering. So far, she had not touched the pile of fresh alfalfa or greens left there for her. That worried Katie. Bats winged across the sky, forecasting the coming of dusk. She'd been sitting there for hours. What was more, she was weary to the bone.

Doc Jake had told her to call if Tulip took a bad turn. Between her and Quinn, Tulip had not been alone since they picked her up. The other reindeer came close to the fence, poking curious noses toward the new member. Tulip's nostrils quivered and she snuffled softly. The others would accept her, Katie knew. Gratitude swelled in her heart at Brayden's generous gift. Though the rescue had almost ended in tragedy, it had still been a rescue and she thanked God that the ailing female had been brought to the ranch. No matter if she lived or died, she would be surrounded by her herd, her family, comfort all around.

An image of her mother rose in her mind along with

a surge of grief. Katie bent her head onto her arms and began to cry. How she'd missed her family with every waking breath right after the accident, and there were moments even now when the ache returned, as painful as ever. And that was why, though she couldn't put it into words, she knew she was doing the Lord's will by taking a leave of absence from her job and coming to the ranch. What happened here was blessed, precious, and no matter what, she had to keep it going. The reindeer family, and her aunt Addie, meant everything to her, but how sweet would it be to have a family of her own someday? It was a thought she had allowed herself to entertain only fleetingly throughout her life. So why now?

"Katie?" The soft voice startled her. She raised her wet face to find Brayden looking at her. Quickly, she rubbed her cheeks on her jacket sleeve.

"Hey, Brayden. What's up?"

"It's getting on toward dark. I came to find you." To her surprise, he sat down next to her. It was an awkward move for the long-legged man and he grunted before he achieved it. Ella settled beside them.

"Ouch, my knee. Man, that probably made me sound old."

She laughed. "No. The reindeer make that noise all the time."

"Well, that makes me feel better, to know I sound like a three-hundred-pound fuzzy animal." He paused. "You...all right?"

"Yes."

"Oh. I thought, uh, maybe you were crying."

"Sometimes…" Should she tell him about the emotional morass she'd sunk into? No, but out it came anyway. "Sometimes I miss my parents so much it hurts, even after all this time."

"Wounds like that never really heal, do they? Just scab over."

"Yes."

"I'm sorry," he murmured.

"I'm fine. Really."

He did not press and she was grateful. Instead, he looked at Tulip. "How's she doing?"

"Holding her own. The antibiotics and fluids should help make her more comfortable. Doc did a treatment on her eyes, too. The hooves will have to wait until she's stronger." Another pause. Katie sighed. "I'm really sorry you got into trouble for what happened. I know the colonel won't hold it against you for advancement or anything."

"Advancement isn't what's worrying me right now." He looked up at the emerging stars.

It wasn't?

"You know, a few weeks ago, my career path was my number one priority, but lately, I've been more concerned about other things."

She watched an owl propel itself on velvet wings through the encroaching night. "Like what?"

"Like you."

She started. *"Me?"*

He nodded. "There's something I want you to tell me."

"Okay, but I have the right to take the Fifth." She waited, plucking at the edge of the blanket.

"You said you saw something that convinced you to tell me about Jamie, even though you knew it would probably go badly."

"Which it did."

"Agreed," he said. "But what was it? I've been racking my brain. I didn't support your hiring, and we hardly knew each other outside of work. As a matter of fact, you probably thought I was a huge jerk."

"Not a huge one exactly," she said lightly.

He chuckled. "All right. A medium-sized jerk."

"I'd go with that, since you didn't take the time to know me. You mistook me for some young, immature woman without the skills and poise needed to do the job, and you treated me like that for a long time after I was hired."

He exhaled. "I did. Like I said, a medium-sized jerk at least. I apologize."

"It's not all your fault. To be fair, I didn't want to know you, either. I keep to myself, as you know, and I don't share my feelings easily. The colonel knows me better than anyone, I guess, even the other cops."

"Yes. The strong, silent type." He teased a smile out of her. "So why *did* you tell me about Jamie?"

She hesitated a moment longer. "Because of Mr. Winkler."

He blinked. "The guy who lives in that run-down trailer in Cantwell?"

"Yes."

He frowned. "I don't get it. What does that have to do with Jamie?"

"Nothing, but it has a lot to do with you."

He arched one eyebrow. "You'll have to break it down for me." He tapped his temple. "My gears work slowly, remember?"

"You arrested Mr. Winkler for a drunk-and-disorderly back in May."

"Uh-huh. I remember. Didn't have much choice. He almost walked into the side of my squad car and he had a fit when I arrested him."

"Right. I was at the county jail doing some business for the colonel when you turned him over to the jailer. I heard him when he was being booked. He was distraught because he kept three elderly dogs and they would be hungry and worried if he didn't come home."

Brayden looked away. "Uh-huh."

"And you took those dogs food. And stayed the night with them, didn't you?"

Brayden was suddenly fascinated by the horizon. "Oh, now, that could be. It was a while ago."

She pressed on. "People say that you still bring Mr. Winkler bags of food sometimes at the end of the month when he runs short of funds."

Now he was squirming. "People say that, huh?"

"Yes, they do."

"Hmm. I didn't know any of that was public knowledge," he said gruffly.

"Hard to keep a secret around here. Why would you want it to be, anyway?"

He shrugged. "It's nothing special and I want to maintain my hard-bitten trooper persona."

She went for a playful tone to match his. "Well, you wanted to know the reason. That's why I told you about

Jamie. I figured under your crusty exterior and your poor judgment beat a heart of gold. That's why I told you."

He was staring at her now, the rising moonlight painting the strong planes of his face, lending a glimmer to his eyes that she knew were the green of new spring grass.

"Thank you for telling me the truth about Jamie," he said. "I never said it before, and I should have." And then his mouth was on hers, a sweet, gentle kiss, light as a breeze, and quickly over.

An electric buzz heightened her senses.

He looked dazed, staying close, as though he might kiss her a second time.

The comfort of his kiss floored her and she felt the wondrous warmth of it, but doubt trickled right along on its heels. What was this thing? This feeling she could not ignore? This kiss?

She was his assignment. He'd already gotten in trouble because of her. He was attracted to adventurous, outgoing women, most definitely unlike herself. The doubt grew strong enough that it propelled her to her feet.

He struggled up next to her. "Katie, I'm sorry. I shouldn't have done that."

"It's okay. Just a thank-you kiss, right? And you're welcome, by the way." Was she babbling? "I'm sorry it all went south with Jamie, but things worked out okay."

"Yes, I guess they did." He looked at his boots. "Helena didn't find any more cameras on the property, but I'd feel better if you were in the house for the night. Do you mind?"

"No problem. I think Tulip will be okay until morning." He bent to pick up her blanket at the same moment she did and their shoulders touched. She backed off and let him gather it up. Her body still felt warm and strange from the kiss.

As they walked back to the main house, she could hear the water sluicing through the riverbed. All at once, another memory returned—cold water, her uncle's face filled with hatred.

*Get off my ranch.*

The shot, the blood, her aunt still and lifeless in the water. Brayden trapped behind broken glass in that same river...

She realized she was shivering.

Brayden wrapped an arm around her shoulders and quickened their pace. He, too, seemed to feel as though the night had gotten especially dark, the rushing river whispering a warning.

*He's still out there.*

*And he's coming back.*

He walked Katie to the main house, sensing her tension. Because of his touch? Had he really kissed her? Yes, the sweet echo of her lips on his told him it was not a dream. He shouldn't have done it. There was a boatload of reasons the kiss was ill-advised. His brain recognized them, but his heart kept on beating a happy rhythm in his chest.

*Stop*, he told himself severely. *There's no room for a relationship here. Keep your kisses to yourself.* And Katie didn't want him in that way, clearly, or had he detected the smallest measure of matched feeling in her?

*There's your imagination going again. You convinced yourself Jamie wanted you. Don't let your own dumb history repeat itself.*

He marched them both toward the main house until Katie tugged at his arm.

"Too fast," she said. "Your legs are way longer than mine. Can we slow to a sprint?"

"Sorry," he said, letting her go and slackening his pace. He wanted to snatch up her hand in his, to feel those slender fingers in his palm. *Stop.* They made it to the main house. Somehow he needed to talk to her about his idea of sleeping in the living room.

As they entered, the old wall phone was ringing. He closed the door and checked the cameras while Katie picked it up.

"Hello?"

There was a pause. "Hello?" she said again.

After a moment, she hung up. "No one there."

*No one there.* The tightening of those lips that he'd just kissed told him she had doubts. No one? Or Terrence, checking to see if she was home? That sealed it.

"Katie, I think I should sleep downstairs on the sofa. I'm sure nothing will happen with Terrence, but I'd feel better if Ella and I were closer." There. He'd stated his case.

He saw her chin go up, the arms folded over her chest that indicated she was evaluating if the idea was a threat to her hard-won independence. "I… Um, okay. I'll get some blankets for you."

And then she went off to the closet, pulling out way too many blankets and pillows.

He smiled to himself. Maybe she was gradually learning to trust him. "Looks like we're sacking out here for the night, El." He turned to find she was already at home on the sofa, paws hanging off the edge of the cushion.

Katie smiled at the dog. "There's peanut butter and jelly in the kitchen if either of you get hungry," she said.

"Appreciate it."

"Is there anything else you need?" she asked.

"No, thank you. Ella and I are self-sufficient."

She nodded. "I know."

His phone rang. "Hey, Charlie," he said, surprised at the butcher's call. "What's up?"

He hit the speaker button so Katie could hear also.

"I was packaging up an order for delivery to the café and I saw him," he said.

"Terrence?"

"Yes. He's in an old banged-up RV headed north toward Pine Gap. I'm following him right now."

Brayden was on his feet. "License number? I'm calling the local cops. Don't approach him, Charlie. He's dangerous."

"Wait—he's pulling off into the woods. I'll have to go on foot or he'll spot me."

"Do not do that, Charlie!" Brayden commanded. "Stay there. PD will arrive soon."

There was a long silence.

"Charlie?" Brayden said. "Are you there?" He waited another beat, heart pounding. "Charlie?" he shouted.

No answer.

Katie's face went white with fear. "He went after him, Brayden."

He looked at the phone in alarm.

Charlie the friendly butcher would be no match for the homicidal Terrence Kapowski.

What could he do? He saw in Katie's expression that she was thinking exactly the same thing.

# ELEVEN

Katie paced the worn family room floor until she almost bumped into Brayden pacing in the other direction. His eyes were glued to his phone, waiting for an update from the local PD. Fifteen minutes had passed since they got Charlie's hushed phone call.

Had the police found Terrence before Charlie did? Was he under arrest and the nightmare was over? She swallowed, considering the alternative. What if Charlie had confronted her terrible uncle? Her nails dug into the skin of her palms. Why did the phone stay stubbornly silent?

She paced another lap until she couldn't stand it. "You have to go help him, Brayden."

His features were locked in that maddening "everything is under control" expression. "Katie, we just had this conversation," he said soothingly. "I can't leave you here unprotected. I won't."

"But Quinn's here and Phil is checking the property every hour. I'm perfectly safe, but Charlie could be in big trouble."

"I am sure everything is going to be okay," he said

again in that irritatingly calm fashion. "The local police are on scene already. They can handle this. We should be hearing from them any minute."

"Brayden," she said, her voice shrill. "Charlie could be dead or dying."

"Let's not jump to the worst-case scenario."

Her self-control dissolved. "Why not? Lately my whole life has been a worst-case scenario." A rising sense of urgency rushed through her. They simply could not let Terrence hurt anyone else. "Please, go. I will be safe. You can leave Ella with me."

"She's only helpful if you get stuck in the bathtub or some other body of water."

Katie would not be charmed away from her point. "She would bark if someone approached the house."

"Katie…" he started again.

"You have to help Charlie," she almost shrieked. In her urgency, she grabbed the front of his sweatshirt. The thump of his heart thrummed against her fingers. "Please, Brayden."

"Charlie is not my case," he snapped. "You are."

His case. Right. Stung, she let go of his shirt, turned and slammed into the kitchen. *You're an assignment, Katie. And he's not going to risk his career by blowing it again.* She wasn't being fair. Brayden didn't want Charlie hurt any more than she did, but to be reminded of her place in his mental hierarchy was painful. Why, she was not entirely sure.

She stayed there, wiping down the immaculate counter and fixing herself a cup of coffee, which she did not drink. Her mind spun with thoughts of Charlie, the good-hearted, kind fellow with an attachment to her aunt and a loyalty to the ranch. If anything happened to him, it would be because he was trying to help. Tears blurred her vision as she scrubbed an old stain that was never going to come out of the cracked tile.

A few minutes later, she heard Brayden enter.

Out of the corner of her eye, she saw him standing there, as if he was drumming up the courage to speak. She wasn't going to help him on that score. The stubborn stain refused to yield, but she scraped at it anyway.

"Katie, I didn't mean to bark at you."

Still, she swiped with the paper towel, hoping she would be able to keep from crying. Now was not the time to turn into a blubbery mess.

"I don't really understand what's going on here," he said.

"What do you mean?"

"Between us."

There was an *us*? Her heart trip-hammered. "I don't know what you're talking about."

He stared at her, eyes clear as an Alaskan spring. "I feel different when I'm with you."

The words both thrilled and terrified her. Should she reply? But too many seconds ticked by while she wrestled with what to say.

A look of something like disappointment flickered across his face. "Uh, well, never mind. I'm just gonna tell you the truth because I have to get things straight for my own sanity. The colonel called me to task for involving you in the Tulip thing. She said it was unprofessional and she was right, but I didn't tell her the real reason."

Katie twiddled with her necklace. "Why did you let me go to the dock, Brayden?"

He huffed out a breath. "Because I wanted to see your face."

She stared at him. "What?"

"That's the truth. Like I said, I feel different when I'm with you, like everything in the world is better and brighter. I was thinking how nice it would be if I could see your reaction when Tulip arrived, and so I caved. I let you be there, and look what happened."

He'd wanted to see her face. His tentative expression and gruff, gravelly tone convinced her it was true. The thought stunned her, that he cared about being with her for reasons other than his job. "No one was hurt," she managed. "It all turned out okay."

"No, it didn't. We were attacked and you were put in danger. You know what that makes me? A bad trooper. I don't want to be a bad trooper again, especially where your safety is involved. I'm sorry if that isn't what you want to hear, but that's the truth. I don't want to lie to you, even if it means sparing myself some embarrassment. You deserve the truth."

And then he about-faced and left the room. She stood there, the cleaning towel dangling from her fingertips. He'd wanted to be with her? Admitting it had embarrassed him to the core, yet he'd felt he owed her the truth. The respect she felt at that touched her deep down. Respect...and something deeper?

*The world is better and brighter...when I'm with you.*

Who was this man? It was as if the old picture she'd had of Brayden was curling up and peeling off, revealing something altogether different underneath. He enjoyed her company? The guy she'd once thought of as a judgmental, arrogant "medium-sized" jerk? She finally put down the tea bag, still marveling at his admission. What was even more difficult to fathom was that she'd enjoyed being with him as well, though she knew she did not have near the same level of courage he did when it came to admitting such notions. Brayden's presence in her life had made things both better and brighter, too.

What was to be done with that confession? Discuss it further to try to ease his mind? Or pretend it hadn't happened?

It was probably best to talk more about it, but she simply could not drum up one single thing to say that wouldn't come off awkward since she did not fully understand her own emotions at the moment. Besides, their focus should be on Charlie, she chided herself. The tension of not knowing the man's status probably drove Brayden's wild conversation. They were both on edge, scared… Ugh… Why was it taking so long to learn what had happened? She began to sweep the kitchen floor to try to pass the time. She'd not finished when she heard Brayden's phone ring. The words were indistinct, but the tenor of his voice made her stomach drop.

She hurried to find him, grim-lipped with the phone pressed to his ear. "Copy that. I'll be there in thirty." He disconnected.

Breath held, she waited for him to tell her.

"Terrence got away. He was spotted in the RV disappearing into the Chugach fifteen minutes ago."

She bit back her frustration. "What else?"

Brayden paused a beat. "He ran Charlie down."

Her hands flew to her mouth. "Oh no!"

"He's alive. I don't know the extent of his injuries. He's being transported now. I'm on the way to the hospital."

"I'll get my coat."

This time, Brayden did not argue as they headed to his car, but he did insist on Phil driving with them to the edge of town. She hardly noticed as they took the main highway.

Charlie, poor Charlie, was all she could think as they once again headed to the same hospital where her aunt Addie was still recovering.

Score another one for Terrence.

Why did he always win?

She began to pray.

Brayden realized he was driving too fast when Katie clutched the door handle. With great effort, he ordered himself to slow down and unclench his teeth. Something close to rage simmered underneath the frustration. He hadn't been able to help Charlie without leaving Katie. It was against his nature to turn away from someone in need, but he would not under any circumstances risk Katie's safety again.

And why had he told her all that soft, squishy stuff in the kitchen, anyway? The mortification was deepened by the fact that she had clearly not felt the same way. And all that business about the world being better and brighter when he was with her, he thought with an inward groan. He'd come off like some sort of sappy greeting card.

What was it about Katie? Being near her made him spill truths he didn't even want to admit to himself. He was turning into mush, both his brain and his heart. Purposefully he kept his eyes on the road and off her, even though he knew she was fighting tears. *Just don't make the situation worse.*

"We're almost there," he said. "Charlie is getting excellent care."

It wasn't the most brilliant platitude, but it was all he could manage. The Alaska K-9 team had been alerted, but there was not much they could do except get some dogs to help search the Chugach. Doubtful there would be much chance of finding him in almost five hundred thousand acres of wilderness. The coward must have spotted Charlie following him and run him down.

Again, he told himself to slow down and relax his jaw before he cracked a molar.

When they got to the hospital, they were directed to a cramped waiting room. Two women were already there. Shirlene he remembered from the Christmas Fair meeting and another lady whose name he did not recall. Ella gave them a sniff as both greeted Katie.

"We heard the news and came right away." Shirlene teared up. "That awful man, running Charlie down. It was Terrence, right?"

"That is how it appears," Brayden said carefully.

"I'm praying Charlie's okay," Katie said.

"Us, too." Shirlene paused. "We'll have to cancel the fair," she said. "Postponing isn't enough. People were already scared about Terrence, and now…"

Brayden heard the catch in Katie's breath. "We've still got time, ladies," he said, in his firmest "trooper" voice, twined with a bit of charm. "Don't give up the ship yet. Come on, Katie. Let me get you a bottle of water." He used the stroll to the vending machine to squeeze her hand. "One thing at a time, right?"

She nodded. "Eyes up, not down?" Her voice trembled on the last syllable.

Before he could stop himself, he'd pressed a kiss on her temple. "Absolutely."

She allowed him to hold her and he did so, relishing the warmth of her, the slender frame that masked the steely strength that had helped her build a life after her family was killed. The same strength that enabled her to be committed to the ranch, her aunt, her work. This woman was magnificent, and she didn't even know it. He realized she was wriggling out of his grasp. *Get yourself together, Trooper. She doesn't share your feelings, remember?* Clearing his throat, he fiddled with his radio as they walked to a couple of seats away from Shirlene and company.

She sipped the water and they sat tensely on their chairs, Ella lounging beside them, until the doctor came out. "He's got a broken ankle and a cracked rib," the physician said. "Considering the impact, I'd say he was fortunate."

Brayden realized Katie was clutching his sleeve. He wrapped an arm around her, acknowledging their shared relief. God had blessed them once again. Terrence had not managed to end the life of a good man. At least they could hold on to that. She leaned against him, her cheek pressed to his shoulder, smelling of the clean Alaskan air. He made a point not to sniff too obviously. Especially since he noticed Shirlene paying attention to their proximity. He could feel her curiosity, but at the moment, he didn't care. Katie was safe and with him. Charlie was alive. Those were enough blessings for one night.

The doctor continued. "We're going to wait for a second scan, just to be sure there's no head injury, but he might be released as early as tomorrow after we get a cast on his ankle. He's on pain relief right now and needs to rest, so no visitors, but you can see him tonight. Trooper Ford, as I understand, there's an investigation in progress?"

"That's correct."

"Okay, then," the physician said with a smile. "Just give us a while to get him settled into a room, okay?"

They thanked him, and Shirlene and the other woman left talking excitedly to each other. He did not doubt news of Charlie's condition would be broadcast all over town in a matter of moments. After updating the K-9 team with a text, he turned to Katie.

"I have a feeling you'd like to pay a visit to a certain aunt while we're here."

"You are a mind reader."

Best to keep things light. "They don't call me Mr. Intuitive for nothing."

"I don't think they call you Mr. Intuitive at all."

"Only my closest friends," he quipped.

They went upstairs and knocked on the door of Addie's hospital room. He waited outside, but after a few moments, Addie insisted he and Ella come in.

"They're finally letting me out tomorrow," she said triumphantly. "I've been telling them for days I'm perfectly well enough to go home. I can't wait to see this new addition we've got. Will she be well enough by the fair time to meet the public? If not, no problem. I think folks would love to see her, is all."

Katie looked uneasily at Brayden.

Addie's eyes narrowed. "What? Has Tulip taken a turn for the worse?"

"No, she is okay. Doc Jake is cautiously optimistic. It's just... Well, first I'd better tell you about Charlie."

"Charlie...as in Charlie Emmons, the butcher?"

"That's the one," Brayden confirmed.

"Has he been suggesting changes to the fair again? I told him he can keep his suggestions to himself. We are not handing out coupons for free frankfurters."

"It's not about the fair." Katie cleared her throat and started in.

Addie listened, her face growing more and more perplexed. "Well, my word! A broken ankle? And he's downstairs right now?" Her look of concern was quickly covered by a flash of irritation. "Well, whatever was that man thinking going after Terrence? Hasn't he been listening? Why in the world would he do such a dangerous thing? He's got all the good sense of a bag of sand."

Brayden almost smiled as Katie rolled her eyes. "If

you must know, Aunt Addie, I think he was trying to help capture Terrence because he's sweet on you."

Now it took all Brayden's self-control not to chuckle at the display of emotion rolling across Addie's face. Her mouth fell open, her complexion turning from white to scarlet and settling on a blotchy combination of the two. Finally, she snapped her mouth shut. "That's ridiculous. You've got your messages mixed up. He fixes up my roasts for me, that's all, and volunteers for the Christmas Fair because he has nothing better to do. He's *not* sweet on me."

"He defended the Christmas Fair at the volunteer meeting," Katie blurted and then stopped.

*Uh-oh*, Brayden thought. The proverbial cat had left the bag.

"Why would the fair need defending?" Addie asked with furrowed brows.

"Oh, um, well…" Katie floundered.

"There's a concern about safety, with Terrence at large, ma'am," Brayden said, earning a grateful glance from Katie. "I reassured them we will catch him soon."

"I keep hearing that word *soon* and I'm getting sick of it," Addie said. "If you don't catch him, he's going to kill me and Katie, too."

If he'd needed any more motivation, that would have done the trick. "I promise, ma'am," he said quietly. "I am not going to let that happen."

Katie kissed her aunt. "Brayden is going to talk to Charlie now and we'll be back in the morning to pick you up."

"I want to talk to Charlie, too," Addie told her, flipping the covers back.

"No," Katie said firmly, putting the sheets back in place. "He can only see police right now, and you'll chew him out and make him feel worse anyway."

Addie fumed. "Tomorrow, then. When you pick me up, I want to have a word with that man."

Poor Charlie, Brayden thought. He was going to get more than a word from Aunt Addie.

Since he did not want to leave Katie unattended, she joined him when they stopped in Charlie's room. The man's eyes were swollen, a bruise on one cheek. His ankle was wrapped and elevated, awaiting the cast.

Brayden leaned close. "Charlie? It's Trooper Brayden Ford. Can you hear me?"

Charlie groaned. His eye opened a sliver. "Did ya get him?"

"No, sir." He was heartily sick of having to repeat that over and over. "Can you tell us what happened?"

"I got out of my car and sneaked into the woods," he croaked. "Terrence was parked there, engine on. In an old trailer with one of those spare tire covers. It said Adventure Time on it."

Brayden wrote it down.

"I took a picture of the license plate with my phone." Charlie struggled to elevate himself. "Where is my phone?"

Brayden put a restraining hand on the butcher's arm. "Cops said you didn't have one on you when you were brought in, but they're still working on the crime scene."

He sank back. "I was gonna stay there and keep an

eye on him until the cops came, but all of a sudden, he put the rig into Reverse and backed at full speed. I didn't react fast enough and he got me."

Katie took Charlie's hand. "I'm so sorry."

"Aw, it's my fault." He sighed. "Who did I think I was, helping Addie by running down Terrence all by myself? I can't even change my own tires anymore since my sciatica flared up. I'm way too old to be a hero."

He looked so down. Brayden was about to speak when Katie beat him to it.

"No, you're not," she said firmly. "You've defended our ranch and you acted courageously because you were trying to help my aunt. I am going to make sure she knows it."

He smiled, but it was wan. "Thanks for saying that. Boy, my ribs hurt something fierce."

"We'd better let you get some rest," Brayden said, but Charlie's eyes were already closing.

They headed to his car. He checked in with Quinn and Phil as well as perused the video camera footage to be sure there was still no sign of the crafty Terrence.

Katie leaned against the headrest. "Why do I feel like we're back at square one again?"

"Not so. We have two important details we didn't have before. A description of Terrence's vehicle and a possible license plate number if we can find Charlie's phone. That's two very big steps forward."

She cocked her head, a wide smile spreading over her features. That smile was worth everything, like a sunbeam after a horrific storm. Charlie was going to be okay, and Katie had gifted him with a beautiful smile that made him feel like not just a good cop, but a good man.

In spite of the tumultuous day and the unsolved case, Brayden realized he was—for a brief moment, anyway—content.

# TWELVE

Monday morning, Katie found Brayden in the living room, bent in half at the waist, fingers reaching for his toes. He didn't make it. She was still uncertain about how to act around him after what had happened between them the previous day.

*Don't interrupt his exercise*, she told herself, attempting a stealthy exit. Ella heard her and her tail wag gave Katie away. Brayden straightened with a hand on his lower back and a flush on his cheeks. Was he warmed up from exercise or embarrassed about what he'd shared the day before?

"Oh, hi," he said. "I was, er, stretching. Sore back."

"Sorry to hear it. Does the stretching help?" It seemed so natural to be talking to Brayden Ford about his back pain. No lofty conversations about feelings.

"Not really. I think Ella is secretly laughing at me."

She smiled. "I'm sure she's rooting you on. Was the sofa uncomfortable?"

"It's not the sofa—it's the hitch in my gitalong. Got it wrestling a car door open for a stranded motorist, believe it or not." He sighed. "Gabriel's always going on about me doing Pilates or some such thing, but I'll just stick with awkward stretching, thank you very much."

She suppressed a giggle as she went to the oven to pull out the casserole dish she'd put in earlier that morning when she was awake worrying about Addie and Charlie. He followed her.

"I heard you cooking at the crack of dawn. Please tell me what that delicious-smelling thing is. And then tell me I am allowed to eat some of it." Ella was right beside him, nose twitching.

"It's chilaquiles."

He raised an eyebrow. "Chil a what?"

"Strips of fried corn tortillas simmered in salsa with cheese and some eggs that poach in all that nice yumminess." She dished up two plates. "And, yes, you can have some. I made extra because it's one thing Addie and I both like that satisfies her carnivorous side and my vegetarianism. I put a portion of it in the freezer for Charlie, too."

Brayden poured Ella some kibble before he sat in the chair opposite her and said grace with particular fervor. He beamed a grin at her after he forked up a mouthful. "I had no idea vegetarianism could be so delicious."

"I'm glad you think so."

They talked about food, fortunately, and Charlie's condition, which Brayden had checked on. Neutral topics. She found the slight tension between them disconcerting, but she did not know what to do about it. As she watched the rising sun play across his face, she realized she'd memorized the features—strong jaw, tiny crow's-feet that framed thoughtful green eyes, the thick thatch of blond hair that had a mind of its own in spite of the short cut, the gentle mouth that had kissed her temple. *You're staring, Katie.* "Uh, would you like some more?"

He was about to reply when the house phone rang. She answered, stomach taut. Would this be another anonymous hang-up? Brayden put his fork down and waited, his wary expression revealing that he wondered the same thing.

"Hi, Katie."

"Hello, Shirlene," she said with a sigh.

"I was told Charlie is going to be okay. Such happy news."

"Yes." The pause became more awkward.

"Um, I felt you should know that we're having a Christmas Fair volunteer meeting at my house tomorrow night to formally cancel."

Katie gulped. How would she tell Addie?

"I think you know, but I want everything to be aboveboard. I'm so sorry, but everyone wants to be done with it and move on to other projects, so we'll need an official vote."

She gripped the phone. "Shirlene, we talked about this. Some volunteers said they would be back on board if Terrence was caught. Why must you cancel right now?"

"Circumstances have changed after this last attack on Charlie. Some of us have to be on the ranch sooner rather than later, getting pictures for the flyers, getting the decorations from the attic to take inventory, building the extra tables to replace the ones ruined by the weather. We need to make a decision as one body and it can't wait any longer. Postponement just keeps everyone on hold."

Katie fought back tears.

"And then if things calm down," Shirlene continued in a brighter tone, "we can always reverse any decision we make."

Another long, awkward beat of silence fell between them.

"I'm sorry, Katie. I truly am. I will call Charlie to get his vote over the phone."

"He supports the ranch," Katie said.

"We all do, but he might not be so willing to be involved anymore after what happened to him. Again, I'm sorry."

She was left staring at the receiver.

Brayden grimaced. "I can guess what Shirlene wanted."

She told him about the vote.

"A lot of things can happen between now and tomorrow," he reminded her.

They finished their breakfast, but she could not shake her worries. She left a foil-covered pan of the chilaquiles out on the porch for Quinn, Phil and Alex, with extra plates and forks.

"Are you ready to go pick up your aunt?" Brayden said.

She nodded. He went through all the safety protocols. When he was assured that no one was lurking on the property, he drove them to the hospital, Phil following until they reached the main road.

Katie had mixed emotions. Though she knew the best

thing mentally for her aunt was to return to the Family K, it had been comforting to have her secure at the hospital with a guard at the door. Plus, it would be impossible to protect her from the fact that the Christmas Fair would be officially canceled as soon as Shirlene's meeting took place.

The thoughts pinballed through her mind as they reached her room. Aunt Addie's door was ajar and she was not there.

Panic flashed through Katie for a moment until a security guard popped his head in. "She's gone to visit Charlie Emmons on the second floor. Don't worry. There's a guard with her."

"We better hurry," she said to Brayden. "Aunt Addie's probably chewing Charlie into little pieces." She decided that she would not mention the volunteer meeting at Shirlene's house until Addie was settled and comfortable back at the Family K.

At Charlie's room, a security guard waved them in. They entered to find Charlie sitting in a wheelchair, a set of crutches lying across his lap. Addie, her shoulder in a sling, stood next to him. Her expression was dour as ever, but Katie wondered if she hadn't finger-combed her silver hair back behind her ears. It made her look softer somehow, or maybe she was imagining it.

Charlie waved at the new arrivals.

"You missed the lecture," he said. "I've been read the riot act for my foolhardiness and colossal lack of good judgment." His face was still lined with pain, but there was a sparkle in his eye in spite of the exhaustion.

"And all-around idiocy," Addie said.

"Yes, that, too, but I'm waiting for the part where I get an embrace for my act of heroism."

"You're gonna be waiting a very long time," Addie snapped. "Because there was *no* heroism involved. Your behavior was ludicrous, pure and simple. Don't try to sell it as anything else."

He laughed. "It's okay. I'm patient. I can wait for my hug."

Addie rolled her eyes, but Katie saw the tiniest crimp of amusement on her mouth. Could it be her no-nonsense aunt was hiding some warmer feelings for Charlie?

She glanced at the other woman. "Are you supposed to be walking around? I thought the doctor said minimal exertion only." Katie hoped the misdirection would prevent Addie from launching a scathing rebuttal to Charlie's remark.

"I am perfectly fine, and how else could I come here and arrange things since this silly man has lost his cell phone on top of everything else?"

Katie frowned. "Arranging *what* things?"

Addie huffed and adjusted the angle of her sling. "Well, Charlie can't go stay by himself in his apartment. He can't even boil water and he won't take his pain medicines properly, I'm sure, if he's left to his own devices. Who is going to cook for him and make sure he doesn't fall?"

Katie gaped. "We are?"

A slight shade of pink stained her cheeks. "Of course. You said Brayden's staying in the main house, so there's a bed in the bunkhouse with Quinn. Lots of room. Perfect for a man on crutches."

Charlie grinned. "How could I say no to such a gracious invitation?"

Again, Addie rolled her eyes. "It's not a vacation. There's plenty you can do to prepare for the fair. Your two hands work, right?"

Charlie chuckled. "Yes, they do."

Katie managed not to come off as too surprised at the details, though Brayden looked on the verge of laughing. She purposefully kept from looking at him.

"Let's ask the trooper how he feels about this," Katie managed. "I would love to have you, Charlie, but the ranch is sort of the bull's-eye of the target, right now. And Terrence has already almost killed you."

Brayden nodded. "She's right. My focus has to be on Katie and her aunt. I'm afraid I can't guarantee your safety." He paused. "But something tells me you might be helpful in keeping an eye peeled, and we can use all the help we can get."

Charlie waved a hand. "We have already established that I am heroic. I'm comfortable staying in the bull's-eye and helping out with security."

Katie could only smile. "Well, all right, then. It will be wonderful to have you stay with us. Brayden, can you fit all of us in your car?"

"It'll be tight, but we'll manage." He opened the door to lead the way when Addie's cell phone rang.

She answered it. Her face went dead pale and the phone slipped from her startled grasp. Brayden managed to catch it before it hit the floor.

"It's him," she whispered.

Katie's blood turned to ice.

*Uncle Terrence.*

Brayden jabbed on the speakerphone. "Terrence? It's Alaska State Trooper Brayden Ford. I've been waiting to talk to you." He began to text Eli, the tech guru of the team, to see if he could triangulate the cell signal. They'd put a tracker on Addie's phone, so there was a slight chance Eli could figure out a general area from where the incoming call had been made.

There was a pause. "I'm calling for my dear sister Addie." His voice was sharp and gravelly. "Is she there?"

"Yes, I'm here," Addie said, recovering somewhat. "How did you get this number?"

"The guy I ran over dropped his phone upon impact. I helped myself, and what do you know? Your number is second from the top. That surprised me. I know he's not a friend, since you have no friends."

Charlie's face went slack. "Yes, she does," he grunted. "I'm her friend."

"Ah. You must be Charlie. Still alive? Word of advice, pal—stay away from my sister. She's a she-wolf and just as cunning. She'll use you and toss you out as soon as she doesn't need anything from you."

Addie's face went scarlet.

Charlie was about to fire off a comment when Brayden held up a palm to stop him. He needed to keep the conversation going to allow Eli time.

"Where are you, Terrence?" Brayden asked.

"Somewhere close. Don't you worry."

Addie's mouth pinched. "What you've done…running into Charlie, threatening Katie… It's going to land you in prison or get you shot. Can't you understand that?"

"Aw, I didn't know you cared about my welfare, sis."

"I don't," Addie said. "But I feel responsible since we are unfortunately related."

"Always the silver-tongued woman," he sneered. "You should have been a politician instead of a rancher."

"Why did you call?" Addie asked.

His tone hitched up an octave. "Because I'm getting tired of trying to push you and Katie off my property."

"It's not yours," Brayden said. "I've seen the paperwork. It's your sister's, willed to her by your parents, legal and tidy."

"It was supposed to be mine!" he shouted. "I'm the oldest child. Mom and Dad meant it for me."

"Careful, Terrence," Brayden murmured. "You sound like a spoiled child who didn't get that new set of marbles for Christmas." He set the phone down and began tapping more messages into his own phone.

"Stay out of this, *Trooper*," Terrence said derisively. "This is between me and my sister."

Addie shook her head. "You squandered every gift our parents ever gave you—money, your car, the savings account they put aside for you. They knew what you were like. Why would they give you the Family K?"

"They would have, if you hadn't poisoned them against me. I know you told them every bad thing I ever did when I wasn't around to defend myself."

"There was no poisoning required," Addie snapped. "You never treated them well. When Daddy broke his hip and couldn't tend the animals when we were teens, you didn't lift a finger. You didn't even come to their funerals or our sister's."

"Mom wrote me off, just like you did. You finagled your way into their graces and got the will changed so you'd inherit the land."

"They didn't trust you," she said. "Why can't you get that through your thick skull? They did not want to give the ranch to you. You're just too deluded to admit it."

"Shut up," he yelled. "No more of your lies, Addie. You'd say anything to keep the land you stole from me."

"Let's meet, Terrence," Brayden said, cutting in. "You and me, man-to-man. You can tell me your side of things. I'll listen and we can get this all straightened out."

Terrence muttered something. "Please. I'm not an idiot. I'm not meeting with anyone, especially a state trooper."

"Well, you're not getting my ranch, either," Addie huffed. "So why don't you just drive your RV into the sunset and find another piece of land to call your own?"

"It's too late for that," Terrence said.

The comment sent a thrill of fear through Katie.

"What do you mean?" Addie demanded.

Terrence chuckled. "At first, I figured I could convince you, but now your chance is over."

"What are you saying?" Brayden said. "Spell it out for me, okay?"

"It's not about property anymore." He paused. "It's about pain…"

Addie and Katie, the two women who were depending on Brayden for their safety, stared at him with unconcealed terror. He could not take a moment to console them. He had to keep Terrence talking.

"There's been enough pain," Brayden said. "Turn yourself in. Save us the trouble of finding and arresting you."

Terrence laughed, one hard animal bark. "It will be over when Addie's dead, lying alongside dear Mom and Dad in the grave."

Addie recoiled. "No, Terrence."

"Oh, yes. But there are worse things than dying."

Now Brayden was leaning toward the phone. "Terrence, listen to me. You're not going to get out of this. How about we end it and…?"

"Oh, I'll end it, don't you worry, but not until Addie endures all the pain and suffering she's got coming to her. Death isn't enough."

The room was so silent, he could hear Terrence breathing into the phone.

"Tell my niece hello, would you, sis?" Terrence said. "She's like your daughter, isn't she? The only person close to you on this whole miserable planet."

Brayden's body went cold and he grabbed for the phone.

"Stop it!" Addie shrieked. "Don't you dare threaten Katie."

Terrence laughed. "Oh, one more thing. Tell Katie that breakfast she made sure smells wonderful. Chilaquiles, right? And you didn't even leave me any. Guess I'll help myself."

Brayden saw the shock that shuddered through Katie's body as the dial tone filled the room.

# THIRTEEN

Terrence was on the ranch. Brayden somehow kept his voice level as he called in hospital security to stay with Katie, Addie and Charlie. But beneath the calm, professional veneer, his blood burned hot as he considered what he would find at the ranch. A quick check revealed that the cameras were disabled. Hopefully Terrence was still there. Maybe the guy was bullheaded enough to force a confrontation.

Well, he'd get one.

"Brayden," Katie called as he started to run down the hallway. He stopped and jerked a look at her.

She looked so small standing there, silhouetted by the harsh hospital lighting.

"You heard him," she said. "He wants to cause us pain, all of us."

"I know."

Her mouth trembled. "Don't give him what he wants by letting him hurt you. I couldn't bear it."

*Couldn't bear it?* Because she cared about him? Of course she did, he told himself. They were friends now, colleagues. But maybe that fear in her troubled gaze was something deeper than affection? No time for that now.

"I'll call when I can." And then he was sprinting to the car and rolling code three to the ranch property. Hunter and Maya were already there, having been diverted from their search of the Chugach. They'd stopped at the main entrance, no lights and sirens.

Quinn was at the Family K, too, with Ella, brow puckered in confusion. "No sign of Terrence. Are you sure he's here?"

"There's a few seconds of him spray-painting the camera lenses before everything went dark. No way to know if he left again. Eli said the call was probably made from the Palmer area, but he couldn't be more specific than that," Brayden said. "Stay here with Ella until we give the all clear."

Brayden radioed Phil. No reply. He tried calling his cell. "Phil's not answering."

"I'll go find him," Quinn said.

"Sarge and I will search the bunkhouse and the other buildings," Maya added.

Brayden nodded. "Hunter, you're with me. We'll take the main house. If he's got a trap waiting, I think that's where it will be."

Hunter nodded. He opened a plastic bag and let his husky take a whiff. "It's Terrence's dry suit we recovered after he shot Addie. If he's in there, Juneau will know."

Guns drawn, they crept past the front porch, which held a soiled dish stacked neatly with silverware, the remnants of a chilaquile breakfast. Probably Quinn's meal. They entered the house. Hunter spoke softly to

Juneau, but the dog knew what to do. He trotted from room to room with his handler, excited at the prospect of finding his quarry.

"In here," Hunter called.

Brayden ran into the living room, where he found a message from Terrence painted in dripping red across the windows.

*MAXIMUM PAIN.*

The room had been thoroughly trashed, cushions ripped apart, paintings torn from the walls, mirrors defaced. Bile rose in his throat.

"I'll call an evidence team in after we're done searching," Hunter said.

Brayden checked closets, under the beds and every conceivable hiding place he could think of without finding anything else out of place. He was not totally surprised. Terrence had to get in and out quickly before Brayden alerted help after the taunting hospital phone call.

An engine sounded in the front. Quinn pounded into the house, with Phil's body draped over his shoulder. "I found him unconscious in his car. He's breathing and his heart is beating."

Brayden called for an ambulance, chafing Phil's hand. The man groaned and opened an eye. "What happened?"

"You were passed out in your car," Brayden said. "But I don't see any sign of injury."

Phil waved away the hands trying to support him and sat up. They helped him into a chair after Brayden set one on its feet.

"I'm okay," the security officer said. "Just groggy." Hunter joined him.

"Nothing from Juneau," he said, rewarding the dog for his efforts with a treat and an ear rub. "Seems like he kept the damage to one room."

Brayden nodded in relief, then called the hospital and talked to Gabriel, who had arrived to help with the security detail. "I'll bring them to you now," Gabriel said. "How did he get onto the property?"

"Looks like he immobilized Phil somehow before he disabled the cameras. Working on it."

"I didn't see Terrence," Phil said, when Brayden hung up. "So I'm not exactly sure what happened."

"Did you start your shift on time this morning?"

"Yes, sir. Like clockwork."

How had Terrence managed to drug Phil without him knowing?

"All right. Sit tight for a minute. We'll have the medics check you over. I need to make a call."

His next call went to Alex, who had done the last night shift. This time he chose FaceTime to connect. The phone rang, three times, then four. If Alex was working for Terrence, he would have to have been on the property sometime around 6:00 a.m., when Katie started cooking.

As the phone continued to ring, Brayden's suspicion mounted. He was about to disconnect when Alex answered, the screen blinking to life. His hair was standing straight up and he wore a striped pajama top. His eyes were puffed as if he had been asleep for a long while. If he had been on the ranch property to help Terrence somehow, he'd done quick work of getting himself back to his house and into bed afterward. A convincing liar? Brayden had met a million of them, including his ex-girlfriend.

"Sorry to wake you."

"I finally got to sleep," the security guard said peevishly. "They're working on the electric lines and they have to drop crews in by helicopter. Noisy."

"Sorry. This will only take a minute."

Brayden asked him a few questions, but the man either was extremely skilled at deceit or he really had no part in Terrence's latest attack. So who did that leave?

The neighbors? But the nearest one was miles away.

His mind pondered the possibility over and over, trying to avoid the truth until he could evade it no longer.

Someone close by was a traitor.

Gabriel walked the threesome to the house. Katie heard Ella's happy bark and knew Brayden was okay. She sighed, letting loose tension she'd been holding on to since he'd left the hospital. Her jaw dropped at the sight of the ruins of what had once been their living room.

"I'm sorry," Brayden said.

*Sorry?* Terrence had violated their home again. There was nothing he could possibly say to make her feel any better right now. Off to the side, Phil was sitting in a chair, looking like he'd swallowed a lemon. "Are you okay?"

"I guess he drugged me," the man croaked.

A muscle ticked in Brayden's jaw and Charlie put

a sympathetic hand on her shoulder. But all she could feel in that moment was that the walls were closing in. Without a word, she turned on her heel and walked back out, gulping in deep breaths, catching her aunt before she crossed the threshold. "Aunt Addie, let's get Charlie settled in, okay?"

She was grateful that Addie didn't argue.

Gabriel shadowed them as they helped Charlie walk on his crutches to the bunkhouse.

Charlie whispered to Katie, "Do you have police following you everywhere?"

"It seems like it," she whispered back. She'd become so used to having protection, she'd forgotten how strange it must feel to people living normal lives. Brayden had become a fixture for her. But Charlie's life had been dramatically changed by Terrence like Katie's and Addie's had.

She and her aunt helped Charlie to his room in the bunkhouse and quickly put clean sheets on his bed. Addie hurried off to fix him a cup of tea. He sank gratefully onto the edge and she realized he was weary. "Why don't you rest for a while." She handed him the new phone Gabriel had brought. "My number is programmed in. Text me if you need anything."

"Thanks, Katie. I am determined to be a help, rather than a burden."

She thought about Addie scurrying to arrange the details of Charlie's stay. Though she grumbled, there was a sliver of happiness in the activity, Katie thought. "You are not a burden, Charlie," she said. "And I am glad you're here. I suspect my aunt is, as well."

The butcher grinned. "Maybe she really will succumb to my charms."

"Who wouldn't?" Katie said. She wanted to smile, but her heart was too burdened.

She tried to prepare her aunt for the mess that awaited in the main house as Gabriel escorted them back.

Addie looked as though she would cry, surveying the damage. "I'm going to go upstairs until you're finished," she said, voice high and tight. "Let me know when I can clean all this up."

Katie's heart broke as she watched her aunt heave herself slowly up the stairs.

"So Phil was drugged, leaving the ranch unprotected. But how?" she heard Quinn say. He stood, hands on hips, listening intently to Brayden and Hunter. Phil must have refused to be transported to the hospital, but the medics were fussing over him anyway.

Ella lumbered over to greet her, and she rubbed the dog's fuzzy ears, trying not to look at the disaster in the living room.

"That's a great question." Brayden's face lacked the usual easygoing smile. "Maybe he had someone else do it for him." He was staring at Quinn now, expression stony.

Quinn stiffened.

*No, not Quinn*, Katie thought, stomach clenching. She wanted to speak out for him, but she knew she should not interfere.

"Are you saying you think I have been helping Terrence?" Quinn said quietly.

"Not saying, *asking*," Brayden said. "Are you?"

Quinn looked at the ceiling. When he turned his gaze back on Brayden, it was filled with fury. "No, I'm not."

"That leaves Phil and Alex. I've talked to Alex and his movements check out."

Quinn fisted his hands on his hips. "Doesn't mean he isn't lying."

"No, it doesn't," Brayden admitted. "But he and Phil were hired by my colonel on recommendations. They're vetted."

"And I'm some out-of-work local with a bum knee," Quinn snapped. "So I'm the liar."

"No," Katie said, unable to stay quiet any longer. "No one thinks you're lying, Quinn." She shot a look at Brayden for agreement, but his demeanor remained rigid.

Quinn glanced at her. "Thanks for the vote of confidence, but I guess I'll tender my resignation."

"Please, no," Katie protested. "We need you."

He glared at Brayden. "I'm not going to work where I'm not trusted."

Brayden stared him down, not angry, but all business. "Quinn, I need to hear from you and Phil. I'm doing my job. Sit down for a minute or two until we get this straightened out."

"Are you asking or ordering?"

"At this point, it's a request."

Quinn hesitated, still obviously angry, but he sat.

Brayden gestured to Katie and drew her outside on the porch.

"Quinn's a good man," she blurted when they were outside.

"It's not personal."

She folded her arms. "It is to Quinn."

Brayden pulled in a breath and let it out slowly. "Katie, I am going to ask you to stay out of this, okay? Let me do my job."

"Stay out of it? While you shred Quinn?"

"I'm not shredding," he said slowly. "I'm investigating. That offends people sometimes. It's what I get paid to do."

"Don't talk to me like a child. I work for the department, remember? I understand what your job is."

He shook his head. "If I was talking down to you, I apologize. I didn't mean to." Steel crept into his expression. "But this is my job and I'm going to do it, and anything else I need to in order to bring Terrence down." He paused. "Can you understand that?"

Deep down in the emerald pools of his eyes, she saw he desperately wanted her to understand. Her upset warred with her newly developed trust in him. She was trying to figure out how to respond when Brayden went back inside. She followed.

A moment later, Hunter and Maya arrived with their K-9s. "Tell me again your movements this morning," Brayden said to Phil.

The man sighed. "Business as usual. I arrived at five forty-five. Stopped at the main house at just before six for a cup of coffee. I checked the cameras. No one on the property who didn't belong, and everyone drank that coffee, so I know it wasn't tampered with."

Katie made sure every morning to fill a carafe with hot coffee and leave it on the porch with mugs, along with whatever she'd made for breakfast that day. She and Brayden had drunk some, along with Quinn, in addition to Phil.

Phil continued. "I drove to the main gate to meet Alex as he finished up his rounds."

"What time was that?"

Phil looked surprised. "Six on the dot."

Brayden nodded for him to continue.

"We debriefed. He left. I started up again. Followed you to the main road when you left for the hospital and continued my rounds until I got the call from you that Terrence might be on the premises."

Brayden was frozen for a moment, chin cocked. "When you stopped at the main house for coffee, did you see anything unusual?"

"No, sir." He smiled at Katie as if he'd just remembered something. "Oh. I wanted to thank you for the breakfast, ma'am. I had a plateful and took more for later. Chilaquiles are my absolute favorite. My sister used to make them for Sunday brunch."

That silly breakfast. Katie was beginning to wish she'd never made it.

"Where did you put it?" Brayden asked suddenly.

Phil blinked. "Put what?"

"The food. You helped yourself to a plate to save for lunch. Where did you put it?"

"In my car."

They all stared at him.

Brayden nodded. "Did you stop anywhere after you talked to Alex?"

"No, I…" Phil stopped, looking sheepish. "I, uh…

Well, I did stop for a smoke. I took a little walk to stretch my legs. I was only gone for ten minutes or so. And when I came back to the car, I…"

"Ate some of the chilaquiles," Katie finished with a groan.

Phil deflated. "Yeah. Just a couple of bites, is all." He rolled his eyes. "I'm sorry, Trooper. I guess I messed up."

Hunter and Brayden exchanged a look. "Terrence must have a hiding spot off the property, near the main gate. He sneaked to the car while you were smoking and drugged the food. We'll send the remainder to the lab for testing. I'll go bag it on our way to check for possible hiding places," Hunter said.

Phil agreed to a ride home from one of the local police, after again declining a hospital transport, since they needed to check his car for prints. Quinn stood, arms folded, staring laser beams at Brayden.

"Not a liar, am I? And neither is Phil, for that matter."

"I apologize, Quinn," Brayden said.

He paused before answering. "You were doing your job. But I don't like being accused."

Brayden clapped him on the shoulder. "And I didn't enjoy asking you about it, but you can understand that I'm not in a position to trust anyone. Can we call a truce, then, and keep you here on the ranch?" Brayden's warmth was back.

Quinn didn't smile, but his frown softened around the edges. "Maybe until I get a better offer."

"Sounds fair." Brayden watched him go.

Hunter and Maya were already heading for the door

with their dogs to check out the area at the main gate where Phil and Alex had debriefed. Maya palmed her phone, and she and Gabriel stepped away to report to the colonel.

Alone with Brayden, Katie heaved out a deep breath. "I owe you an apology."

Brayden shrugged. "No, you don't."

"You were doing your job, and you did it with respect. I shouldn't have made it harder for you than it needed to be." She grimaced. "I would make a terrible cop, wouldn't I?"

"Nah," he said. "As long as you could learn how to manage a furry tank, you could step into my shoes any day."

He was so gracious, and his manner so warm, she could not resist reaching out and giving him a hug. His arms went around her waist, strong and gentle at the same time. Her pulse beat quicker at the comforting weight of his chin resting on her head.

*We fit together*, she thought with a start. But she'd never fit with anyone, not allowed herself to. Was this right or wrong? An evolving blessing or a step toward disaster? Hastily she let him go. "One thing is certain— I'm not making chilaquiles again for a long while."

"Now, that really would be a crime."

Addie came down the stairs with an armful of blankets. "Well?" she demanded. "Did you figure out how my dirtbag brother got onto the ranch?"

Brayden launched into an explanation until his phone rang. "Hunter says he's found Terrence's hiding place. It's a hollowed-out tree right near the main gate."

Katie slapped her forehead. "I used to hide there and pretend it was a castle. I forgot all about it. I can't believe it's still standing."

"We thought about taking it down," Addie said. "But there were always other problems to tend to. The thing is massive, so it would require a professional to remove it."

Katie's stomach churned. "It's still a perfect hiding place, not ten feet from the main gate. Terrence could have heard every word Phil said to Alex and tampered with the chilaquiles."

"And wrecked my front room." Addie's nostrils flared with rage and she appeared exhausted.

"Ma'am, why don't you let me clean this up," Brayden said.

"No… I…"

"Brayden and I will do it," Katie said quickly. "Together."

Her aunt hesitated only for a moment. "All right. I appreciate it. I surely do." She went back upstairs.

Katie stared into space, brought back by Brayden's touch on her arm. "You're deep in thought."

"Yes. Terrence didn't just happen to be listening at the right moment. He must have been watching Phil and Alex closely for a while, memorizing when they come and go. He's getting ready to put his plan into place." *Death isn't enough.*

"But we're not going to let him," he said.

Terrence intended to torture them both before he ended their lives.

Through the twang of fear, she felt her inner resolve

crystallize and harden. He would *not* win. He would not take away the ranch. She would fight to her last breath.

Brayden was still gazing at her, the resolve showing in his own expression.

"No, we won't let him win," Katie said, holding out her hand.

He took it and gripped her fingers tight. "Sure as eggs in April."

Katie smiled despite herself. "Where did that expression come from? Another bit of your mother's wisdom?"

"No, my gran's. We always thought it was strange, since she grew up in the city and never raised chickens."

She laughed. "Somehow that makes it even better."

There was danger and stress and uncertainty, all mixed up with a mega portion of fear, but with Brayden's hand holding hers, she felt a strong surge of hope, and another smile broke across her face.

"Sure as eggs in April," she echoed.

The police would catch Terrence.

They had to.

Her job was to keep the ranch going and Aunt Addie safe until they did so.

Thinking about Terrence hiding in the hollow tree, listening, watching, like some feral beast, made her pray that Brayden would succeed soon.

April seemed like a very long time away.

# FOURTEEN

The next day, Brayden was mulling over a new schedule and routes for the security team. Following that, he'd need to figure out a plan to remove the dead tree near the front gate. The thing was a monster, so it would be a job he'd have to hire out. He was considering how to get that done without asking Quinn for his input.

Quinn was still on the frosty side, but Brayden figured he was entitled to his feelings. The guy had pride and Brayden couldn't fault him. He'd give him the space he needed and deserved. There was some improvement in Quinn's mood later that afternoon when a shipment of alfalfa arrived and Brayden helped Quinn stack it in the barn. Ella took interest enough to have accumulated several stalks in her thick fur. They both returned smelling of alfalfa to the main house.

Katie and Addie sat with Charlie in the cleaned-up family room discussing Tulip's progress. Charlie's ankle was propped on a footstool.

"She's stronger," Addie said. "Ate some leaves from my hand. She's showing a lot of interest toward the other members, which is a wonderful sign."

"Can her lameness be corrected?" Charlie asked.

Addie nodded. "She'll require many hoof trims, but Robby is optimistic. He's the best farrier in Alaska. He'll have to wait until the spring to do much more since her hooves are hardening for the winter."

Charlie cocked his chin and grinned.

"What?" Addie demanded. "Why are you staring at me?"

He shrugged. "Can't a guy admire his woman's skills and talents? You're an expert with those animals, truly."

"I'm not anybody's woman." Addie waved off the comment, but even Brayden could detect she was pleased to some degree.

While they were occupied, Brayden stepped outside to check in with the K-9 team via a video call. He spoke over the rustling of papers. "If Terrence keeps driving that clunky RV, I figure he's going to have to stop for gas regularly. That thing's a dinosaur. I've touched base with the three gas stations closest to the ranch, so they're on the lookout. But it's way more likely that he ditched it for something harder to spot."

The other troopers chimed in with suggestions on how to tighten the net around Terrence, followed by updates on the Violet James case.

"I found a clinic that is pretty centrally located with lots of traffic, so she might have gone there. They provide prenatal care, but they're serious about the privacy of their patients. Not to mention the fact that Violet is probably using a fake name," Poppy said.

"Ariel keeps sending her texts, even though they come back 'undeliverable.'" Hunter's concern was written all over his face. "She's trying to stay positive, but it's getting harder."

The colonel cut across the chatter. "Full confession, people. I am becoming weary of progress reports that don't get us anywhere. Violet is still unaccounted for, Lance and Jared are as well, and Terrence isn't any closer to landing in jail. I want these cases closed before anyone else gets hurt. These investigations trump all your other duties. Am I clear?"

There was agreement from the gathering.

"All right. We'll adjourn, then. Brayden, stay on the call, will you?"

*Uh-oh*, he thought. "Yes, ma'am."

When everyone disconnected, he found himself alone on screen with his boss.

"Needless to say, Addie was outraged at my suggestion that she come to a safe house. Are you the least bit surprised?"

"No, Colonel. I am unable to get her to comply with telling me when she wants to leave the main house. Ella and I are on our toes every moment trying to keep tabs on her."

"I don't doubt it." Lorenza massaged her temples, an unusual show of fatigue. "I need to tell you something. Addie let slip some info I thought you should know about."

"What's that?"

"She had to mortgage the ranch property to make ends meet during the flooding we had last spring."

Something tightened in his chest. "And?"

"There's a balloon payment due in January. She pays it, or she loses the property to the bank."

He tried to absorb that new round of bad news. "Why are you telling me this?"

"You reported before this last go-round with Terrence that the Christmas Fair volunteers have backed out. If that fundraiser doesn't happen, it will be the death knell for the ranch."

He sat up straighter. "You don't have to tell me that we need to catch Terrence fast. I'm well aware."

"I know. I'm merely filling you in on the stakes so you can properly understand the timeline. If Terrence succeeds in prolonging his reign of terror, it's not just another lean year for the Family K. It's the end."

"Does Katie know this?"

Lorenza shifted on her chair. "That's the other sticking point. Addie said she had not told her. She wanted to handle the matter herself."

He stifled a groan. "I'm not sure it's the right thing to tell her now. She's got so much on her plate as is, trying to keep Addie healing and Charlie…"

The colonel cut him off. "Katie needs to know. Her aunt means everything to her, and she won't want to be kept in the dark. She's a strong, independent woman. She can take it."

He hesitated. How could he add that burden to the pile she was carrying already?

"This whole situation has gone on too long," she added.

*Way too long.* Brayden was silent for a moment. "Colonel, what if we made something happen?"

"I'm listening."

His thoughts coalesced into an honest-to-goodness plan. "It's time to force Terrence to show his hand."

"How?"

"By giving him what he wants."

She pursed her lips. "Brief me on the particulars and then convince me it's not going to result in any injuries to Katie or her aunt."

Brayden breathed a silent prayer. And then he said, "I think I know how we can trap Terrence by using a look-alike." When he finished, she stayed quiet, tapping her pen on the top of her immaculate desk.

"All right. You sold me. I'll send Hunter and Helena to back you up on this, but we only get one shot. If Terrence figures it out…"

He didn't let her finish. "Yes, ma'am. I know. High stakes."

"The highest."

They finished the call.

High stakes indeed. Katie's life, her aunt's and now the future of the ranch hung in the balance. *No pressure, Brayden.*

It took a couple of hours of concentration on the front porch to set the wheels in motion for his scheme to trap Terrence. By the time he was done, his fingers were numb with cold. Ella rose and stretched, her furry behind up in the air. It didn't require a dog's sniffer to catch the tantalizing scent of cheesy pasta wafting from the kitchen. He and Ella followed their noses and found Katie putting plates on the table.

"I can handle that job," he said, taking them from her.

"You sure? You spill stuff," she teased.

"I am offended, but I will forgive you because quality chefs can be temperamental."

"That's me. Temperamental." Laughing, she headed back to the kitchen for the food, her hair rendered luminous in the failing sunlight that streamed through the front window. Like copper, or the tawny autumn leaves. If he could pick his favorite color in the world, it would be that shimmery auburn hue.

Jamie had been everything opposite Katie—chatty, elegant, dark-haired, always in the most beautiful clothes and smelling of perfume. All the things he'd thought he wanted. How could he have been so wrong?

Brayden didn't fully snap out of his musings until Charlie and Addie settled at the table, the poor guy landing in the chair with a clatter of crutches. Quinn joined them, as well as Hunter and Helena, who had arrived to help him roll out the plan. When the pasta, salad and fragrant rolls were passed around and grace spoken, he unpacked his idea for them. They listened with rapt attention until he sat back.

"What do you think?"

Addie glared at him. "I'm not going to let myself or Katie be used as bait…" she began.

"No, ma'am. A trooper will be impersonating you, driving off the ranch. We'll have Phil sow some false information to make Terrence believe you're running an errand, but you'll both be safe in the bunkhouse, just in case. Quinn will have it under watch. If this goes right, Terrence won't ever set foot on the property."

"Still…" Addie said.

"And even if he slips by us and gets back, he would head for the main house, not the bunkhouse," Hunter put in.

"I think it's a *fantastic* plan." Katie's face was shining in a way that made his breathing shallow out. "It will finally be over. No more waiting around for Terrence's next move. When do we do it?"

"We'll set it in place tomorrow morning. We'll use Phil and Alex to plant the seed that Addie will be leaving the property at seven thirty, by herself. Hunter and I will stake out positions on the main road, where he will hopefully try to intercept her."

"And who will be impersonating Addie?" Charlie asked around a bite of pasta from his second helping.

"That'd be me," Helena said, "with my hair tucked up and wearing a borrowed plaid shirt. I'll drive your truck, Addie. Okay?"

Addie nodded, brows furrowed. "What do you think, Charlie?"

The butcher looked every bit as surprised as Katie that Addie had asked his opinion. Brayden covered his smile by taking a sip of water.

Charlie wiped his mouth, brows drawn as he considered. "I think we should go for it. With this many eyes keeping watch, we're bound to get him."

"All right, then," Addie said. "I'm on board."

With the plan out of the way, Brayden could enjoy a second helping of pasta. He'd never thought dinner would be complete without meat, but he might have to reconsider. He'd already reconsidered a lot of preconceived notions where Katie was concerned. He sneaked another glance at her.

She looked honestly hopeful for the first time in quite a while. If his plan worked, they could restart the Christmas Fair and Addie would be able to keep the ranch. The missing reindeer would be found and returned home. He was still struggling with the decision not to tell Katie about Addie mortgaging the ranch, but seeing her happy cemented it for him. She'd earned a little lightness, hadn't she? A moment of ease? And hopefully the balloon payment would be paid off without a hitch.

The house phone rang, and Addie hopped up to get it before Katie could manage. She returned with a look of puzzlement. "It's Shirlene," she said. "She wants to talk to you about some kind of a vote, Charlie."

Katie's face went white as Charlie heaved himself up onto his crutches and answered. When he finished, he rejoined them, expression grave. "Shirlene said they're voting to officially end support for the Christmas Fair. They wanted my answer."

Addie gaped. "They can't walk away from the Christmas Fair. Not now."

Charlie fingered his mustache. "Um, my vote doesn't really make a difference. It was a formality, really. I'm sorry, Addie, but they said they made it official." He frowned at the tortured gasp that bubbled up from Addie. "It's okay, honey. We can tell them about the plan to trap Terrence and they'll change their minds."

"No, we can't," Brayden and Hunter said at exactly the same moment.

"The fewer people who know the better," Helena explained.

"Oh, of course," Charlie said. "But tomorrow Terrence will be captured."

"But what if he slips away again?" Katie lamented.

Charlie raised a calming hand. "Even if the Christmas Fair doesn't fly, we'll find the funds to keep the ranch going until next year."

But Addie stood there, stricken. She shook her head. "No, we won't." The words came out as a whisper. She began to sway.

Katie ran to her aunt's side before Brayden could rise from his chair. She helped Addie to sit.

"Tell me what's wrong," Katie said. "All of it."

And then, in tortured stops and starts, Addie told the story. A balloon payment, the ranch heavily leveraged, no choice but to sell without the Christmas Fair. Katie listened openmouthed. "Why didn't you tell me any of this?"

"She didn't want to worry you," Brayden said.

Katie's head snapped around. "You knew about this?"

He nodded. "Just since this morning."

"And you didn't tell me?" He saw her flinch, absorbing his omission, the shutters falling across her heart.

"Katie, I…"

Addie's breathing grew labored. "That's it. The penny has dropped. I have nothing else now. If it doesn't work tomorrow, Terrence will have the satisfaction of watching me lose the ranch to the bank and then he will kill both of us."

"No," Katie said. "That's *not* going to happen. He's going to be caught."

"How can I put my hopes in that when he's terrorized us for months? I want to believe it will work, but I can't. I'm sorry, Katie," Addie said. She threw her napkin down and hurried from the room. Katie followed, without looking at Brayden.

The rest of them sat in stunned silence for a moment.

Hunter cleared his throat. "If our plan works, maybe the committee will change their minds."

"Maybe," Charlie said.

"It's going to work," Helena reassured them. "Ranch or no ranch, we have to get an attempted murderer locked up and we will do that. Tomorrow's the day." She patted Brayden's shoulder as she carried her plate to the kitchen. "Things will be different once we get him," she murmured. "Katie will understand why you didn't tell her."

But the look on Katie's face told him otherwise.

He'd kept something from her, something important. *I'll explain it, make her understand.*

The breath burned in his lungs. As soon as he caught Terrence Kapowski, Katie would be safe. She could resume her life, free of terror.

But time was running out.

And Terrence was determined that he would destroy Katie and Addie at any cost.

Katie consoled Addie as best she could. She'd never seen her stalwart guardian so completely undone. Addie was no longer crying, but she sat hollow-eyed, staring out the bedroom window at the darkening night. "I am sorry you had to find out that way. I didn't know what else to do. We needed feed, and the barn collapsed. Our truck transmission failed. The washing machine conked out. I had no choice but to mortgage the ranch."

"It's okay," Katie said, squeezing her arms. "You did what you had to do. There's no shame in that."

She gulped. "If I'd done things better, not taken in so many animals…"

"Stop blaming yourself," Katie chided. "You're not a quitter and this isn't over. Tomorrow will change everything."

Addie shook her head. "Don't you understand? I have nothing to pay that mortgage. It will take everything I have to care for the herd. The Christmas Fair was going to bring in enough, barely, for the bank payment. I don't have any more options."

Addie's helplessness scared Katie. "The committee will change their minds once Terrence is caught. And we won't need to be scared every minute about what he's going to do next."

"I pray that happens, but if it doesn't, you need to be prepared. Find homes for the animals, but the older ones…" She grimaced. "Who will want to take them?"

"Aunt Addie," Katie said more loudly. "Stop getting ahead of yourself. Terrence is going to be arrested tomorrow. The threat will be gone."

"Do you believe that?" Addie said. "My brother knows this land, these roads. He's wily and cunning. Do you trust Brayden to finally bring him down?"

Thinking of Brayden sent a pain through her chest.

He'd known, and not told her, but that was a separate issue. Did she think he could capture Terrence? In spite of her hurt and anger toward him, she nodded. "Yes, I do. So can you hold on for one more day?"

Addie clutched her hand. "I'll try."

Katie closed her aunt's door and walked slowly to her own room. Brayden was in the hallway, leaning against the wall, hands shoved in his pockets. "I didn't mean to hurt you," he said before she got a word out. "I thought it best that you not know."

"*You* thought it best? What gives you the right to keep my aunt's situation from me?" she snapped. "I'm her niece, her kin."

"I'm sorry. You're already so stressed and I…"

"Didn't think I could handle it?"

"No," he said firmly. "I didn't want to burden you further."

"Family isn't a burden. It's always been me and her against the world. Addie is all I have, all I've ever had since I was ten years old."

"Not all…" he started, then stopped. "I mean, you have me. At least, I hope you see it that way."

She shook her head. "Let's be clear. You didn't come here because you had any fondness for me, Brayden. As a matter of fact, you arrived under duress, as I recall."

"Things changed. You're making this a bigger issue than it needs to be."

Was he serious? Her anger ticked up a notch. "No, I'm not."

He shook his head. "I don't understand this. Did I threaten your independence? Is that what this is? Did it ever occur to you that you use your independence as a way to keep people away? You and Addie against the world. That doesn't leave much room for anyone else to get in."

She could only stare at him, mouth open. Her chin went up. "I don't need anyone else."

He matched her. "I think you do."

"Because *you* know what's good for me? You're talking like we're friends, but the truth is I'm an assignment. You can't deny that."

His hands came loose from his pockets and he leaned forward. "I don't deny it, but my feelings toward you have changed since I arrived. I mean… I thought yours had, too. We're closer now, right? Friends at least? Or more? Was I reading that wrong?"

All the frustration and fear boiled over into a hot stream. "You got something wrong, because real friends, *true* friends, don't hide things from each other. You, above all people, should know that."

His eyes narrowed. "Me, above all people? What are you saying?"

She felt the prick of hot tears. "Jamie didn't tell you the truth and that devastated you, yet you didn't come clean to me."

He straightened as if she'd struck him. "I…" He closed his mouth abruptly. "I care about you and I didn't want to cause you pain. I may have messed up, but my motives were clean. Unlike Jamie's."

"Jamie was your whole world and come to find out you were in love with a liar," she said. "Maybe you learned a few tricks from her." She was aghast at herself. The acid just kept pouring out, burning him, scorching her.

"I didn't expect you to bring *her* up."

"You overstepped. You're here on a detail. That's all."

His jaw tightened, an angry tilt to his mouth. "I thought you knew me better, but I guess to you maybe I am still that jerk you always thought I was."

His stare was so intense she was rendered mute by it. He shook his head. "And I was trying to figure out a way to tell you how much you mean to me. Well, I won't make that mistake again, believe me."

Without a word, he marched away, boots heavy on the staircase.

She stared after him, numb and sick.

*I was trying to figure out a way to tell you how much you mean to me.*

She was that important to Brayden?

Katie stumbled into her own room and flopped on the bed. What had she done? Yes, he'd kept something from her, something big, and it reawakened all those old doubts she'd had about having the strength to manage her life on her own. But deep down did he still think of her as that flighty, unsavvy girl who was not qualified? Just an assignment, like she'd accused him of?

No, she thought. He didn't. He'd shown that in a million small ways and many big ones. His choice to keep Addie's secret stung, but more because of who she was than how he'd treated her. She'd let him in, allowed him to become crucial in her life, and the price of that was disappointment.

*I was trying to figure out a way to tell you how much you mean to me.*

*Things are better and brighter when I'm with you.*

The thoughts stunned her and underneath was the faintest layer of elation. Her own tenderness toward Brayden had not been one-sided. The happy tune that played in her own heart echoed in his. How important was he to her?

Regret almost choked her. All the vitriol she'd poured out replayed in ugly discord. She'd repaid her anger and hurt in kind and dumped it on him.

And what did that leave in the way of the future? If tomorrow's plan was successful, the ranch would likely be saved, but Brayden would pack up and return to the police headquarters at Anchorage. They'd go back to being only coworkers.

*You and Addie against the world.* With Brayden here, her world was better, bigger, brighter. She would apologize to him, but she feared it would not change anything. He was a proud man and she'd struck out at the very most vulnerable spot in the most cruel way. Her own behavior shamed her.

She went to the window. Dusk played across the hard-packed earth, shadows growing to swallow up the remaining light. Brayden was watching Ella lope circles around the yard. His back was to her, his tall form hunched against the cold. Her heart twisted. As if he'd felt her watching, he tipped his face up to her window. She pressed a hand to the glass, hope rising for the briefest of moments. Maybe he could forgive the hateful things she'd said, but then he turned abruptly away.

Tears blurred her vision at that silent dismissal. Sinking down on her knees, she asked God to help her find the words to apologize to Brayden and she prayed that Terrence would finally be caught.

Tomorrow...

Everything hinged on tomorrow.

# FIFTEEN

Brayden didn't partake in the early breakfast. Bleary-eyed from lack of sleep, he told himself he'd been busy briefing Phil and Alex, checking and rechecking the plans with Hunter and Helena. A self-deception, he knew. He didn't want to see Katie. Thinking of her burned a hot coal straight through his insides. He had a brain in his head, he was pretty sure. Why had he decided yet again to love another woman who didn't love him back? And Katie not only did not love him, she thought him an interfering liar. Why in the world had he admitted to her that he loved her? *You were in love with a liar... You learned a few tricks from her.* That one hurt most of all.

He sat in the bunkhouse, staring at his phone, willing the time to pass until it was seven thirty. It would all go down soon and he'd put the Family K behind him. Ella sensed his mood and bopped a nose into his thigh until he stroked her ears. "I'm glad you still have faith in me, El."

There was a discreet clearing of the throat. He jerked

a chin up. Charlie stood at the doorway, balanced on crutches. "Am I…interrupting?"

"No, not at all. I was going over last-minute details."

Charlie's smile was knowing. "I'm familiar with those kinds of details."

Brayden realized the older man must have overheard what had happened between him and Katie. He fiddled with his radio. "How's Addie this morning?"

"Resolved. Chiding herself on her uncharacteristic display of emotion, which she equates with weakness. Right as rain outwardly, but I can tell she's nervous." He paused. "The Kapowski women are a spirited clan."

Didn't he know it? "That's for sure."

"But they don't always say things in the most comforting way."

Brayden's gaze sharpened. "What do you mean?"

He sat on an edge of the couch. "I mean… Addie is afraid to trust anyone since she's had to rely on herself all her life. Seems to me, maybe Katie leans a bit in that direction."

Brayden sighed. "True enough. But it doesn't leave a way for people to get close, does it?"

"No. I'm not an expert on anything but roasts and chops, but it appears to me that extra patience is required to weed out the common from the exceptional where women are concerned."

Brayden quirked an eyebrow at him. "Has that been your strategy with Addie?"

Charlie laughed. "It has indeed, son. I had to package a lot of dinner roasts before she'd even exchange more than a comment about the weather with me. We were going on months before she joined me for coffee. But I'm a patient man." He winked. "And I'm willing to wait for the exceptional."

*To wait for the exceptional.* But what if the exceptional woman didn't want you? Brayden was still pondering Charlie's wisdom when Addie and Katie arrived. He studiously avoided looking at Katie, but the heat licked his cheeks anyway. It felt as if everyone in the room knew how she'd told him off in the hallway. He got to his feet as Quinn arrived. "All set?"

"Yes," Quinn said. "You?"

"Hunter and Helena are waiting at the car. If anything goes wrong, I'll call or text. You do the same."

"Got it."

He thought Katie might be sending glances his way, but he did not dare look at her for fear any more lunacy would slip from his mouth. For all Charlie's pep talk, Katie had made her feelings abundantly clear. The worst part of all was that he really did love her, in spite of what had happened. Of course he did. Textbook Ford, loving a woman who could not care less about him. Same story, different day.

Avoiding any more small talk, he exited the bunkhouse and let Ella into the back seat of his car. Hunter pulled out behind him. They both passed Helena in her vehicle, engine idling. She gave them a go-ahead nod. With the hat and glasses, and her hair pulled up, she could pass for Addie with no trouble. She would depart through the main gate.

He and Hunter drove out the rear entrance, circling around to the road and taking up their positions a half mile apart. Brayden was concealed in a patch of shrubbery and Hunter behind a pile of rocks. Time dragged on, the minutes crawling by so slowly that Brayden rechecked his phone to be sure the clock was still working.

That morning before sunup, Phil had reported he'd said the words Brayden had scripted out verbatim as he stopped by the hollow tree to debrief with Alex. Good thing Brayden hadn't acted too quickly on having Terrence's hidey-hole removed from the property.

"That Addie is a stubborn woman," Phil had recited. "She's bound and determined to drive into town this morning without an escort. In broad daylight, no less, seven thirty sharp. A sitting duck, if you ask me, but I don't get paid to make decisions around here."

So the trap was laid and all they could do was hope Terrence walked right into it.

He thought of Katie again and tried to shut down that line immediately.

*Do your job. Get Terrence out of her life.* So she could live it without him. The pain waxed fresh until he heard a car on the road behind him. Helena. Showtime.

Helena drove slowly past him. No sign of anyone in pursuit as she crunched along the road.

*Come on, come on.* He drummed his fingers on the steering wheel. Seconds ticked into minutes that piled up. Where was Terrence?

Hunter's voice was hushed over the radio. "You got anything? Why haven't we seen him? He'll want to get Addie now to avoid being seen by anyone when the road widens."

"I don't see any sign of him." He radioed Helena. "Stop for a minute and pretend you're getting something from the glove box."

She did as instructed without answering, lest Terrence see she was speaking to someone. Nothing. No movement from the trees or road.

Helena continued on. She'd almost gotten to Hunter when his phone pinged with a text from Quinn.

Guy near the dock.

Brayden's pulse leaped. He activated the new ranch camera he'd installed on his phone. It was at the far end of their range, but he saw it, a man sneaking along the road near the dock.

"Hunter..." he started.

And then to his horror, he saw Addie appear on the screen, running from the bunkhouse toward the man. "No," he pleaded.

Quinn appeared behind Addie at a full-out sprint.

*No. No, no, no.* How could Terrence have gotten wise to their plans? What was Addie thinking going after him? He radioed Hunter.

"We're blown. Terrence is on the ranch."

*"What?"* Hunter's question went unanswered as Brayden floored the gas pedal and raced back onto the Family K. His pounding blood almost deafened him. Why hadn't Terrence gone after the Addie impostor? What had tipped him off?

That was spilled milk. All that remained was to catch him before he hurt Addie or Quinn.

The wheels bumped and juddered over the packed earth of the frontage road. He jerked the car to a stop at the dock and ran flat out, Ella galloping along behind him. Quinn was pulling Addie back, trying to shove her behind him as she confronted the man moving fast toward the edge of the weathered boards.

"You wanted to come for me," Addie screamed. "Well, here I am. You leave Katie alone."

Brayden pulled his weapon. "State trooper. Stop right there, Terrence."

Now the man accelerated and, after a quick look behind him, dived feetfirst into the river. Ella launched herself in directly. He trained his gun on the flailing body.

"Don't fight against the dog," he yelled. "She'll get you out." Ella towed the sodden figure to the edge of the muddy bank just as Helena and Hunter arrived, panting from their own sprint to the dock.

Brayden's stomach was a ball of tension, as Ella paddled her way out of the icy water with her rescue in tow.

Hunter and Helena kept their weapons on the fugitive as Brayden holstered his gun and climbed down the ladder to the bank to receive Ella's burden. "Good girl, El," he said. It hadn't gone like he'd expected, but they'd made the arrest. The dripping man lay on his side while Ella licked at his hands.

"You're under arrest, Terrence." Brayden flipped him over and his heart stopped.

It took a few seconds for him to realize how thoroughly he'd been duped. It was not Terrence, but Phil, disguised to look like him. They were in league together after all.

"It wasn't supposed to happen like this," Phil sputtered, wiping the water from his forehead. "Terrence promised me five thousand dollars and that I'd be well away before you got back."

Brayden felt like he was the one in the water, slowly drowning in his own failure. "You were on the take this whole time."

"Sorry," Phil said with a shrug. "Security jobs don't pay very well."

And then the full impact of the betrayal hit Brayden between the eyes. Terrence had paid off Phil to cause a distraction and Phil had given him all the details of the plan. Phil had been tipping him off the whole time, sharing important information when Terrence was nearby, probably texting or calling with other key facts. He should have trusted his earlier suspicion that it had to be someone working on the ranch.

Quinn, Hunter, Helena and Addie stared at him with various expressions of horror as they understood, too. The bottom line was inescapable.

Katie and Charlie were now alone and unprotected in the bunkhouse.

And he'd practically left the door open for Terrence to get to them.

Getting into his car, he rammed it in gear and drove as if his life depended on it.

Charlie had restrained Katie from running from the bunkhouse after her aunt. "Let Quinn get her," Charlie said soothingly. "Brayden wouldn't want you out in the open."

Charlie was right, but Katie was electric with fear since her aunt had run from the house when she'd seen someone out by the dock. It couldn't be Terrence. She was not able to see clearly what was going on since the bunkhouse windows faced the other direction, but she'd heard the sirens.

"Something must have gone wrong," she said. "I'm going to call Brayden."

"Brayden is a busy boy right now," a voice said.

Charlie and Katie whirled to see Terrence standing in the doorway. "I thought maybe I'd find Addie here, too, but she couldn't stay put, right? Ran right out like a silly child."

Before Katie had a chance to scream, Charlie raised up a crutch and charged to deliver a blow to Terrence's midsection.

Terrence batted it aside easily. He stripped the crutch from Charlie and dealt him a kick to his cast that sent him tumbling into a pile. He staggered to his feet and lowered his head, rushing like a bull right at Terrence. But Terrence was younger, stronger and wasn't dealing with a broken ankle. He hooked a foot out and sent Charlie crashing to the floor again. Then he clubbed him in the head with the crutch.

"Stop," Katie cried, rushing to help Charlie.

Before she got to him, Terrence grabbed her arm. She fought him, kicking and screaming, but he rammed a knee into her kidneys. Pain exploded through her body and she went down onto her stomach, the breath driven out of her. He immediately began to wrap her wrists behind her with duct tape. When she recovered enough to scream again, he stuffed a dirty handkerchief into her mouth, which made her gag, and taped over it. Fear flooded her senses like a wave of icy river water. How had it gone wrong? Why hadn't he taken the bait?

"It would be so much faster to strangle you right now," Terrence said, voice harsh in her ear. "But I promised maximum pain, didn't I?"

Desperately she tried to get up, but he kept a heavy knee on her lower back.

"Addie will be devastated when they find your body. Poor, poor sis. All alone in the world."

For a second, the pressure of his knee eased. Katie thrashed, but there was no way to escape as he hoisted her up by her bound wrists. The throbbing in her arms was intense.

No way was Terrence going to win. No way. *Come on, Katie. Fight back.*

He lugged her to a standing position. Through her haze of pain, she realized he hadn't secured her ankles. Easing back a step so she was as close as she could be, she donkey kicked behind her, aiming for his knee. The sole of her boot connected with his patella. She detected a satisfying crunch. Terrence buckled, cursing with pain. She ran for the door. It wouldn't be easy to pull off, but she had an escape plan in mind. She would turn backward, open it with her bound hands, yell for help. Less than a foot from the door, her hopes soared, until a thrown chair knocked the legs out from under her. She collapsed with a muffled cry of pain, striking her head on the door frame. Then she lay there with stars dancing in front of her eyes.

Terrence leaned on one leg, panting from the exertion of throwing the chair. He clutched the knee she'd damaged. Anger sharpened his features and made his eyes gleam. "You'll regret that, Katie. Maximum pain, remember?"

*Get up. You have to get away.*

But her limbs felt leaden and her senses buzzed.

She could hardly get a breath. Through her tears, she saw that Charlie lay crumpled and groaning.

"Charlie." Her scream was locked in by the soiled handkerchief.

"Ready to go, niece?"

*Don't let him take you.*

But she could think of no way to escape. The room grew fuzzy around her and she slipped toward unconsciousness.

"Maximum pain" was the last thing she heard.

# SIXTEEN

Brayden saw the open door of the bunkhouse. Phil's security vehicle, with Terrence driving, had vanished through the main gate with Hunter in hot pursuit. He'd escaped... But what had he left behind for them to find?

"Katie! Charlie!" he shouted as he sprinted into the bunkhouse. There was no reply that he could hear over the pounding of his own heart. He shouted again, pushing in farther. Where were they? Had he been too late? Did Terrence kill them before he escaped?

Helena appeared in the doorway. "I can't find them," he told her. "I'll check the bedrooms." He almost fell over Charlie's prostrate form partially concealed behind the sofa.

"Here," he yelled. Brayden knelt by the man. Was there a bullet hole? A stab wound? As he felt for a pulse, all he could make out was blood coming from Charlie's nose.

Helena helped him drag Charlie away from the furniture so they could begin first aid. Addie and Quinn arrived at a run. Addie let out a scream when she saw Charlie.

Helena put her cheek to Charlie's mouth. "He's breathing and I've got a pulse."

Addie's mouth trembled. "Thank You, God," she said. Then her wide-eyed gaze traveled around the bunkhouse. "Where's Katie?"

Brayden did not acknowledge her tortured question because he was already moving toward the back of the house. She had to be there somewhere.

He tore apart the tiny rooms, looking everywhere she might have hidden or anyplace that Terrence might have confined her. She wasn't there. He could feel it, though he'd forced himself to be thorough.

Brayden rattled off information on his phone as he charged back in the living room to join Helena. "Katie's gone." They locked eyes as they came to the same truth.

"Terrence took her," Brayden croaked. His brain spun with shock. He didn't have to ponder the *why*.

What would be the only thing worse for Addie than having her niece found dead in the bunkhouse? Having her abducted, powerless to whatever anguish Terrence had in store for her.

*Maximum pain.* And Brayden had handed the opportunity to Terrence on a silver platter.

He walked outside, praying Hunter had intercepted Terrence. Phil was already handcuffed in the back of Helena's car. Brayden went to him. "Where's Terrence?"

"I don't know."

"You're lying," Brayden growled.

"No. He contacted me only by phone. I never met with him, never knew where he was staying. Never even saw him when he was hiding in the tree, listening in on our conversations."

"From what number did he call?"

Phil shrugged. "A local number. You can check my phone if it's still functioning when you pull it out of the river." He wiped at the top of his damp head. "I didn't plan on jumping in. You were supposed to spot me on the camera and I'd be gone in the woods by the time you made it back, except my knee went out on me and I couldn't get away in time."

He spoke calmly and practically, as if they were talking about the weather instead of a woman's life. Brayden wanted to grab hold of him and toss him into the river all over again. "The cops are going to interrogate you until you spill everything you know about Terrence."

He shook his head. "I figure as much, but it's a waste of effort. I worked for some cash, that's all. He'd ask me to do something and then leave payment in the hollow tree. Told him your movements, mostly, like when you went to get that old reindeer so he'd know where to set up the ambush. Cash, always cash."

Brayden shook his head in disgust. "You handed Katie over for cash."

Phil grimaced. "I was going to stop helping him anyway, since I didn't appreciate having to drug myself so he could trash the living room. I only swallowed a little, a few bites, so that if you insisted on a blood test it would show. Way too much risk. The guy's a real loose cannon. It's too much stress for the money, so I was going to tell him I was out."

"But you didn't, did you?" Helena said.

"No." Phil squirmed. "You had us set up this whole plan to catch him on the road. I figured, you know, he'd be real grateful to me for filling him in. He paid me off and asked me to do one last thing before we parted ways, making an appearance on the dock to lure you away from the bunkhouse and leaving my car where he could get it. I agreed. It wasn't personal, just money."

Brayden knelt to stare him straight in the eye. "It was very personal to me and I will make sure you get the maximum sentence." He slammed the car door shut so hard the window rattled before he returned to the bunkhouse.

Quinn and Addie still knelt next to Charlie, who was now starting to stir. At least Terrence hadn't killed him. Surviving Terrence a second time was certainly a feat in itself. Addie struggled to her feet, took two unsteady steps toward Brayden and tried to speak… But nothing came out of her mouth. Her legs shook. Quinn grasped her under the forearm to steady her.

Time stood still in the tension that stretched between them. He'd give anything not to have to tell her the truth.

"Katie?" she whispered. "Did he tell you where she is?"

Brayden managed to get it out. "No. Phil said he doesn't know. Terrence didn't tell him that part of the plan."

"What?" It was no more than a whisper from Addie, soft, like a prayer. She searched his face, desperate for him to cut down the fear that had to be infecting her like a virus.

He swallowed, mouth dry, no comfort to give. "Phil was the diversion so Terrence could abduct her."

Helena drew close to him, expression dour. He could feel their sense of defeat that echoed his own. "We've got the BOLO out," she said grimly. "Roadblocks will be in place within fifteen minutes, but…" She paused. "Hunter didn't catch him. I'm going now to help."

*Didn't catch him.* Brayden's last thread of hope unraveled.

Helena held up a baggie. In it was the forget-me-not necklace, the one from Katie's mother, the one she never took off. "This was on the ground. I'll see if Luna can track Katie's scent from her being forced in the car, at least detect which direction Terrence turned on the main road."

Forget-me-not. His senses numbed.

A whine of sirens announced the paramedics. Quinn waved in the ambulance. The medics hurried to assess Charlie. He looked dazed and he tried to argue when they explained he was going to the hospital. "I'm okay. I want to stay with Addie."

Addie did not even supply her usual no-nonsense rebuttal. She held his hand and kept staring at Brayden, beseeching, until he had to look away.

They loaded Charlie onto a stretcher against his protests.

"I'll go with him," Addie said. "Unless…" She looked again at Brayden. "Is there anything I can do to help you get Katie back?"

He had to force out a reply in the face of her anguish.

"We'll handle it and keep you posted," he gritted out. "I promise."

"I'll drive her to the hospital and stay there as long as I'm needed," Quinn assured him.

Brayden nodded. He hoped there was enough gratitude in his expression to show his thanks to Quinn, since he still did not trust himself to speak. Fury and fear swept through him in waves.

Quinn guided Addie toward the main house. She walked as if she was plowing through a dense drift of snow.

He was left standing there, Ella shaking off the water, as the ambulance rolled away. Helena started to crouch next to Luna, but instead she rose and put a tentative hand on his arm.

"I'm just going to say it because I know what you're thinking. This isn't your fault. There was no way you could have known that Phil was on the take." Then she opened the baggie and gave Luna a good whiff of the necklace and followed the wagging tail.

*This is every bit my fault*, he thought as he watched them track. He went back to the main house, which he knew in the next few hours would be turned into the center of operations for the flood of law enforcement that would descend upon the place to search for Katie. He would call the colonel from there. He surveyed the ranch once more, the sweep of autumn sun brushing the acres, the reindeer huddled together in the distant pens, the soft warbling of the river.

Addie's home. Katie's home. A sanctuary for the unwanted animals that had nowhere else to go. He would set the official wheels in motion.

And then he would personally tear up the acres one single inch at a time until he brought her home again.

*Katie, I will find you.*

From far away came the sounds and sensations, strange, unfamiliar, frightening.

Katie felt prickles under her chin as she swam toward consciousness. At first, she was too deeply lost in the dark to do anything more than acknowledge the sensation. Agony pounded her skull as she fought to wake up. Something terrible had happened. Fear circled around her, darting and biting without coming fully home to roost.

There had been pain. Terror.

Charlie unconscious.

And Terrence... Her eyes flew open, heartbeat zooming. She was lying on grass—not grass, *hay*, someplace gloomy and cold. Where was she? Fighting through the pain that pierced her skull, she got to her knees, where she realized her hands were no longer bound behind her. Her thighs trembled. Forcing her head up, she looked around. A barn... She was inside a barn. The hay strewn across the floor was dirty and clumped. How? She swam through her fractured recollections. The last thing she remembered was falling in the bunkhouse.

*Charlie!* Had he been badly hurt? Using a raggedy hay bale as a level, she pulled herself to her feet. Wobbling, she grabbed hold of the rough-hewn wall. Her vision blurred, then cleared.

Terrence had not left her to die. He'd brought her to this barn. Why?

The answer was obvious. He was delaying her murder in order to torture Addie. Anger slithered through the fear. *You're not going to hurt my aunt*, she silently promised. As long as she had one more breath in her body, she'd fight him with everything she had.

He'd given her time and she'd use it to plan her escape. As she sucked in some lungfuls of the dank air, trying to steady her breathing, she heard a soft clicking. She knew that sound.

She jerked a look around so fast it made sparks fly in front of her eyes. As her vision cleared, she saw the two reindeer, penned into a corner of the barn. Thunder had lost his antlers, but she recognized the big male right away. And next to him, Lulu, the sweet mother who had been separated from her tiny baby when Terrence abducted both animals. Their agitated movements produced the clicking of their hooves. She half crawled, half staggered over to them.

"Hi, sweethearts." She put her hand through the slats to stroke Lulu. Tears threatened but she swallowed them down. "It's okay," she crooned nonsensically to the animals. "I'm going to get you out of here."

And how exactly was she going to do that? Brayden probably had no idea where Terrence had taken her. Thinking about Brayden and how he must be feeling fueled her resolve.

She stepped over a ruined saddle cast on the floor, walked over to the big barn doors and pushed at them. They swayed on their rusted hinges but did not give.

Locked. Not surprising. There was no back exit. The only other way out was the enormous loft window some fifteen feet above her head. The ruined ladder indicated she would not be able to climb up there, even if she wanted to. The light that shone in told her it was probably late afternoon. How long had she lain there? A couple of hours? An entire day? And she had no clue where she was...

Her phone. She fumbled only to discover it gone. Of course Terrence would have taken it, or it was on the floor of the bunkhouse. Where was he right now? Had he stayed in the vicinity of the ranch, or driven for hours to spirit her away? She returned to the wall and found a missing knothole where she could see out. Crouching, she pressed her eye to the spot. There was a flat swath of dirt that vanished into a dense brushy area. A few scraggy trees poked through the low foliage, but it gave the impression of untended property that was isolated from any neighbors.

Katie felt a swell of desperation. "Now isn't the time to panic." A pile of soiled hay half concealed a car. Phil's security vehicle. She didn't know whether he was working for Terrence, or if perhaps Terrence had taken the vehicle by force. Whatever the case, there might be a way she could get the radio to work, or at the very least, find something she could use to defend herself.

She was about to go investigate when she caught the sound of the barn door slowly creaking open.

She swallowed down a scream as Terrence let himself in.

He wore the same faded jeans and long-sleeved

sweatshirt. "Awake? Good. I was worried about freeing your hands, but it was too hard to lug you over my shoulder with them taped behind you."

She glared at him. "Did you kill Charlie?"

He shrugged. "Who knows?" He held up a chain and a manacle. "Look what I brought you. Jewelry."

Her muscles went limp. If he chained her, she would not be able to reach the car. The upside was it did not appear he wanted to kill her immediately. "Where is this place?"

"Old barn. That's all you need to know. Nice and cozy."

"You've made a mistake, kidnapping me. You should run. The police will be all over the area. They'll catch you."

He laughed, showing yellowed teeth. "Alaska is a great big place. They'll try their best, but they won't find this barn. It's all they can do to keep electricity going to this area." He jerked a thumb upward. "Gotta bring in the crews by helicopter to work on the lines because the roads are terrible."

Her spirit sank, but she was determined not to let him see her discouragement. "You're wrong. They'll find me."

He shrugged. "I'm only gonna keep you here a little while anyway, until I have a chance to touch base with Addie. She's going to give me the cash equivalent of what the ranch is worth."

Katie gaped. "She doesn't have that kind of money. The ranch is mortgaged. You're wasting your time."

His lips thinned. "Then she'll fork over to me all she

has and that will have to be enough for me. As long as she's ruined, I'll be happy. Maybe she can borrow from that doughboy with the mustache. I don't care. She'll pay until it hurts."

"And then you'll kill me anyway, won't you?"

His smile was wolfish. "Like I said, maximum pain." He moved closer.

Could she fight him off? She didn't think so. Her body was still trembling and she felt dizzy. Kick out at his knee. That worked last time. She shifted her weight.

"Sit down," he commanded. "I'm going to fasten this to your ankle."

"I won't."

He looked at her with eyes cold as Arctic snow. "I can knock you out with a shovel, if you'd rather. Then I don't have to listen to your yammering."

She sank down on the dirty hay. He fastened the iron manacle around her ankle and clamped the chain end to a metal rack that was probably used to hang harnesses and other equipment. He tugged on it to test the strength. "That should do."

"I'll scream," she said. "I'll keep on screaming so loud that someone will hear."

"Now, I'd like to see how long that would last. Go ahead. Scream the place down. There is no one to hear you." He bent so his face was closer to hers. "There is no one coming to save you. You are going to die in this barn, so if you want to spend your last few hours screaming until you're hoarse, go ahead. I think it will upset the reindeer, though." He laughed. "Then again, they're going to wind up dead here with you, depending on how long it takes them to find your body. Dumb animals. Useless, except for eating."

Chuckling to himself, he left the barn, slamming the doors shut behind him.

Even as she watched the dust settle to the floor, she knew she would not let him win.

Ever.

# SEVENTEEN

Colonel Gallo came to direct operations for the search, along with several local cops and all the Alaska K-9 officers who could be spared. The tension was palpable; even the canines were subdued. Brayden pushed to be involved in every conceivable route. He and Ella drove the ranch property, combed the woods alongside Hunter and Juneau. Helena reported that Luna could not pick up a scent for Katie on the main road. She graciously offered to bring Addie home from the hospital along with Charlie, who had been checked over and cleared of major injuries by early afternoon. He managed to avoid Addie, who spent the rest of the day alternately sitting with Charlie or wandering through the house, listening in to see if there had been any progress.

There hadn't. The roadblocks had possibly been set up too late, or Terrence had headed off-road in Phil's vehicle. They'd found his RV parked in the woods behind the ranch. It was being processed for evidence. The sheer enormity of the task was daunting. Alaska was 665,000 square miles of rough terrain, some of it nearly inaccessible. But Katie was out there somewhere, if Brayden could have only some slight indication of which direction Terrence might have headed.

When it was almost two, he was moving to his car again to start on the next search grid. He and Ella drove countless miles, his frustration mounting with each passing hour. Why hadn't Terrence been in contact?

To prolong the torture was the obvious answer.

"Brayden," Lorenza said, stopping him with his hand on the doorknob. "Take a break."

"Don't need one. I'm going out again."

She folded her arms across her chest. "You're tired. It's time to stop for a while."

"I'm all right."

"That's an order, not a suggestion," she snapped. Then she heaved a breath. "Look. Things went bad here. That happens in police work. I know how you're feeling."

"All respect, Colonel, I don't think you do."

Her shoulders stayed erect, but her face was creased with fatigue. "I love Katie like she was my own."

"I love her, too," he blurted.

The comment surprised her. She raised both eyebrows.

He should feel embarrassed, dismayed by his own admission, but he felt nothing but the burning desire to find her, to *save* her.

"I didn't know that's where things stood between you."

*It doesn't*, he should have said. *Just on my end.* But there was no point in bringing that up now. So he simply said, "I'm going to search. If you need to take my badge, do it. I'm going anyway."

"All right, Brayden," she said slowly. "This isn't the time to lose a good trooper. Do one more search route. Report back in an hour." She paused. "And you can keep your badge, by the way."

"Yes, ma'am."

He'd almost cleared the porch with Ella when Hunter called out. He'd been assigned to monitor any calls on Addie's cell phone. "It's Terrence," he said, covering the mouthpiece. "He wants to talk to Addie."

Brayden's hands itched to grab the phone and savage Terrence with all the anger that flashed through his nerves. Instead, he moved as close as he dared and waited.

"Just a minute. I'll get her," Hunter said to Terrence.

Addie was summoned. She took the phone with a quaking hand, poking the speaker button on. Brayden strained to hear every syllable.

"Where's Katie?" Addie demanded.

"With me. Still alive, unless you don't cooperate."

"What do you want?"

"Money. Five hundred thousand dollars should do."

Addie gaped. "I don't have that kind of money."

"Then you'll have to borrow it. I'll give you two days."

"And if I can't come up with it?" she asked.

"Aw, you know the answer to that. She dies, slowly and painfully."

Brayden's teeth ground together. Hunter scribbled a note and handed it to Addie.

"How do I know you haven't killed her already?"

Addie said, prompted by Hunter's message. "I want to talk to her."

"No. You don't make the rules anymore. I do." A whirring sound caught Brayden's attention. A fan? He leaned closer and motioned for Addie to stretch out the conversation.

"Where…? I mean… How do I get you the money?" Addie said.

"I'll call you tomorrow and give you a bank account number. You'll transfer the money and I'll tell you where Katie is."

Again, the thwop of something spinning. A washing machine?

"Don't…" Addie whispered. "Don't hurt her, please. I'll give you anything you want. The ranch…"

"Nah. I heard that comes with a nice big mortgage. Too late. I want money. If you don't give it to me, she's dead. And tell all those cops if I see a sign of any of them she dies." The call clicked off.

"He has to be close," Hunter said. "I'll see if Eli can get a ping off a cell tower."

But Brayden was lost in thought.

"You have something?" the colonel said.

Brayden didn't answer. He had to think. He walked out onto the porch and stood there, letting the conversations whirl around his brain as he stared at the sun low on the horizon.

Terrence couldn't have gone too far. Somewhere isolated. But that could be a million places in the area. That whirring sound.

The whop of a rotor? He recalled Alex's remark.

*"They're working on the electric lines and they have to drop crews in by helicopter. Noisy."*

He leaped over Ella and ran back inside. "The power company," he said. "We have to ask which lines they were working just now when Terrence called."

"What?"

"That noise in the background of the call. It's a helicopter crew working on the lines. There can't be too many crews out in this area at once."

The colonel was already on her phone. "I'll find out." Her question was clipped and urgent. When she disconnected, they stood staring at each other. Brayden willed Lorenza's phone to ring. It might be a goose chase, but he knew in his gut it wasn't.

It was the break he needed to find Katie.

It took five endless minutes before the answer came back. Colonel Gallo went to the map spread out on the table. "They have two crews working on the lines in this quadrant," she said, stabbing a finger at a spot on the map. "It's rugged terrain, which Phil's car would be hard-pressed to tackle, but there are three fire roads. Let's pull it up on Google Earth and see if there are any kinds of structures or landscape features where he could have hidden the car."

Helena tapped her laptop screen and zoomed in. "Fifty miles is a lot of area to cover," she said. Hunter and Brayden yanked out their laptops and each of them took different zones to search. He stared at that screen until his eyes burned. It was a whole lot of flat ground, blurred green and gray, without a farmhouse to be seen.

Could he have been wrong? *Again?* Had he sent them

along a false trail in a direction that would take them farther away from rescuing Katie? Then it materialized in a small clearing, with one tiny adjustment of the mouse. An old, dilapidated barn. He zoomed in. It could be accessed from a fire road and was within ten miles of the spot where the electric crew was working on the line.

Lorenza was watching over his shoulder. "Is this it?"

"I don't know," he said, "but there's a solid chance."

"Go," she said. "And watch your backs. Terrence may be ready to deal with intruders."

Brayden ran for his car, along with Helena and Hunter.

Terrence might be on the lookout, but he had no idea what was in store for him.

And if he had already hurt Katie...

Brayden shut down the thought. He would follow his own advice and his mother's.

Eyes up, not down.

*I'm coming for you, Katie. Hang on.*

Katie pulled at the chain until the manacle cut into her ankle. The chain was not going to come loose from the wall, on that count she was certain. Only two choices remained—either she forced the iron band around her ankle to give way, or she got her foot out. The reindeer watched; in her mind they were quietly urging her on. The creeping shadows told her it was late afternoon, and her urgency increased. Escape in this nowhere spot would be exponentially harder when night fell.

A protruding nail in the barn wall finally came loose

under her persistent wiggling. When it dropped into her hand, she immediately set about scraping at the rusted spot on the manacle. She worked until her nails were torn and bloody, but the iron held fast.

"Okay. Then we're going to go it the other way." She slipped off her shoe and sock. The cold air immediately numbed her toes. It was a matter of maneuvering, she told herself, just like easing a very large reindeer out of a very tight stall. With effort, she could point her toe and the manacle would slide clear to the bottom of her heel, and there it would stick. Try as she might, she could not get it to ease past that point. With a groan, she lay on her back, panting. If she didn't get free, Terrence would kill her. Even if she did, she might not make it out of the barn, but at least she wouldn't be a passive participant in her own destruction.

Shoving her hands into her jacket pockets, she tried to warm her fingers, which were stiff and cramped. Her fingers touched a tube of ChapStick. *ChapStick!* She sat up, uncapping the tube and slathering it on her heel until there was nothing left in the cylinder. Now she tried again, working the manacle lower and lower across the slippery ointment. Just when she thought she'd gone and permanently jammed the steel bracelet across her heel, the iron slipped free, taking some skin with it. Tears of relief gathered in her eyes. Tossing aside the manacle, she pulled on her shoes and ran to Phil's car.

The driver's door was unlocked. She eased it open, praying it did not squeak. The keys were tucked under the sun visor. She put them in her pocket. There was no radio affixed to the dash like in Brayden's car. The glove box? Nothing much in there but some paper and a stack of old napkins. She checked under the seats and throughout the vehicle, but there wasn't any weapon like she'd hoped, not even a can of pepper spray she might use against Terrence.

She popped the trunk and found a lug wrench. It wasn't the best alternative, since Terrence was strong, but it was better than nothing. She grabbed it. It was possible she could take him by surprise, hide while he was unlocking the barn door and wallop him. Then she'd drive the car for help and come back with a bunch of cops and a trailer for the reindeer. Brayden would be impressed.

What was he doing right now? She thought about the way she'd treated him, broken his heart. And he loved her. Or at least, he *had* before she lashed out at him. And now he was probably feeling tortured over his botched plan to catch Terrence.

Just what her demented uncle would want.

Well, Terrence was in for a surprise, because she wasn't planning on dying in this stinky barn. She would survive for herself, for Addie…and for Brayden. She owed him an apology.

And so much more.

The sudden bird squawk outside made her jump. Through the open loft window she heard it rocket into the sky and away. The reindeer reacted uneasily to the noise, too, eyes rolling as they shifted from hoof to hoof. Scooting to the knothole, she peeked out. At first, she saw nothing save the thick shrubbery.

Then there was the glint of something moving slowly

along the fire trail. She pressed her face to the hole and tried to track it. A vehicle? Another glint. Two vehicles? Terror and hope warred inside her. She wanted to scream, but then Terrence would hurry to make sure she was dead before anyone came to her aid.

Uncertainty made sweat prickle her forehead. The minutes ticked by and she heard nothing but the pounding of her own pulse. And then there was another sound of movement, a crash from the wrecked farmhouse. With a flush of terror, she saw Terrence bash out the remaining glass from the front window as he aimed a rifle into the bushes.

Katie barely contained her scream.

"I see you," Terrence shouted. Then he let loose a volley of shots into the shrubbery. Katie clapped her palms to her ears. There was return fire and now she could see the top of a police car peeking out of the greenery. A dog barked somewhere, muffled. *Ella.*

Her breath caught. It was Brayden and Ella. Somehow they had found her. Elation and fear whirled inside her. Terrence had a good position from which to shoot, protected by the house and at a higher elevation than the police cars. Another blast from Terrence's rifle almost made her scream again. She had no doubt that he was well stocked with ammo and willing to keep shooting until the bitter end. Would he take the lives of Brayden? Hunter? Helena? Any of the other troopers who might be out there?

"Stop shooting," Brayden yelled. "Terrence, we've got you. Throw down your weapon."

Her pulse exploded at the sound of his voice.

"That's not going to happen," her uncle called out. "Let Katie go and you'll get out of this alive."

"She's already shot, bleeding to death in the barn," Terrence sneered.

"No," she yelled. "He's lying." But there was so much shouting from outside and she wasn't sure anyone could hear her.

"Put down your weapon," Brayden commanded again.

Terrence fired another burst of gunfire. She had to do something to help. As she stood there, thoughts reeling, she noticed the weathered boards to the right of the big barn doors. They were fractured with cracks, warped and weakened by the elements. Weak enough? Only one way to find out. Racing back to Phil's car, she turned on the ignition and aimed the wheel straight for the moldy-looking board on one side of the swinging doors.

It was now or never.

# EIGHTEEN

Brayden heard the revving engine one second before Phil's security car exploded through the barn door, showering bits of wood in its wake. Katie… It had to be. He charged from the cover of his vehicle, doing his best to stay concealed behind the shrubbery. If he could cut Terrence off before he took aim at the car…

But there wasn't time. Terrence turned his weapon onto Phil's front windshield, shooting repeatedly into the vehicle. Glass showered everywhere. He returned fire. The vehicle raced madly on until it smashed headlong into a rusted tractor, the front end crumpling. Terrence stumbled into view, ready to start firing again, when Ella exploded from the squad car barking so loudly that he jumped in surprise.

Brayden didn't stop to consider. He flat out sprinted after Ella and aimed a flying tackle that knocked Terrence flat. Hunter and Helena moved in. Helena kicked the rifle away and Hunter snapped on the handcuffs.

Brayden left the arrest and first aid to them. There was only one thought on his mind. He ran toward Phil's ruined vehicle. Terrence had fired directly into the driver's-side window. There would be no way he could have missed.

An agonized cry spilled out of him as he ran, skidding and slipping. Ella galloped after him.

*Katie.* Reaching the vehicle, he yanked open the door.

His senses could not understand what he was seeing. The engine was still running, the accelerator weighted in place by a half-wrecked saddle.

No Katie, only a trick.

He spun around and charged for the barn just as she came running out. There was straw stuck in her hair and her face was slack with fear, eyes wild.

His heart leaped and spun at the sight of the dirty, disheveled, magnificent woman rushing toward him. He gathered her up in his arms and squeezed her tight. Ella ran over and danced up and down in excitement.

*Thank You, God* ran through his mind in an endless loop. In surprise, he realized he was saying the words aloud. She raised a trembling finger to his lips and quieted the stream of words. "I'm saying the same thing, that Terrence didn't hurt you." She shot a look around. "Any of you. We're all okay, aren't we?"

He simply could not speak until he swallowed hard. "Yes… We are."

She heaved in a breath. "Is Charlie alive?"

A question. He could answer and maybe get his body back online, though he could not remove his hands from around her. "Yes. He's going to recover."

She sniffed and sobbed, and he held on tight.

"She all right?" Hunter said, jogging over. "Ambulance is rolling."

"She's okay," Brayden affirmed, earning a smile from Hunter. He shot Helena a thumbs-up to where she stood guarding Terrence. Her wide grin shone clearly, even in the failing light.

Brayden stroked Katie's hair. "You figured sending Phil's car through the barn wall was the best course of action?"

She nodded, still sniffling. "Yes. It worked, didn't it?"

He smiled and resisted the urge to kiss her. Instead, he cupped her cheeks in wonder. "Yes, it certainly did."

"Guess what?" she said.

He stared adoringly at the woman before him whom he loved with all his heart. "What?" he rasped.

"Thunder and Lulu are inside." Fat tears rolled down her face and she began to tremble harder.

Delayed shock, probably. "Let's get you to the car with a blanket around you."

She allowed him to guide her away from the filthy barn, Ella close by her side. "We can bring the reindeer home, back to the herd. Can you think of anything more wonderful than that?"

As a matter of fact, he could, but he wouldn't trouble her with it at the moment. "Addie will be thrilled." He sent a text to the colonel before he handed his cell phone to Katie.

"Tell her right now. I think it will be a call she won't forget."

It would certainly be a day he would remember until he drew his last breath on earth.

Terrence was in custody.

Katie was safe.

He closed his eyes and offered a proper prayer of heartfelt gratitude.

The following day was crammed with cleanup details. There was evidence to be painstakingly cataloged, reports to write, various online briefings to participate in. Brayden felt the spark of excitement in the K-9 team and in Colonel Gallo herself when he drove to Anchorage to have the official team debrief. Even Ella perked up when the cheer broke out that Terrence would stand trial for his crimes and the Christmas Fair would go on as planned.

"Got him," Gabriel said, pumping a fist. "One case down, two to go."

"And I've got some news to add on the Seaver investigation," Poppy said. "Remember the kid I talked to in the Chugach, the one I gave the note to? Well, I did some good old-fashioned legwork and I have some intel on him. His name's Xaviar Lemark. I don't have an address yet, but I'm getting closer. He's seventeen, same age as Harrison Seaver, Cole's son. When he talked to me, he said they were friends—at least, they used to be. And that Harrison is apparently unhappy living off the grid."

"Well, that's something to work on. Keep on it, Poppy," Lorenza said.

Brayden sensed a new energy circulating through the room. Another step forward on locating the Seavers for Eli's godmother. Maybe they'd catch a break on the whereabouts of Violet James, too. There was plenty more work ahead for the K-9 team and now he would be free to participate in the ongoing investigations. It was what he'd wanted, yet he felt as if his spirit still lingered behind at the Family K Reindeer Ranch.

He hadn't talked privately with Katie since the rescue, not properly, but when Colonel Gallo cleared her throat, he had a feeling he knew what was coming.

"And I'm sure some of you may have already guessed that our wonderful Katie Kapowski has tendered her resignation. She's decided to live with her aunt on the Family K full-time."

So she wouldn't be returning to her job with the Alaska K-9 Unit. He should be sad about it, but honestly, he couldn't picture Katie apart from the ranch, now that he'd seen her joy at tending to her precious reindeer family. It was where she belonged.

The meeting disbanded and he found his boss standing next to him in the empty room.

"Ready to get back to work, Ford?" she asked.

He hesitated. "I...uh... I think there's something I need to finish first at the ranch."

She cocked an eyebrow. "With Katie?"

He felt himself blush to the roots of his hair. "Yes, Colonel."

A savvy smile crept over her face. "Very good, Trooper. You go do that."

"Uh, ma'am? I'm not exactly sure that, you know, the whole thing will work out in my favor."

She stared intently. "Remember why I chose you for this case, Brayden? I wanted someone determined, averse to failure..."

He looked at his boots.

"With a touch of the goofball," she continued. "That's you to a tee."

"But…"

"You're dismissed, Trooper Ford. Go finish what you started." And then he was watching the door close, a plan forming in his mind.

In the early afternoon, Katie and Addie watched the herd as they greeted their long-lost members through the slatted wood. Thunder and Lulu had been given a quick vet exam and a clean bill of health, and it was time to reintroduce them to their family.

Katie unlatched the gate and allowed the herd to meander out, offering snuffled greetings. Tulip had revived enough to join them, too. Though she limped a good deal, she was welcomed by her new family. They might be three-hundred-plus-pound deer, designed with survival utmost on their priority lists, but it was clear as the ice crystals that formed on the morning pasture that these animals had missed their two abducted members.

And then Sweetie hopped along, bringing up the rear. He froze in surprise on gangly legs as he caught sight of Lulu. Katie clutched Addie's hand. Had the separation been too long for the baby to remember his mama? Sweetie twitched and trotted a few steps closer to Lulu. Katie realized she was holding her breath. Lulu shook her antlers and stretched out, bringing her velvety nose to rest on Sweetie's head. Her warm breath riffled his fur. And then he was snuggled up beside her and the two walked side by side to rejoin the herd.

Katie's face was damp with tears, as was Addie's.

God had put everything right. There would be wounds to heal, residual memories to be dealt with, financial uncertainty ahead, but they *would* survive.

She hugged Addie gently so as not to aggravate her healing shoulder. "Will the volunteers come tonight?" Shirlene had shown up in person that morning with a plate of muffins and a report that the committee had reversed their vote.

"Not tonight," Addie said vaguely.

"Oh? I thought they were eager to get started."

"Well, tonight wasn't going to work."

"Why not?" Katie asked.

Her aunt shrugged. "Are you sure about this decision to leave your job?"

"Yes. Completely." She would miss her work with the K-9 unit, but she knew God wanted her here. "I want to thank Brayden before I go, though," she said softly. And there was a long-overdue apology she'd not been able to offer. Thinking of him made her heart squeeze uncomfortably, as if it was trying to beat with a missing piece. She reached up to fiddle with her forget-me-not necklace, only to be reminded that it was not there anymore. Another missing piece.

"Come on, honey," Addie said. "There's a pen to be cleaned. Let's start there, okay?"

"Yes, ma'am," she said.

They got to work. When they were finished, Quinn joined them.

Katie smiled at him. "I am so happy you've decided to stay on here. How could we run the place without you?"

Quinn ducked his head. "Aw, you'd manage. I like

it here and my girls are going to love it on take-your-kids-to-work day," he joked, checking a message on his phone. "I was told to inform you that dinner will be ready in fifteen minutes."

"Dinner?" Katie frowned. "Who's the cook?"

But Quinn had already turned away.

"You go on and get a shower," Addie said. "You're a mess. We'll be right behind you."

Her suspicions prickled, but she followed directions. Clean and adorned in comfortably worn jeans and a long-sleeved T-shirt, she headed for the dining room thirty minutes later.

She was flabbergasted to find Brayden there, wearing the pink reindeer apron over his jeans and flannel shirt. His hair was newly cut, a mischievous smile playing around his mouth. Ella greeted her with a friendly bark.

Her pulse skittered at the sight of the handsome trooper who knew her better than anyone except maybe her aunt. "I didn't know you were coming."

He saluted her with a spatula. "That is because I am a master of stealth. I cooked dinner for us."

"You…*cooked*?"

He raised an offended eyebrow. "Don't sound so surprised. I can cook chicken and steak, and my pork ribs are…" He trailed off. "Okay, well, I haven't had much practice at the vegetarian options," he said, untying his apron and tossing it over a chair. He led her to the dining table and swept a hand toward a plate that held a peanut butter and jelly sandwich. It was cut into the shape of a reindeer, with pretzel antlers, raisin eyes and a bit of red grape for a nose.

She took it in, laughing in utter delight. "You made this for me?"

"Well, I made enough sandwiches for everyone, but you get the special reindeer version." He pulled out her chair. "Would you care to sit, madam?"

She knew she could not let another second go by. Instead of sitting in the proffered chair, she turned to face him. "This is so special, absolutely sweet and perfect, but I can't enjoy a mouthful of it until I tell you something."

A look of trepidation crept across his features. "All right. I'm listening."

"I'm sorry, Brayden, so sorry about what I said to you before when I learned about the mortgage payment. I was upset, but it didn't give me the right to talk to you like I did. I've been thinking and praying about it, and you were right. I have used my independence as a way to keep people from me, but... I... I don't want it to keep me from you."

"Katie..." he started, but she cut him off.

"Please, Brayden. I have to finish. I'm sorry I hurt you. Those things I said, especially about Jamie, I wanted to justify my need to push you away. It was hurtful and unfair. I think... I mean..." She swallowed. "It hurt especially because... I love you."

Now his mouth opened in shock. She could not read the expression. Embarrassment? Reluctance?

"You love me?" he said hoarsely, as if the words felt strange on his tongue.

She wanted to run away, but there was no way to go past the awkwardness except to find a way through it. She swallowed hard. "I know things are different now, but I wanted to be honest and tell you that, since you were courageous enough to be straight with me. I don't expect you to return the feeling. But I hope we can be friends, in spite of everything. Can you forgive me?"

He blinked, as if he'd received a blow to the head. "Katie…"

"I get that we are probably not going to see each other much anymore, but I don't want things to end badly between us. Do you understand? I—"

"Yes," he said quickly. "I do. As a matter of fact, if you weren't such an interrupter, I was about to state my case." To her complete surprise, he dropped to his knee and opened a velvet box. Inside were two things: her forget-me-not necklace and a sparkling diamond solitaire engagement ring.

She went completely silent. "You were going to…to do this? Before I apologized?"

He smiled at her, the sweetest boyish smile she'd ever seen. "I love you, my darling Katie. I decided that I was going to go for broke and risk asking you even if you sent me packing. You're that special, that exceptional." His voice broke, and he cleared his throat. "And besides, I already asked Aunt Addie for your hand in marriage, and if I can get through her interrogation, I can handle anything."

Tears sprang to her eyes. "I can't believe it. I thought you were going to go back to Anchorage and I'd never see you again."

"I am going back to my job, of course, though I'll miss your gorgeous face at the office. At least I'll be able to go home to you every night, which should make up for things. Aside from my trooper duties, I think Ella and I are going to have plenty of time on weekends to come help out my wife's family outfit… *If* she says yes to marrying me, that is." He shifted uncomfortably. "And I hope she does soon, because my knee is starting to cramp up."

She realized he was still kneeling there, holding the box. "Yes," she said, eyes dripping with tears as he slid on the ring. "It will be the greatest honor of my life to be Mrs. Katie Ford."

"I love the sound of that." He got to his feet and swept her into an embrace, kissing her deeply. Ella added her bark to the excitement.

The kiss lasted until the applause broke out, and she pulled away to see Aunt Addie and Charlie holding hands, watching the proceedings. Both seemed to be grinning from ear to ear.

"He's kind of a klutz," Addie said, clearing her throat, "but if I can tolerate Charlie, I suppose I can handle Brayden."

Charlie laughed. "A ringing endorsement. And speaking of rings, when are you going to accept mine, Addie? I'm going to keep asking until you say yes."

Addie rolled her eyes, but her cheeks were pink with pleasure. "Let's talk about it after the Christmas Fair. I have a lot to do."

"Anything you say, buttercup."

Addie waved him off, but not until he pressed a kiss to her cheek. "Let's leave these lovebirds to their plans."

Brayden smiled as they left. "Cute couple, aren't they?"

Katie laughed and kissed him. "Are you sure you want to trade in your relaxing weekends for work on this scruffy ranch?"

He looked at her with a smile full of love, and life and promises.

"I'm sure as eggs in April," he said, catching his bride-to-be in his arms.

\* \* \* \* \*

Aside from her faith and her family, there's not much **Shirlee McCoy** enjoys more than a good book! When she's not hanging out with the people she loves most, she can be found plotting her next Love Inspired Suspense story or trekking through the wilderness, training with a local search-and-rescue team. Shirlee loves to hear from readers. If you have time, drop her a line at shirleermccoy@hotmail.com.

## Books by Shirlee McCoy

### Love Inspired Suspense

*Hidden Witness*
*Evidence of Innocence*

### FBI: Special Crimes Unit

*Night Stalker*
*Gone*
*Dangerous Sanctuary*
*Lone Witness*
*Falsely Accused*

### Alaska K-9 Unit

*Blizzard Showdown*

Visit the Author Profile page at
LoveInspired.com for more titles.

# BLIZZARD SHOWDOWN

## Shirlee McCoy

But ask now the beasts, and they shall teach thee; and the fowls of the air, and they shall tell thee: Or speak to the earth, and it shall teach thee: and the fishes of the sea shall declare unto thee. Who knoweth not in all these that the hand of the Lord hath wrought this? In whose hand is the soul of every living thing, and the breath of all mankind.

*—Job* 12:7–10

To the members of Chesapeake Search Dogs who volunteer their time and resources to bring home the lost and missing, and to search-and-rescue professionals everywhere who selflessly give so that others might live. You are wonderful examples of what sacrificial love looks like. May He guide and protect your efforts and multiply your strengths.

# ONE

Violet James didn't want to step outside.

Not because of the cold wind that beat against the windows of the medical clinic. Not even because she had her newborn daughter strapped to her chest.

She didn't want to go outside because she was terrified.

Even now, after seven months of hiding in the Alaskan outback, she wasn't safe. She would never be. Not unless the police caught her former fiancé, Lance Wells, and tossed him in jail where he belonged.

She shuddered, trying not to picture his handsome face or remember his crooning voice and sweet promises. She'd believed every word he'd said. All the I-love-yous and the forever-afters.

She'd been a fool, and it had almost cost her best friend, Ariel Potter, her life. It *had* cost the wilderness guide Violet had hired his. Violet had been planning a small wedding. Just her best friend and Lance's. The guide, Cal Brooks, was going to take them into Alaska's pristine wilderness for a weeklong adventure. When they returned, they'd exchange vows at a beautiful little cabin on Eklutna Lake.

Instead, the guide had been murdered.

Ariel had been pushed off a cliff.

And Violet had run for her life.

She didn't like remembering that day.

The helplessness she'd felt when she'd discovered Cal's body, blood pooling beneath his torso, still sent chills down her spine. She'd tried to render aid, calling for help and hoping someone in the wedding party would hear her. But there'd been no one else around in the vast expanse of Chugach State Park. After she and Lance had gotten engaged, she'd set the wedding date in April and had rented two cabins as far away from the bright lights of Anchorage as she could get. She'd thought it would be romantic…that they'd create unforgettable memories.

Her memories were unforgettable, but not for the reason she had hoped. Instead of following through with her plans to exchange vows with the guy of her dreams, she had found herself fleeing from the man of her nightmares.

She had made *so* many mistakes. Missed so many red flags. She hadn't had a chance to talk to Ariel about it. But she knew what her best friend would say: *Give yourself a break. You couldn't have known.*

Maybe not.

She liked to think she had not been blinded by love. That she had gone into the engagement the same way she went into business meetings—clear-headed and focused.

The truth was, she had been swept away by her deep need for connection and family. She had allowed herself to be blind to Lance's less-than-desirable personality traits because she had craved closeness and had been tired of being alone.

She had been desperate for family after her parents' deaths.

Lance had offered her a chance to, once again, be part of a loving home. He had known all the right things to say to make her mourning heart feel joy again.

And she had bought into it.

Even when he had balked at the idea of signing pre-nups. Even when he had asked her to change the way she dressed and the way she wore her hair. Even when every sign pointed to the fact that he wasn't ever going to love anyone as much as he loved himself, she had allowed herself to believe the lies he'd told her.

She had wanted family so much that she had been willing to compromise on things that she shouldn't have. Like the vacation home in Florida—a multimillion-dollar property that Lance had made a cash offer on.

Her cash, of course.

The plan had been to fly to Florida after their wedding, complete the purchase and then honeymoon in their dream vacation home.

Only it hadn't been her dream.

It had been his.

She had been the bankroll, paying his way.

Despite the bragging he had done about the small business he owned, he never seemed to have money. After the first few months of their relationship, when I-love-yous had been exchanged and the future was being planned, he had stopped paying for dinners and trips. She had paid for their dates, fueled their cars and told herself that it was all perfectly normal.

She had known it wasn't.

Deep in her heart, she had understood that something was very wrong with her relationship. She just hadn't been able to admit it.

When he had insisted they put the money for the Florida property in a joint account, she'd balked, but he'd hounded her about it, accusing her of selfishness and arrogance, until she'd complied.

He had been a master manipulator.

She only wished that she had realized that before they had gone to the bank together and opened a new account. She had transferred two million dollars of the money she had inherited from her parents.

Lance had been thrilled. He'd treated her to a lovely dinner. Praised her beauty. And told her they would spend the rest of their lives together, splitting time between Anchorage and Miami. Then, later that night, he had given her a diamond bracelet to wear on their wedding day. She should have been charmed, but she'd noticed that the money had come from the account they'd just opened. She'd been embarrassed for him and for her. She would rather he have given her a card with something lovely written inside than an expensive gift that she had paid for.

That night, she'd transferred the house money back into her account, leaving nothing but a few thousand dollars.

She hadn't told him.

If she hadn't been pregnant, she probably would have ended the relationship. But there'd been a baby to think about. An unexpected complication to a relationship that had already gone from romance-of-the-century to having her question whether her groom-to-be had ever truly loved her. She hadn't told Lance she was pregnant. She had been worried about his reaction.

That should have been another huge clue to the fact that he wasn't the right person for her.

She frowned, staring out into the bright sunlight, wishing she had made dozens of different choices.

She didn't regret having her daughter, but she regretted the decisions she'd made that led her here—a medical clinic on the edge of Anchorage, desperate, scared and on the run from Lance *and* the police.

"Are you okay, hon?" a receptionist asked.

"Fine," Violet said, shoving open the door and stepping outside without looking back.

She couldn't afford to make a spectacle of herself.

Even sleep-deprived and ever more anxious to return to civilization, she had to make decisions that would protect her baby and protect the survivalist family who had taken her in and helped her stay hidden for the past seven months.

The Seavers lived off the grid in Chugach State Park. Violet had learned a lot from them, but she didn't want to raise her daughter in an underground bunker in the wilderness. She wanted to bring Ava home to the beautiful house she had grown up in and offer her little girl the same security and sense of belonging she had felt growing up.

"We'll get back there, sweetie," she murmured, patting the baby's back as she hurried along the sidewalk. Brisk October air stung her cheeks and ruffled her hair. She pulled her hood up, more to cover her face than to keep her warm.

Violet wore a dark wig and heavy makeup, thick glasses and layers of clothes, but despite her meticulous disguise, she still worried that Lance would find her. If he did, she knew he wouldn't hesitate to kill her. She had no idea what he would do to their daughter, and that scared her more than anything.

She touched Ava's back, feeling for the subtle rise and fall. At just a few weeks preterm, her daughter had arrived during the first major storm of the season. Labor had been quick and brutal, over almost before Violet had processed the fact that it had begun.

Dana Seaver, the matriarch of the family, had helped her through the birth. It certainly hadn't been the kind of labor Violet had planned or imagined. She had thought she would be at the medical clinic where she had been going for prenatal care, with doctors, midwives and nurses available during labor.

Instead, Ava had been born in an underground bunker. All the necessary things had been sterilized, but that didn't change the fact that the walls were packed earth, lined with shelves that contained all the supplies the Seaver family would need for the winter.

There had been no natural light. Oil lamps had illuminated the birthing area Dana had created once she had realized there would be no time to get Violet to the hospital.

If things had gone wrong…

But, fortunately, they hadn't.

One of the things Violet had been trying to learn during her exile was that dwelling on the past did nothing to change the present or the future.

That would be easier to do once Lance was in prison.

And when the authorities finally apprehended him, she planned to turn herself in to the Anchorage police department, tell her side of the story so she could clear her name and then finally move on with her life.

*Please, God, let it be soon.*

Bright sunlight reflected off the pavement and flashed on the windshields of passing vehicles, hiding the drivers from view. That made her nervous. Anyone could be driving past.

If Lance did, would he recognize her? She knew that was a long shot because of her disguise, but still, she couldn't afford to let her guard down. Or take their safety for granted. As always, keeping Ava away from her father was foremost in Violet's mind.

She walked across another street, forcing herself not to rush. She had to act as if she had all the time in the world. A woman with no worries…with no one hunting her. A mother and child out enjoying a beautiful fall day.

There were storm clouds in the distance, hovering over the mountains and threatening to bring snow showers and heavy winds. The Seavers listened to the weather report religiously, always prepping for the next change in the forecast. Cold weather was coming, and they had spent the past few months preparing. Violet had helped as much as she could, understanding that her presence had strained the survivalists' resources. Ava's birth had added to the burden. The family needed more of everything to sustain the two lives they had added to their fold.

One day, when this was all over and she was home with her daughter, Violet would find a way to repay them for all they had done.

She passed several shops, glancing into the windows, pretending to look at parkas and coats, clothing and fishing gear. In reality, she was studying the people behind her.

She had learned to be careful without being obvious about it.

Seven months on the run did that to a person.

She turned onto the road that led out of town. The trailhead wasn't far away, and she felt confident in her ability to find it and then find her way back to the bunker. It had taken months to get to that point. Up until recently, she had always been accompanied by one of the Seavers—usually Harrison, the Seavers' teenage son. Sometimes Cole. Father and son were confident in the wilds of Alaska and comfortable in urbanized settings. Dana preferred to stay close to home, tending herb and produce gardens in greenhouses she'd built far off the beaten paths.

The family would have been happy to let Violet stay in their quiet sanctuary forever, but even though Violet had never been the social butterfly the press had painted her to be, she missed all the trappings of civilization. She liked going to the grocery store when she needed food or supplies. She enjoyed seeing other people when she was out shopping. She had no desire to spend hours making candles or heating water to wash clothes in deep tubs.

She wanted what she'd had before she had met Lance—a quiet life filled with the people she loved and admired.

At long last she reached the edge of a neighborhood that abutted the park. The sky had darkened, wispy white clouds gathering into steel-gray masses. Soon the storm would hit. She wanted to be back at the bunker by then. She *needed* to be. As terrifying as Lance was, the Alaskan bush during a blizzard was even more terrifying.

Suddenly, a car engine revved, the driver accelerated off a side road and appeared to be heading straight for Violet.

Lance!

It had to be!

Shocked, she jumped sideways, stumbling behind a hedge grove between two properties. The driver braked hard, barely missing a vehicle parked on the curb, then backed up and sped forward again.

She ran around the side of a house, flying across the yard and into the woods behind it. As she sprinted between sparse trees, the sound of a slamming car door filling her with dread. Her wig caught on a branch and was yanked from her head. She left it there, every cell in her body focused on escape. One hand cupping the delicate curve of Ava's skull, the other shoving aside leaves as she raced headlong into the park, she prayed that somehow, *someway* she could outrun the man who wanted her dead.

The first flakes of snow fell as Gabriel Runyon got out of his vehicle. They splattered on his cheeks and melted, icy rivulets running into the open collar of his coat. He pulled up his hood and grabbed his emergency pack. Dry clothes. Material for building a shelter. Fire starters. Food for Bear. Water. Energy bars. Enough to keep him and his K-9 partner going for a few days. *If* the weather didn't worsen.

He glanced at the darkening sky. The meteorologists were calling for a blizzard. If that happened, and he and Bear were stranded, they could survive, but could a woman who who had just given birth?

Could a newborn baby?

He, along with members of his Alaskan K-9 unit, had spent the last seven months trying to locate Violet James, Lance Wells and Jared Dennis. They were all wanted for questioning in the murder of a wilderness guide and the attempted murder of Ariel Potter—a woman who had been pushed off a cliff and left for dead. He and the K-9 team had followed tracks through the Alaskan wilderness, visited every medical clinic and hospital in Anchorage, and spent hours following up on leads. They had even reached out to church groups and charities, hoping that Violet would eventually make an appearance and that Lance would make a mistake.

There'd been sightings, calls from concerned citizens that came in a little too late, near misses that had given him hope that he was on the right track. But today had been different. He'd been following an anonymous tip that a woman named Violet James had a newborn baby and was at Helping Hands Christian Medical Clinic at the southwestern edge of Anchorage. Gabriel hadn't expected to find his quarry there, but he had followed up on the lead, arriving just in time to see a dark-haired woman step outside.

Violet had blond hair.

He had pored over photos of her. He knew she was small-framed, thin and delicate-looking. Not the sort of woman he would have expected to survive seven months alone. She'd been pampered as a child, raised by parents who had enough money to lavish her with every luxury.

He knew nothing about that lifestyle.

Gabriel had been orphaned at seven, tossed into the foster system and raised by a series of apathetic foster parents. He had no resentment about that, but he certainly had no clue what childhood stability and comfort looked like.

What he did know was that people raised with plenty often struggled when they didn't have enough. In the past several months, Violet James hadn't accessed her bank accounts or used her cell phone. She hadn't logged on to social media. So, aside from a letter she'd sent to her best friend last April, claiming her innocence in the murder of a wilderness tour guide and attempted murder of Ariel, Violet had stayed off the radar.

Had she suddenly reappeared?

Gabriel had kept his distance from the dark-haired

woman, inching through midmorning traffic, his unmarked SUV helping him blend with morning commuters traveling to jobs in the center of the city. He'd lost sight of her when she'd turned down a one-way street, and by the time he'd followed the grid-like pattern of traffic onto the side road, she was gone.

As near as he could tell, she had disappeared into the Chugach State Park.

Someone had followed her.

He had flagged tire tread marks leading into shrubbery across from the park entrance. A dark sedan was abandoned there, tires stuck deep in muddy earth. Gabriel had called it in.

Now, he was going hunting.

"Ready, Bear?" he asked as he opened the back hatch.

His K-9 partner lumbered to the ground—one giant step for the St. Bernard. Trained in avalanche rescue, Bear could find a needle in a haystack. He loved cold weather, snow and the hunt. For him, this was a game, the prize a few rousing games of tug.

"I'll take that as a yes," Gabriel murmured as he pulled a search vest over Bear's boxy head. The St. Bernard stood still as Gabriel snapped straps and slid a glow stick into a pocket on the back. Night fell quickly this time of year. They both needed to be prepared.

He attached a lead to Bear's collar, called in their location again and walked into the park. A dusting of snow covered the ground. No footprints visible. Or obvious track marks.

He allowed Bear to sniff the area.

"Ready, Bear? Go find!" he called.

The K-9 took off, trotting through sparsely forested land and out onto a trail. Chugach State Park covered 495,000 acres of pristine wilderness. Even after decades of exploration, Gabriel respected the vastness and the biodiversity. Lakes. Rivers. Streams. Mountains. Forests and plains.

There was a little of everything in Chugach, and a lot of danger for the foolhardy. It would be easy for someone who didn't know the area to get lost. From what he had learned about Violet, while she had been off the grid for seven months, living in the Alaskan wilds alone didn't seem feasible for someone with her background.

Bear veered to the right, crossing a stream and bounding up a hill. Snow swirled through the shadowy forest, coating the ground in glistening white. Gabriel didn't think they were far behind their quarry. Bear's tail was high, his head up. He knew the game, and he loved it. He could go for hours if necessary.

Bear stopped as he crested the hill, snuffled the ground and raised his head to the air. His nose twitched, and then he growled.

Seconds later, a shot rang out. A bullet whizzed past, slamming into the ground a yard or so from Gabriel's feet. A warning shot meant to drive him back.

He dived behind a tree, shouting for Bear to drop. The dog obeyed immediately, dropping down in an emergency stay that would hold him in place until Gabriel gave the release command.

"Alaska State Police! Drop your weapon! Now!" he called, even though he knew the perpetrator would refuse the command. Out of visual field and completely hidden, his quarry had the advantage.

For now.

Backup would be arriving shortly, but Gabriel didn't want to waste time. He crawled along the forest floor, keeping ground cover between himself and the gunman as he attempted to take a higher position. Uphill, through dense undergrowth and then along a ridge, he headed in the direction the gunshot had come from. His trek became more challenging as the wind picked up, branches bowing and swaying as snow continued to fall, but he stayed the course.

He finally reached the top of the hill and waited, listening for the sound of approach or retreat. It took just moments. Branches broke and pebbles skittered along the rock face on the far side of the hill. The perp was on the run, probably heading back to the park entrance, using the trail that wound along the top of the hill.

Gabriel followed, whistling for Bear to heel.

They moved together, pressing through the trees and stepping onto the trail. He spotted footprints in the snow. Larger ones heading west toward the trailhead and smaller ones heading east, deeper into the park. His fellow K-9 officers were heading for the park entrance. They could apprehend the shooter. He wanted to follow the smaller prints. After all these months, it was time to finally meet Violet James face-to-face and get her side of the story of how a wilderness guide had ended up dead and her best friend at the bottom of a cliff.

He turned east, following the footprints across the crest of the hill and down the nose. The trail meandered along a clear stream that gurgled over smooth rocks. The footprints veered in that direction, leading to the bank of the river, deep prints in the muddy shoreline. Then nothing.

Whoever it was didn't want to be followed and was making it as difficult as possible.

That was fine.

Gabriel liked a challenge, and he had no intention of giving up before he found his prey.

"Bear! Find!" he commanded.

Bear loped into the water, splashing to the opposite shore, his head to the wind as he darted away from the safety of the trail and deep into the Alaskan wilderness.

# TWO

The temperature was falling, snow pouring from the sky. Daylight had turned dusky with storm clouds. Even dressed for the weather, which she was, a person could only survive so long outside in conditions like these.

Swirling snow was creating whiteout conditions, and she didn't dare travel through the park without a good visual of the surroundings.

Violet shoved through thick foliage, Ava's warm body pressed against her chest and tucked carefully beneath her parka. She had heard a gunshot a while ago. Since then, there'd been nothing but the rushing sound of the river, the babble of brooks and the soft sigh of wind through the trees. She picked her way up steep drainage, careful not to slip on the snow-coated rocks as she laser focused on what she needed to do.

Get to shelter.

Build a fire.

Wait the storm out.

Return to the bunker.

Go back into hiding until Ava's next well-baby checkup.

Repeat it all again.

Ava wiggled against her chest, letting out a quiet mewl and reminding Violet that she hadn't nursed since they had left the bunker that morning.

"It's okay, sweetie," she murmured, patting Ava's back as she crested the hill. She stood at the top, looking for some clue as to where she was and where she needed to go to reach safety. Everything looked the same. Trees. Deadfall. Ground cover. All blanketed with white. The forest had gone eerily quiet. No crunch of deer hooves on leaves or rustle of vixens readying their dens for spring litters.

She was alone, and she felt it. All the animals had gone to ground as they waited for the storm to pass, and she was standing on a hill, being blasted by arctic wind, a helpless newborn in her arms.

Her heart thumped heavily against her ribs, her pulse racing as adrenaline poured through her. It had been a while since she'd been this afraid and this certain that she would be lost forever in the wilderness.

"Calm down," she snapped. "Panicking will get you nowhere. Look around. You know this area. You've hiked it dozens of times looking for berries and mushrooms. You've fished in the river right below this hill."

She blew out a breath. Unless she missed her guess, Lance had given up chasing her as soon as she had left the trail. Her former fiancé had never been an outdoorsy type and had conceded going on a guided wilderness adventure only because she had wanted it so badly. At the time, she had thought he was trying to please her because he loved her. He had convinced her that he would always put her needs first, sacrificing his own desires to make her happy. In truth, the only needs he had cared about were his own. He'd wanted her money. Plain and simple. He would have done anything to get it.

Knowing she had to keep moving or freeze, Violet continued on, stumbling over deadfall, one hand pressed to Ava's back, the other pushing branches out of the way. She struggled forward, shivering, legs nearly numb. She needed to get inside and warm up, but snow fell like a shroud, blinding her. Pausing, she listened for the river. Just the way Harrison had taught her.

*Follow the sound of the river. Then walk along it. There are dozens of little cabins tucked along the shoreline. You never have to spend the night in the forest without shelter as long as you can make it to the river.*

The storm drowned out sound, the whipping wind and whistling through the treetops mixing with the groan of old spruce trees bowing beneath the onslaught.

"God, please. Protect me and my daughter," she prayed, snow pelting her face and flying into her eyes. She thought she heard the gurgle of water over stones and headed in that direction, hoping with every fiber of her being that there was a cabin at the base of the hill.

Every hill looked alike in the wilderness.

Every tree was one of millions.

People got lost. They disappeared. Often, they were never found again.

She shuddered, forcing her mind away from the gruesome thought as she scanned the area, probing the white cloud of snow that surrounded her. Something dark rose up in front of her. There and gone as the wind shifted and the snowfall increased.

She moved toward it, nearly falling in her haste.

Ava was whimpering.

Soon she would be squalling, the sound certain to draw any hungry predators. Somewhere in the distance, a dog barked, the sound making the hair on the back of her neck stand up. There were wolves in the park, but she'd only heard them howling at night. This time of day, a barking dog almost always meant there were people nearby. On a day like today, the only people she could imagine wandering through the wilderness were police officers and first responders.

She shivered. She'd been hiding for a long time, terrified of turning herself in to the police. What would they do if they found her? Would they question and release her? Would they take her to prison for eluding them for so long and take her daughter away?

The thought terrified her.

The wind shifted again, and the cabin was in front of her. Dark stone walls. Trees pressed in close. She hurried to the front door, used the lock pick Harrison had given her to unlock it and stepped inside. The windows shuddered beneath the onslaught of the storm, the wind pushing against the door as she closed it. The Seavers, and survivalists like them, left canned goods and supplies in abandoned buildings all over the park. A failsafe that ensured survival if they were ever surprised by a storm and unable to get back home.

That would serve Violet well.

But dare she light a fire? She hesitated, rubbing Ava's back as she considered her options. There were blankets in a small chest. Dry clothes. But even with those things, the interior of the cabin was below freezing, wind seeping in through cracks in the log walls and through the thin panes of the windows.

If someone was wandering around with the dog she'd heard, she didn't want a smoke plume from the chimney to draw him to her hiding place.

On the other hand, she didn't want her baby girl to freeze.

She glanced out the window. The snow was falling faster, sheets of it limiting visibility. If anyone was out in the storm, they wouldn't last long.

Shuddering, she hurried to the fireplace and snatched up a log from a stack of wood nearby. There were matches and Vaseline-soaked cotton balls in tins on a shelf above the mantel. She grabbed both, knelt beside the hearth and prepped the fire.

The door burst inward.

Shrieking, she pivoted around, her hand cupping Ava's head, her heart hammering against her ribs. She expected to see Lance striding toward her.

Instead, a large animal barreled inside.

A *bear*?

She shrieked again, scrambling to her feet and grabbing a long piece of wood from the pile, ready to swing at the beast's head.

It stopped a few feet away, dropping onto its belly, like a…

Dog?

"He won't hurt you," a man said. "So how about you drop the wood?"

She jerked her gaze away from the giant dog.

A man stood in the doorway, his broad shoulders blocking the grayish light. He wore a dark blue coat and heavy cargo-style pants. A hat. Gloves. And winter boots made for hiking back trails.

"How about you tell me who you are and why you're in my cabin first?" she responded, her voice shaking.

She was terrified, but she didn't want him to know it.

There was a back door. If she could get to it, she could escape.

Out into the storm and the cold.

But better to be out in a blizzard alive than to be dead in a cabin. She didn't think or plan. Instead, she'd acted, swinging the wood back and tossing it at him with as much strength as she could muster.

Violet didn't wait to see where it landed.

She ran through a small doorway in the back wall, into a room that had once been sleeping quarters. Abandoned cots and shelves filled with bottles and jars of canned goods surrounded her. Too bad she didn't have time to grab blankets from the old chest.

She had barely reached the back door, her hands fumbling to lift the bar that held it closed, when her parka was snagged and she was pulled back.

She whirled, ready to fight.

Determined to free herself and her baby.

She had fought too hard to stay safe during her pregnancy to let herself be taken down now.

Violet swung a fist at Gabriel's face, but she was a foot shorter, her reach limited.

He stepped back, avoiding the first punch and grabbing her arm when she lunged at him again.

"How about we not play this game?" he suggested, Bear growling softly beside him.

"It's not a game," she snapped. "Back away and leave me alone."

"So you can go out into the storm with a newborn in your arms? I can't let you do that, Violet."

"How do you know my name?" she asked, her free hand cupping the head of the tiniest baby Gabe had ever seen.

"I'm Gabriel Runyon, a state trooper with the Alaskan K-9 unit. We've been looking for you for seven months." He fished out his badge.

She studied it for a moment, a small frown line marring the smooth skin of her forehead. "How did you find me?"

"We got a tip that you were at the clinic with a newborn. Bear and I followed you from there."

"So did my former fiancé," she muttered, her hand still on the baby's head. "You should have put your time into tracking him down instead."

"We have troopers waiting at the park entrance where I found his abandoned car. If Lance returns there, he'll be captured. Making sure you and your baby were safe was my first priority. There's a blizzard blowing in, and you have a newborn."

"I'm very aware of that fact," she said, sidling past him and moving away from the door. Cold air was blowing in through cracks in the log walls, and the door shuddered beneath the onslaught of howling wind. "But we'd have been fine. I know how to take care of myself and my daughter."

"I'm sure you do, but Bear and I plan on helping in any way we can."

"Bear?" She led the way into the main room, grabbing a log from a small stack near the fireplace and placing one in the hearth. The baby was mewling, the sound catching Bear's attention.

"My partner." He gestured in the St. Bernard's direction. Bear had his head cocked, his brown eyes focused on Violet. He was obviously curious about the noises the baby was making.

"He's…big," she said, picking up a few cotton balls that had fallen on the floor. She tossed them into the fireplace, shoved some dry kindling under the log she'd thrown into the hearth, then used flint to spark a flame.

It burned bright for a moment. Then died.

She sighed, dropping to her knees, the baby's mewls turning to a full-out cry as Violet struck the flint again.

"How about I take care of the fire and you take care of the baby?" Gabe suggested.

"I can do both," she insisted, but she didn't protest when he took the flint from her hand.

He sparked another flame, blowing gently so that it caught dry kindling. It didn't take long to get a decent fire going. That was the good news.

The bad news was that the plume of smoke rising from the chimney could attract unwanted attention.

He'd need to be vigilant until backup arrived.

By the sound of the wind and the fury of the storm, the team might not be able to make it out until dawn.

For now, they were safe.

Bear huffed quietly and settled down in front of the fire, his fur still glistening with melted snow. He rested his head on his paws, his gaze on Violet. He'd had good manners trained into him, but Gabe knew he wanted to go take a look at the crying creature Violet was holding.

"I don't think your dog likes me," Violet said uneasily. She stood a few feet away, still in her outdoor gear. Heavy parka. Small pack. The baby bundled up and held in a sling near her chest.

"He's curious about the baby. I don't think he's ever been around an infant," he responded, hoping to put her at ease. He had some questions he wanted to ask. Some things that he wanted to clarify. When Lance Wells had called 911 to report a shooting, he had told the responding officers that Violet had gone crazy with rage when she'd learned that the wilderness guide she'd been having an affair with had been secretly seeing her best friend and maid of honor, Ariel Potter. She'd shot the guide, pushed Ariel over a cliff and then attempted to kill Lance and his best man, Jared Dennis.

According to his story, they had barely managed to escape with their lives. It hadn't taken long to realize the story had been fabricated. Lance had become a suspect in the murder of the wilderness guide, but he and his best man had gone into hiding before they could be taken in for questioning. Since then, Gabe and his fellow troopers had been hunting for the suspects and for Violet. She was the key to understanding what had happened and why.

"I hope he doesn't think she's a tasty little treat," Violet said with a nervous laugh.

"Bear prefers his kibble. He would never take a bite out of a human," he replied, watching as Violet dropped her pack, shrugged out of her coat and took the baby from the sling carrier. "That is one tiny little baby," he commented.

"Ava was born a few weeks early, but the doctor says she's healthy." She settled into a rickety chair that sat against a wall. Despite having recently given birth, she was almost too thin, her face gaunt beneath what looked like a thick layer of makeup. She was a beautiful woman. Nothing could hide or diminish that, but the last seven months had changed her. She wasn't the carefree socialite he'd seen in the photos and newspaper stories. She was somber and scared, her eyes large in her thin face.

"I'm glad to hear that. The wilderness isn't the best place for a newborn baby."

"I know," she agreed. "But I was afraid to return. Lance is dangerous, and I didn't know what he'd do if he got his hands on our baby."

"I understand that, but the two of you will be safer with police protection than out on your own."

She frowned but didn't respond.

After she'd gone missing, Gabe had expected her to succumb to the elements.

She'd survived.

And continued to elude the police.

He admired her gumption, but he wasn't going to

risk her escaping again. She needed to answer questions, and he needed to make certain she stayed safe.

"Sounds like she might be hungry," he commented as the baby whimpered.

He didn't know much about infants. Everything he *did* know, he'd learned from hearing coworkers and friends talk about their children. Babies needed to eat, they needed diaper changes and they needed to sleep.

That was the sum of his knowledge.

"She is," Violet responded, pushing to her feet wearily, the baby clutched close to her chest. "I'll go in the back room and feed her."

"No need. I'll go. You stay near the fire."

He grabbed her backpack and parka as he left the room.

He wasn't giving her an opportunity to run off.

"I'm not planning on leaving," she grumbled as he stepped into the larger room. "And the pack has Ava's diapers in it."

He didn't respond. People said a lot of things. Told a lot of lies and a lot of half-truths. Maybe she hadn't planned on leaving. Or maybe she had. But in any event, he wasn't taking chances. Gabe and the K-9 team had been working to close the murder investigation for several months. Violet was the key to doing that. And now that he had her, he didn't plan to let her go.

Plus, whether she wanted to admit it or not, she needed his protection.

As soon as the weather cleared, backup would arrive to transport them out of the park and to the Anchorage police department. He had already contacted the team, sending coordinates so that they could head in as soon as it was safe to do so.

He walked into the back room, checking the window and the door. Neither was secure enough to make him comfortable. If Lance decided to track through the blizzard, if he made it to the cabin, he would try to break in. But, fortunately, that would not be so easy to do without Bear alerting them first.

That was one of the blessings of working with dogs. They had exceptional senses and could hear and smell what humans couldn't.

Gabe pulled out his cell phone. No reception. Not with the storm raging. He knew the team, though. They'd be in as soon as it was possible. He paced the small room, listening to the wind and the groan of old wood. Bear was still in the main room, lying on the floor where he had been told to stay. Probably getting hot with the fire going.

"Bear, free!" he called.

Seconds later, the K-9 padded into the room, his tongue lolling, his tail up, his body relaxed. He sniffed Violet's pack, then sat in front of Gabe.

"Thirsty, buddy?" Gabe guessed, sliding out of his pack and pulling out water and a collapsible bowl. He gave Bear water, then pulled off his coat, hanging it from a peg near the door.

"She's done eating," Violet said quietly, suddenly appearing in the doorway between rooms. "You can come back in here. It's warmer."

"Bear enjoys the cold," he responded.

"Your dog has a thick coat. You don't." She turned

before he could respond, the baby's head visible just above her shoulder. Fuzzy white infant curls against the bright blue fabric of Violet's flannel shirt. That wasn't what she had been wearing the last time she was seen by her friend Ariel. Violet's bridesmaid had photos of the day. She'd captured the soon-to-be groom and his best man before they'd left for wedding. Both had looked happy. Violet, dressed in jeans and a cable-knit sweater, had been smiling, but there'd been something in her eyes—a bit of fear or trepidation that had caught Gabe's attention.

She had been pretending to be happy, but she hadn't been.

Regrets?

Misgivings?

Hours later, she'd fled the scene of what should have been her wedding. Gabe and the canine team had found her trail and followed it until the dogs lost the scent.

"Is this where you've been holing up for the past few months?" he asked as he walked back into the main room.

She hesitated, then shook her head. "No."

"A cabin like it?"

"I'd rather not say," she murmured, settling back into the chair.

"Why not?"

"Because… I don't want to betray the trust of people I've come to care about."

"Someone helped you hide?"

She didn't respond.

"I'll take that as an affirmative."

"They didn't do anything wrong, because *I* didn't do anything wrong," she replied. "It isn't like they were harboring a fugitive. They were helping a very scared woman whom they happened to find wandering around in the woods." She shrugged, patting the baby's back as she settled into the chair again.

Violet looked tired, her skin pale through layers of heavy makeup. She'd been hiding for months. Pregnant. Scared. Probably traumatized by what she'd seen and what she'd been through.

She had been betrayed by someone she'd loved. Someone she had planned to marry. That couldn't be an easy thing to deal with.

He'd told himself that he wouldn't have sympathy for her.

She could have turned herself in to the police, gone into protective custody and stayed safe. Instead, she'd stayed a step ahead of the team, always eluding capture and making it difficult for them to do their jobs and finish their investigation.

So, yeah, the hard-nosed cop in him felt that she'd gotten what she'd deserved, and he didn't want his opinion of Violet to soften. But the protector in him? Well, he couldn't help feeling for her. She was young and tired, her sweet, innocent baby sleeping peacefully in her arms. For months, she'd lived in terror, doing everything she could to keep her baby from harm. She had stayed away from everyone and everything she knew to keep her child from harm.

He could respect that.

He could understand it.

In her position, he'd probably have done the same.

"We could have helped you," he said sternly. "If you'd turned yourself in to the authorities, we'd have kept you safe."

"How? By locking me in a jail cell? I heard news reports, and I know you thought of me as the prime suspect in the crime."

"For a short period of time, we did. But it didn't take us long to sort things out."

"You thought I was culpable," she pointed out. "I heard the reports. The police were calling me a person of interest."

"We still are," he said. "We have questions that need answering. Ariel didn't see who pushed her off the cliff, and she has no idea who killed the wilderness guide you hired."

"How is Ariel?" she interrupted, leaning forward, her eyes deeply shadowed. "I've been worried sick about her."

"She's made a full recovery, but she's spent seven months worrying about you."

"I know," she said quietly, her gaze shifting away. She had to have thought it all through, weighed all her options, all the people she would worry, all the responsibilities she was abandoning. Somehow, in her mind, staying hidden had been the only viable option.

He couldn't understand the decision, but he couldn't help respecting it.

"But you still stayed away. Why? What happened that made you think that was your only option?" he asked, curious to hear her version of what had happened all those months ago.

"I saw Jared Dennis push her off a cliff. I'd run to get her after…"

"What?"

She swallowed hard, the memory obviously upsetting. "I found Cal. He was bleeding. I felt for a pulse but couldn't find one. I ran for Ariel's help, and I saw Jared shove her off the cliff. She was taking pictures of eagles. Minding her own business. She tried to save herself, but she toppled over. I screamed, and Jared came after me. He was yelling for Lance to grab the gun and take care of me. I didn't even know they'd brought a gun on the trip. I had to run, but all I could think about was my friend tumbling over the cliff and Cal lying on the ground." Her voice broke.

"You did what you had to," he assured her, knowing she had to be carrying a terrible burden of guilt.

"There might have been something else I could have done. I don't know. It all happened so fast, and it was all so confusing. If I had just been thinking about myself, I might have gone back toward our vehicles, but that seemed like the obvious choice, and I was worried Lance would catch me before I could escape. I had learned I was pregnant two weeks before, and I knew I wasn't just running to save my life. There was another life to worry about."

"You can't beat yourself up over what happened. You did what you had to. You know that, right?"

"Sometimes," she responded. "Other times, I think

that if I had made better choices, Cal would still be alive and Ariel wouldn't have been injured."

"Better choices?"

"I...wasn't always certain of how much Lance loved me. I wanted to believe the things he said, but his actions didn't always bear up to the emotions he claimed to feel."

"Meaning?"

"I think he wanted my money more than he wanted me." She said it dispassionately, but he could see the pain in her eyes.

"What does that have to do with Cal's murder and Ariel being pushed off the cliff?" he asked, curious to know what she thought her former fiancé's motive had been.

She shrugged. "I don't know, but I'm sure Lance had something to do with both things. Jared is a follower. He does what he's told."

That had been Gabe's impression as well. During questioning, Jared had given what sounded like scripted responses that perfectly matched the information Lance provided. No veering from the topic. No adding extra details. That had been Gabe's first indication that both men were being deceptive.

"What happened after you ran?" he asked, switching gears before she got upset enough to shut down.

"I tossed my phone over the side of a hill. Lance had a tracking app, and I was afraid he'd be able to find me. I was trying to get on the trail so I could return to the vehicles and get help, but I got turned around and ended up wandering deeper into the park."

"You spent that night in the woods?" He and the team had scoured the area, but Chugach State Park was vast. The dogs had found and lost her scent numerous times before sunset. They'd suspended the search until dawn and began again the next day.

"Yes. I tried to find my way out the next morning, but I was so turned around, I had no idea which way to walk. That's when I ran into…" She shook her head. "I was found by some survivalists. They took me in."

That made sense.

He and the team had been certain she would succumb to the elements. She'd had no survivalist training and hadn't been prepared to stay outside for any length of time.

"And helped you for the past seven months."

"Yes." The answer was terse, her gaze dropping. She was uncomfortable with the direction of the conversation. Either she was lying, or she was worried about getting the people who'd helped her in trouble.

"We aren't going to charge them with anything, Violet," he said. "But we'll probably want to talk to them. A name and location would be helpful."

"I'm not providing either."

No apology. Or explanation. She was still looking away, her gaze focused on the fire, her hand resting on the baby's back. Snow had melted in her hair and dripped down her temple, leaving white tracks through her heavy makeup. She was exhausted, scared and still willing to stand up for what she believed in, still intent on protecting people who had protected her.

He respected and admired that. He'd thought she would be spoiled, haughty and demanding.

She wasn't any of those things.

Realizing that made him want to be gentle rather than tough. Good cop rather than bad cop. He was known for his tough-as-nails approach to the job, but he couldn't be tough with someone who had been through so much and fought so hard to protect others.

"Why not?" he asked.

"Because they helped me when I needed it most, and they don't want to be found. If I bring civilization to them, how is that repayment for all they've done?"

"I understand your feelings, but we need to ask what they saw the day of the murder, what they heard, if they have anything to add to our investigation."

"Like I said, I'm not giving you that information." She pressed her lips together, her muscles tense.

"That's fine. For now. We'll discuss it again once we get out of here," he responded gruffly, his heart softer toward her than he wanted it to be. He wouldn't take no for an answer. He *couldn't*. They'd been chasing down leads for months, trying to find Violet so that they could get her version of events. They had wanted to question her about Lance, their relationship, his habits. He and his buddy Jared had taken off as soon as they'd realized the focus of the investigation had shifted to them.

They'd been on the run ever since.

Why they hadn't left the area was a mystery that needed to be solved. Most criminals fled and went into hiding far from the scene of their crimes.

Lance and Jared had stayed local, eluding police by

using the park and the vast wilderness that surrounded Anchorage. They weren't survivalists. They were scavengers and predators, breaking into winterized cabins, using them for shelter until unwary owners showed up.

Bear lifted his head, his gaze focused on the window. He growled, his attention never wavering as he charged toward the glass and barked.

"What's wrong?" Violet asked, pulling the baby close as she stood and moved to the back of the room. Away from the window and whatever or whoever was outside.

"Could be an animal," he responded, but Bear wasn't the kind of dog to bark at wildlife.

"You don't really think that, do you?" She looked scared, her muscles tense, her gaze riveted to the door as if she expected someone to kick it open.

"I'll check it out," Gabe told her. He wasn't going to lie about the potential danger, but he didn't want to scare her more than she already was. And he certainly didn't want her running into the blizzard with her newborn. She'd survived the first time she'd fled in terror. She might not be as fortunate the second time around.

He closed ratty fabric curtains over the windows, blocking some of the grayish light that had filtered through the glass. Then grabbed his coat and pack, quickly sliding into both.

"Stay away from the windows, and don't open the door until I tell you to."

"I—I won't. Be careful. Too many people have already been hurt because of me. I don't want you to be another tragedy."

"Don't worry. I know how to take care of myself,"

he assured her, smiling to try to reassure her that everything was going to be okay.

Then he pulled the door open and stepped into the storm. Bear barreled out beside him, nose up to the wind, fur ruffled by it. The dog's thick coat would keep him warm for a while.

"What do you think, Bear? Anyone out here?" He surveyed the small clearing in front of the cabin. His K-9 partner was a few feet away, staying close until he was told to search. Until Gabriel knew what they were hunting, he wouldn't send the St. Bernard out. Bear was a large target, strong and powerful but not trained to attack. He would defend himself if necessary, but he wasn't going to take down an armed criminal the way other dogs on the team might.

Bear veered right, heading toward the edge of the woods. Gabriel pushed a branch aside as he walked into the forest, his ears straining for any unusual sounds. It was impossible to hear more than the howling of the wind and the groaning of trees bending beneath its fury. Gabe had GPS coordinates for the cabin and wasn't concerned about finding it again. His top priority was tracking down Lance. Seven months into the murder investigation, and he and the team were ready to get the perps into custody. As long as Lance and Jared were on the streets, no one in Alaska was safe.

He edged deeper into the woods, watching as Bear sniffed the ground, then dropped down to his haunches. He'd found something. A boot print pressed into snow and dirt, leading away from the cabin.

Had a transient walked through? Maybe thinking

about using the cabin during the storm and then realizing it was occupied? It was possible.

It was also possible that Lance had found them and had run when he'd heard the dog bark.

"Let's go," he said, still not willing to give Bear the command to find. Lance was dangerous. If he was out there, he wouldn't hesitate to kill anyone or anything that tried to prevent his escape.

Bear growled and swung his head to the left, his body suddenly stiff, his muscles taut.

Gabriel stepped behind a tree.

A bullet slammed into the rugged pine, splinters of bark and wood hitting his face. He dived to the ground, blood oozing from a gash in his temple as he pulled his weapon and fired.

# THREE

Violet could hear nothing over the wild roar of the wind. The old cabin shook beneath the onslaught, the windows rattling with the fury of the storm.

She needed to feed the fire.

She needed to change Ava.

She needed to plan what she would do if Gabriel Runyon didn't return.

Violet had almost begged him not to go out into the storm. She had too many horrible memories of the day she'd fled into the wilderness. Back then, she'd felt helpless and alone, the faith that she'd turned her back on after her parents died suddenly the only thing that stood between her and abject hopelessness.

*God is present always.*

*Waiting for us to turn to Him.*

Her parents had instilled that in her—the idea that God cared and that He would intervene in the lives of His people. But as she had entered her teenage years, she'd fallen away from their teachings. She'd begun to question their faith, and she'd wondered if God really was concerned about the matters of men.

Didn't He have more important things to do? More vital matters to worry about? Her life had been easy and good. She'd had parents who had loved her. Everything she'd needed and most of the things she'd wanted. She'd had no reason to need God's help.

Violet had stopped attending church in her early twenties.

She regretted that now. Regretted that her parents had died worried about her faith and eternal security. Regretted that they hadn't lived long enough to know that she finally understood how deeply she needed God in her life.

"You can't live in regrets, Violet," she muttered. "You've got to live in the moment. Do what has to be done right now. Prepare for what will need to be done later."

Those were things she had learned from the Seavers.

They hadn't survived years in the Alaskan wilderness by sitting idly. Rather, they spent their days pursuing the things that would help them survive and thrive. During the spring and summer, they planted, hunted and foraged. In the fall, they harvested and preserved fruits, vegetables and meats. And in the winter, they hunkered down, tending to daily chores while the weather raged.

Violet didn't want to spend her life in their underground bunker, but she had become stronger, more confident and more capable because of her time there.

She sure wasn't the same idealistic young bride-to-be who had ventured into the wilderness seven months ago—a rich, spoiled socialite playing at understanding the great outdoors. She had become someone who could light a fire, build a shelter, raise a baby without help. She was independent, strong, and filled with a desire to raise her daughter to be the same.

She didn't need or want anyone in her life.

All she wanted was to be able to return home. She wanted to give Ava a warm house with windows that let in the light, a backyard with views of the mountains and the security that came from a roof overhead and neighbors nearby. She understood that the Seavers didn't need or want those things, but Violet craved them. More with each passing day.

"Focus," she grumbled, grabbing a few logs from the stack and tepeeing them over the flames.

"Always tend your fire first, Ava," she said. "Shelter and warmth are your first priority when you're out in the wilderness."

Ava stirred, her soft hair brushing against Violet's jaw as she burrowed closer. She was too tiny to understand the lessons Violet wanted to teach, but eventually she would be old enough to learn.

"Right, precious girl?" she murmured against the baby's hair, her heart thudding painfully as the windows and doors rattled. She was trying to focus on the job at hand, but her mind was skipping from thought to thought.

Was Lance outside?

What would he do if he found her?

Kill her for sure, but what about the baby? *His* baby?

Would he murder his own flesh and blood?

Or would he take Ava to some far-off place and raise her?

Either thought was horrifying.

"But we're not going to think about that. We're going to concentrate on keeping the fire going and staying one step ahead of trouble."

She grabbed her coat and shrugged into it, then opened the back door, scooping snow into an old pot that had been left on a shelf near the fireplace.

If they got snowed in, they'd need water. Plenty of it.

Violet tried not to think about Gabriel and his dog out in the storm, possibly being stalked by a predator. She certainly didn't want to imagine Lance outside the cabin, watching as she set the pot on the fire, so she focused on the task at hand, then quickly changed Ava.

Suddenly, something bumped the back door.

She jumped, spinning to face it.

As if, somehow, watching danger's arrival could make it less horrible.

"Please, God, don't let it be Lance. You've protected us for this long. Please keep us safe awhile longer," she prayed aloud, her lips pressed to Ava's downy curls.

The door shook as something slammed into it again.

She stepped back, using her free arm to blindly search for a weapon. There was an ancient rifle standing in the corner behind the rocking chair. Not loaded. No ammunition. Months ago, she and Harrison Seaver had stopped in the cabin on the way back from the clinic. The place had been abandoned long ago, the old rifle left to gather dust and rust. It probably wasn't functional, but it might scare someone away.

She placed Ava back in the carrier, relieved when

she snuggled in easily. Then she checked the rifle's cartridge chamber. Empty. Just as she had expected.

She could use the heavy wooden weapon as a club or as a scare tactic. No one who hadn't been in the cabin would know it wasn't loaded.

There hadn't been another thud or bang. The wind was still howling, cold seeping through her layers, her body shaking.

She was cold.

She was scared.

She was alone.

Just as she had been when she had run into the wilderness to escape Lance and Jared.

She hadn't known the area. Hadn't known how to survive the late-spring temperatures, which fell to below freezing at night. But she'd had no choice. Jared and Lance had been chasing her, Lance screaming that she was going to be sorry if she didn't stop running. She hadn't stopped.

She had run until she was out of breath, her heart skipping beats, her legs trembling. Then she had found a hole left by the roots of a fallen tree. She had crawled in and stayed there.

After the sun had set, and she was certain she had escaped, she had climbed hills attempting to see the lights of Anchorage. All she had discerned was darkness. By the time the Seavers had found her, she was dehydrated, hungry and wanted by the police.

She was a different person now…and she needed to remember that.

Something slammed into the front door again, and

she ran in that direction, rifle in hand, pointed at the shuddering wood.

"I have a gun!" she announced, waiting for the old wood to be kicked in and for Lance to appear.

A dog barked, the sound carrying over the wild howl of the wind.

"Bear?" She yanked open the door, slamming it shut after the giant dog barreled in.

Snow-covered, tongue lolling.

Alone.

"Where's Gabriel?" she asked, as if the dog could respond.

He whirled back to the door, scratching the wood frantically.

"Is he hurt?"

*Worse?*

She opened the door again, hoping the ruggedly handsome trooper would be there. But she couldn't see anything. Visibility was almost zero, the snow swirling in a thick cloud of white.

Bear grabbed the hem of her shirt, tugging her outside.

"No," she yelped, pulling back.

Undeterred, the dog moved behind her, nudged her toward the door, whining loudly. Melting snow dripped from his coat and muzzle, his dark eyes focused on Violet, asking her for something.

"All right. I get it. You need me to help you find Gabriel," she said as she pulled rope from her emergency pack and tied it to her waist, her heart pounding crazily in her chest. Something horrible must have happened for Bear to have returned without Gabriel. She didn't want to imagine what that could be. She only knew she had to try to find and help him.

She'd go as far as the length of the rope. No farther. It would be too difficult to find her way back in this storm if she weren't tethered to the cabin. And she couldn't subject her baby to these harsh elements for long. She walked outside and tied the other end of the rope to a tree near the front door, fighting the wind, struggling to see Bear through the whiteout conditions.

*Please, God,* she prayed silently as snow pelted her face and the wind stole her breath, *help me find him.*

Bear stayed close as she struggled forward, seemingly unfazed by the blustering storm.

"Okay. Slow and steady," she muttered, giving the rope a hard tug to make certain it wouldn't untie. She had the rifle under her arm, Ava close to her chest, her hood pulled up over her hair. She was already cold. Already wondering if she was making the right decision. She had to protect her daughter.

But she couldn't leave Gabriel out in the storm.

Bear barked, his big body so close, her free hand brushed against his shoulder. She hooked her fingers through a strap on his vest, determined to stay tethered to him as they walked farther from safety and deeper into the storm.

Snow swirled in thick waves of white, limiting visibility to just a few feet. No lights in sight. No sign of the cabin. Any footprints he and Bear had left were covered by fresh snowfall. It couldn't be much farther to the cabin. Gabe counted paces out. He knew how much distance he had traveled—he had marked the cabin location on his GPS and had been following that back—but satellite reception was iffy in this kind of weather.

Still, he knew they had to be close.

The fact that Bear had charged ahead seemed to confirm it, but five feet was too much when a person was hypothermic.

Which he was.

His feet and hands were numb, his body shaking with cold. He had been outside too long. Even dressed right, a person could only last so long outside in weather like this. Soon his body would stop trying to produce heat. Blood would be shuttled to his vital organs. Everything else would shut down. His brain functions would slow, and he'd start making poor decisions.

He knew all the facts. He had studied them in emergency preparation classes, wilderness first aid and search management courses.

He needed to get to shelter before he became a statistic.

Gabe glanced at the GPS unit. A moving light tracked Bear's movements. He was two hundred meters straight ahead. Moving slowly in Bear's direction, trying desperately to close the distance between them. He wanted to rush, but he needed to be careful. Deadfall was slippery on good days. During inclement weather, the old logs and branches were hidden hazards that could easily cause broken bones.

He couldn't afford to be injured.

"You can't afford to be hypothermic, either," he muttered, wishing the storm wasn't preventing the K-9 unit's arrival. Gabe had sent coordinates as soon as he had located Violet. He trusted the men and women he worked with and knew they would be there as quickly as they could, but traveling in whiteout conditions wasn't possible.

That meant he would have to deal with Lance on his own.

And if Lance had his buddy Jared with him, and the men were still out in the storm, Gabriel would have to face down both.

He'd been certain he'd heard an ATV motor just after he'd fired a warning shot into the storm. Based on Bear's more relaxed behavior, he'd felt confident the shooter had backed off.

For now.

He touched his forehead. The blood had stopped oozing from the wound. He stumbled through ankle-deep snow, his focus on the yellow blip on his GPS screen. He was closing in on it. Once he reached Bear, he knew he could get back to the cabin. The St. Bernard had an uncanny ability to find his way through snow. He could find a missing person in some of the most challenging terrain. There was no way he wasn't going to be able to get them back to Violet.

Gabriel stopped, listening for the unmistakable sound of Bear's excited barks. He heard nothing. Usually his K-9 partner would be running toward him, eager to be reunited. Gabe had no doubt that Bear could smell him. The wind was moving toward the dog, sending a scent cone that even a rookie search dog would be able to follow.

So why wasn't he running? Or barking?

Gabe waited impatiently while the wind howled and snow flew in his face. When the blip was nearly on top of him, he could finally see the outline of Bear. Someone was with him. Dark against the white landscape, holding him by the collar. Not tall like Lance or Jared.

*Violet?*

Had she left the safety of the cabin?

That hadn't occurred to him, but it probably should have. She'd been on her own for months, learning to survive in the wilderness, sometimes sneaking in and out of Anchorage without being seen.

The ornery woman certainly wouldn't hesitate to run if she thought it was necessary, but he doubted that she was trying to escape in the storm. She'd come looking for him.

Bear barked. Just once.

"Good boy," Gabriel called. "Stay."

The dog stopped, and Violet followed suit.

Then they both stood and waited as Gabriel approached, Bear shifting excitedly, Violet looking tense and unsure.

"Gabriel?" she called as he drew closer.

"If it wasn't, Bear would be letting you know," he responded, sliding his arm around her slender waist and turning her toward the cabin. He could feel smooth rope beneath his finger. She'd taken precautions.

That was good. What would be better was getting them both back inside the cabin. "Are you okay? I was worried when Bear came back without you," she shouted above the howling wind.

"I'll be better once we're both inside," he admitted. "Bear, lead!" he commanded.

The St. Bernard took off, loping in front of them, a dark shadow against the snow.

Gabe kept him in sight, fighting the urge to rush. Violet had the baby strapped to her chest, tucked away under a coat. They were both vulnerable, both in need of protection. Until the team was able to get through the storm, he and Bear were all they had.

It would be a long night. Even longer if Lance decided to reappear. Gabriel hoped that wouldn't happen, but if it did, he was prepared to do whatever it took to keep Violet and her baby safe.

# FOUR

Violet wanted to run back to the cabin, but she was afraid of falling and injuring Ava. She moved cautiously, using the rope as a guide. Thankfully, she could see Bear, walking in front, leading the way. But he was a dog, and she was worried he'd take off after a moose or decide to chase a scent in the wind.

The last thing she needed was more time outside in the storm. She was already shivering. So was Gabriel. She could feel him shaking violently as they made their way through the storm.

"We're almost there," she said, hoping she was right.

It felt like they'd been walking forever, pushing against the wind and hiking through the snow.

"There it is," Gabriel said.

"Where?" Violet couldn't see anything but white. Snow. Trees. Wind. All of it a misty blanket that shrouded the world. Beside her, Gabe was a solid and comforting presence, his arm around her waist, his fingers pressing against her ribs.

She didn't want to need anyone.

Not after what she had been through.

But she pressed closer to Gabe's side, relieved that she wasn't in this alone. That she had someone standing beside her, fighting the battle with her. They would survive together.

Or die together.

She refused the thought.

She was a fighter.

She would fight through this, and she would come out the other side better and stronger and more capable.

"Straight ahead. I caught a glimpse when the wind shifted." Gabe's hand tightened on her waist, and his fingers pressed against her ribs. He oozed confidence and self-assurance, towering over her in a way that was protective rather than intimidating.

"Are you sure?" she asked, shivering from the cold, terrified for her daughter.

"Absolutely," he responded. "It's just a little farther."

"I hope you're right," she replied, her words swallowed by the storm. She had no choice but to trust him, to move with him as he took one step after another. She had just met him, but she was putting her life and the life of her child in his hands.

That was a strange and uncomfortable feeling, but she would rather be in this with someone than alone.

A few more steps, and she could see the dark wall of the cabin.

Bear was waiting by the door. If he was cold, he didn't show it.

Gabriel dragged the door open, holding it against the wind as Violet stepped inside. The fire was still going, the snow melted and boiling. She hurried to it, using a fireplace poker to move the pot from the flames.

"That's quite a storm," Gabriel said, closing the door and dropping the heavy latch into place.

"Hopefully it'll keep Lance away," she responded, taking off her coat and hanging it over the back of a chair. Ava still seemed content, sleeping soundly in her sling. Hair dry. Skin warm. She had weathered the journey well.

Meanwhile, Violet felt frozen to the bone.

She crouched near the flames, taking off her gloves and holding her hands out to the warmth. "I boiled water. How about some tea?" she suggested as Gabriel joined her.

"I've got soup. How about that instead?" he suggested, shrugging out of his pack and pulling out several packets of freeze-dried food. "Chicken noodle or tomato?"

"Chicken noodle," she replied.

She wouldn't say no to calories. She'd lost too much weight after Ava's birth, and she couldn't afford to go into the winter any thinner than she already was. The Seavers ate sparely during the coldest months, and she was nursing a baby. She had to stay healthy enough to continue nourishing her daughter.

But eating had lost its appeal after Ava's birth.

She'd felt melancholy and tired, unmotivated and ambivalent. The thought of spending winter in the underground bunker filled her with dread. She wanted to go home. She wanted Ava to have her own bed rather than sharing with Violet.

A crib would be nice. As would a rocking chair and changing table… "You okay?" Gabriel asked.

He was holding out a steaming bowl of rehydrated soup.

She took it, her hands still nearly frozen, her fingers curving around the warm porcelain. "I'm fine."

"You don't look fine." He opened a packet of soup, dumped it into the other bowl and ladled water out of the pot with a mug he'd taken from his pack.

"That's just what every woman wants to hear."

"I'm not here to make you feel good. I'm here to make sure you stay safe," he muttered, sipping the soup and watching her over the rim of the bowl.

"I was plenty safe until this morning. I'm not sure how Lance found me, but I'm not going to give him another opportunity. Once I get back to the bunker…"

She realized she was saying too much, staring into his eyes and forgetting that he was a police officer. For all she knew, he might come down hard on the family that had harbored her when she'd been wanted by the police.

"The bunker?" he asked, setting his soup on the hearth and taking a collapsible bowl from his pack. He used his water bladder to fill it, setting it down in front of Bear, who lapped greedily.

"I told you. I was helped by a family. That's where they live. In the bunker."

"In a national park?" He raised a dark eyebrow.

"And this is why I refused to give you information about them," she responded, taking a careful sip of the soup.

"Hey, I have no authority in the park, and I'm not questioning you so that I can go in and disturb a family that isn't bothering anyone," he replied. "I'm just curious."

"Why?"

"Because that's what I do. I get curious, I ask questions, I get answers. It's part of the job." He shrugged. "So, you've been living in a bunker. That explains why drones and airplanes couldn't spot you."

"It isn't like I had a choice," she replied.

Violet hadn't meant to cause trouble. She certainly hadn't wanted the police to send out drones and planes to find her. All along she'd been doing what she thought was right. And had been prepared to go to any lengths to protect her baby. She still was, but she thought she might be able to trust Gabe to help her, to get her to civilization and help her navigate the legal ramifications of the choices she had made. "I understand you felt that way," he said gently, his eyes the deep blue of the sky at dusk.

How many evenings had she spent sitting outside the bunker, staring up at sky? Watching as the moon rose and the stars appeared? How many times had she wished she wasn't so alone? Even with the Seavers nearby, she had felt isolated. She had longed to have someone to sit beside late at night when she couldn't sleep, when worries and fears kept her awake.

She'd turned to her faith for comfort, reaching out to God in those horrible dark days after Cal's murder, but she had still wanted human companionship and friendship. The Seavers had been wonderful, but they saw the world in a vastly different way.

"I didn't just *feel* that way. I ran from Lance thinking I could go to the police and get the protection I needed. By the next day, it was all over the news that I was the primary suspect in two assaults and a homicide. I couldn't just turn myself in and hope for the best. Not when I had a baby to think about." Violet got to her feet, carrying the soup across the room and settling into the chair. She was still cold, but she didn't want to sit close to Gabriel. She didn't want him looking into her eyes and seeing the shame and guilt there.

If she wasn't terrified for her life, and that of her unborn child, she would have had the Seavers bring her to the police station, and she would have turned herself it.

"I understand," he said, still watching her.

She expected more questions.

Thought he'd be filled with recriminations.

After all, she'd spent seven months eluding police. But instead, he remained silent. She tried to wait out the quiet the way she had done so many times when she lived with the Seavers. Dana was warm and caring, but she was a woman of few words, and Violet had learned to wait and give her a chance to speak.

But Gabriel didn't seem compelled to fill the silence.

In many ways, he was an enigma, and a part of her wanted to find out what made him tick. He hadn't hunted her down and interrogated her harshly. She would have understood if he had. She'd been hiding from the police, eluding capture, for months, and he had to have been frustrated by that.

But he had been gentle, kind and compassionate. He hadn't pushed hard for the things he obviously wanted. He'd asked questions and let her answer, giving her space to think things through.

She studied his profile as he sat in front of the fire, sipping hot soup, a bloody scratch on his temple. He was handsome. There was no denying that. Masculine and strong, with a soft side that he might not allow everyone to see.

"You're hurt," she said, nervous energy forcing the words out. She shouldn't be noticing the way he looked, or the warmth that filled her when he met her eyes.

"My head?" He touched the scratch. "It's fine."

"What happened?"

He hesitated. "Someone took a shot at me. He missed, but I got hit by shrapnel."

"Lance shot at you?" She wasn't shocked. She was appalled. The thought that someone she'd loved could do something so horrible filled her with guilt and remorse.

"Probably, it was Lance, but I don't know that for sure," he told her.

"Who else would shoot at a police officer?"

"Plenty of people, actually. I've made some enemies during my time on the force," he said with a tired smile.

"I'm sorry," she replied softly. "I wish that weren't the case."

"If wishes were horses, beggars would ride," he replied, unzipping his coat and finally removing it.

He had been outside longer than Violet, and he was still shivering from it. He had done so much to help her, and she'd let him sit there shivering and cold while she warmed up near the fire.

"There are blankets in the trunk," she said, pointing to the old cot and the trunk that sat beside it. "I can get one for you. You've been out in the cold awhile, and you need to warm up."

"I'll get them. With the way the wind is blowing through this place, it's going to be difficult to stay warm. Even with a fire." He walked to the trunk and pulled out several wool blankets. He draped one around his shoulders and put another around hers, tugging the ends so that they covered Ava. "Hopefully, the baby won't be too cold tonight."

"She should be fine," she managed, secretly touched by the overture. "The Seavers…"

She pressed her lips together, frustrated that she'd said the name. She had no intention of giving any information about them to the police. They'd helped her more than anyone else could have, and she owed them her life.

"*Seavers?*" he asked, settling down near the fire again.

Bear had made himself comfortable, spreading out near the front door, his quiet snores indicating that all was right in his world.

"Forget I said that," she replied, finishing her soup and setting the bowl on the floor beside the chair. She was too tired to stand. Caring for an infant was hard work. Caring for one out in the wilderness was even harder. There were no electric lights. No quick way to warm up water. No tub. No real shower. The Seavers relied on candles for light and propane for heat. Washing clothes required muscle power and time.

Her hands were raw from scrubbing diapers and onesies.

Dana seemed to love the lifestyle. But Violet? Well, she wasn't quite as enamored.

Not that she was unappreciative. On the contrary, she was truly grateful for all the Seavers had done for her and Ava. But deep down she longed for normalcy. She craved the hustle and bustle of civilization, the hum of a heater and the purr of motors. The sounds of voices carrying through the evening air.

"I wish I could forget what you said, but unfortunately, I can't," he replied. "There's a guy that I work with who has been searching for Cole Seaver. Any relation to the people you've been staying with?"

Violet hesitated.

She knew what this was about and couldn't in good conscience pretend otherwise. Harrison had recently filled her in about his encounter with Trooper Poppy Walsh, who had told him that she was searching for the Seavers because of a dying woman's last wish to be reunited with her son and his family.

"Yes," she finally admitted.

"It's important that we speak to him. His mother is terminal."

"He knows."

Gabriel frowned. "He does?"

"Harrison ran into a state trooper who shared the information."

"Harrison?"

"Cole's teenage son," she explained. "We've been trying to talk Cole into returning to town to visit his mother, but it's a hard sell."

"Why?"

"I don't really know. He won't say what happened, but whatever it was, he's still angry about it."

"Anger isn't a good reason to deny a mother's dying wish," Gabriel said harshly.

"I agree. If my parents were still around, I wouldn't let anything stand in the way of my being with them. I told Cole that, but he said I didn't understand the dynamics." She had never seen Cole angry like that before. In fact, in all the months she'd lived with the Seavers, he had never raised his voice. He was kind, faith-filled, reasonable and loving, but when it came to his relationship with his mother, he refused to budge.

"I hope he changes his mind," Gabe said, pulling out his phone and frowning. "Looks like my colleagues are trying to get out to us. I'm going to see if I can get through to them on the phone."

He stood, dropping the blanket onto her legs as he walked past and taking a moment to make certain it was wrapped around her thighs. She shivered involuntarily. It was still warm from his body, the heavy wool giving an extra layer of protection from the cold seeping through log walls.

"Thank you," she whispered, but he had already stepped into the back room.

To Gabriel's surprise, the call went through, Hunter McCord picking up on the first ring.

"Gabriel?" he asked, his voice tinged with worry. "Do you have shelter? The weather is horrible, and it isn't going to let up until the early-morning hours."

"Yes. In an old cabin. We've got a fire going and enough wood to keep us warm until the storm breaks. Any idea when the team will be able to deploy?" The sooner the better. He felt safe enough for now, but as soon as the storm let up, Lance would be on the move again. If he didn't already know where the cabin was, the smoke coming out of the chimney would give away their location.

"Should be around dawn," Hunter replied. "We're hoping to be out before first light. We've already gathered the team, and we'll deploy as soon as we can get all-terrain vehicles out. Any sign of Lance or Jared?"

"Someone shot at me. I'm fairly certain it was one of them, but I think they've left the area. No way are they waiting outside in this mess." He paced to the window, pulled back the tattered curtains and watched the snow swirl. There was no sign of anyone or anything. The fact was, Lance would be a fool to be out on a night like this one. He might be a criminal, but he was a smart one.

"I don't like that he knows where you are. If he's found a place close by to wait out the storm, he could be on you before we arrive."

"I'm prepared," Gabriel assured him.

"I have no doubt about that, but it's not just you I'm worried about. What about Violet James? Is she cooperating?"

"Cooperating?"

"Not trying to run again? Not causing any kind of

trouble? With Lance and his buddy out there, you have enough to worry about without having to chase her down in a storm."

"She's...quiet." Gabe glanced at the doorway to the main room. He doubted Violet could hear above the storm, but he lowered his voice. "And cautious. I don't think she trusts that I have her best interest at heart."

"I can't say I blame her. She's been hiding for months. Terrified for months. She probably has no idea who she can count on."

"She also has a baby to protect."

"So, the reports that she was at the clinic with a newborn were accurate." It wasn't a question, but Gabe responded.

"Yes. I don't know much about kids, but this one is tiny. Violet is definitely concerned about protecting her. If nothing else motivates her, that should keep her from attempting an escape."

"There's that, then. How does she seem? I'm sure Ariel will ask."

"The baby? Fine. Violet? Tired. Too thin. Stressed," he responded. "It might not be a bad idea to get Ariel involved. She could assure Violet that we only have her best interest at heart."

"If you're suggesting a phone conversation, I'm all for it."

"I was thinking more along the lines of a meeting when we get back to Anchorage." A phone conversation would be fine, but he thought that the best thing for Violet would be to see her friend face-to-face. Familiarity and comfort could go a long way in helping her open up about what she'd seen and experienced.

"That's not happening until we've apprehended Lance and Jared," Hunter growled. "I don't want to give that guy any reason to think he should go after Ariel again. She's safe as long as she stays away from Violet."

Gabe could have argued that the team could keep Ariel safe, but he understood Hunter's concerns for the woman he loved. She had nearly been killed. He didn't want to risk putting her in harm's way. No matter how small the chance that she'd be hurt. "Understood. The good news is that Violet's version of events substantiates our belief that she is innocent of the crimes she was being accused of. When I questioned her about what happened in Chugach State Park that day, she told me she found the guide dead, ran to get help and saw Ariel pushed off the cliff. She thought for sure she was dead, so she took off, hoping to get help. And it was only later on that she learned her best friend had survived."

"Yeah, that matches with the evidence and with what little Ariel can remember about that day." Hunter always sounded soft when he spoke of Ariel Potter. She'd survived a lot, and she'd proven to be tough and resilient. It hadn't surprised anyone on the team when the two had fallen in love.

"From what I've been able to gather, Violet stayed hidden because she was afraid of Lance. She was afraid going to the police would make her an easier target," Gabe continued.

"She has good reason to be. Did she give you any idea as to why he wouldn't just flee the area?"

"The conversations haven't gotten that far," he said. "She's guarded, and I don't want to push. She seems... fragile."

"She's been surviving in the wilderness alone, Gabe. *Fragile* isn't a word I'd use to describe her."

"She hasn't been alone. She was taken in by a survivalist family. Get this," he said, glancing at the doorway again. "She's been staying with Cole Seaver and his wife and son."

"Cole Seaver, the guy Eli has been searching for?"

"Yes."

"Strange coincidence."

"I don't put much stock in coincidence. I'd call it an act of divine intervention. Violet has been trying to convince Cole to see his mother before she dies."

"I'll pass that information along to Eli," Hunter promised. "He'll be happy to hear that someone is trying to help."

The team's tech guru, Eli Partridge, was close to his dying godmother—Cole Seaver's mother—and he was determined to make her last wish come true.

"I appreciate it."

"And I'll appreciate it if you stay in one piece until the team can get to you in the morning," Hunter deadpanned.

"I'll keep that in mind," he said. "Text when you're heading my way."

"Will do." Hunter ended the call, and Gabriel shoved the phone in his pocket. Hopefully he could check in with the team during the night, but the storm wasn't abating, so the chances were low.

He was on his own until morning.

Well, not quite alone.

He had Bear. The dog might be a lover rather than a fighter, but he was a great early-warning system. If anyone approached, he would let Gabriel know.

In the meantime, he was going to make good use of the time he had with Violet. There was more to her story, and he had every intention of hearing it. He needed all the details, every bit of information that she could offer.

Once he got her to safety, he planned to go after Lance, and Violet might be the key to understanding how her former fiancé thought and how he might act.

Information was the key to successfully stopping a cold-blooded killer, and Gabriel wasn't opposed to twisting arms to get what he needed.

But something about Violet made him hesitate to use a more aggressive approach.

He might be a hard-nosed, hard-hitting cop, but he had a soft spot for the underdogs.

In this situation, Violet was that.

She had everything against her. No background in survival, no experience in the wilderness, absolutely no skills that would have helped her survive.

Somehow, she had done it.

He respected that and her.

He might need answers, but he was going to be gentle in his approach to getting them. She deserved that and more, after everything she'd been through.

# FIVE

No crib.

No bed.

One musty cot sitting against a log wall.

Despite the fire, the cabin was cold. Not a good place to settle a newborn down for the night. But that was fine. Violet had experienced plenty of sleepless nights during her wilderness exile. When she'd first been taken in by the Seavers, she'd lain awake staring into the darkness, terrified that Lance would find her. After Ava's birth, she'd worried that something would happen to the baby. She'd wondered if the dirt walls of the bunker were safe for little lungs, and she'd been afraid that Ava would fall asleep and not wake.

Staying awake all night was easy. But spending the night in a cabin with a stranger was far more complicated. Because she didn't trust people...not anymore. Gabriel might wear a badge and carry a gun, he might be kind and protective, but she didn't plan to put any faith in him.

Sighing, she watched as he walked to the trunk and emptied it. There were several old quilts and a few threadbare flannel shirts. No mice or other critters. She was thankful for that. She had gotten used to sharing space with shelter-seeking animals, but she still didn't like it.

"This might work for the baby," he said, carrying the crate across the room and setting it closer to the fire.

"I don't mind holding her." She loved being a mother. After all the horrible things that had happened since she'd met Lance, having a baby in her arms felt a little like redemption, renewal and hope.

"You need rest. You're a new mother, and you've been through a lot these past few months." He dragged the cot next to the trunk, folded two flannel shirts and used them to pad the trunk. "If you don't want to lay her in here, I can hold her while you sleep."

She lifted a brow. "Do you have any experience with babies?"

"No, but I raised a puppy who got into a lot more trouble than your baby seems capable of. And he survived." He smiled, obviously trying to lighten the mood. Maybe trying to create camaraderie and work on gaining her trust. She didn't mind that. She trusted him to help her and Ava, to work to get them out of the situation safely.

She wasn't going to trust him with more than that.

Even if her heart skipped a beat and her cheeks warmed when she looked into his eyes. Even if she could see his integrity and kindness in everything he did and hear it in every word he said.

"There's a big difference between a large and sturdy

puppy and a newborn," she pointed out. "But I appreciate the offer."

"That's a very polite way of saying you don't think I can be trusted with your child." He laughed, brushing dust from the cot and spreading a blanket over it. "How about you both lie down here, then?"

"I'm fine. Really."

"Suit yourself." He settled on the edge of the cot, back to the fire, hair deep black and glistening with the remnants of melting snow. "Tell me about Lance," he said, staring into her eyes as if he could see every secret she'd kept from Ariel—all the doubts she'd had near the end of the engagement, all the worries.

"What do you want to know?" she asked. Ava stirred, and she rubbed her back, enjoying the rhythmic movement of her daughter's breathing. Up until she'd found out she was pregnant, she had never thought about what it would be like to be a mother. She hadn't been all that interested in finding Mr. Right and settling down with him. Sure, she'd dated, but she had kept the relationships short and light.

She'd been in her midtwenties when her parents died. And hadn't been in any rush to find love.

There were too many gold diggers in the world, and she had no intention of being used by someone who only wanted her money. She'd gone to college, gotten a degree in business administration and had worked for her father's oil company. Nothing high-tech or glamorous. She'd been his assistant, and while it hadn't been fulfilling work, she'd enjoyed spending time with her dad. Eventually she had planned to open a nonprofit that helped underprivileged youth find jobs and attend college.

When her parents died, those plans had gone out the window.

She'd suddenly become CEO of her father's business and owner of three properties in Anchorage. Keeping up with everything had taken all her time and attention.

And then Lance had come along.

Visiting a friend of a friend.

Smiling at her at a dinner party hosted by one of her sorority sisters. He'd given her his number and told her to call. She'd been charmed enough to do it.

Worst mistake of her life...

"How likely is it that he'll stay out in weather like this?" Gabriel asked.

"Not very. He doesn't like to suffer. He likes to be comfortable, and he enjoys pursuits that don't take a lot of energy."

"Like?"

"Spending other people's money," she replied, despising the tinge of bitterness in her tone. Aside from the steel-cold edge of terror at the thought of him finding her, she no longer felt anything but apathy for Lance. But what she *did* feel was regret and shame for her actions and for the fact that she had been duped.

Gabriel watched impassively, his hair damp, the cut on his temple a dark slash on tan skin. He wore a police uniform, the shirt open at the collar, a black under layer visible.

Handsome.

Confident.

Quiet.

Watchful.

Violet shifted beneath his steady gaze, wishing he would say something. Because she had nothing to add. No insight into why Lance had committed murder or why he seemed so determined to find her.

"If you want to know what motivates him," she finally said, "he likes nice things. Cars. Houses. He isn't as interested in people. Unless they can do something for him. I wish I had realized that before I got involved with him."

"I hope you aren't blaming yourself for what happened."

"I take responsibility for my part in it."

"What part? Being fooled by someone you loved? That's not your fault. It's his. You own no part of the guilt for that. It all belongs to Lance," Gabe said quietly, leaning forward so that his elbows were resting on his knees, his big, strong body just feet from hers.

She leaned toward him, somehow desperate for his strength and confidence, his kindness and warmth.

"That's nice of you to say, but it doesn't change how I feel," she murmured.

"Feelings are fickle, Violet. Facts are what matter, and the fact is, Lance is a criminal who uses people to get what he wants. He has made a habit of finding people who can payroll his hobbies. His sister has a lot to say about his skills as a manipulator and liar."

"That doesn't mean I should have fallen for him." She glanced down at Ava. She had gotten a beautiful little girl out of the relationship, but she still regretted it.

"Let's focus on the here and now, okay? The past is what it is. You can't change it, but you can make sure Lance doesn't hurt anyone again." He touched her hand, and warmth spread up her arm. Not the quick excitement she'd felt when she was around Lance. This was deeper, stronger and much more real. It was the kind of thing that lasted. She knew that as surely as she knew that the heartbreak she'd felt when she'd realized the truth about Lance was nothing compared to the heartbreak losing someone like Gabe would bring.

"You don't have to convince me to help you, Trooper Runyon," she said, trying to bring the conversation to a less personal level. She needed to steady herself before she did something she regretted. Like grabbing his hand and holding on to him like he was a lifeline in the raging storm of her life.

"Gabe," he corrected, glancing at Bear, who was sleeping beside the door. Jowls splayed on either side of his boxy head, snoring loudly enough that she could hear it above the sounds of the storm.

She couldn't help smiling.

"He seems to enjoy his downtime," she commented, wanting to turn the conversation away from her mistakes. He was correct. The past couldn't be changed. She needed to focus on the present. On getting through the storm and getting back to the bunker.

She frowned.

"You're not going to let me go back, are you?" she asked.

Gabe met her eyes. "No."

The answer was simple and direct.

No hedging. No pretending. No promises he didn't plan to keep.

"At least you're honest," she murmured, leaning her head back against the chair and closing her eyes.

"How about you be the same?" he suggested.

Her eyes flew open. "I have been."

"Do you want to go back to living in a bunker? Is that really where you plan to raise your daughter?"

"No, but until Lance is apprehended, it's the safest place for her."

"It *was* the safest place before you had the state police beside you," he responded. "I'm not going to let anything happen to you or your baby, Violet. I give you my word that Bear and I will do whatever it takes to keep you both safe."

It sounded good.

It sounded like everything she had been hoping for during her long months away from home—the police on her side, promising to make certain Lance didn't harm her or Ava.

But things that sounded good weren't always the case. She wouldn't trust blindly. Not again. There was too much at stake. Ava was depending on her to be smart and safe, and she would do anything for her daughter.

Even go back to hiding in the underground bunker. With or without Trooper Gabriel Runyon's permission.

The storm abated a few hours before dawn, the onslaught of snow and wind ceasing. Gabriel opened the back door and let Bear out, watching him bound through foot-high drifts, his huge body nimble and swift as he made a circuit around the area behind the cabin. Nose up, tail high, body relaxed, he made quick work of searching for trouble.

He found nothing.

That was a relief, but Gabe wasn't counting on things staying quiet. If the suspicions of the K-9 team were correct, and if what little information Violet had shared was true, Lance had committed murder, colluded with Jared Dennis to kill Ariel and then spent the past seven months hunting Violet.

To silence her?

Seemed like a lot of effort to go through.

Especially because the K-9 team had made it clear that they wanted to question Lance and Jared in connection to not only Cal Brooks's homicide but also in regard to the double murder of that older couple in Anchorage who'd been slain during a home invasion/burglary.

If the men had been smart, they'd have left the area.

A successful business owner, Lance owned and operated an import-export business. He had plenty of connections who could have easily flown him out of Alaska.

But instead he'd stayed, going into hiding soon after the police had questioned him, claiming that he and Jared Dennis were afraid for their lives and hiding in a safe house until Violet was apprehended.

At first, the K-9 team had believed the story.

They'd been called to the scene of Cal Brooks's murder soon after the park police had discovered the crime scene. The wedding party had been slated to return from a wilderness tour. When they hadn't, park police had been called to search for them. They'd discovered the body of the tour guide but had lacked the resources for a canine search.

Alaska K-9 had been happy to help.

At the time it had seemed like a cut-and-dried case. Lance and his best man had called 911 from the safety of a cabin close to the park entrance. Jared had been shot in the arm—wounded, he claimed, by Violet. Gabe and his colleagues Hunter McCord and Maya Rodriguez had brought their dogs to the scene and undertaken a lengthy search of the area. They'd been certain they were hunting a killer, and they'd been anxious to get her in custody.

As weeks and months passed, they'd realized they might be looking for the terrified victim of a crime. They'd wondered if she'd survived, worried that she might not have. The dogs had worked Chugach State Park, searching for any sign that Violet was still alive. They'd found her cell phone and a diamond bracelet that Ariel said had been a wedding gift from Lance.

To Gabriel, it had looked like a gaudy piece of costume jewelry. Huge stones set in bright yellow gold. He'd been surprised to learn that it was worth tens of thousands of dollars. If he'd had that kind of money to spend on a woman, he would have purchased something a little more personal and a lot less ostentatious.

After Lance's refusal to turn himself in to the police for further questioning, the K-9 unit had subpoenaed his bank records. They'd discovered that his business was in the red and his condo was mortgaged to the hilt. He enjoyed the finer things in life, but he didn't seem to have the means to pay for it.

Marrying Violet would have changed all that.

As a matter of fact, the two had a joint bank account that they'd opened the day before they'd gone on the wilderness adventure. Close to two million dollars transferred into the account from Violet's trust funds. She had transferred most of it back out a few hours later.

Why?

Had she had misgivings?

Was she planning on backing out of the marriage?

Had that caused Lance to go on a murderous rampage that had ended in Cal Brooks's death? Those were questions Gabe needed to ask, but he hadn't had the heart to subject Violet to an aggressive interrogation. Not while they were hunkered down in a cold cabin, huddled near a fire trying to keep warm, and not while she seemed so exhausted.

She'd fallen asleep sitting in the chair, Ava held close to her heart. He'd let her sleep, allowed all the questions he needed to ask to simmer on the back burner. There would be time to ask them once he got her to safety.

"Is everything okay?" she asked.

He turned to face her, surprised at the way his heart jumped when he met her eyes. Ava was still in her arms, held snug against her shoulder, little hands fisted near a tiny perfect face.

He'd never been a baby kind of person. He preferred puppies. They were hardier and more predictable, in his opinion. But there was just something about this precious baby girl that made him melt. "Yes. Just had to let Bear out. He prefers the snow to the indoors."

"I guess if I had a fur coat like his, I'd do the same." She smiled tiredly. Looking more relaxed than she'd been the previous night, but obviously still on edge.

He didn't blame her.

Violet had been through a lot, and she'd survived it by staying hidden. Now she'd been discovered. Not just by the police, but also by a deranged man who seemed intent on harming her.

"Hopefully we'll get cell reception shortly. Now that the storm has cleared, the team should be able to deploy. We'll have you back in Anchorage by midday."

"I'm not sure that's the best thing for me and Ava," she said, patting the baby's back.

"No?"

"We've been safe because we've stayed hidden," Violet pointed out. "And if Ava and I go back to the Seavers', you can concentrate on apprehending Lance."

"You know I can't let you do that, right?" he asked, calling for Bear and closing the door after the dog walked inside.

"I don't remember asking permission." Her tone was haughty, but she looked scared.

"Violet, Lance followed you into the park. Which means he knows you're hiding somewhere out here. Do you really think he's going to stop searching now that he is certain you're still in the area?"

She didn't respond.

"I'll take that as a negative."

"You don't understand," she murmured.

"Then explain it to me. What's making you think you need to run from people who are trying to help?"

She was quiet for a moment, her hand smoothing down her daughter's tiny back. "Ava is my responsibility. I have to do what is best for her. If that means I spend another seven months in a bunker in the wilderness, that's what it means."

"We can put you in a safe house, Violet. The two of you will be well protected. There's no need to hide in a bunker, and the risk of Lance finding you has increased exponentially now that he knows you've been hiding in the park."

"The park is huge. There's no way he could track me through it," she responded, but he knew she was thinking about what he said.

Her expression was guarded, her body tense. He didn't want to push too hard, but he needed her to understand that he wasn't going to let her return to the bunker. It was too dangerous. His phone buzzed, and he looked at the screen. Hunter had sent a quick text. The team was on the way. "What's going on?" Violet asked nervously.

"The team is readying to deploy. They'll be here within the hour."

"I need to go." She hurried into the main room, grabbed her coat from the back of the chair and hurried into it.

"You know I can't let you leave, right?" he asked.

She froze, her hand on the strap of her pack. "I'm not under arrest, am I?"

"No, but you're wanted for questioning in regard to the murder of Cal Brooks."

"You already questioned me. I told you what I know."

"We need an official statement," he responded.

It was the truth.

More importantly, though, he needed to get her out of the wilderness and away from the imminent threat of Lance's return.

Gabe was armed. He would do whatever was necessary to protect Violet and her baby, but he would feel better surrounded by his colleagues. Men and women that he respected, trusted and counted on. "If I give my statement now, will you let me leave?" she asked.

He shot her a disbelieving look. "There is a foot of snow out there," he replied. "And you have a newborn."

"We'll manage." But she did peek out the window."

"You know that's not the best decision for your child. Bringing her out into the cold. Risking getting lost. Leaving obvious tracks for anyone to follow."

"Maybe you're right," she murmured, settling into the chair, seemingly exhausted. Her shoulders bowed, her face gaunt. Despite her natural beauty, she didn't look like any first-time mother he'd seen. No healthy glow. No excitement or enthusiasm.

She had lived in fear for months.

That had to have taken a toll.

He wanted to get her to safety, remove the threat that had been stalking her and then watch her bloom. Pink cheeks. Excitement. Joy. Those were the things he wanted for Violet.

"I'm not going to let anything happen to you or your baby," he promised.

"We're not your responsibility," she reminded him,

but there was a catch in her voice that betrayed her fear. She was trying to be strong, but she was tired. He could see that, and he was going to do what he could to ease her burden and allow her the rest she so desperately needed.

His phone buzzed again. The team was on the move, heading into the park and following GPS coordinates to the cabin.

It wouldn't be long before backup arrived.

Gabe just had to keep Violet and her baby safe until then. That was his mission and his goal, and he wouldn't be satisfied that his job was done and done well until he knew the threats against them had been removed.

# SIX

Violet was torn between excitement at the thought of returning to civilization and dread at the thought of what that would mean. She'd be back in her comfortable home with an oven, a refrigerator, a heater and fireplaces. Plenty of blankets and clothes. She could buy Ava a bassinet, a crib and all the little accoutrements that babies needed. But she'd also be easier to find. She hadn't been to town much, but on the few occasions when she'd risked it to get prenatal care, she'd bought newspapers and pored over articles that related to her disappearance.

The tragedy of her parents' deaths combined with the intrigue surrounding her disappearance had made her front-page news for a while. No doubt, when she reappeared, reporters would be vying for her story.

She could handle that. But what she truly worried about was Lance finding her.

He had chased her into the wilderness the day he'd murdered Cal Brooks, shouting that if he didn't catch her, the police would, and she would pay for the crimes she'd committed. Violet had no idea what he'd meant. She'd only known she had to escape him.

Now, after months of replaying the horrible events, she'd realized that Lance had planned everything. That he'd gone along with her wilderness adventure in order to get her alone, far away from help. The stories he had told the police—about her supposed affair with Cal, her violent rampage, her dash into the wilderness—had all been fabricated to make her look guilty. He hadn't intended for her to survive. He had probably planned to kill her and dump her body far from the scene of the crime, leaving it for scavengers.

All for what?

The two million dollars he had talked her into placing in a joint account?

She watched as Gabe walked to the window and looked outside. He seemed even taller than he had the previous day. Sunlight streaming through the window reflected off his badge and glimmered in his black hair. He had broad shoulders and lean muscles, and he seemed confident in his ability to stave off danger.

She hoped he was as capable as he was confident.

She thought he was. He had found her in a snowstorm, protected her and Ava through a long, cold night. He had made sure they were safe, even when that meant risking his life. That was something she could respect and believe in and trust.

"You okay?" Gabe asked.

He had turned to face her, his eyes vivid blue. Handsome, fit and at ease with himself, he was the sort of guy most women would take a second look at.

Violet was no exception, but she had fallen for another handsome face. She had no intention of ever making that mistake again.

"I want this to be over," she admitted. "I want to move on with my life and put this behind me and make a good life for my daughter."

He nodded. "I can understand that, and I'm going to do everything I can to make certain it happens, but you're going to have to cooperate with us."

"I wasn't planning to do anything else," she assured him, shifting Ava so that the baby was cradled in her arms. Wispy blond hair peeked out from beneath a cap Dana Seavers had knit. Yellow and white with little snowflake patterns in it.

"I'm glad to hear that." He dragged the trunk over and sat in in front of her, perched on the old wood, his intense gaze locked on her face. "Maybe you can help us understand what Lance wants. He has resources available that would make it easy for him to leave Alaska, so why did he stay? What is his goal?"

"Aside from killing me because I ruined his plans?" She shivered and pulled a wool blanket tighter around her shoulders.

"He's risking a lot for revenge. If he's caught, he's going to spend his life in prison. There has to be something more," he prodded.

"Money. We opened a joint account the day before we went on our wilderness tour. We were going to buy a property in Miami. Lance had made a cash offer and wanted the money to come from a mutual account. We planned to honeymoon in Miami and close the deal while we were there."

He didn't speak, and she was certain he was processing the information, trying to decide how much validity it had. "Is that the account that had money transferred out in the early morning the day of the murders?"

"Yes."

"Was Lance aware that the money was no longer available to him?"

She hesitated, almost embarrassed to admit that she'd had suspicions but had planned to go through with the wedding anyway. "Not that I'm aware of. If he had been, he would have confronted me about it."

"So, he had two million reasons to think he could escape Alaska after the murders," he said as much to himself as to her.

She nodded. "I've had plenty of time to think about it, and I'm sure that was his plan. What I'm not entirely sure of is if he went out there planning to kill Cal, or if something happened that made him think he *had* to do it. Either way, he was expecting to leave Anchorage with the money and, probably, without me."

"My suspicion is that he never planned to kill anyone. He probably planned to skip town with the money and start a new life somewhere. Criminal and malicious, but not a crime that could get him tossed in jail for life. Jared was probably in on that plan, and Cal may have overheard them discussing things. It's possible he threatened to go to you with the truth, and they killed him because of that." The words were mater-offact, his expression neutral. This was the kind of thing he dealt with all the time, but it was new to Violet. The betrayal still hurt. The depth of Lance's depravity still made her shudder.

"You broke that down nicely, Gabe. It sounds very neat and tidy. No emotion or betrayal behind it. If only it felt that way," she murmured.

"I'm sorry. I didn't mean to sound cold."

"You didn't. I'm just… I guess I still can't believe Lance could be so evil."

"I'm sorry. You deserved better." He touched her arm, looked into her eyes, made her feel as if she were a victim rather than a fool who had gotten what she deserved.

"I should have been more careful. If I make it through this—"

"You will."

"I'm going to spend the rest of my life raising Ava to be the strong, independent and confident woman I wasn't. With the right tools, she should be able to avoid getting herself into this kind of trouble."

"You're carrying a lot of blame for something that wasn't your fault," he commented, his gaze shifting as Bear lumbered to his feet.

"You've said something similar before, and I know you're right. I couldn't have predicted any of this, and I couldn't have known Lance was using me, but I still feel like a fool."

"He was the fool. You're a strong, intelligent, beautiful woman. He obviously was too blind to realize that he was giving up the real prize in exchange for monetary reward." His gaze returned to her, and he smiled, the sweet curve of his lips making her pulse race.

"That's a nice thing to say."

"*Nice* is not an adjective most people would use to describe me. Honest, honorable, driven. Those are my things." He touched her cheek, his fingers tracing a line to her jaw. "So, take what I said for what it's worth, and know that I wouldn't say it unless I absolutely believed it. Lance was a fool, and if I had been in his shoes, I'd have spent every day of my life proving just how wonderful you are and how worthy of affection, love and respect." His hand slipped away, but the warmth of his fingers lingered.

Bear growled, breaking the sudden silence. Head cocked, eyes focused on the door, the dog growled again, the fur on his nape standing up.

"What's wrong? Is someone out the—" she began, but Gabe put a finger to his lips, cautioning her to stay quiet.

"Listen," he whispered.

She did, waiting in the silence, her heart thundering in her chest.

At first, she heard nothing but the quiet rasp of her breath and Bear's low growl. Then, another sound drifted into the cabin. An engine rumbling in the distance.

"Is that your team?" she asked, terrified that it wasn't and that Lance was back.

"I don't think so," he replied. "Stay here."

He was up and in his coat before she could think to question his plans. Leather gloves on his hands. Bear by his side. "I'll be back soon. Don't leave the cabin," he cautioned as he stepped outside with the St. Bernard and closed the door.

She wanted to call him back, but the words stuck in her throat, terror making her mute.

If she hadn't had Ava to think about, she might have gone out the back door and run. She had a head start and knew she wasn't far from the bunker. But the snow was deep. Her tracks would be easy to follow, and she didn't dare bring danger into the lives of people who had helped her.

So she stayed where she was, huddled beneath a blanket, holding Ava close and praying that Lance would be stopped before anyone else was hurt.

Gabe sent a text to Hunter McCord asking for an update on the team's ETA. It was possible they had made excellent time and were closing in on the cabin, but he expected them to be farther out. If they were, someone else was approaching in a snowmobile.

As the engine roared closer, he made his way up a nearby hill and studied the landscape, searching for signs of the vehicle. Bear stood beside him, body alert, tail up. His K-9 partner had his face to the west, and Gabe focused his attention there. There was a trail in that direction—a hiking and biking path that wound through the park and around Eklutna Lake. Anyone familiar with the area would know of it.

As he watched, two snowmobiles came into view. Just specks of black against the pristine white trail. He couldn't make out details, but the team would have more manpower with it.

Bear growled again, his muzzle lifted to the air.

"I see them, buddy," Gabe assured him.

His phone buzzed, and he checked the message. The team was still twenty minutes out. But the two snow-mobilers would be on them in ten. *If* they were heading for the cabin.

He typed a quick message, giving what little information he had about the vehicles, still watching the dark specks curving around the icy blue water of the lake. Maybe they were nature lovers out for a snow-day ride.

The lead snowmobile turned off the path, disappearing into the trees and heading in the direction of the cabin. The second vehicle followed.

His adrenaline spiked.

"Not what I wanted to see," he muttered, updating Hunter and hurrying back inside.

Violet was where he had left her, sitting in the chair, a blanket over her shoulders. The fire had died down, the flames eating at the wood he had tossed in earlier.

"Is everything okay?" she asked, standing up and grabbing her pack from the floor. She pulled out the baby sling and tried to put it on while still holding Ava.

"Someone is heading this way," he said.

She froze, the sling dropping from her hands, her face pale beneath layers of thick tan makeup. "Not your team?"

"No. We need to be prepared to take off at a moment's notice."

"You'll get no argument from me!" she said, reaching for the sling again and fumbling to get into it one-handed.

"I can take the baby," he offered without thinking. He wanted to expedite the process and get Violet ready to run, if they had to. But holding her baby was honestly the last thing he wanted to do.

She hesitated, looking into his eyes, her expression still guarded but so filled with fear, that he had the urge to pull her into his arms and assure her that everything was going to be okay.

"You have to support her head," she said quietly. "She's still too young to do it herself."

He nodded.

In theory, he knew what she meant. He had friends with kids. He'd even helped out in the church nursery a few times when it was understaffed and in need of an extra set of hands. But he had always avoided newborns.

He knew nothing about them. Except that they were completely helpless, completely dependent and absolutely fragile.

When Violet passed Ava to him, the swaddled bundle of tiny humanity fitting into the crook of his arm, he looked into the baby's face. Found himself drinking in her soft cheeks and pink lips, her closed eyes and one miniature fist that had escaped the blanket.

His heart jumped. A quick thud of fear and wonder and worry. This innocent child was out in the wilderness being hunted by her own father. A man who had killed once and would not hesitate to kill again.

Ava was being raised in an underground bunker away from medical help and friendships and sunlit windows. She deserved better. Gabe had felt protective of many things and many people during his time as an Alaska state trooper. He had a deep desire to see justice done and to protect the innocent, but he had never felt such an intense need to shelter someone, to hide them from the world and to make certain that nothing ugly or mean ever touched them.

"I'm done," Violet said, reaching for the baby.

He handed Ava back, that fierce need to protect still lodged deeply in his heart.

The snowmobiles had stopped, the engines silenced. He imagined Lance and his lackey, Jared, hiking closer, trying to be surreptitious in their approach. Silent predators stalking their prey.

"Are we leaving now?" Violet asked, Ava already in the sling, her coat on. She zipped it so that only the baby's tiny knit cap was visible.

"I was planning to leave, but I think it's better to have walls around us if Lance is close," he responded, pulling his focus away from the baby and meeting Violet's dark blue eyes.

"Walls don't keep out bullets."

"No, but they'll offer some protection," he replied, sliding into his pack and helping Violet into hers. "My team isn't very far out. They're aware that Lance and Jared may be nearby, and if we stay here, that will give them an opportunity to move in on Lance and Jared."

"Jared is out there, too?" She glanced at the window, the fear in her eyes belying her calm tone.

"I saw two snowmobiles. If Lance is on one, Jared is on the other."

She nodded, her hand dropping to the baby's back, the protective gesture touching him to the core. He had interviewed enough people to know when someone was being honest. What little she had said had rung true.

She was an innocent victim in this. The woman's only "crime"? Being duped by a man she loved.

"I'm sorry for what you've been through, Violet. I know it's been tough, but we're almost on the other side of it. You're going to get back to your old life and to normalcy. You're going to be safe again," he vowed.

"I hope you're right," she replied, her voice catching on the last word. As if she had used up every bit of faith she had, as if hope were a fragile snow-covered blossom, waiting for the sun to bring it to life.

Bear barked, the sound jolting Ava.

She wailed, a kitten-like cry that startled Bear into silence. He padded to Violet, gently nosing her coat, sniffing Ava's hat and head.

Violet didn't back up. She didn't ask Gabe to call off the dog. Instead, she merely watched as Bear nosed Ava's cheek. The baby stopped crying, and Bear retreated, rushing to the door and pawing frantically at the wood.

"Is someone out there?" Violet asked. This time, he could hear the anxiety in her voice.

She was backing into the other room, probably trying to get closer to an escape route.

"Yes," he responded honestly.

There was no sense in trying to hide the truth.

"Is it Lance?"

"I think we're about to find out," he replied tersely. "Stay away from the windows and stay low."

She nodded, dropping to her knees, one hand supporting Ava as she crawled to the threshold of the back room.

A gunshot exploded, the window shattering, cold air sweeping in.

Not an attempt to kill.

A warning, perhaps?

"Come on out of there, Violet!" a man yelled. "Unless you want your new friend and his dog to get hurt."

"Lance," she mouthed, her pulse pounding frantically in the hollow of her throat. He could see it there, beating beneath pale skin.

He moved closer, whispered in her ear, "We just have to hold him off for a few minutes. The team will be here soon. See if you can engage him in conversation."

She nodded. "Go home, Lance. Leave me alone!" she called, her voice shaking but her tone firm.

"Honey, why would you want me to do something like that? We're going to spend our lives together, remember?" he crooned.

"You're a cold-blooded murderer! I want nothing to do with you."

"Well, now, isn't that a shame. After all the times you claimed to love me, you're going to abandon me in my hour of need?"

"You tried to kill me."

"If I'd tried, you'd be dead. A little poison in your morning coffee, dump your body in the lake—it would have been done." He nearly spat the words.

Gabe eased toward the window, hoping to get a good visual and a good shot. If he had to, he would take Lance out. He was prepared to do whatever it took to protect Violet and Ava.

"You know what your problem is, darling," Lance said. "You lack vision. Your parents did you the favor of dying and leaving you with a fortune, and you spend your days sitting in a musty office running a company that you could sell for billions of dollars. Me? I'd have taken the money and retired. As a matter of fact, I *was* planning to take the money and retire. That cool two million was my ticket out of here. I was heading to Bangkok. You ruined that."

Gabe made it to the window and motioned for Violet to keep talking. Bear was still near the front door, whining softly and scratching the wood. Gabe signaled for him to heel, and the dog joined him, glued to his left side.

"You lied about everything, didn't you?" Violet demanded. "You never cared about me. You never loved me."

"Of course I didn't. Did you really think someone like me would want someone like you? You're a mousy little girl with no interests outside of books and business. The only thing exciting about you is your money."

Gabe scowled, the urge to climb out the window and shut Lance up so strong, he had to remind himself that Lance hadn't come alone and that flying off the handle would accomplish nothing.

Logic and careful planning trumped emotional responses.

*Always.*

He'd learned that while growing up in foster care. Gabe had had no one to show him how to be an adult. He hadn't had anyone invested enough in his life to teach him what it meant to have emotional control. And instead had to learn through trial and error, a ton of mistakes and missteps.

He eased to the window ledge, peered out into the bright day. As he suspected, Lance was just feet away, a shotgun resting against his shoulder. He wasn't planning to let Violet out of this alive.

And even though he couldn't see Jared, he knew the guy was out there, too.

Gabriel pulled his firearm, prepared to draw Jared out by threatening Lance.

"Freeze!" he called. "Police!"

Lance jumped back, stumbling in his haste to duck behind a tree.

"Now!" he shouted.

A soft pop followed his command.

For a moment nothing happened.

Then the door exploded in flames, smoke billowing up to the rafters, fire lapping at the old log walls.

Violet screamed, jumping to her feet and running to the back door. He caught her before she could open it.

"Don't!" he said. "That's what they're expecting."

"We have to get out!" she cried, her hand on the latch.

"We will, but we're not going out the door." He took her arm, hurrying her back to the window where Lance had been standing.

Footprints were clearly visible in the snow, leading from the trees toward the back of the cabin. They were waiting there, probably hoping to kill Gabe and take Violet and Ava alive.

He gestured for her to wait, then climbed silently through the window, making sure there were no shards of glass. Bear followed, bounding out with little effort. In the distance, engines roared, the sound of backup arriving filling Gabe with relief. Soon the men and women he trusted most would be there to help.

His coworkers. The only real family he had ever known. He reached for Violet, helping her navigate through the window, then pulling her into a full-out run toward the trees. Bear turned his head, growling ferociously as a shadow appeared at the corner of the cabin.

Gabe didn't hesitate.

He fired.

The person dropped with a howl of pain.

Gabe kept moving, running into the trees, Violet beside him, Bear on his heels. The sound of engines was growing louder. The team was getting closer. He just needed to hold the perps back until help arrived.

# SEVEN

Violet raced into the woods, Ava tucked securely in the sling under her coat. Fabric wouldn't protect her from a bullet. Love couldn't keep her from being hurt or worse. But as she pushed through knee-deep snow, Violet prayed that she and her baby would survive this ordeal as she unconsciously began moving in the direction of the bunker.

Gabe's hand was on her wrist, his fingers tight as he tried to steer her downhill toward Eklutna Lake. She changed course, forcing herself to ignore the knee-jerk desire to return to the one place she had felt safe during her pregnancy.

She didn't want the Seavers hurt. Didn't dare bring trouble to their doorstep. Not in the form of Lance or the police. If she was going to return, she'd have to be very careful about how she did it. *If* she was going to return. She craved safety and security. That, more than anything, was what home meant to her, and it was where she longed to be.

"Get down!" Gabe yelled, yanking her behind a tree.

Moments later, a bullet slammed into the trunk, bark

ricocheting into the snow. Violet winced, her arms crossing over Ava's tiny back. She had an obligation to protect her daughter, a duty to keep her safe, and she would do anything necessary to accomplish that.

Gabe hurried to a pile of deadfall and urged her to stay down.

Violet curled up on her side, desperate to shield Ava. The downed trees were nearly two feet high, but even that couldn't keep them safe from flying bullets.

Her eyes darted toward the trooper, and she saw he had his firearm drawn and was peering through cracks between dead branches. Someone was calling for help, shouting that he had been shot and needed an ambulance. Not Lance. She knew his voice as well as she knew her own.

It had to be Jared.

"Put your weapons down!" Gabe shouted. "Now!"

"Violet, I don't want to hurt anyone, but if you don't come out here and give me what I want, I won't be responsible for my actions," Lance responded. He sounded closer than she'd expected. Yards away, maybe, waiting for Violet or Gabe to lift their heads.

She didn't respond, didn't move. Bear was beside her, his big head close, his gaze focused on his partner. "I said, drop the weapon," Gabriel demanded.

"I did!" Jared hollered back. "I'm unarmed. Please, I need help. I'm going to bleed to death."

"It's a flesh wound, you idiot," Lance snapped. "Pull yourself together."

"We'll get you the help you need. Step out where I can see you. Hands up," Gabe called.

"Don't be a coward," Lance growled. "Violet, come on out and let me see my baby. Boy or girl? I need to know how to decorate the nursery when I leave town."

She bit her lip, refusing to be baited into speaking.

Lance wasn't father material. Trusting him, *loving* him, had been terrible mistakes. She wanted to believe she was smarter and wiser now, no longer the sheltered and naive young woman who had been swept off her feet by charming words and focused attention.

"Cat got your tongue, baby?" he called. "Or is your new buddy calling the shots like I always did? He says jump, you jump. He says hide, you hide. He says keep your mouth shut, and you do?"

She glanced at Gabe.

He seemed unfazed, his focus never wavering, his gun aimed in the direction of Lance's voice. She had never known anyone like him—someone who could face down a threat without flinching, a man willing to sacrifice himself for a stranger.

She wanted to thank him now, just in case there wasn't a chance later, but she didn't dare speak.

"I can forgive you for betraying me, babe," Lance continued. "We can still have the life we planned together. We can take our baby and leave Alaska together. Just the three of us. A happy little family. That's what you wanted, right?"

He knew it was.

She had poured her heart out to him, reveling in the attention he had given. Thinking about it made her cheeks heat and her stomach churn.

After her parents died, she had been desperate for

connectivity. She had craved the comfort of family bonds. Her mother and father had been older, both of them only children. Her arrival had surprised and delighted them. They had given her love and time, but they hadn't been able to give her siblings or cousins, uncles or aunts. Their friends were their family.

In the distance a dog barked.

"Last warning," Gabe called. "Put down your weapons and step out where I can see you. Hands up. No sudden moves."

"Please, help me!" Jared cried once again.

"I said *shut up*," Lance screamed.

The boom of a gunshot followed.

Then silence.

The dog had stopped barking, and the world seemed to be holding its breath. Even the trees seemed to have stopped rustling.

Violet shifted, terrified of what it meant.

Gabe inched closer, his shoulder warm against hers, his presence as comforting as dawn after the darkest, longest night. She had felt alone for so long, she had forgotten what it felt like to be together. Gabe made her feel that—as if she were part of something more than just herself. Two people facing trouble together were more powerful than one person alone.

She felt that to her bones as Bear dropped his big head on her legs, the warmth of his muzzle seeping through fabric and into her chilled skin.

"Violet! Get out here. Now!"

There was an edge to Lance's voices, a frantic energy that she had never heard before.

Bear barked in return, the dog shifting his attention downhill.

She did the same, surprised to see a Siberian husky darting through the trees, heading straight for them.

Another shot was fired, this one slamming into a tree a dozen yards away.

"He's on the move," Gabriel said, and she realized he had his phone in hand and was speaking to someone. "Heading west. Probably back to his snowmobile." He slipped the phone in his pocket.

"Stay here," he said. "A trooper is just below us. He'll be here shortly."

He gave Bear a command to stay, then jumped over the deadfall and took off.

Should she make a run for the bunker? She shifted onto an elbow, her free arm wrapped around Ava as she peered between dead branches. A man lay on blood-stained snow, arms and legs splayed. Gabe paused beside him, touching his wrist and neck before moving on.

Was it Jared lying dead in the snow? She couldn't make out details. Wasn't sure she wanted to. Violet had never liked Jared. She'd thought he was crass and seedy, and she'd often wondered how a charming person like Lance could be friends with him.

Now she understood that they were cut from the same cloth, and that Lance was the worse of the two—hiding his true colors beneath a coat of manners and civility. Jared had been his lackey, doing what he was told and following blindly.

She hadn't liked him, but she certainly hadn't wanted him dead.

Bear lifted his head, his gaze still on the husky.

It darted toward them, rushing in to sniff Violet's hair before running off again. Minutes later, she heard a man yell, "Good job! Show me!"

Two police officers appeared, running after the husky and heading straight toward Violet.

She stayed down and quiet as they reached her.

"Ma'am, I'm Trooper Hunter McCord. This is my colleague, Trooper Maya Rodriguez. She's going to escort you down to our ATVs and get you back to civilization."

"Gabe is still out here. I can't leave without him," Violet said, her voice thick with nerves. She wasn't used to being around people, and her communication skills felt rusty. Aside from the Seavers and a few medical professionals, she hadn't spoken to anyone until Gabe had found her the previous day. They had been a team all night, working together to stay warm and safe.

She wouldn't leave him behind.

She couldn't.

"We have several officers joining him. He's going to be fine," Trooper Rodriguez said kindly, her gaze shifting from Violet's face to Ava's head. "It's cold, though, and we've got another storm blowing in soon. Let's get you and your baby inside and warm."

She offered a hand.

Violet hesitated. "I can't leave him out here."

"Do you really think he would want you and the baby to stay in the cold waiting?" Trooper Rodriguez asked.

He wouldn't.

Violet knew that.

She took the offered hand, allowing herself to be pulled to her feet. Bear stayed down, head resting on his paws, not the least bit concerned about the commotion that was going on around him. "What about the dog?" she asked.

As if on cue, someone whistled. Bear jumped up, bounded over the deadfall and ran.

"Gabe just whistled. Bear will make quick work of reuniting with him," Trooper Rodriguez reassured her, turning her head as another dog ran out from between trees. "Sarge! Heel," she called.

The K-9 immediately took a position on her left.

"I'm heading out. Radio if you have any trouble," Trooper McCord said, hurrying away, the husky by his side.

"Ready?" the female trooper asked, meeting Violet's eyes. She had a kind face and an easy smile. Maybe that was why she'd been chosen to escort Violet out of the park.

"Yes," Violet responded, but she wasn't sure she was.

She had been dreaming about this moment for months, praying about it, begging God to allow her to return to civilization and her life. But now that it was happening, she didn't feel ready. She'd been away for too long, had lived with a family she'd grown to love. And now she was leaving everything she had known, everything that had kept her safe, and walking into the unknown.

Violet sighed. She had no idea what the police were thinking. For all she knew, she was still a suspect in Cal's murder and they were going to take her to jail and toss her in a cell.

She must have looked as anxious and unsure as she felt.

"Everything is going to be okay," Trooper Rodriguez said as she and her dog headed down the hill.

Violet followed, a feeling of finality and sorrow filling her. She was saying goodbye to the survivalist lifestyle, carrying all the lessons she had learned and heading back home.

To a new beginning.

A fresh start.

She and Ava. The two of them facing the world together.

"It's going to be fine," she whispered, patting Ava's back and praying that she was right and that the police would apprehend Lance. That he would be put in prison and that he would stay there.

He had killed Cal, and he had shot his best friend. Probably killed him, too.

Why? To shut him up? To keep him from turning himself in? Whatever the case, Lance's actions proved what Violet had already known—he was a very dangerous man. One without a conscience and without a heart. If he found her again, if he had the opportunity, he would kill her.

*I forgive you for betraying me, babe.*

He certainly hadn't been talking about her relationship with Cal. There hadn't been one. Maybe he had been putting on an act for Gabe's benefit.

Or, maybe, he was talking about the money she had transferred from their account. Money he would have had access to while she was hiding in the bunker. Money that would have made his escape easy. She'd taken it from him.

Probably worse in his mind, she had stepped out from under his control and done something he hadn't anticipated. Their relationship had always been about him. What he wanted and needed. What he felt and believed. She had worked hard to be the woman he wanted, jumping through every hoop he had set in front of her because she had been afraid to lose him. And he had probably firmly believed that would never change.

She had fooled him, and he couldn't forgive that. Now he wanted to make her pay. She shuddered, hurrying to keep up with Trooper Rodriguez.

It was time to leave Chugach State Park. Time to face the police. Time to do whatever it took to make sure Lance never hurt anyone again.

She glanced back, hoping to catch a glimpse of Gabe. He had stepped in and helped when she'd needed it most, and he was sacrificing his safety for her and Ava's sake. She wanted to thank him. She needed to tell him just how much she appreciated the safety he'd provided and the kind words he had offered. More than anything, she wanted to tell him to be careful. She couldn't bear the thought of anything happening to him, but he was gone, swallowed up by the forest and heading back into danger.

Gabe followed Lance's tracks through the snow, Bear loping a few meters ahead, both of them flanked by other K-9 teams. Helena Maddox and her dog, Luna, to their left. Will Stryker and his dog, Scout, to their right.

Of the three K-9s, Luna would be the most useful in this situation. Trained in apprehension, she would track Lance and take him down as soon as she was given the command.

"You want me to send her ahead?" Helena asked, her gaze focused on her dog. They were a great team. Tough and no-nonsense. Always ready to do what it took to capture suspects.

"He rode in on a snowmobile. I'm worried about him running over Luna if she gets too close," he responded.

"Luna doesn't let anyone get the best of her," Will said.

He was right. The Norwegian elkhound was sweet and accommodating when she wasn't working. When she was on the job, she was ferocious.

"It's your call, Helena. She's your partner."

She nodded, then gave Luna the command to work.

Luna took off, shooting into the woods and disappearing from view. Seconds later, a snowmobile motor roared to life. Lance had reached his escape vehicle. Gabe knew Luna was fast, but not fast enough to chase it down. "I'm calling in for park rangers to be on the lookout for a snowmobiler," Will said. "You want to let Maya and Hunter know he might head down to the road?"

"He'd be an idiot to do that," Helena muttered.

"He shot a man in front of me. I wouldn't give him high points for intelligence," Gabe muttered.

He hadn't expected Lance to shoot his best friend in cold blood, and he regretted not pulling the trigger and firing into the trees. Unfortunately, he hadn't had a clear line of sight, and firing blindly was a good way to get an innocent person killed. So he'd waited, hoping to catch a clear view and bring Lance down.

Waiting had cost Jared his life.

"Don't beat yourself up, Gabe," Will said as if he could read his mind and knew his thoughts.

Maybe he could, and maybe he did.

They were a family built by their strong desires to protect and serve the community. There wasn't a member of the team who didn't value every human life. Jared was a criminal, but his crimes should have been judged by a jury of his peers, his punishment decided by a court of law.

"I should have tried to take Lance out."

"Did you have a clear shot?" Will asked.

"No."

"Then you did the right thing. If Jared didn't want to be shot and killed by his best friend, he should have chosen a better one."

"Lance is a loose cannon, and he needs to be apprehended," Helena added. "He's unpredictable and dangerous, and as long as he is free, the community isn't safe."

"I'd like to know why he's hanging around. He could have flown out of Alaska seven months ago and left us chasing down Violet, thinking she was the prime suspect in the Brooks murder." Will whistled for Scout. The border collie rushed to his side. Small and nimble, Scout was trained in narcotics detection.

"Money is my guess," Gabe replied. "The joint account that was opened and then emptied out the night before the wilderness excursion? That may be key. I suspect he planned to leave town with the cash either before or after the wedding."

"And found out there was no money to leave with?" Helena asked.

"I'm not sure if he found out before or after the shooting," Gabe admitted. "Violet wasn't in the mood to talk, and I didn't want to press her for too many answers when she was taking care of a baby."

"I understand," Helena said. "But the sooner we ask the hard questions, the sooner we'll have a clear picture of what is driving Lance. He could have left Alaska months ago, but he's stayed. Why? What is he hoping to achieve? Once we know that, we'll be able to stop him."

"Money?" he suggested. "Violet said material possessions are his motivating factor."

"If that's the case," Will cut in, "and Lance was planning to empty the account, leave town before the wedding and live off the two million, it's possible Brooks overheard them talking about their plans."

"And was killed to ensure his silence? Just about anything is possible, but I think you may be on to something," Gabe responded. "Two million dollars can buy a really nice lifestyle in South America. Lance has his pilot's license and access to a plane. We already know that his business was deeply in the red, that he was tens of thousands of dollars in debt and that his condo was going into foreclosure."

"So he preyed on a vulnerable woman and planned to rob her blind, then killed a man to make sure she didn't find out? Nice guy," Helena muttered.

"I sure wouldn't want him on my friend list," Gabe said.

"I wouldn't want him on my enemy list, either. The guy has no conscience. He shot his best friend dead. I can't imagine what he'd do to someone he didn't like." Will shook his head.

"Stalk her for months? Make her live in fear? Try to kill someone she loves?" Helena suggested.

"Kidnap her baby, if he has the chance," Gabe added, every cell in his body rebelling at the thought of a thug like Lance getting his hands on Ava. She was fragile and tiny, and the thought of anyone hurting her made his blood boil.

The sound of the snowmobile's engine had faded to a muted rumble, and he bit back a groan of frustration. "I think he's managed to escape again."

"He can't run forever. Eventually we'll catch him and make him pay for what he's done." Helena called for Luna.

Minutes later, the elkhound appeared, glossy black against the bright white snow.

Clouds were moving in again, crowding close to the sun. More snow was arriving. Winter was just around the corner. And soon the park would be more difficult to travel. Would Lance finally give up and leave Anchorage? Or would he stay for as long as it took to accomplish his goal? Without his lackey, he might not have the guts to stick things out, but he'd proven to be a masterful manipulator and a seasoned liar. He'd almost had the K-9 team convinced that he and Jared were victims of Violet's violent rampage.

After months of interviewing her friends, coworkers and acquaintances, Gabe was certain Violet had too much compassion and empathy to hurt anyone.

She and her daughter needed to be protected.

He felt compelled to be the one to do it. He had looked into Violet's eyes. He had seen the fear and the strength there. She would do what it took to keep her baby safe, and he was determined to stand beside her, fight with her and make certain they both survived until Lance was caught and tossed in jail.

If that meant twenty-four-hour security, that's what she'd get. Gabe had assured Violet that everything would be okay. He intended to make certain it was. No matter what it took, no matter how many hours, he would find Lance and he would toss him behind bars where he belonged. Violet and her baby deserved to have peace in their lives, and he would do whatever it took to make certain they got it.

# EIGHT

Violet expected to be taken to the Anchorage police department, and she had braced herself for an intense interrogation.

Instead, she had been transported to the federal building. The white facade gleamed in muted sunlight as she was hurried inside and up a flight of stairs. Offices lined the long hallway of the historic building, and she could hear the normal sounds of busy office life.

It felt odd to be there, a trooper flanking her to either side, two dogs padding beside them. Life in the Seavers' bunker had become normal, whereas the hubbub of Anchorage life had become strange. Electric lights. Gleaming floors. Heat chugging out of ceiling vents. She felt overwhelmed and overstimulated, and she worried that Ava would feel the same.

She patted the baby's back as she was led into a small conference room.

"Violet, if you'll have a seat, we'll have someone with you shortly. We have a few questions to ask before we release you to return home," Trooper Rodriguez said. Tall and slender, she held the lead of a small Malinois that looked like it was still a puppy. She looked as relaxed inside the building as she had out in the woods, confidence and kindness seeping out in everything she did.

"Do I need to call an attorney?" Violet asked. Her father had always had lawyers on the payroll, and he had never been afraid to utilize their services. He had lived his life with integrity and purpose, but running a multibillion-dollar company often made him a target of false accusations and lawsuits.

Trooper Rodriguez frowned, her dark eyes spearing into Violet's. "If you feel the need to have an attorney present while you're being questioned, that is your prerogative."

"Am I being questioned because I'm a suspect in a crime?" she asked. That was another skill she had learned from her father—don't be afraid to ask questions. You can't formulate good plans of action without accurate and complete information. Without those things, you were just fumbling around in the dark.

"You're being questioned as a witness to the murder of Cal Brooks and the attempted murder of Ariel Potter," the trooper said. "But, like I said, if you want an attorney present, you're welcome to call one."

"I don't have a phone," she pointed out.

"We can bring you one. Have a seat. Do you want coffee? Tea? Cocoa? Something to eat?"

"No, thanks."

The trooper nodded and stepped into the corridor. "I'll be back shortly."

She shut the door, leaving Violet and Ava alone.

There were windows on the far side of the room,

and Violet opened the shades, letting muted sunlight filter in. Clouds dotted the horizon, another storm on the way. She had weathered several spring storms in the bunker, snow and rain and cold making life in the wilderness even more complicated.

The Seavers had their lives down to a science.

They knew when to plant, reap and harvest, knew how much meat they would need for long winter seasons, and they went to town every couple of months to trade fur and leather for supplies.

Violet admired them, and she appreciated everything they had taught her, but she hadn't wanted to spend her life off the grid. She liked being in touch with friends. She liked going to the office every day, returning home to a warm house and comfortable furniture. The Seavers' seventeen-year-old son, Harrison, felt the same. When his parents had made the decision to go off the grid, he had been old enough to have strong memories of living in a house, enjoying modern conveniences. He had admitted to Violet that, while he enjoyed the outdoors and appreciated the survival skills he had, he wanted to return to civilization, attend college and go into veterinary medicine. She knew he was smart enough to do it and had secretly planned to help.

After all his parents had done for her, the least she could do was pay for him to pursue his dreams.

The door opened, and a young man stepped in. Tall and lanky with dark hair, he wore jeans, a gray button-down shirt and a bright blue vest.

"Ms. James?" he asked, pushing round black glasses up his nose and smiling.

"Yes."

"I'm Eli Partridge. I work tech for the Alaska K-9 unit. I heard you needed a phone." He placed a cell phone on the table. "You can use this one. We have landlines, but we think it's best if you stay in here until we get a handle on what's going on with Lance."

"Thank you," she murmured, staying near the window.

She felt skittish and unsure. An odd development, as she had always been confident in social settings. Violet might have been a loner, but her parents had always included her in social gatherings and events. She had learned to be at ease no matter where she was.

Seven months in a bunker away from civilization seemed to have changed that.

"No problem." He crossed his arms and shifted his weight, staring at her intently.

"Did you need something else?" she asked.

"Actually, yes. I heard you've been staying with the Seavers. Is that correct?" He shoved his glasses up his nose again and leaned a shoulder against the wall.

"Yes."

"Would you be willing to tell me where they are? I've been trying to get in touch with Cole. My godmother is his mom. She has cancer, and she really wants to see him."

Her stomach dropped.

After Harrison had run into a state trooper who had asked about the family and requested that Cole get in touch with his mother, he had tried to talk his parents into reaching out to her. Violet had joined him in the campaign, explaining how important it was for everyone to have the closure a final meeting would bring. Despite their efforts, Cole had dug in his heels and refused.

Violet didn't agree with his choice. She would have given anything to have one last conversation with either of her parents. She had told Cole that repeatedly, but he hadn't changed his mind. Despite disagreeing with his decision, Violet couldn't give away the Seavers' location. Not after everything the family had done to make certain she and Ava were safe.

"I'm sorry, I can't," she murmured.

"Can't? Or *won't*?"

"Both," she admitted. "The Seavers took me in when I had nowhere to go. They offered me a place to stay, and they didn't ask anything in return. I can't betray them by divulging where they are living."

"I understand, and I appreciate your loyalty to them, but as I explained, Bettina is really sick, and she wants to be reunited with Cole and his family before she dies." Eli rubbed the back of his neck and shifted his weight. He wasn't happy with her answer, she could see that, but he didn't argue, and he didn't try to force her into giving him the information.

"I can pass a message to Cole through Harrison. He and I have been trying to convince Cole to get in touch with his mother. It does seem like the right thing to do." Violet would be heartbroken if she reached the end of her life and had a severed relationship with Ava.

"I'd appreciate that, and I appreciate that you and Harrison have been trying. How old is he now? Seventeen? Eighteen?"

"Seventeen."

"And he likes living off the grid?"

"He is good at it," she said, hedging around the truth, because she it wasn't her place to speak for Harrison.

"Being good at something doesn't mean you enjoy it. What does he want to do with his life? You ever talk to him about it?"

"He's interested in veterinary medicine, but he's young, and that could change tomorrow."

"Sounds like he has a good head on his shoulders. I'd like to meet up with him one day. Just to get to know him. If you can pass that along, too, I'd appreciate it. He can contact me here." Eli set a business card next to the phone. "I'll grab the phone later. Just leave it on the table."

He stepped out of the room without saying goodbye, closing the door behind him.

The silence in the wake of his departure was almost deafening, the weight of his disapproval and disappointment hanging in the air. She almost followed him into the hall. Not because she planned to change her mind and give up the Seavers' location, but because she wanted to find out where Gabe was and if he was okay.

He had taken every action with her and Ava's best interest at heart, doing everything he could to make sure they got back to Anchorage safely. He had risked his life to protect theirs. She would never forget that, and she could never repay the debt. His warmth and compassion were genuine. They had nothing to do with where Violet came from or what he hoped to get from her. He cared because it was part of who he was. Deep down, where it counted most, he was a decent, upstanding, heroic human being. Being around him made her feel safe and protected, and that was something she had needed and longed for while she was living off the grid.

"We're strong, independent women, Ava, but that doesn't mean we can't appreciate and admire a man who steps in and helps us," she murmured, pulling off Ava's knit hat and kissing her downy head. Her hair was damp from sweat, the layers of bundling Violet used to keep her warm in the bunker too much for the interior of the building.

"Sorry, love," she said. "Mommy wasn't thinking. Let's get you more comfortable."

Violet took off her coat, dropping it on the back of the chair, then took Ava out of the sling. Once that was done, she unzipped the tiny snowsuit and pulled it off, smiling at her daughter.

"Is that better?" she asked, her heart filled with a terrible kind of yearning, a deep-seated need to protect the precious life God had given her.

She hadn't intended to get pregnant. She couldn't say she had been thrilled when she'd learned the news, but she had never doubted that she would love her child, and she had been wholly committed to the task of being a mother.

What she hadn't known was how quickly and deeply love happened, or how desperate she would be to make certain Ava was safe and cared for.

Violet had no family, but she knew Ariel would step in if something happened to her. She'd be the mother

Ava deserved, but there was nothing official. Nothing in writing. Ariel had yet to meet the baby.

Violet picked up the phone, settling into a seat to nurse Ava. She knew she probably should call a lawyer, but the voice she really wanted to hear, the only person she really wanted to talk to, was Ariel.

She dialed the number and waited for her best friend to answer.

The team made it back to headquarters before the first flake of snow fell, but Gabe doubted they'd be there long. Paramedics had pronounced Jared Dennis dead, and the medical examiner had indicated that he had died from a gunshot wound to the head. He'd had a shallow bullet wound in his arm. One he would have easily recovered from if his best friend hadn't decided to kill him.

The cold-blooded murder shouldn't have surprised Gabe.

He had seen plenty of the uglier side of human nature.

He frowned, opening the back hatch of his SUV and letting Bear out. This was the part of the job he struggled with—doubting his decisions, worrying that he had done the wrong thing at the wrong time.

Lives depended on his ability to make good decisions under incredible pressure.

Today, he had failed.

But he had protected Violet and Ava. That had been his priority and his focus. As hard as it was to feel like he had made a mistake, he had at least done what he had set out to do.

"I hope you're not still beating yourself up about this," Hunter McCord called from across the parking lot. They had worked together for enough years to know each other well. "Will told me you were blaming yourself about what happened."

"Second-guessing my choices, maybe, but I was more worried about Violet and Ava than I was about a guy who was trying to kill us all. How are they?"

"Violet and the baby? Back at headquarters and fine, from what I've heard." Hunter opened the back of his SUV and released Juneau. The husky shook out his fur and greeted Bear with a friendly bark and play bow.

"Good. Let's make sure we keep them that way."

"You know we will."

"I'd like to have interrogated Jared. He was the weak link in their little criminal gang. If we'd apprehended him alive, he would have spilled the beans on where Lance has been hiding."

"He did," Hunter said with a quick, hard smile.

"What do you mean?"

"I just got off the phone with the ME. Jared had a wallet in his pocket. There was a key card for a motel room in it."

"What motel?" Gabe asked, ready to get back in his vehicle and head there.

Lance was an incredibly dangerous man.

He'd shot his best friend dead in front of the police.

He needed to be stopped.

"Mountain Terrace."

"The one east of Anchorage?" Gabe was familiar with the place. He'd done a few drug busts there in his younger years. A seedy motel that catered to people who didn't want to be found, it served a community that lived right on the edge of the law.

"Yes. I already called the colonel, and she's getting us a search warrant for the motel room. Should have it in hand in the next few hours."

The founder of the K-9 team, Lorenza Gallo, had been one of the first female Alaska state troopers to work with a K-9. Ten years ago, she had put together a team of top-notch handlers and dogs to help work some of Alaska's toughest cases. Driven, high-energy, fair and to-the-point, Lorenza knew how to get things done.

"Are we planning to head over there after we question Violet?" Gabe asked. He wanted to see her, make sure she was okay and that she and her baby didn't need anything.

He also wanted to hear her side of the story.

It would be easier to ask the questions, and easier for her to answer them, when they were safe in headquarters.

Hunter's phone buzzed, and he glanced at the screen. "Ariel just texted. Violet called her. Apparently, Eli let her use a precinct phone."

"Did she say anything helpful?"

"Ariel didn't elaborate. Just said she called, sounded good and wanted her to meet the baby. Just in case."

"In case what?" They stepped into the federal building, the 1930s architecture streamlined and minimalistic. The K-9 training facility was behind the historic building, and Gabe often spent more time there than at his apartment.

"She's worried that Lance will get to her. That he'll kill her and that there won't be anyone willing to take the baby."

"Foster care is no joke. It would be better for Ava to be with someone who loves her and will be invested in her future," he said. After spending most of his childhood in foster care, shuffled from one ambivalent placement to another, he'd never felt like he belonged. And while Gabe had muddled through as best he could, he'd always longed for parents who cared about him. His mother had died when he was in elementary school, and his father had never been part of his life.

"Not that we're going to let anything happen to Violet," he added.

"Absolutely not," Hunter agreed. "Ariel is champing at the bit, wanting to see Violet and the baby, but I've asked her to stay away until we apprehend Lance. I'm concerned he'll kidnap her and use her as bait to draw Violet out."

"We're not going to let that happen, either," Gabe said. Hunter and Ariel had become close during the investigation. Now they were engaged, their lives together starting from a tragedy and turning into something wonderful.

"Back so soon, Hunter? What? Your thin blood couldn't take the cold?" Maya Rodriguez joked as she walked past with her dog, Sarge.

"You know it," he laughed as he hurried up to the stairs that led to their offices.

"How are Violet and Ava?" Gabe asked.

"Fine, but you know Violet asked for an attorney,

right?" Maya said. "It might be a while before we can actually speak with her."

"Has the attorney arrived yet?" Gabe asked.

"No, but she has enough money to pay for the best, so I'd say whoever it is will be here soon with plenty of rules about what we can and can't ask and what she can and can't say." Maya sighed. "I hope she gets released soon so she can take her daughter home. The baby is adorable."

"Yes, she is," Gabe returned gruffly.

"She's in the conference room at the far end of the hall," Maya told them. "I'm going to type up some reports. If you need me, you know where to find me."

She walked off, her dog on heel beside her.

"A lawyer isn't my idea of a fun afternoon," Hunter muttered as he opened the door to the conference room and stepped inside.

Gabe followed.

Violet was seated at a table, muted sunlight streaming in through the windows and highlighting the pale gold strands of her hair. The makeup she'd been wearing had worn off, and her skin was alabaster with a few freckles on her nose and cheeks. He'd studied photos of her during the months she'd been hiding, and he had never noticed them.

She smiled as she met his eyes, the kind of welcoming smile that passed between friends. They had spent a long night in a cabin in the woods, cut off from the world and waiting for trouble to find them. Maybe that had created a bond between them. Whatever the case, his heart responded, his pulse ratcheting up as he looked into her eyes.

"Ms. James," Hunter began, taking a seat across the table from her. "I hear you've requested an attorney. Any idea when your counsel will arrive?"

"I've changed my mind and am going to waive my right to an attorney. I haven't done anything wrong, and I don't have anything to hide," she responded.

"Mind if we get that on tape?" Hunter asked, pulling out a small recording device and setting it on the table.

"Not at all."

He began the recording, and she repeated her statement, Ava cradled in her arms, tiny fingers curled into fists, cheeks pink. A fragile life that Gabe felt fiercely protective of.

He didn't like seeing kids hurt.

It bothered him to hear them crying.

In a perfect world, no child would ever be homeless, loveless or neglected. It wasn't a perfect world, but he had striven to do his part to help kids in the community. Gabe ran the rec program at his church, supervising after-school basketball and football games and offering plenty of activities for at-risk youth. He also volunteered at a local shelter, mentoring young men looking to make better choices in their lives.

His protective nature ran deep, but what he felt for Violet and Ava surprised him. It felt personal, as if they were more than just another mother and child who needed help. As if they were somehow connected more deeply than that.

He'd never thought about what it would be like to have a family of his own. He'd only known that if he did, he would do everything possible to make certain they felt safe and loved.

But Ava wasn't his child. And Violet wasn't his wife. He had no reason to feel such a deep tug of protectiveness toward them, but he couldn't deny it, and when the baby started fussing during the interview, he offered to walk her around the room to calm her.

Violet placed her in his arms, and he held her close, gently patting her back. It still felt awkward and unnatural. His years of not being around infants hadn't prepared him for comforting a fussy, tired newborn, but holding Ava felt…right and good. He met Violet's eyes, and she smiled gently, her expression tender. His heart swelled with the need to keep her and her baby safe, to stand beside her and do everything he could to make sure they had what they needed to thrive.

The feeling took him by surprise.

He considered himself a hard-hitting, tough cop who had been through enough in life to not be swayed by emotion. He was a pragmatist with just enough cynicism to keep himself from falling for every sob story he heard during interviews with suspects. He didn't expect or want to be drawn to someone the way he felt drawn to Violet, but he couldn't deny that he felt something compelling when he looked into her eyes.

He walked to the window, looking out into the fading day.

The sun was being swallowed by dark clouds, the few flakes of snow that had been falling suddenly turning to sheets of ice and rain. Not good weather to be out in. Maybe that would drive Lance back to the motel.

Troopers had already been dispatched there and were sitting in unmarked cars, waiting for his return.

If he tried to set foot there, Lance would be stopped. Until then, Gabe was going to stick close to Violet and Ava. He might not be an expert at taking care of newborns, but he knew how to protect the people he cared about. Right now, they were at the top of his list of priorities. He had found them in the cabin in the woods, and it was his responsibility to make certain that didn't cost either of them their lives.

# NINE

Violet answered every questioned she was asked.

Some of them she answered two or three times.

Trooper McCord finally finished the interview, hit the stop button on the small recording device that sat on the table and leaned back in his chair. "We appreciate your cooperation, Ms. James. You and your baby have been through a lot. It wasn't my intention to make it worse. I hope that you understand, we're just trying to get to the bottom of what happened."

"I do," she assured him, glancing at Gabe, wondering if he planned on questioning her, too.

Up until now, he'd been mostly quiet, pacing the width of the room with Ava in his arms, his hair blueblack in the overhead light.

He met her eyes and offered a reassuring smile.

She should have felt nothing. No tiny little thrill of attraction. No acknowledgment that Gabe was very handsome, very charming and very heroic. But apparently her heart had other ideas.

"I can take her now," she murmured, her pulse thumping wildly in her chest. This was what the beginning of love felt like. She didn't know how she knew it, but she did. What she'd felt before was nothing compared to the deep, soul-stirring need she felt when Gabe was around.

*Don't go there*, she warned herself sternly, Whatever she might be feeling was pointless. She'd been there and done that. Looked into the eyes of a handsome and charming man. Believed his smile and his lies. She'd paid for that in ways that had permanently changed her.

There was no going back, no trusting blindly. She was wiser. Smarter. More confident of herself and her place in the world. She didn't need a man to validate her worth, and she certainly didn't need one for financial support. Living with the Seavers had taught her how easily she could adapt to different places and different circumstances. It had also taught her how to be content with herself. At night, when the Seavers went to their small rooms and she lay on the cot in the living area, she'd had no one to talk to. Just her thoughts and her prayers.

It had been enough.

It would continue to be enough.

But she still felt her heart melt as Gabe walked toward her.

"She's out cold," he said softly, handing her the baby, his fingers brushing her knuckles. Warmth spread up her arm, and her cheeks heated.

He had a way about him. A confidence that was more appealing than she wanted it to be.

"Thanks," she murmured, placing Ava in the baby carrier and standing.

She moved a few feet away, shoving her arms into

her coat, ready to leave. But, of course, she had no car and no money.

Aside from the borrowed phone that still lay on the table, she had nothing but the clothes on her back and the few things in her pack. "If we're done here, I'd like to go home. I'll need to call an Uber," she said.

"You're really planning to return to your home?" Gabe asked.

"Yes. There's another storm blowing in, and I'll feel better having Ava in a safe place," she replied.

"I'm not sure your house is the safest place for the two of you." He frowned, his attention shifting to Trooper McCord. "What about the safe house outside town? Is it available?"

"Should be. I'll give Lorenza a call. If she approves it, we can head over there now. Then go to the motel."

"Motel?" Violet asked, her head pounding with fatigue and hunger. She'd barely slept the previous night, and she hadn't eaten since the evening before. Nursing a baby and hiking through the snow burned calories that she didn't have to spare.

"Lance and Jared were holed up in one. We found the key card in Jared's wallet," Gabe explained.

"Did Jared…survive?" she asked, knowing that he hadn't but wishing she were wrong. So many horrible things had happened because of choices she had made. If she'd broken up with Lance the first time she had wondered about his intentions, two people might still be alive and Ariel never would have been hurt.

"I'm afraid not," Gabe said gently.

"Did Lance shoot him?"

"Yes."

"They were friends for most of their lives," she whispered, trying to wrap her mind around the fact that a man she had thought she loved had killed two people in cold blood. One of them his best friend.

"People like Lance don't care about friendship. They care about getting what they want. Jared had an injury to his arm. Lance probably thought he was going to be a liability. Rather than leave him behind and risk him becoming a witness for the state, he killed him." Trooper McCord was matter-of-fact, his expression hard, his gaze sharp. "If you think he won't do the same to you, you're mistaken."

"I'm not that much of a fool."

"You aren't a fool, Violet," Gabe cut in. "Lance is an exceptional liar and manipulator. He had us conned until we got a good look at the evidence."

"I still feel responsible for what happened to Cal and to Jared."

"The responsibility for their deaths rests on Lance's shoulders, not yours," Gabe said. "He committed the crimes, and he is the one who is going to pay. But he's dangerous and unpredictable. Until we have him in custody, the best thing you can do is allow us to offer the protection you and your daughter need."

Gabe was right... Violet knew it. A safe house would keep her hidden until Lance was behind bars, but she was desperate to go home. Just for a few minutes. Just to check on the property, to see it through fresh eyes, to grab a few things that would remind her of her parents and the happy life they'd had together. "If I agree to go to the safe house, will you let me stop by my place first? I've been away for seven months, and I'm feel like I've forgotten what it's like to be home." Her voice broke, and to her horror, tears welled in her eyes.

She'd never been much of a crier.

There were better ways to deal with emotions.

She turned away from Gabe and Trooper McCord, walking to the windows and staring out into the fading day.

A few moments later, she heard the door open and close. But she didn't look to see who had come or gone. She didn't want anyone to see the tears that were sliding down her cheeks. Still, voices carried through the door. A discussion between Gabe and Trooper McCord, she thought, but she didn't get closer to the door to try to hear what they were saying. For the past few months, it had seemed as if her life was out of her control. She'd had no choice in how or where she lived, because she'd had to stay hidden. She'd hoped that returning to Anchorage would change that.

The door opened and closed again.

Violet wiped the moisture from her cheeks, hoping she didn't look as dejected and defeated as she felt. She'd fought so hard for so long to keep moving forward and believing that one day things would go back to normal.

But how could things ever be normal if Lance was on the loose?

"Violet?" Gabe touched her shoulder. "It's going to be okay."

"You can't know that, and neither can I."

"Maybe not, but I can do everything in my power to keep you and Ava safe."

"Why?" She turned to face him.

"Because I'm a police officer. My job is to protect and serve."

"I don't want anyone else hurt because of the choices I made." Lance had done enough damage, and she was terrified of what he might do next. Would he go after her friends? Her coworkers?

Would he try to harm Ava?

The thought made her cold with dread.

"We're going to do everything possible to bring him into custody quickly. Until we do, the safe house is your best option. I spoke with Hunter. We can bring you to your place before we go there. You can pack a few things for yourself and Ava."

"I appreciate that," she said, her throat tight with more tears. But she didn't let them fall. She needed to focus on gathering the things she'd missed most from home—photos of her parents. Her mother's worn Bible. The quilt her grandmother had made.

She'd lived a life of privilege. She'd always known that. Her parents had instilled a sense of grateful acknowledgment. They'd taught her to be generous with what she had, to appreciate it and to understand how fortunate she was. She had always valued the house, the heat, the food, but she had overlooked the smaller things—the trinkets, the keepsakes, the items that had no intrinsic value but were rich in memories.

Those were the things she had missed most when she was in the bunker.

"You ready to head out, Gabe?" Maya Rodriguez walked into the room, her Malinois at her side. "Sean and Grace are already in his vehicle."

"Are you ready?" Gabe asked Violet.

She nodded. Scared. Excited. Ready to return home. Even if it was just for a few minutes.

"Let's head out." Gabe took her arm, his fingers curved around her bicep. The gentle touch reminded her of all the things she'd never had with Lance. He had never made her feel safe, and she had never really felt she could count on him.

He'd been attentive, showering her with words of praise, with gifts, with dinner dates and flowers. She'd been so desperate for love that she had convinced herself that those things were true signs of commitment.

But Gabe's hand on her arm? That felt more real than anything Lance had done.

She didn't allow herself to dwell on that as she stepped outside and got in Gabe's vehicle. She had more important things to worry about.

Lance was still on the loose.

No matter how determined Gabe was to protect her, the threat was real, and she would be foolish to ignore it. She'd go inside the house, gather the things she wanted, and then she'd allow herself to be taken to the safe house. As much as she hated the idea, she'd stay there until Lance was apprehended.

That was the smart thing to do.

Not just for herself, but for her daughter.

And right now, Ava's well-being was the most important thing in the world to her.

\* \* \*

Violet's house sat in the middle of ten acres overlooking Campbell Lake. The impressive facade hid an equally impressive interior. Hardwood floors. Plush throw rugs. Huge fireplaces.

Gabe took in the details as he followed Violet up a curved staircase and into a large bedroom suite. He thought she'd grab clothes and toiletries. Maybe a laptop or electronic gadget of some sort.

Instead, she put several photos into a small suitcase. Then she walked into an adjoining room, and he stood on the threshold as she took folded baby clothes from a tall dresser.

"I bought a few things when I found out I was pregnant," she said as if she needed to explain herself.

"There's nothing wrong with that," he responded, walking to a window that overlooked the front yard. Maya and Sean were in their vehicles, keeping their eyes out for trouble.

"No. There isn't, but I was buying things and hiding them from Lance. I didn't want to tell him about the baby. I was afraid of what his reaction would be."

"I'm sorry," he said, turning to face her again. "No woman should ever have to feel that way."

She looked tired, sad and very, very beautiful.

He wanted to tell her that.

Tell her just how lovely she was. Just how deserving she was of all the things that every person should have—acceptance, friendship, admiration and kindness.

"Don't be. I made my choices, and I got the consequences of them. I have no one to blame but myself for how things played out." She tossed a pack of disposable diapers in the suitcase. "I almost called off the wedding the day before we went on our wilderness tour. If I had, none of this would have happened. Lives would have been saved. No one would have been hurt."

"We've been down this road before, and you know what I'm going to say—you can't blame yourself for Lance's actions."

"And you know what I'm going to say," she responded with a tired smile. "I can blame myself for being an idiot. My parents raised me to be smarter than this." She dragged the suitcase into the hall and walked into a large office. A mahogany desk sat in the center of the room, facing windows that looked across the lake.

Violet took a photo from the desk and tucked it into the suitcase, then opened a drawer and pulled out a well-worn leather Bible. "My mother's," she explained. "She read it every morning and evening. She'd be disappointed if she knew some of the choices I've made."

"Or, maybe, she'd be proud that you've persisted and overcome enormous adversity," he suggested, not wanting her to cry again. He'd seen the tears on her cheeks at headquarters, and it had taken all he had not to brush them away, pull her into his arms and promise that everything would be okay.

She walked to an oil painting and pulled it off the wall, revealing a wall safe. "Maybe," she said with a half smile. "My mom and dad were always accepting of others, and they didn't hold things against people, so I guess she wouldn't hold my poor choices against me."

"Sounds like your parents were exceptional people."

"They were." She unlocked the safe and took out a stack of bills. "This is legal, by the way. No ill-gotten gains in the safe. My father always insisted on keeping enough cash at the house to pay bills for a month."

"Obviously, your father's bills are way higher than mine," he joked as she put the cash in her suitcase.

"Probably higher than most. He liked to help people, and he never turned someone away if they needed it. I usually just leave the cash in the safe, but my wallet was at the cabin the day of our wilderness excursion. I don't have access to my bank cards, and I'd really like to buy Ava a crib. She deserves a comfortable place to sleep." She kissed the top of her daughter's downy head.

"I'm not sure shopping is the best idea right now." Not with Lance still on the loose.

"I wasn't planning on making the purchase myself. I was hoping someone could give the cash to Ariel Potter. She could buy it for me."

"We'll make sure Ava has a crib," he said, sidestepping the request to get Ariel involved. She hadn't seen who pushed her off the cliff, but the renowned husky trainer hadn't wavered in her belief that Violet was innocent of any crimes. Her insistence that the team focus in other directions had been part of the reason why Lance and Jared had become suspects so quickly.

"I know it probably seems like a silly thing. She can sleep with me, and that will be fine, too, but the day she was born, I felt like such a horrible mother. I had nothing for her. Just some clothes Harrison bought at the thrift store and some makeshift diapers."

"You said she came early," he commented, wishing

she wasn't berating herself over something she'd had no control over.

"I'd had eight and a half months to prepare, and I'd done nothing. I guess I kept hoping things would change and I'd be able to return home before she arrived. I should have pulled my head out of the sand months before I went into labor. The Seavers tried to get me focused on getting ready for her arrival, but I kept putting it off."

"You were dealing with a lot, Violet. Don't beat yourself up over it."

"She deserves better," she replied, her voice breaking, a tear trickling down her cheek.

"What is better than love?" he asked, nudging her chin up so that she met his eyes. "What is better than giving your child every bit of your heart?"

"A home with four walls and some windows. A real floor. Light streaming in," she responded, not stepping away from his touch. Instead she just stood there, looking into his eyes and studying his face, searching for something.

Maybe honesty. Integrity. Honor.

"Those are things, Violet. I had them when I was a kid. Walls. Windows. Light. Yards to play in. But after my mother died, I didn't have love. I'd have traded it all for that."

"Gabe, I'm so sorry," she said, another tear slipping down her cheek. Only this time, he thought she might be crying for him. For the confused kid he'd been, shuffled from home to home, uncaring placement to uncaring placement.

"Hey, it's okay. I grew up, and I used what I learned

from my time in foster care to help me do better for kids in Anchorage. I've been a big brother for years, and I'm involved in foster education and training," he responded, brushing the tear away and giving her and Ava a gentle hug.

It wasn't meant to be more than that.

Just a quick and easy expression of friendship, understanding and comfort, but she fit perfectly in his arms, her hands fluttering near his ribs for a moment before settling on his waist, her forehead resting on his chest. Ava was between them, her small body sheltered by two people who would do anything to protect her.

Gabe felt it all deeply.

The two vulnerable lives he was holding close.

The vastness of the wilderness they'd survived.

The danger that lurked just beyond the walls of the house Violet had spent her childhood in.

He brushed her hair back, the thick strands falling past her shoulder. Flax and honey. Burnished by days spent outdoors. "Don't cry," he rasped.

"I'm sorry," she repeated, finally stepping back, her cheeks pink, freckles dancing across her nose.

With distance between them, he could think again.

Bear was near a window, staring out into the dusky light. Icy rain was falling in sheets, mixing with flakes of snow and pea-size pieces of hail. Lance had proven that he wasn't averse to bad weather. He hadn't returned to the motel.

He could be anywhere. And Gabe would be smart to keep that in mind. He needed keep his thoughts and his attention on the case. Getting too deeply involved could only cause problems.

He watched as Violet walked to the dresser, opening drawers and grabbing clothes. She didn't seem to notice or care what color or what item she was taking. Rather, she just shoved everything in the suitcase, added a brush and toothbrush from the bathroom, and then hastily zipped it closed.

"Everything okay?" he asked.

"Yeah." She sighed. "I was just hoping to spend the night here."

"I wish we could allow that, but it's not safe. It won't be until Lance is behind bars." He grabbed the suitcase and called to Bear.

"I know." She sounded tired.

She *looked* tired. There were dark circles under her eyes, her shoulders were bowed and he could see the vertebrae in her neck, each one clearly delineated.

Gabe recalled that they hadn't eaten since the previous night, and she was a nursing mother. That concerned him.

Her gauntness concerned him.

And her pale skin and the shakiness of her hand as she set the security code and stepped outside made him wonder if he should be taking her to the hospital rather than a safe house.

"Maybe we should get you checked out by a doctor," he suggested as she closed the door and used a code to lock it.

"I was at the doctor yesterday morning. Well, the

midwife. But she gave me a physical and a clean bill of health."

"Really?" he asked, waving to Maya, who had jumped out of her car and was hurrying toward them.

"She wants me to eat more, but other than that, I'm in good shape."

"We'll make sure the safe house has a fully stocked pantry," he promised.

"Some extra diapers would be nice, too," she responded.

"We'll make sure you have those as well." He opened the passenger door and waited while she climbed in.

He needed to buy an infant car seat. Violet hadn't mentioned it, but he put it on his mental list. Safety was paramount. Even in situations like these.

"Gabe!" Maya called. "Can I talk to you for a second?"

"Sure." He closed the door and joined her. Bear lumbered beside him, happy to be outdoors, the rain and sleet bouncing off his thick coat.

"What's up?" he asked, surveying the area while he spoke, looking for any sign that Lance was nearby.

"We got the search warrant for the motel, and patrol officers have already made entry. Lance isn't there."

"Did we expect him to be?"

"No, but there's plenty of evidence that he was. Clothes. Shoes. A watch with his name engraved on the back. They also found a couple of plane tickets as well as fake IDs for Lance and Jared. Passports. Driver's licenses. Everything they needed to leave the country without being detected."

"So, why didn't they?" he wondered aloud, brushing icy rain from his cheek.

"Interesting question, and I think we have an answer. The tickets were dated for the day after the wilderness tour began. Looks like Lance and his buddy planned to skip out, get on a plane and leave the country."

"A runaway groom?"

"That would be my guess. When we subpoenaed his financials, Violet and Lance had a joint account. Remember? Approximately two million dollars transferred in to open it. Then all but a couple of grand transferred back out the night before the excursion?"

"I remember," he said, glancing at his car, wondering if Violet had any idea that Lance had planned to leave before he'd married her. Gabe had spent hours interviewing her friends and the people she worked for. According to them, she was intelligent, hardworking and compassionate. She didn't get duped in business and ran the family oil company with the same efficiency and focus as her father.

How had someone like that ended up with someone like Lance?

No doubt the guy was a chameleon, changing colors to match his environment. People who knew him through his business called him a shark. Old friends hadn't had very flattering things to say. New ones loved him, praised him and thought he could do no wrong.

Even his family was at odds when it came to Lance. His parents thought he was a perfect son with perfect manners who lived a nearly perfect life. But his sister called him a liar and a manipulator. Gabe thought her opinion was closest to the truth.

"You feel sorry for her," Maya said.

"She didn't ask for this. She went into the relationship believing Lance was everything he claimed to be."

"She's fortunate she's alive to talk about it. We'd better head out. The storm is going to come in hard in the next few hours. The safe house is nice, but it's out in the middle of nowhere on that back road. Not easy to get to when the ice gets thick."

"Did Lorenza approve officers to stay at the house with Violet?" he asked, scanning the yard, the lake, the shrubs that lined the driveway.

"Yeah. You probably have the text."

"Want to give me a recap?" he replied, still scanning their surroundings. The dogs seemed relaxed, but something felt off. He couldn't put his finger on what, and he couldn't see anything alarming.

"She has a few of us running shifts, but you're scheduled to do the overnights. I let her know that I'd be happy to switch out with you."

"I'm currently the one with the freest social schedule, so that makes sense," Gabe said. In the past year, most of the members of the team had fallen in love and gotten engaged or married. They were just as committed to their jobs, but they also had other priorities. People who loved them. Families that needed them.

Gabe was still a bachelor, living in a one-bedroom apartment. That was what he'd wanted. It was how he had always planned to live. He'd done his time on the dating circuit when he was younger and had even been engaged at one time. But his long hours and commitment to work had created tension with his ex-fiancée. Destiny had wanted time and attention that he hadn't been able to give.

Or, maybe, he hadn't wanted to.

The day she'd tossed the engagement ring in his face and told him she was done, he had been more relieved than heartbroken. That had made him wonder if he was like his father—a man who had walked away from his wife and child without a backward glance. Gabe had no memories of him, and he had very few of his mother. He had no idea how to parent or how to create the kind of happy family he had longed for when he was a child.

He hadn't thought he wanted to learn, but meeting Violet had changed that. Watching her with Ava had made him long to be part of something bigger than his job, bigger than his career. He wanted to go home to people who were waiting with open arms and open hearts.

"Like I said, I can switch out with you. When David was the security chief for the cruise line, he worked all kinds of odd shifts, so he totally gets what it's like not to have a nine-to-five job. Plus, he isn't the type of guy who would give me a hard time about my schedule, anyway. If he was, I wouldn't be with him."

Maya had met David Garrison while working undercover on a cruise ship, and the two had been inseparable since. Gabe couldn't deny the affection and love he had seen between them.

"I appreciate it, but I'll be fine." He opened the back of the SUV and called for Bear to get in. The temperature was dropping, hail falling in sheets and bouncing off the ground. Ava fussed, a quiet mewl that reminded him of a kitten.

He needed to get them to safety.

The nagging feeling of danger wouldn't leave, and he had learned to always trust his gut.

"Let's head out," he said, closing the hatch and rounding the side of his vehicle.

Maya hurried to her SUV and hopped in.

The community was posh, the properties spread out and sitting on several acres each. Most of them gated. The long driveway that led back to the road was lined with lights. Even so, visibility was low, the evening dusky and gray. The gate into the property was open. Just as it had been when they'd arrived. Nothing looked out of place or seemed amiss. But Gabe was tense and on edge just the same. He was certain trouble was coming.

Maya drove through the gate first. Sean followed. Gabe was next, cruising toward the gate at slow speed, that odd disquiet still lodged in his chest. The gate swung shut, blocking their exit and preventing anyone's entrance in.

"It doesn't close on its own," Violet said. "It stays open unless you punch the code in from the house to close it or use the remote I have in my car."

"Is there a keypad on the gate?" Gabe asked.

"Yes, but you have to get out to punch it in, and I don't think that's a good idea." Her voice was shaking, and she'd shifted in her seat to look toward the house.

He was on the radio, calling for immediate backup, when she grabbed his arm. "I think I see flames."

"Where?"

"The house is on fire!" she shouted, opening the door.

The first bullet hit the window, pinging off bullet-proof glass. He had the door closed before the second hit. "Stay down, Violet!"

He glanced at Ava, felt his heart shudder with fear and the desperate need to protect them both.

Bear barked, the frantic warning coming seconds before a barrage of bullets hit the front of the SUV.

Gabe was on the radio, shouting information above the chaos. Maya's vehicle was outside the gate, Sean's parked beside it. Both of them were taking cover behind open doors as they tried to get a clear shot, but the evening had gone quiet again, the barrage of bullets ending as quickly as it had begun.

Lance would be a fool to stay nearby.

He'd taken his shots. He'd tried to get Violet out of the vehicle. He'd failed.

He'd be on the run.

And he was about to have three K-9 officers chasing him down.

"What's the gate code?" Gabe asked after helping Violet back into her seat.

She gave it.

"Stay here."

He jumped out of the SUV, opened the back hatch to free Bear and locked the doors. A patrol car pulled up outside the gate as he entered the code. When the gate swung open, the officers raced inside. Gabe couldn't resist looking back at Violet and Ava before following suit. He reminded himself that they were safe as long as they remained in the vehicle.

Plus, he had a murderer to chase down.

But for the first time in his career, he felt hesitant to go on the hunt. Not because he was afraid of finding the perp, but because he was worried about what he was leaving behind.

A vulnerable woman and newborn.

Two innocent people who had done nothing to deserve the trouble they'd found themselves in.

He wanted to make that right.

He needed to.

He called to Bear, radioed his location and headed away from the lights and sirens.

# TEN

The fire was minor.

Just a pile of debris lit with accelerant near the front corner of the house. No damage to the facade. Just a few smudges of soot on the fieldstone used for the foundation.

Violet had been shown the photos, but she hadn't been allowed to go back to the house. A K-9 trooper had ushered her and Ava into a waiting vehicle and driven them away.

They'd wound through Anchorage, taking back roads and main roads. She knew the area well, and she tracked their progress. They were going in circles, revisiting routes. She assumed the trooper was making certain they weren't being followed.

Ava whimpered from the infant car seat the trooper had provided.

She was hungry. They were way past feeding time. She probably needed to be changed.

"It's okay, sweetheart. We'll be there soon," she cooed.

"Won't we?" she added, directing the question at the

auburn-haired officer who was escorting her to the safe house. The giant dog lying in the back lifted its head and sniffed the air.

"Yes," the trooper said. "Sorry this is taking a while. We want to make certain Lance can't follow us to the safe house. I'm Trooper Poppy Walsh, by the way. Should have introduced myself earlier, but I had orders to get you out fast. My dog, Stormy, will let us know if there's anything to worry about once we arrive at our destination. She goes after poachers and is good at detecting people who are lurking where they shouldn't be."

"I appreciate the effort you're putting into keeping me and Ava safe," Violet said. "I'm sorry that I caused so much trouble."

"Honey, you didn't cause a thing. Lance Wells did. But we'll find him, and we'll put him in prison. Then your life can go back to normal."

*Normal?*

Violet wasn't sure she knew what that was. Not anymore. She'd had normal with her parents, and after they'd died, she'd thought she'd found it again with Lance. That had been a charade.

When she returned to her old life, what would it be?

Living with the Seavers had made her realize how little she had been doing for herself. Sure, she washed her own clothes, made her own meals and drove where she needed to go. Her parents had taught her to be self-sufficient, but she had never had to worry about where a meal would come from. She certainly hadn't had to tend a fire through the night to keep warm.

That said, she'd tried to give back before she'd gone on the run.

She'd contributed to the community. Had given to charity. She'd even volunteered in soup kitchens and women's shelters. Violet had always had compassion for the people she was serving, but she had never really been able to empathize, because she'd had no idea what it felt like to rely on the charity of others.

Now she knew.

She understood how tenuous an existence that was. How humbling and how hard to have to ask for help and pray you would receive it.

The Seavers' kindness had kept her fed, clothed and warm for seven months. The medical clinic had offered free pregnancy care without asking for anything in return.

She would never forget that.

Her view of the world, of life and of her place in it had changed, and she needed to change with it.

Violet didn't just want to return to her old life. She wanted to return to her community. Be better. More committed to making a difference.

She planned to start with the medical clinic. It was run on a shoestring budget by doctors, nurses and midwives who volunteered their time to help pregnant women.

Once this nightmare with Lance finally ended, she would volunteer her time and experience to help expand the clinic's service to the community. She had the resources, and thanks to her father's tutorage, she had the business know-how.

"You doing okay?" Poppy asked, breaking the silence.

"I'm fine. Just anxious to get to the other side of all this."

"You've been running from Lance for a long time. It seems like a little peace is past due," Poppy said kindly.

"I just hope Lance doesn't hurt anyone else. He's already done enough damage."

"We're doing everything we can to keep that from happening." The SUV left the main road, the pouring sleet and hail pinging off the windshield. The road might have been gravel or dirt. Violet couldn't tell. She could barely see the trees that crowded to either side.

It was dangerous weather to be out in.

Especially dangerous for someone hunting a killer.

She had been trying not to think about Gabe and Bear, out in the dark and the cold, going after a man who wouldn't hesitate to kill them, but her thoughts circled back to them again and again.

They were risking their lives for hers.

She couldn't forget that.

Gabe had said his job was to protect and serve. She got that. But when push came to shove, most people looked out for themselves first and worried about everyone else later. That was a lesson being involved in a multibillion-dollar corporation had taught her. It was what having wealth had taught her. Her parents had been kindhearted and compassionate, but they had raised Violet to understand that people would take advantage if they could. It still shocked her that she had fallen for Lance…that she had set herself up to be victimized, and she hadn't even realized she was doing it.

Never again.

She could do life on her own, and she would.

But she couldn't deny Gabe's integrity, his honor and his commitment to his job. He had proven himself again and again, protecting her and Ava when he could have simply protected himself.

Poppy pulled up in front of a log cabin–style home, parking under a portico that sat near a detached three-car garage.

"This is the safe house?" Violet asked, surprised by how nice it was.

She wasn't sure what she'd been expecting. Maybe a small hunting cabin out in the wilderness?

"Yes. It belonged to a senator who left it to the state when he passed away. We have a few properties like this. They stay in the family's name, but we pay the taxes and upkeep. That makes it difficult for criminals to identify them as safe houses."

Poppy got out of the SUV, released her dog and helped Violet unlatch the infant car seat.

They walked inside together, entering a foyer that opened into a hearth room. A fireplace was central to the design, old river stones gleaming in dimmed chandelier light.

"Your bedroom is the first one to the right upstairs. I'm going to get a fire started. You go make yourself and your daughter comfortable. Doesn't look like you brought anything with you?"

"I had a suitcase in Gabe's car," she responded.

"He'll be here shortly. So you'll have all of it then. In the meantime, we were able to get a crib and some baby stuff. It's all in the room."

"That was fast."

"We have been chasing Lance for seven months, so from our perspective things are going slowly." Poppy walked to the fireplace and tossed kindling in. The trooper seemed done talking, and Violet was tired, her head pounding, her body leaden.

She headed up the curved staircase and onto a wide landing that served as an office area. Her room was the only one with an open door. She walked in, her heart stuttering when she saw the white crib set up against one wall.

Whoever had purchased it had also bought a changing table.

There was a rocking chair in the corner with a few throw pillows tossed on the wooden seat. A twin bed stood against another wall. Two doors flanked a tall dresser. One led to a bathroom. The other led to a closet.

Violet took Ava from the car seat and changed her, humming softly as the baby fussed. It had been a long day. It wasn't surprising that the newborn was disgruntled.

"It's almost time to eat," she said, wrapping Ava in a blanket she found in the changing table. There were packages of onesies, a few sleepers and bibs.

Someone had thought of everything, and that kindness made Violet's eyes well with tears.

"We are going to repay all of them, sweetheart," she

murmured as she sat in the rocking chair and began to nurse.

The house was quiet. Nothing but the soft sound of sleet hitting the roof drifted into the room. Heat poured from a vent in the floor, warming Violet's cold toes.

*This* was what she had imagined the beginning of motherhood would be like.

Peaceful.

Secure.

Filled with warmth and love.

*Please, God, help me provide those things for my daughter*, she prayed, wishing she had the Bible she'd packed.

She was too tired to read, but it would be nice to hold it, to feel the leather cover worn smooth from her mother's hands. To know how often her parents had read it together, praying over each other and over her.

Violet had wanted that for her daughter.

She had been willing to compromise, to go through with a wedding that had begun to feel like a mistake in order to give her a family, but that had been a foolish mistake. Even if she had married Lance, it never would have worked out. He wasn't the kind of man Gabe was. He didn't have the same set of values.

Gabe.

She couldn't stop thinking about him.

He had been there for her when no one else could be. She would never forget that, and she would never forget him, or the way she felt when she looked into his eyes. Ava finished eating, and she patted her back gently, rocking to a tune playing in her head. Some old song her parents used to dance to.

She missed them. Missed the life they'd had. But she could create something special for Ava. She could make it a good life. Even without family connections.

Stormy barked, the scrabble of her feet on hardwood floor drifting into the room. No panic, though. No shouted warnings from Poppy. Just the quiet murmur of voices that let Violet know more troopers had arrived.

Had Gabe?

Her heart skipped a beat at the notion of seeing his handsome face again. Despite everything, she wanted to gaze into his kind blue eyes. Hear his deep, comforting voice. Because when she was in his presence, she felt safe. Cared for. A little less alone. And beyond that, she was worried about him, terrified that he would have a fatal run-in with Lance. He and Bear weren't the targets, but Lance had shown that he would kill anyone who got in the way of what he wanted.

He wanted the money.

Two million dollars that he probably would have transferred to a personal account and left town with, if she had given him the opportunity.

If she gave it to him now, would he leave town?

Leave *her* alone?

Let her raise Ava in peace?

She couldn't predict what he would do, but if she had a phone, she could access her accounts and let him have what he wanted. Anything to see an end to this nightmare.

She crossed the room and put Ava in the crib.

A real mattress. Real sheets.

Those things seemed so precious now.

"Sleep well, sweet one," she whispered, kissing the baby's cheek. Then she turned on a bedside lamp, turned off the overhead light and walked out of the room.

The office area was set up with a desk and a computer. She pulled out the chair and took a seat.

"Planning to do some work?"

She whirled around, met Gabe's eyes.

His hair was wet from melting sleet, his jaw shadowed by the beginning of a beard. He had her suitcase in one hand and Bear's lead in the other, and he looked better than any man who had been out in the elements for a couple hours should.

"I was hoping to use the computer," she said, trying to ignore the way her pulse jumped and her stomach flipped when she looked into his eyes.

"For?"

"Online banking," she admitted.

"The cash you brought isn't enough?" He frowned.

"I was thinking about transferring money to the account I opened with Lance."

"Why?" His expression was cold, hard and unreadable. Whatever he thought about her idea, he was keeping to himself until he had more information.

"Because it's what he wants. It's all he wants. He can take it and go to Bangkok, or wherever else he might like to live."

"He's a criminal, Violet. He'll be a fugitive. You'll be aiding and abetting."

She hadn't thought about that.

Sighing, she glanced at the room where Ava was sleeping.

So many people had already been hurt. Two people had died. Ariel had nearly lost her life. All over money.

"How long would I be in jail?" she asked.

"You aren't serious?" He scowled, putting the suitcase down and motioning for Bear to sit.

"I can't risk anyone else being hurt, Gabe. Not if I can stop it."

"Violet, you *can't* stop it. That's what I need you to understand." He crouched in front of her, holding both her hands, his palms warm against her cold skin. "He'll take the money, and he'll still come after you. If not because he wants revenge, then because he thinks he can get more financial reward."

"I won't give him more," she argued. "Just the amount he thought he was going to have."

But deep down she knew she wasn't being rational. Desperation and fatigue weren't a good combination. "I can see that you know I'm right," he said, staring into her eyes, studying her face, looking at her the way no one ever had. As if he wanted to know everything. All the easy things and the hard ones.

"Maybe." She shifted her gaze, uncomfortable with how much he could see. How easily the truth was reflected in her face and eyes.

"I have something for you, but I don't want to give it to you if you're going to use it to transfer the money into that account."

"What?" she asked, looking into his eyes again.

Her breath caught. Her thoughts fled.

He was close enough that she could see the fine lines near the corners of his eyes, a small scar just below his left ear. Specks of brown in his dark blue eyes.

"Your phone. We'd collected it as evidence. Eli, our tech guy, got it working and put in a new SIM card to make certain Lance couldn't track it. We don't need it any longer, and I got permission to return it to you. I thought you could call your friends and employees. Let them know that you're okay." He took it from his pocket and set it in her hand.

"You're not going to make me vow not to transfer the funds before you let me have it?" she asked, deeply touched by the gesture.

"I trust you to make the best decision, Violet. You're an intelligent and savvy woman. You know what's best."

He was right.

She did.

As much as she hated to admit it.

And no matter what it cost her, she knew she couldn't give Lance what he wanted to accomplish her goals.

"Thank you," she said, leaning forward and kissing his cheek.

A quick gesture of friendship that she had exchanged with dozens of people over the years.

Only he wasn't other people.

Heat spread across her cheeks, and she jumped up.

Too quickly.

The world spun. The phone dropped from her hand. Gabe said something she couldn't quite hear.

And then she was falling, body numb, unable to fight whatever was pulling her down.

* * *

Gabe caught Violet before she hit the floor, scooping her into his arms and shouting for Poppy before carrying her into her room.

A single lamp glowed on a small table near the bed. He laid Violet on top of the blanket.

"Violet? Can you hear me?" he said, his pulse racing, adrenaline rushing through him as he touched the pulse-point in her neck.

Poppy rushed into the room, her eyes wide with surprise and worry.

"What happened?" she asked.

"She passed out."

"She's a new mom. That could mean a lot of different things. We need to call an ambulance and get her to the hospital."

"No. I'm fine," Violet murmured, opening her eyes and struggling up onto her elbows. "I don't need to go to the hospital."

"You passed out. You *aren't* fine," Gabe growled, relieved that she'd regained consciousness but also incredibly frustrated that he couldn't do more for her. That he couldn't snap his fingers and make her world right. That he couldn't change what had happened and give her back her life.

She had been so thankful for the phone. Legitimately grateful in such a profound way that his heart had ached for her. Seven months with no contact with friends, family and coworkers was a long time. Being pregnant, living out in the wilderness, cut off from everyone and everything? Not because you wanted to? Because you were forced to?

That wasn't something he would wish on any woman.

"I just need to eat, I think. It's been a while, and nursing Ava takes a lot of calories." She sat up, crossing her legs, her skin several shades too pale.

"Did you feed her?" he asked.

"Yes. She's changed, fed and down for a few hours."

"You need to take as good care of yourself as you do of her," he said, helping her out of her coat and hanging it from a hook near the bedroom door. She was still in her boots. Still wearing several layers. She hadn't eaten. Probably hadn't had anything to drink.

"I'm going to make some soup," Poppy offered. "It's canned, but it'll be hot. How about a grilled cheese, too?"

"Soup is fine," Violet said. "But I can make it myself."

"No," Gabe said.

Both women frowned.

"Do either of you really think it's a good idea for her to go up and down the stairs when she just passed out?" he asked, knowing he sounded abrupt and not caring.

He was worried.

Violet was too thin, too pale and too exhausted. She'd fought hard to survive a situation that many people would have found untenable, and it showed.

"He has a point, Violet," Poppy said. "Just relax for a few minutes. I'll be right back with the food."

She hurried away.

Violet was still frowning.

"Should I apologize?" he asked.

"For?"

"Telling you what you can and can't do. Most people aren't thrilled about that."

"I wasn't thinking about that," she admitted, taking off her boots and setting them beside the bed.

"What were you thinking about?"

"How strange it is to be back in a world where it just takes a couple of minutes to make soup. Cooking at the Seavers' took time. We had to get the fire going and bring everything up to temperature."

He lifted a brow. "No propane stove?"

"They had one but didn't like to use it. Propane wasn't sustainable. They couldn't go out into the woods and find it. They had to go to town to buy it. They liked to limit trips to once every couple of months. When I lived there, I'm sure they went more. They were worried about me having enough to eat." She took off the sling she'd carried Ava in, stripped off a thick flannel shirt. Beneath it, she wore a silky, long-sleeved shirt that clung to her slender arms and narrow rib cage.

"Eli has said that the Seavers were always kind to him."

"They were probably kind to everyone before they went off the grid. In all the months I lived with them, I never heard any of them say a mean word about anyone. Maybe that's why they left civilization behind. Maybe they were tired of not getting back what they put out into the world."

"Is that how you feel?" he asked.

She shook her head. "Lance is an exception to all the rules my parents taught me. Most of the people in my life are genuine and warm. They care about me. Not just what I have to offer."

"I'm glad your experience hasn't made you cynical."

"It's made me *cautious*. I certainly don't intend to fall for another handsome face and charming smile. Ava and I will be fine on our own."

"You don't want her to have a father?" he asked, curious to hear her answer. She had what his mother hadn't—financial security and the support of a community of friends.

She hesitated, glancing at the crib. "I want her to have a life filled with love, security, faith and hope. I had two parents, and that was wonderful, but I don't think she'll be ruined forever if she doesn't have a father figure in her life. I hope." She bit her lower lip, a frown line appearing between her brows.

Obviously, she was worried.

No parent wanted to think they were shortchanging their child.

"She'll be fine," he assured her.

"I hope you're right."

"I turned out fine, and my father was never in my life. I didn't have a mother after the age of seven. That's when she passed away and I was placed in foster care."

She met his eyes, and he could see the compassion in her eyes, the sorrow for his losses. "I'm sorry, Gabe. I can't imagine how tough that must have been for you."

"It was fine. I learned to take care of myself at a young age. It's served me well, and now I do a lot of work with kids in the community who don't have fathers in their lives." He smiled, not wanting her to think he dwelled in the past or mourned what he'd hadn't had.

"Do you want children of your own one day?"

He almost said no, but he glanced at Ava, sleeping in the crib, her cheeks pink, her downy hair curling around her tiny ears.

"A few weeks ago, I might have said no, but Ava has won me over. She's a sweet baby. I guess I'll see what God does and not rule anything out."

"I never thought I wanted a dog," she replied with a smile. "But then I met Bear."

"Seems we both may have changed our minds about a few things," he said, tucking a strand of her hair behind her ear. "Who knows what we could change our minds about next?"

"I'm not going to change my mind about enjoying the trappings of civilized life," she said with a quiet laugh. "I like having a bed and a real floor and windows."

"Me, too, but I thought I liked being a loner. Doing the bachelor thing, just me and Bear, but maybe I'm changing my mind about that, too. It's not a bad thing having companionship."

"It depends on who the companion is and what he or she wants from you."

"Sometimes, a companion wants nothing except your company." He touched her cheek, his hand lingering on smooth warm flesh before dropping to her shoulder. He could imagine a future with her and Ava in it, and if he hadn't been afraid of scaring her away, he'd have told her that.

She studied his face, looking for whatever truth she thought she'd find there. "My father always said it was good to be open-minded, to not close yourself off to possibilities and to allow yourself to go wherever God leads."

"That's excellent advice."

"It is. Maybe when this is all over, we should both follow it."

She might have responded to that. She looked like she was going to, but the door opened.

"Soup's ready," Poppy said, stepping into the room with a tray. Her gaze landed on Gabe's hand, still sitting on Violet's shoulder.

She smirked but didn't comment.

"I brought you crackers and cheese, too. Also some fruit. You need to nourish yourself if you're going to nourish your baby."

"Thank you," Violet said, taking the tray and setting it on the bedside table. "I appreciate it."

"The patrol officers are here, Gabe. You planning on going to the motel with the K-9 team? We're hoping to track Lance from the room, maybe figure out where else he might be holing up."

"Yes, I'm coming." He called to Bear, letting his hand drop away from Violet.

He didn't want to leave her or Ava. That was the sharpest thought in his mind. He wanted to stay with them, make certain they had what they needed and were well guarded. But they'd never be safe until Lance was apprehended.

He'd run from Violet's home, gotten in a car and escaped again, but he couldn't escape forever. Eventually he'd be caught.

Gabe would do everything in his power to make sure that happened.

# ELEVEN

Nearly two weeks after moving into the safe house, Violet was finally adjusting to life back in the civilized world.

Not that there had been a whole lot of adjusting to do. Living in the cabin was as easy as living in the bunker had been difficult.

Hot showers every day.

Hot meals any time.

Lights.

Heat.

Music, if she wanted it.

Violet had found a piano in an alcove off the hearth room, and she played nearly every day. Gabe had brought her sheet music and a hymnal from his church.

In the evenings, he'd hold Ava while Violet played through some of her favorites.

Light streamed through the windows, warming the hardwood floors, and the newborn had plenty of time to lie on the blankets on the floor or sit in the baby swing one of the K-9 officers had brought.

It was a good place to be. But Violet still longed for home.

Each day, when Gabe returned from work, she asked if they were any closer to finding Lance. His response was always the same—they were working on it.

Lance had disappeared.

The same way he had after he and Jared were questioned by the police. He hadn't made an appearance since he'd gone after her at her house. There'd been no sightings and no leads.

Some of the K-9 officers had questioned whether he was still alive.

Violet thought he was. His sense of self-importance and self-preservation were too strong for him to have taken many risks.

"It's going to be okay, love," she murmured against Ava's hair. Despite eating well, she was still tiny, and Violet was beginning to worry that she wasn't thriving. She had a well-baby checkup scheduled for the following day but had been hesitating to bring it up to the police.

It was a big deal to take her out of her hiding place. If she left, she risked Lance finding her again. But if Ava wasn't healthy, that was another risk.

One Violet wasn't willing to take.

She paced her bedroom, listening to the muted voices of the patrol officers who were stationed at the house during the day.

At night, Gabe and one of the other K-9 officers took turns patrolling the area with their dogs. She had gotten used to having them around. But there was something *more* with Gabe.

Violet wasn't just used to him. She enjoyed his company. Looked forward to his return. And she made certain she was awake in the morning to say goodbye when he left for the day.

He had become part of her life.

Someone whom she counted on for advice, for conversation, for laughter. She hadn't been allowed to see Ariel. She'd called her friends and texted them, but she couldn't sit face-to-face, looking them in the eyes.

Gabe had filled the gap, his strength, kindness and faith drawing her in.

She grabbed a fresh diaper and changed Ava, frowning at the thinness of her arms and legs.

Weren't babies supposed to be chubby? Shouldn't they have rolls on their thighs and dimples on their knuckles? The thought that something was horribly wrong with Ava had settled deep in the pit of her stomach, and she couldn't stop thinking about it.

Her phone buzzed, and she glanced at the text, smiling when she realized it was Gabe.

Checking in. How are you and Sweet Girl? Need anything from the store? he asked.

I'm worried, she typed quickly, afraid if she didn't say it, she'd decide not to. She didn't want to endanger herself or anyone else, but she also didn't want to neglect her daughter's health and well-being.

About?

Ava. I'm afraid she isn't gaining weight.

Have you called the doctor?

She has an appointment with the midwife tomorrow at 9:00 a.m.

Okay. I'll get it set up set up with the team so we can get you both there safely. We'll talk when I get home.

*Home.* The place where love lived. Where people felt safe and happy and accepted. She'd had that growing up…then lost it when her parents died. She had thought she had found it again with Lance, but he had never made her feel like Gabe did. As if he had her back. No matter what. As if he wouldn't just fight for her, he'd fight *with* her.

Her phone rang, and she glanced at the number, hoping it was the Seavers. She's been calling every day, but the family had one cell phone that they only used when they left the bunker. Harrison had made her memorize the number the first time she'd gone to the medical clinic. She'd borrowed the clinic's phone to call him and let him know she was ready to return to the bunker.

Unfortunately, when the phone wasn't being used, it was turned off. Cole worried his family could be tracked, and their lives could be upended, if he kept it on.

She hadn't been able to reach them, but she still kept hoping they'd somehow reach out to her.

They had to be frantic with worry.

As much as she had longed to return to town, she couldn't deny how kind the Seavers had been or how accepted they'd made her feel. She didn't want to cause them trouble or stress, but the number on her caller ID wasn't theirs. It didn't belong to anyone she knew.

It could have been anyone wanting anything, but her skin crawled and she tensed, waiting to see if whoever it was left a message.

Lance wasn't patient.

He didn't believe in letting life happen.

He went out and got what he wanted.

Someone knocked on the bedroom door, and she jumped, her heart in her throat as she hurried to open it.

Trooper Hunter McCord stood in the hall, his husky beside him. K-9 officer Will Stryker was a few feet away, a small border collie at his side.

"Sorry to bother you," Hunter said. "I hope we didn't disturb the baby."

"She's sleeping," Violet responded, stepping into the hall. "What's going on?"

Had something happened to Gabe? Had he been injured after he'd texted? Had Lance somehow hurt him? The thought filled her with dread.

"We came on the behalf of one of our team members. Eli Partridge. He works the tech side of our investigations," Will explained.

"We've met."

"Did he mention his connection to Bettina Seaver?" Trooper Stryker asked.

"Yes. He wanted information about where the Seavers are living, but I can't give it to him."

"Bettina is critically ill," Trooper Stryker said.

As he spoke, his dog cocked his head and looked up

at him, totally focused and alert, ready for any command. "She may not survive the next few weeks, and her dying wish is to see her son and his family."

"I'm sorry about that. I have deep sympathy for Bettina, but—"

"Hear me out." He cut her off. "Harrison Seaver walked into the police department to ask if we had any information on you. He wouldn't give us much regarding how he knew you. He just said he had reason to be concerned. He'd already been to the local hospitals."

"I've been trying to contact them. I knew they'd be wondering what happened to me."

"We assured him that you're safe, and then we asked him to wait at the station while we met with you," Trooper Stryker told her. "We think that if you write a letter to Cole asking him to visit his mother, he might capitulate and agree."

"As I explained to Eli, I did discuss this with Cole. Harrison and I tried to get him to put aside whatever bad feelings he has, but he dug in his heels and refused."

"Did he say why he's upset with his mother?" Hunter interjected.

"No, and I'm not even sure it's just about his mom. He worries about going back to town and getting caught up in the kind of life he left behind. Cole eschewed all the trappings of modern life, and I wonder if he thinks that going back will remind him and his family of what they left behind."

"She's still his mother," Hunter said. "There has to be some part of him that wants to reach out before she dies."

"Maybe, but even if I thought I could convince him, there's no way he'd ever believe I wrote the letter. He'd believe you did it to try to draw him into to town. Cole can be little…conspiracy theorist. He doesn't trust anyone he doesn't know."

Trooper Stryker frowned. "What if you gave the letter to Harrison? Would Cole believe it then?"

"Probably," Violet said. Cole trusted the people who were close to him. Everyone else was subject to suspicion.

"Can we do it?" he asked, shifting his gaze to Hunter.

"We can do it. I'm just trying to decide if it's a good move with Lance still at large. Let's discuss it with the rest of the team," Hunter suggested. "Do you mind waiting here for a few minutes?" he asked Violet.

"Not at all," she replied, wondering where he thought she would go. There were police stationed inside and outside the house. Every time she even looked at an exterior door, one appeared.

"We'll be back in a moment."

The men walked downstairs, and she returned to her room.

Ava was still sleeping, her chest rising and falling gently.

She seemed more comfortable and content since they'd left the bunker. If only she would start gaining weight, Violet could stop worrying.

She touched her daughter's cheek, imagining what their relationship would be like in the future. She couldn't fathom a rift so wide and deep they never spoke, never visited, never spent time together. Just the thought was enough to nearly break her heart.

Violet walked back into the hall.

She could hear voices and the quiet patter of dog feet on the floor. She still didn't think writing a letter would change Cole's mind, but she had to try.

She opened the desk drawer, found a piece of paper and pen, then sat down and started to write.

The afternoon sky was deep azure, sprinkled with white clouds, the sun bright and warm as Gabe returned to the safe house. The log structure was tucked neatly among tall pine trees, mountains looming behind it. It was a picturesque location, far from the main road and hidden from view. A nice place to stay, but he knew Violet was getting restless. She wanted to return to her childhood home and her life.

He could understand that, but his goal was to make sure she and Ava remained safe. In his opinion, that meant staying hidden here until Lance was apprehended.

No excursions into town except for emergencies.

Ava's doctor's appointment was an emergency.

Bringing a letter to Harrison Seaver at the police station was not. The team had deemed it low risk. Lance hadn't made an appearance in two weeks. No sightings. No leads. As far as anyone knew, he'd left town.

Maybe he had.

Maybe murdering his best friend in front of a police officer had made him flee Alaska.

Gabe doubted it.

A guy who had stuck around for seven months wasn't going to change his MO. He'd continue to hunt his prey, lying low until he sighted her again.

Bringing Violet into town gave him that opportunity, and that was something Gabe wasn't comfortable with. He'd made his misgivings known, but the team had everything in place to keep her safe. Four K-9 team members would escort her to and from the precinct. Several patrol officers would stay with Ava.

The dirt road leading to the safe house was three miles long and stretched through private property. Ava was safe with at the house with patrol officers. No one but the team and patrol officers should be on it. If Lance spotted Violet in Anchorage and attempted to follow her back to the safe house, he'd be seen, and he'd be stopped.

But Gabe was still concerned.

He had gotten close to Violet during the weeks he'd been staying at the safe house. He'd watched her with Ava, listened to her play piano and hum old hymns, heard stories about her childhood and her parents. They'd spent late nights chatting about life, about faith and about all the things that they each valued.

Surprisingly, the two of them had more in common than he would ever have believed possible.

He and Violet both valued family and friendship, hard work and integrity. They enjoyed being home but also enjoyed the outdoors. No bars. No late-night outings. None of the things so many people their age seemed to gravitate toward.

Additionally, they both were invested in the community.

Violet had mentioned helping to expand the medical clinic where she had gotten pre-and postnatal care. She had said she had the means and the business acumen, and he had no doubt she'd accomplish anything she set her mind to.

He admired that.

He admired *her*, his feelings deeper and stronger than he should have been comfortable with. Even though he had lived the last few years as a die-hard bachelor, he didn't play the field. He wasn't that kind of guy. But after his engagement ended, he'd gone out with a few women over the years, enjoying their company but never allowing the relationship to go deeper than surface connections.

He was past that point with Violet.

They had bonded their first night together, when they'd sat out the storm, waiting and wondering if Lance would show up.

That bond had continued to grow, and he couldn't imagine a future where they weren't friends, where they didn't spend evenings in front of a roaring fire, taking turns rocking Ava while they talked...

Gabe sighed. He had a job to do and he'd better get on with it. He got out of the SUV, opening the back hatch and offering Bear a bowl of water. There was no sense getting him out. They'd be leaving as soon as Violet was ready.

"Gabe!" Hunter called, stepping out the front door and hurrying toward him. "We've got everything in place at the precinct. Violet has finished writing the letter, and Harrison Seaver had agreed to carry it to Cole. We should be leaving shortly."

"You know my feelings about this," he said, scratching Bear behind the ears as the dog lapped up the last of the water.

"I understand your misgivings, but we've thought this through, and I've run it by the colonel. The only way Cole is going to believe that letter is from Violet is if someone he trusts assures him that it is. Harrison can let him know she delivered the letter under no duress. The colonel agrees this is low risk, and we're not putting Violet or Harrison in danger. The likelihood Lance is hanging out near the police station is minuscule."

"I agree, but I'm still not comfortable with taking Violet out when it's not necessary. Ava has an appointment at the medical clinic tomorrow, and we're going to have to bring them to town for that. Why not ask Harrison to meet us there tomorrow?"

"There's snow in the forecast for the morning, and he's coming on foot from somewhere in the park. He may not make it. Is there any way Violet can get the baby in this afternoon? We can bring Harrison to the clinic and have her hand him the letter there."

"I can ask," Gabe said. He would still rather not bring Violet into town at all, but she was worried about Ava's growth and development, and a medical checkup couldn't be put off.

He texted her, asking if the medical clinic could see Ava a day early. Minutes later, she responded with an affirmative. She'd get the baby ready and be out shortly.

"She can bring her daughter today," he said, tucking his phone into his pocket and meeting Hunter's eyes. "I know the team is hopeful that Lance has moved on and left the area, but hopes don't keep people safe. We're going to need a K-9 team in front of the clinic and one in back. Do we have some patrol officers who can run cars past the address?"

"I'll get it set up. I know you're worried, Gabe, but the team is strong and capable. Violet and Ava will be fine."

"I know," he agreed.

He planned to make certain of it.

# TWELVE

Violet was terrified, her stomach a jumble of knots that she couldn't dispel. She tried to focus on the scenery—the gorgeous mountain views and the pristine sky. It was a beautiful fall day, the air crisp without being too cold. In a few weeks, the ground would be coated with snow, but for now there was still a carpet of green beneath a layer of fall leaves.

She loved Anchorage in every season. Snow-peaked mountains, rain-shrouded summer, spring flowers and colorful fall days. She wanted to raise Ava with the same appreciation, introducing her to the outdoor activities that she'd spent her childhood involved in.

But first, they had to get through this tumultuous season.

"You okay?" Gabe asked as he pulled onto the main road that led into Anchorage.

"Just a little nervous."

"A *little*? You're digging holes in your palms." He touched her hand, smoothing his palm over her fisted knuckles.

"Okay. I'm a lot nervous," she admitted, opening her hand and letting the blood flow back into her fingers.

"That's understandable. To be honest, I wasn't excited about bringing you to town this afternoon. My priority is your and Ava's safety. I have all kinds of sympathy for Bettina Seaver, but I don't want to risk your life to try to convince a man to do something he has already refused to be part of." He wove his fingers through hers, holding her hand as he navigated the two-lane highway.

She didn't tug away or question the warmth that spread through her at his touch. "Is that why you asked if I could bring Ava to the clinic today?"

"Yes. Getting her checked out is a priority. If we can do both things today, we won't have to take risks tomorrow."

"I hope she's okay." She glanced at Ava, tucked into an infant car seat and sleeping soundly. "I had most of my prenatal care, but not all of it. If I harmed her by—"

"Violet, you did everything you could for her. You're still doing everything you can. If there's something wrong, and I don't think there is, it has nothing to do with anything you have or haven't done." He gave her hand a gentle squeeze and offered a quick smile.

Her heart leaped in response, her body humming with sweet contentment and a gentle longing for things she had stopped believing she could have. Love, companionship, friendship and passion had been the cornerstones of her parents' relationship. She had been looking for those things when she'd met Lance. He had allowed her to think she'd found them.

Now that she'd spent time with Gabe, she understood that what he'd offered had been a pale facsimile of the real deal. Lance's friendship had been one-sided, his passion selfish and his love and companionship offered with strings attached.

Gabe asked for nothing. Demanded nothing. Over and over again, he had proven he cared selflessly.

She couldn't help being smitten by that.

By *him*.

"I wish I'd met you sooner," she blurted, the words slipping out before she realized she was going to say them. "I'm sorry. I shouldn't have said that," she added quickly, embarrassed for herself, for the neediness she felt when she was with Gabe.

She'd always prided herself on her independence.

But there was a piece of her heart that did need the handsome trooper—his quiet strength, his confidence, his easy companionship. She craved that the way she craved sunshine after a long Alaska winter.

"Why?" he asked quietly, still holding her hand.

Anchorage was in front of them, the city sprawling out across the landscape. They'd be at the medical clinic soon. Violet had been told how things would go down—she'd be escorted in by Gabe. There would be patrol officers on the street, K-9 officers outside. Lance wasn't going to get a chance to harm her or the baby. Not if the state police had anything to say about it.

Yet she was still afraid.

"Why am I sorry I said it?" she asked, her stomach flip-flopping as they drove past a restaurant where she and Lance had once eaten.

"Yeah. Why do you wish you'd met me sooner?"

"If I had, none of this would have happened. Lance never would have been part of my life. Two people wouldn't be dead. Ariel wouldn't have been hurt."

"You wouldn't have Ava," he pointed out.

She nodded. "I wouldn't trade her for a do-over, but… I feel tainted by Lance. I didn't realize how much of myself I'd given away until after I spent time with the Seavers."

"You didn't give it away. You put it on a shelf for a while. Now you've taken it down again. Which is good. I like the person you are. Your integrity. Your kindness. Your enthusiasm for the community and the people in it. Your strength." He lifted her hand and kissed her knuckles, the gesture sweet and surprising.

"If I were strong, Lance never would have taken advantage of me."

"Cut yourself some slack. Your parents hadn't been gone long. You were vulnerable, and like any predator, Lance can sense that in people." His gaze shifted to the rearview mirror as they entered downtown Anchorage.

Four K-9 vehicles were behind them, each containing a trooper and a dog, ready and willing to do whatever it took to keep Violet and Ava safe.

She couldn't put into words how that made her feel. That they would risk so much for a stranger touched her in a way not many things had.

She would find a way to thank them.

When this was over, she'd donate to the K-9 development program, but she wanted to do something more personal, too.

"Thanksgiving is coming," she said, her heart in her throat as Gabe turned onto the road that led to the clinic.

"Just a couple weeks away," he agreed.

"I was thinking, if Lance is behind bars by then, we could have a Thanksgiving celebration for your team. I've got plenty of room at my house to host everyone."

"That sounds nice," he said, pulling up in front of the clinic and parking the SUV. "But we're talking a lot of dogs and a lot of people. Your house may never be the same."

"I don't want it to be," she replied. "I want my first memories after this is over to be of people enjoying the home my parents built, filling it up with laughter and conversation and love."

He nodded, looking into her eyes, studying her face, his expression soft. "You're a special person, Violet. Someone I'm glad to know."

"I'm glad to know you, too," she said.

"Good." He smiled, leaning close, his lips brushing hers. A surprise, but not. They had been moving toward each other from the moment they'd met.

The tenderness of the kiss, the sweetness of the gesture, made her heart ache.

If she had to put a name to it, she'd have called it love. But was she truly ready to take a leap of faith with this man after everything she'd been through?

"Ready?" he asked, squeezing her hand as he broke away.

"As I'll ever be," she responded.

"Bear and I are going to escort you inside. Harrison is already there. Once he has the letter, he's taking off and you'll go back for Ava's appointment. I'll be in the waiting area. Trooper West and his dog, Grace, are stationed by the back door. If things go south, one of us will get you out of there."

"Okay," she said, her voice shaky, her hands trembling as she unhooked Ava's car seat.

"It's going to be okay, Violet," Gabe said.

She hoped he was right.

Prayed he was.

Because more than anything, she wanted this to be over.

She wanted to go home so she could get back to the world she'd left behind. And she wanted the Thanksgiving celebration she'd described, with all the K-9 team members and their dogs filling the empty house.

*Just four walls and a roof if you don't have love to fill it.*

That had been her parents' motto and the reason they'd opened their home so frequently. Neither had wanted to squander the blessings that God had poured out on them. They'd wanted to share with those they cared about, and they'd often hosted parties for hospital staff and for business associates.

She hadn't followed in their footsteps.

After they died, she'd moved back into the house, but she hadn't filled it the way they had. She hadn't brought in friends and coworkers or practiced the hospitality her parents had so clearly demonstrated.

Violet wanted to change that.

Because deep down, she desperately wanted to have

a second chance at creating something wonderful out of the tragedy she'd suffered.

"Stay here until I open your door," Gabe said as he got out of the SUV.

She waited while he freed Bear.

There were a few people around. Walking on the sidewalk or getting into cars. None looked like Lance, but that didn't mean he wasn't nearby.

Her heart was racing frantically when Gabe opened the door.

He lifted the infant seat and stepped back, his gaze on the street and the surrounding areas. Bear seemed relaxed, his tongue lolling out, his tail high. If there was trouble nearby, he didn't sense it. Across the street, a patrol car pulled into a parking lot, the marked vehicle idling there. Would Lance dare make an appearance with so many police nearby? She prayed not.

Gabe hurried her into the clinic. The waiting room was nearly empty. Just two people sitting in chairs, staring at the television mounted to the wall.

Two others stood near the front windows. One of them was Trooper Maya Rodriguez and her dog, Sarge. Beside the female K-9 officer was a tall, lanky teenager who was as familiar as sunshine and a sight for sore eyes.

"Harrison!" Violet cried, running to greet the young man who had become as close to her as a brother. "I'm so sorry that I worried you and your family. I tried to call, but you know how hard it is to get through."

"I do, and it's okay," he said, giving her an awkward

hug. "The police explained what happened. I'm glad you and Ava are okay."

"How are your parents?" she asked as Gabe stepped up beside her. His presence was comforting. Just knowing he was there made her feel as if everything would work out. He was an anchor in the storm, a steadiness she desperately needed.

"The same. Although, now that you're gone, Mom seems a little…sad. I guess that's the right word. With you there, she wasn't alone when Dad and I went hunting and fishing. Without you, I guess she's realized how lonely it can get out there."

"I'm sorry, hon."

"For what? You didn't cause it. Our lifestyle did. To be honest, I feel sorry for her, but I'm also hoping it might be the catalyst that brings us back to town. You know how Dad is. He's stubborn, but he'll do anything to make her happy." He grinned.

"I know, but if they stay out there, remember what I said—my doors are always open. If you want to attend college, you'll have a place to stay."

"Thanks, Violet. I'm planning to take you up on that. I went to the library earlier today and filled out a few college applications."

"Good for you! You're going to keep me updated on your progress, right?"

"You know it." He glanced out the window. "It's getting late. I'm going to need to start back now if I'm going to be back before dark…"

"Right. This is for your dad. I included my cell phone number so he can get in touch with me if he wants to discuss things." Violet pulled out the letter she'd written. She'd poured out her heart to Cole, explaining how heartbroken she'd be if she were in his mother's position. She could only hope that inspired him to change his mind.

"I'll pass it on to him. Hopefully he'll decide to visit Gram. I haven't seen her since I was a baby, and I don't want to miss out on getting to know her." He folded the letter and zipped it into his pocket.

"Be careful on your way home," she said, knowing there was no need to caution him. He was aware of the dangers, and he knew how to avoid them.

True to his nature, he nodded politely. "You know I will. I'll try to call you the next time I'm in town."

He leaned down to kiss Ava on the cheek.

"Tell your parents I said hello and thank you."

"I will." He waved and walked out the door.

Confident for his age.

Self-assured.

She wanted so much for him and for his family.

The door to the treatment area opened, and a nurse peered into the waiting room. "Vivian and Annie," she called, using the phony names Violet had provided.

"Right here." Violet grabbed the car seat carrier and met Gabe's eyes. "This shouldn't be long."

"I'll be out here when you finish. If anything goes wrong, stay in the exam room and wait for me to come for you."

Violet didn't ask what could go wrong. She'd seen what Lance was capable of. He knew how to set fires, to track through snow, to find her when she didn't think she could be found.

"I will," she said, praying it wouldn't come to that.

She wanted the appointment to go smoothly, and she wanted everyone to get back to the safe house without incident or injury.

The nurse led her to an exam room at the end of the hall, the back exit just yards away. If she had to, Violet could take Ava out that way. There were police patrolling the streets, K-9 officers inside and outside.

She had to believe that everything was going to be okay.

Lifting Ava from the carrier, she removed her coat and knit cap. She'd just set her back in the carrier when the door flew open.

The nurse was there, pale faced and terrified, a man beside her. Dark hair. Thick glasses. A beard.

Holding a gun.

It took her a second too long to realize whom she was looking at.

*Lance!*

"Do not make a sound, or I will shoot this woman and kill your baby before I kill you," he growled, his eyes flashing with hatred.

"She's your baby, too," she said, her voice shaking with fear.

"Do you think I care? I didn't want a baby. That's why you hid the pregnancy from me. You're a liar and a thief!"

He was dressed in scrubs, a stethoscope around his

neck, and she could only imagine that he'd faked his credentials and taken a job working for the clinic.

He had known she would bring Ava there for check-ups, and he had made sure that he would have access to both of them.

"What do you want?" she asked, her voice raspy, her heart beating wildly.

He grinned. "Everything. You wouldn't give me the two million, so now you'll give me every dime. Grab the baby and let's go."

She wouldn't allow him to have Ava.

"She'll slow us down. And with all the police out-side—"

"Shut up!" He grabbed her arm, yanking her to his side and pressing the gun to her temple. "I make the decisions."

"She's right. A baby is going to slow you down and draw attention to you," the nurse said, her voice shaking as she stepped between Lance and the car seat. She was obviously trying to protect Ava, and Violet could have cried with gratitude.

Lance pointed the gun at the nurse's head and removed the safety.

She flinched, and he laughed.

"How about you stay out of our business?" He put the safety back on then turned back to Violet. "Fine, the baby can stay, but you and I are outta here. Come on, let's go."

He dragged Violet into the hall.

She wanted to break free and run, but she knew he'd kill her and anyone who tried to stop her if she did.

They were at the back door in seconds, outside in the bright sunlight.

She heard a dog growl, saw an officer lying near the street. Sean West. She recognized his blond hair and his beautiful Akita, Grace. She barked wildly, her lead caught underneath his prone body.

"What did you do?" she gasped.

"Just hit him over the head. He wasn't expecting a doctor to attack." Lance chuckled maniacally. "Now, stop worrying about him, and start worrying about yourself. Move!"

Violet thought Sean moved as they hurried past. She wanted to go to him, jerked sideways trying to help.

"Move it!" Lance snapped, dragging her across the road.

Sirens were blaring.

Another dog barked.

She glanced back, saw Bear and Gabe running out the back door of the clinic.

"Stop! Police!" Gabe shouted, but Lance had made it to the corner of the street, and he dragged her into a parking garage, shoving her toward a stairwell.

"Move faster or you're going to die right here," he snarled.

She bounded up the stairs, breathless with terror, grief-stricken over what had happened to Trooper West.

*Please, spare his life*, she prayed.

"This way!" Lance grabbed her ponytail, yanking her sideways toward the third floor of the lot.

A beat-up green pickup truck sat in a stream of sunlight near the exit ramp.

He shoved her toward it, and she fell, sprawling on her hands and knees and sliding across the concrete floor, her jeans ripping, her hands bloodied.

"Get up!" He dragged her to her feet, shoving her into the now-open driver's side door of the truck. She climbed into the seat, desperate to find a way out.

He had the gun pointed at her head, his gaze cold and hard. "Scoot over. I'll drive. Just like old times."

"What do you want, Lance?"

"I already told you, and it isn't about what I want. It's about what I'm going to *have*. After all you've put me through these last few months, you owe me."

Sirens blared, strobe lights flashing as a patrol car raced into the parking garage.

Lance swore, opening the door and dragging her back out of the car. "See this!" he shrieked. "See the trouble you've caused! I had it all planned out, and you ruined everything!"

She didn't speak, she didn't want to waste her breath or risk riling him up more.

"We need another exit. We can't take those stairs," he muttered, rushing toward the other stairwell, the gun pressed to her side as he forced her along.

They headed up another four levels.

Dogs were barking below, the sound echoing hollowly through the structure.

Was Gabe there? Following Bear through the maze of vehicles? Her heart jumped at the thought, her soul aching to see him, to have the comfort of knowing he was there.

She thought she'd known what love was, and then

she'd met Gabe. He was everything she had ever wanted, every dream she'd ever had. That he had come into her life when she'd needed him most didn't surprise her. God had known exactly who and exactly when and exactly how. And He knew this moment. He was in control. She had to believe that.

They reached the top level, sunlight streaming down from the pristine sky. Mountain and water views. Snow-capped peaks.

A perfect day in Anchorage, and she didn't plan to die. Not when she had so much to live for.

She glanced around, searching for a weapon or an escape route. She was desperate to see Gabe but terrified of the danger he would face if he appeared. She needed to act before Lance had a chance to hurt anyone else.

"What are you doing?" Lance barked, shoving the gun against her cheek, his eyes wild.

"Looking for a way out," she replied honestly.

"The only way out is down. You want to go first?" he asked, pushing her backward against the exterior wall, her ponytail dangling into open air. A little more effort on his part and she'd be over the side, falling to the ground.

The second stairwell was to their left, a fire extinguisher attached to the wall nearby.

If she could reach it, she could use it.

"We can take the other stairs. The police are stupid. They'll expect you to be leaving in a vehicle. Their dogs are following us up, but they won't know we're heading back down." She tried to sound confident and helpful rather than desperate.

Lance scowled, easing back so that she was no longer hanging over the wall. "Don't try to fool me, Violet. I don't like it."

"I'm not doing anything except trying to get out of this alive. If you want my money, you can have it. We just have to get to a safe place so I can transfer everything."

"Right. Let's go." He yanked her away from the ledge, shoved her toward the stairwell.

She went. Eyes focused on the fire extinguisher, body numb with fear.

She could hear the dogs. They were getting closer. What would Lance do if they appeared? Would he shoot the dogs? Would he shoot her? Use her as a shield? He had been willing to kill his own child. He wouldn't hesitate to kill Violet.

She reached the stairwell. The fire extinguisher was right there! *Do it!* her mind shouted.

She pretended to stumble, her hands hitting cement, then feeling the cool metal of the canister.

"Hurry up!" Lance yelled, grabbing her arm.

She had the extinguisher in her hand, and praying for the strength she desperately needed, she swung around, slamming it into his face.

The gun went off, the shot pinging into the wall beside her.

A man shouted.

She didn't hear what he said.

Because she was running, sprinting down the stairs, taking them two and three at a time, Lance cursing viciously as he followed.

\* \* \*

"They're heading back down!" Brayden Ford shouted into the radio. He and his Newfoundland, Ella, had made it to the top floor of the parking garage just ahead of Gabe.

"Who fired the shot?" Hunter responded, his voice tight with tension. Sean had been hit over the head and knocked unconscious by Lance. He was up and moving, talking and coherent, but the team was still concerned for his welfare.

"The perp. Our victim hit him in the face with a fire extinguisher," Brayden answered. "They are in the stairwell."

"Let's go get them. I want to take this guy down and put him in jail where he belongs," Gabe said, adrenaline coursing through him as he passed the abandoned fire extinguisher.

There was blood on the cement stairs. Drops of it leading down. Had Violet been injured? Or had Lance?

Bear snuffled the air and shook out his fur, a habit he had when he was getting close to a scent source.

They reached the third floor at a dead run, and Gabe expected to continue down. Instead, Bear loped into the garage, Ella right beside him.

"What do you think?" Brayden asked, scanning the area.

"She made it down here and hid. He heard us coming and did the same."

There were dozens of cars lined up in rows. Plenty of places for the perp to hide.

"I don't know about you, but I don't want to risk my

dog. Ella's not trained for this, and this guy has already proven that he has no conscience," Brayden said grimly. "He'll shoot anyone or anything who gets in his way."

"I feel the same. Let's text this in. I don't know how close he is, and I don't want him to hear radio comms. We'll have the team stationed on level two of all stairwells. Helena and Luna on the way up. When they get here, we'll have the advantage. If he tries to get out the parking garage, he'll be caught."

But Gabe had a feeling he wouldn't try to escape. Not without Violet. He wanted her money, and he wanted revenge.

Both were powerful motivators.

"Lance! Police! Throw down your weapon and come out with your hands where we can see them!" he commanded, calling Bear back with a hand signal and putting him in a down-stay position.

He wouldn't move again until he was told.

No response from Lance, but Bear's head swiveled, his dark eyes focused on some cars near an exterior wall.

"I said come out!" Gabe repeated, motioning for Brayden to break to the left.

He'd head right.

Lance couldn't take them both out at once.

Bear growled, the warning making the hair on Gabe's arms stand on end. He dived for cover seconds before a bullet whizzed by.

Lance appeared to his right, gun raised and pointed.

Not at him.

At Bear.

Gabe raised his weapon, would have fired, but Violet darted out from behind a van, throwing herself at Lance and knocking him off his feet.

"Police! Surrender or I'll send in my dog!" Helena shouted as she raced out of the stairwell.

Luna was on a lead, snarling wildly.

The world was chaotic, everyone in motion. Violet struggling to break free. Lance dragging her to her feet, pressing a gun to head.

Everything suddenly went silent and still.

For a heartbeat no one moved. Even the dogs were quiet.

Sirens blared from below.

Feet pounded on cement stairs, but this part of the garage seemed held in a strange tableau, caught in a spell that prevented action. Three dogs and their handlers standing with guns drawn.

The perp fifty yards away, a gun pressed to Violet's temple.

The sound of traffic and pedestrians drifted in on the cold wind, a reminder that life was playing out all around them while they stood still, held hostage by the moment.

"Everyone, back off!" Lance snapped, blood pouring from his nose and dripping onto the floor.

Violet was pale but seemed uninjured, her eyes wide and filled with terror. Gabe wanted to reassure her. He wanted to tell her that everything was going to be okay. He wanted to tell her how much she meant to him, how deeply he cared for her and for Ava and how important they were in his life, but his focus had to be on getting the gun out of Lance's hand.

"I said back off!" Lance bellowed, his voice echoing off the cement walls. His eyes were wild, his free arm wrapped around Violet's upper body, locking her close to his chest.

Using her as a shield. Like the coward he was.

"Let's all give him some space," Helena suggested, shifting back a few feet.

Gabe and Brayden did the same. Let him relax and think he was winning. Cockiness would lead to mistakes. Once he made one, they'd have him.

"That's it," Lance muttered. "That's better. Just stay back and no one has to get hurt."

He dragged Violet back a few feet, moving toward the cement wall that opened out onto the street.

"Put the weapon down," Gabe said. "You know you can't get out of here."

"I can do whatever I want. Haven't I proven that already? You and your team have been looking for me for months, and you've never once gotten close to finding me. Ironic, since you've got those dogs out searching for missing people all the time." He laughed, the sound harsh and erratic.

"We have you now," Helena said. "How about you admit it and stop fighting?"

"Why would I want to do that?" He sneered. "I've always loved a good fight. I've always been really good at winning them."

He reached the wall, glanced down as if contemplating jumping.

The thought made Gabe's blood run cold.

If he went over, would he try to take Violet with him?

"Here's how things are going to work," Lance said. "I'm going to give you and your friends five minutes to clear my path out of here. Then I'll to take my lovely lady and we'll walk down the stairs and out onto the street. If any of your buddies or their dogs try to stop me, I'll shoot Violet and will kill every civilian I see."

He glanced at his watch.

"Tell you what. I'm a generous guy. I'll give you six minutes. Starting now."

He pressed the gun firmer into Violet's temple and smiled.

Lance wouldn't get what he wanted, but Gabe would allow him to think he was in charge.

He lifted his radio and called in the request for all officers to stand down.

# THIRTEEN

Lance loved to be in control.

Violet had realized that soon after meeting him, but it hadn't set off alarm bells. After all, her father had always been a take-charge kind of guy, and she hadn't seen that as a negative attribute.

However, Lance didn't just take charge. He forced people to do his bidding.

His import-export business had floundered because everyone he hired quit. The only good friend he had was Jared.

*Had been* Jared.

Most people couldn't abide his arrogant assumption that his way was the *only* way. Violet had made excuses for him, of course. Didn't every person in love do the same? She'd thought Lance needed time to mature, to grow into the role of CEO of his small company. So she'd tried to give him pointers and even lent him cash to help keep his business floating.

He had pretended to listen and acted like he'd appreciated the influx of money. Now she wondered if he had even used it for his business. Not that it mattered.

Because in the grand scheme of all the atrocities Lance had committed, that was drop in the bucket.

"I should have killed you the minute you transferred that money. You've caused me way too much trouble," he muttered as Gabe and two other K-9 officers took a few steps backs. He was arrogant and foolish enough to believe they were really going to let him leave.

Violet knew they wouldn't.

She had to get herself out of his arms and away from his gun. Once she did that, the police could do whatever was necessary to apprehend him. He dragged her back, the gun pressed so hard into her temple she thought the bone might crack.

"Four minutes," he crowed. "I hope they're gone. Violet wasn't planning to die today. Were you, honey?"

"Don't call me that," she spat, hating him for everything he had done.

Hating herself more for what she had allowed.

"Would you rather I call you cupcake or cutie pie? Didn't you love those nicknames when I gave them to you?"

"I hated them."

She'd specifically told him not to call her either. But rather than deterring him, he had made it a point to do so in front of colleagues and business associates.

Another red flag that she had ignored.

"Because you're a boring little bookworm who doesn't like fun things," he grumbled, the gun easing away from her temple. Just a fraction of an inch, but enough to give her hope that he might be losing focus.

"Lance, let her go and we'll clear your path out of

here," Gabe called out. "Otherwise we're sending the dogs after you."

"My dog," Helena Maddox added.

Her Norwegian elkhound growled, eyes laser-sharp focused on Lance.

"That wouldn't be a good idea," Lance responded.

She could feel the shift in him. Like the tide changing course. She'd seen it before. Good humor quickly replaced by rage. He would be in control one minute and out of control the next.

If that happened now, would he kill someone?

She met Gabe's eyes. She could see the calmness in his face, the focus.

"It's okay," he mouthed.

She wanted to believe him, but Lance was dragging her closer to the cement wall again. Three stories down to asphalt and cars. Pedestrians wandering along a sidewalk with no idea that a horrible drama was playing out above them.

*It's not okay*, she wanted to respond.

"Two minutes, folks, and I'm losing my patience. Is the path clear or not?" Lance shouted.

"I already told you what needs to happen. Release Violet. We'll clear your path to leave." Gabe looked into Violet's eyes, and she could see love there, shining out, asking her to believe that everything would be okay. She wanted to tell him that she did, that she trusted him, that she knew he would come through for her.

"Violet and I are leaving together or she's not leaving at all. We had plans. Big plans. Didn't we, baby doll?"

"I have a name," she replied. "How about you use it?"

"Right, your name. The one that attracted me to you. I was hoping you'd be more exciting. The only plus side to being with you was that you were easy to manipulate."

It was true.

She had been, but she was stronger now. Wiser. More capable of standing up for herself and the people she loved. And she knew the truth about love and what it felt like. Gabe had taught her that. She met his eyes again, tried to tell him without speaking just how much he meant to her.

"I already told you, I'll give you what I have. Just let me go. I have a baby to go home to," she said, forcing herself to beg, hoping to give Gabe and the K-9 team time to move in.

"You should have thought about that before you took what was mine out of the account."

She wanted to remind him that none of it was his. That he hadn't had a dime to contribute to their house fund, and that he had bought her wedding gift with money she'd provided.

She bit her tongue. She didn't want to poke the tiger. She just wanted to distract him.

"We had an agreement, and I broke it. I understand why you're upset."

"I'm not upset, you little fool. I'm furious. I had tickets to Bangkok and a property I planned to buy that has now been sold to someone else. You ruined everything." He jabbed her with the gun, but it fell farther away from her face as he pulled her to the farthest stairwell.

Gabe and the other troopers were following their progress, watching silently. Inching closer.

She'd seen the subtle movement. One step. Then another. Each of them closing the gap while Lance raged. The elkhound was still on its leash, teeth bared, fangs gleaming.

"Time is up. If the stairwell isn't clear, people die. And, just to prove I mean business, how about I give you a taste of what I'm capable of."

Violet felt his muscles tense and his gun arm shift.

He was planning to shoot. She had no time to shout a warning. He swung the gun toward Bear, but she couldn't let the dog be hurt. She grabbed Lance's arm, yanking it down as he fired. The shot went wild, and so did he.

Turning on her, he slammed the butt of the gun into her cheekbone. The skin split, blood pouring down her face, as he cursed and shoved her backward over the cement wall.

Bowed over, she fought to gain control. The street below was a kaleidoscope of dizzying colors. People shouted commands, but Lance was past hearing.

"Die," he growled, pointing the gun at her face.

Her hand was on his wrist, but she was half over the wall. Nearly falling to the street below.

She had no control.

No way to stop him.

A dog snarled, and Lance screamed, his arm dragged away by the K-9.

Violet scrambled away, blood still pouring from her face as she tried to separate herself from the fray.

The gun clattered onto the ground, skittering a few feet away.

"Off!" Helena commanded.

The dog immediately released its hold on Lance's arm.

"Get on the ground! Now!" Gabe yelled, his gun pointed straight at Lance's heart.

Lance obeyed. Going quietly. A surprise. And, with Lance, surprises were generally not good ones.

Violet was dizzy, off balance and weak. She sat on the ground, leaning against the wall.

A cold nose touched her hand, and she looked into Bear's gentle face. He nuzzled her hair, then settled down beside her.

She had never been a dog person, but Bear wasn't just a dog.

He was a friend, a buddy, a partner.

She touched his head, her hand resting on his velvety fur as Gabe leaned over Lance.

"You have any other weapons on you?" he asked.

"Would I be stupid enough to tell you if I did?" Lance spat.

Gabe frisked him, cuffed him and backed off.

His gaze shifted to Violet, and she could see the fear, anger and relief in his eyes. "Are you okay?"

"Yes. Thanks to you, Bear and the K-9 team." She wanted to throw herself into his arms and hold on until she stopped shaking.

"I've never been that terrified," he admitted, pulling her to her feet and tugging her into his arms. He felt like warmth and safety and home, and she wanted to stand there forever. "And I will never stop being thankful that you're okay."

"I will never stop being thankful for you," she responded.

He pulled back, looking into her face and smiling gently. "You're going to need a few stitches."

"A few stitches are a small price to pay for having him in custody and for putting an end to this nightmare. I'm ready to move on with my life, and I feel like I can finally begin building new dreams," she responded.

"I hope I'm in them," he said.

Her heart swelled. "How could you not be? You've given me a foundation of hope to build those dreams on"

"And, you've helped me believe that the things I dreamed of as a kid could actually be possible—home and family and all the blessings and challenges those bring. Come on. Let's get you to the hospital and get you stitched up. Then, I'll take you home. It's time to start living again."

"My home? Or the safe house?"

"Yours," he replied as Helena yanked Lance to his feet.

Cold air whipped over the wall, ruffling Violet's hair and chilling her skin.

"You people didn't seem to understand the rules of the game," Lance said, his voice monotone, his expression blank. "If I don't get out of here, she doesn't."

He broke free, barreling toward Violet, head down like a battering ram as he tried to throw them both over the wall and onto the street below.

Gabe took milliseconds to respond.

Bear was faster.

One moment he was on the ground. The next, he was launching himself at Lance. His 150-pound body hit like a ton of bricks, throwing Lance sideways and sending him sprawling. Lance was up again in moments, flying toward the wall, scrambling onto it.

"Don't do it!" Gabe commanded. "You still have a trial ahead of you. Plenty of time to prove your innocence."

"We all know I'm not innocent," he exclaimed, his eyes wild with frenetic energy. "And we all know why this all happened."

His gaze shifted to Violet as he teetered on the edge.

"It's your fault, Violet. All of it. The guide died because of you. Ariel was hurt because of you. Jared died because of you. If you had just done what I wanted, no one would have been hurt. I hope that haunts you. I hope you spend the rest of our life knowing you could have saved everyone if you'd just been less selfish." He howled the last part, sidling closer to the edge.

Brayden was feet away, moving in from the left.

"You have a point," Gabe said, trying to buy time. "It's possible there will be charges pressed against Violet. For her part in all this."

"There should be. She has just as much responsibility as—"

Brayden yanked him down, rolling him onto his stomach and placing a knee in the small of his back. "You can finish that thought later. Right now, I'm going to read you your rights," he said.

He did so quickly, then dragged Lance upright and marched him out of the garage.

"That dude is delusional," Helena said, putting Luna back on her lead and giving her a treat. "Do you think he'd have really jumped?"

"No," Gabe said. He wasn't certain, but he thought Lance's sense of self-preservation was too high for him to take his own life.

"Maybe he would have," Violet said quietly. "That would have been the final word, you know? His way of placing the blame without giving me or anyone else a chance to state our side of the story."

Helena shook her head. "I, for one, am glad he's off the streets. All these months of searching, and we finally have our man. It's a good day's work, Gabe, and Bear did awesome! Maybe we should train him for suspect apprehension." She grinned.

"I think he'll stick to snow detection, but if there's ever a need for someone to be knocked to the ground, Bear's your dog." He scratched the St. Bernard's head, smiling when his tail thumped happily.

"I'll keep that in mind," Helena said. "I'm heading down. Do you want an ambulance for that gash?" she asked Violet.

"No. I'll just go to urgent care for stitches."

"I'll take you," Gabe offered.

"As long as it's not going to be a bother."

"Never," he replied gruffly.

"Hmm. Interesting." Helena smiled. "I'll leave you two to work out the details of that, and then I'll see you back at headquarters, Gabe." She walked off, Luna by her side.

"I meant what I said," Gabe said, taking off his jacket and dropping it around Violet's shoulders. "Helping you is never a bother."

"That's really sweet, but I've given you more than

enough to do these past few weeks." A lump rose to her throat. "I'm sure you want to get back to a normal routine—"

"Is that what *you* want?" He took off his button-up shirt, folded it and pressed it against the wound in her cheek.

"I thought I did. When I was in the Seavers' bunker, all I could think about was getting back home. Getting back to the life I'd built for myself after my parents died. Without Lance, of course. I was looking forward to being single. Raising Ava on my own. Being a strong, independent woman. I didn't plan to rely on anyone ever again. I didn't want to open my heart. It hurts too much to be fooled and used." She swiped at a tear, her hand trembling. This was an end for the K-9 team—closure on a case they'd been working for seven months.

But it was a beginning for Violet.

The very start of her healing. The very first day of her freedom from Lance and his control and manipulation.

"I understand," he said, tilting her chin so she was looking into his eyes. "And I'm not pressuring you for anything. Okay? The way I see things, you've got a fresh start, and you should do whatever you want with it."

"Can I be honest?" she whispered as he put her hand over the shirt and had her hold it in place.

"You know you can."

"The only future I can imagine is one with you in it. A fresh start and a new beginning will only make sense if you're part of them. You mended my broken heart, Gabe, and helped me believe in a dream I had stopped hoping for."

"Funny you should say that," he said, helping her to her feet. "Because I was thinking the same thing about my life. I've been a bachelor for a long time. It's time for something different, but only if that something different includes you."

"Just me?" she asked, and he could see a hint of anxiety in her eyes. She was a package deal.

That was fine.

He was, too.

"Of course not," he assured her. "You and Ava. And Bear, and any other kids and dogs and people we gather into our home."

"Be careful what you say. I've got a big house with lots of rooms to fill," she said with a laugh.

"True, but home isn't a house. It's a place in our hearts where the people we love live. When I'm with you and Ava, I'm there. You're deep in the part of my heart where no one else has ever lived. I love you both more than I ever imagine possible."

"I love you, too," she murmured, taking his hand, her fingers curving through his. "So, how about we go get Ava, get my stitches and get to work on our future?"

"That's the best idea I've heard in a while," he said, giving her a tender kiss, his heart beating hard for her, for Ava and for the life they'd have together.

"Come on, Bear," he called as they headed for the stairwell.

The K-9 lumbered after them, tail high, head proud.

He'd done an excellent job protecting a person he cared about, and he knew it.

It had been a tough journey to capture Lance, but the payoff was worth it. The team had closed another case, a killer was off the streets, and Gabe had found something he had never imagined was waiting for him.

Family.

Love.

Home.

All the things he had dreamed of as a child.

All the things he had stopped hoping for.

They were his, and he would never stop being grateful.

# EPILOGUE

*Thanksgiving Day*

No pressure.

Just every one of the K-9 team members, their spouses or significant others, and their dogs, all gathered at the house for a feast and celebration that Violet was hosting.

She wasn't panicking. Not at all. Well, maybe a *little*. She wanted to do a good job. Not just for herself, but for Gabe.

Because his work comrades were his family.

She had grown to know and care about all of them while she was at the safe house. Now, two weeks later, after spending hours being interviewed about Lance and sharing the truth about their wildly toxic relationship, she felt she knew them all enough to know they wouldn't be judging her efforts here today.

Still, she wanted Gabe to be happy.

She supposed that was part of being in love with someone who loved her back. In fact, Gabe had helped her plan the whole event. He'd bought the turkeys, helped her choose a menu, and he had even offered to take care of Ava while she was getting the house ready. And while Violet certainly could have catered everything—could have hired people to do all the work—she knew her mother and father had felt that preparing for guests was part of extending hospitality.

So, other than asking the housekeeper to help make certain the turkey didn't overcook and the appetizers were ready on time, she'd done all the work herself.

Not an easy job with an infant around.

"But I don't mind, love. You're worth it," she told Ava, lifting her out of the baby swing and kissing her chubby cheek. "What do you think? Nice?" She spun around to face the table with the bright white china and flower centerpieces.

Ava cooed.

"I thought you would. The guests should be here soon. Hopefully Gabe will arrive first. I want to make sure he's happy with everything."

As if any of it mattered to him.

He would have been content to host the Thanksgiving feast at the office. In fact, he'd even suggested setting up tables in the conference room, because he hadn't wanted to put pressure on her. Gabe had been worried about how the investigation and the looming trial were affecting her.

Sometimes she woke up in a cold sweat, reliving those moments in the parking garage, hearing Lance's taunting words.

She'd always call Gabe, and he always answered.

He'd talk her through the bad moments, help her reason through her fear, and he'd encouraged her to focus on other things.

Violet had been turning her attention to her father's business and to helping the medical clinic. She had visited them two days ago and gone over plans to expand the facility.

She owed a lot of people, and she planned to repay them.

To that end, she had already offered Harrison funds for college. She was prepping a room over the garage—his own place where he could be free to come and go but still have all the modern conveniences he craved. He was incredibly grateful to her, thanking her repeatedly even though she'd told him there was no need, and she smiled when she recalled how touched he'd been when he learned she had invited his entire family to her Thanksgiving banquet.

Though she had no idea if all the Seavers were coming.

Eli still hadn't heard from Cole, and Bettina was getting sicker every day.

Life was fragile.

Time was fleeting.

Violet was sorry that a man she respected couldn't see that he was squandering both.

The doorbell rang, and she hurried to answer it, glancing out the peephole, her heart swelling when she saw Gabe and Bear.

If love were a photograph, it would be blue sky and white clouds, snow-capped mountains and a cabin in the woods. It would be this man and his dog, stepping into the foyer, Gabe in a suit, Bear wearing a bow tie.

They took her breath away.

"You two are looking very handsome," she said, standing on her toes to steal a kiss. She had never loved anyone the way she loved Gabe. Freely and without self-consciousness. This man had seen her at her worst, and he had never judged her for it. He knew her secrets and her scars, and he loved her anyway.

"And you both look beautiful," he murmured against her lips, his hands sliding down her back and settling at the curve of her waist. "Did you eat today?"

"You ask me that every time you see me," she said with a laugh, stepping back but not going far. She liked being close. Knowing that he was there. A best friend, a companion, a partner.

"Because you forget every time I don't see you," he chided.

"I had toast. Danielle made it for me while I was putting the turkeys in the oven." Danielle had been her parents' housekeeper for a decade before their deaths. She'd continued to work for Violet, but they were more friends than employee and employer.

"I guess the bribe to keep you fed paid off," he said.

"You did *not* pay her to get me to eat," she responded with a laugh, leading the way into the dining room, the scents of turkey and dressing filling the air.

"Okay, you're right. I didn't, but I thought about it. I worry for you, Violet. It's not just you you're nourishing." He touched her chin, kissed her forehead.

"I know. I'm doing better. It's just been so busy since

I've returned. Once the banquet is over, things will be calmer."

"And then you'll be prepping for some big Christmas shindig," he commented, his lips quirking in a half smile.

"Would you mind?"

"What makes you happy makes me happy," he responded. "Besides, I never had big gatherings when I was a kid. No family to gather, so this is nice." He walked to the table, lifting one of the placeholders she'd made. "This is amazing, Violet. You're amazing."

"I learned from my parents. They were fabulous hosts."

The doorbell rang, and her heart jumped.

"This is it! The first guest is here," she said, breathless with sudden anxiety and nerves. What if the turkey was dry? What if the veggies were tasteless? What if she gave everyone food poisoning?

"Honey, don't look like the world is about to end, okay? Everyone coming today cares about you. Not the food or the table or the flowers. Just you." Gabe kissed her deeply, passionately, wiping away all thoughts of dry turkey or dissatisfied guests.

Bear gave a quiet woof, and they broke apart, breathless staring into each other's eyes.

"If you were trying to distract me, it worked," she said.

"Good, because here comes Eli, and from what I hear, he can eat!"

"I have enough to feed a small army," she said, her cheeks warm with excitement and nerves.

The rest of the team arrived in pairs.

Hunter and Ariel with Juneau and Ariel's young husky, Sasha.

Poppy and her new husband, Lex, and his toddler son. They'd married right after the case wrapped up. Stormy loped in beside the happy newlyweds and made herself at home near the fireplace.

Maya and her significant other, David, arrived next, Sarge prancing in front of them, eager to play with his canine friends.

It wasn't long before the hearth room was filled with people—Helena and her fiancé, Everett, Luna standing protectively between them. Will and his beloved bride-to-be, Jasmine. Their dog, Scout, playing happily with Bear. Sean and Ivy West with their son, Grace lying near the little boy's feet. Brayden and his fiancée, Katie Kapowski. Katie was the assistant to Colonel Lorenza Gallo, who stood in the center of the room, petting Brayden's dog, Ella.

Violet's housekeeper, Danielle, was standing near the doorway, dressed in a beautiful pink sheath. Violet had wanted her to attend. Not just to help with the banquet. She was family, and Violet wanted her to know it.

"It looks like everyone is here," she called above the chatter. "The food is ready, so how about we go ahead and say grace? Then we'll go into the dining room to eat. We're doing buffet style. Danielle and I have already set everything out. Gabe has offered to pray."

Gabe's prayer was heartfelt and sincere, filled with thanksgiving for all God had brought to the team. The relationships. The friendships. The solved cases.

When he finished, the group moved to the dining room, gathering around tables laden with food.

"A feast fit for a family," Gabe whispered in Violet's ear.

"You haven't tasted it yet. You might say something different once you do," she responded playfully.

He, more than any other person she knew, could make her heart sing. Not with joy or passion. Although she felt those things, too. With contentment.

He was the right fit. The puzzle piece sliding right into place.

As everyone took their seats, the doorbell rang.

Surprised, Violet hurried to the door, Gabe right beside her.

She glanced through the peephole and was shocked to see the Seavers standing on her porch.

She fumbled with the doorknob, yanked the door open and dragged Dana Seaver into her arms, Ava sandwiched between them. "You came!" she cried.

"We wouldn't have missed it. I'm sorry we are late. It's a bit of a trip out here, and we had to hire a car to bring us." Dana glanced at her husband and son. "We also didn't have suits or dresses or anything. I mean, this is kind of a fancy place. If you'd rather us not come in…"

"Don't be silly! You're dressed perfectly." She stepped back, ushering them into her house and seeing it through their eyes. The gleaming floors and bright lights. The excess.

"I can take your coats," Gabe offered. "I'm Gabriel Runyon. Violet's friend."

He hung their coats in the closet, making small talk and doing everything he could to put them at ease.

Violet appreciated that about him.

The way he strove to make everyone feel accepted and valued. Watching him made her heart go soft and her eyes misty.

"Friend, huh?" Harrison whispered as they walked into the dining room.

"*Good* friend," she corrected.

He laughed.

The boisterous conversation quieted as the Seavers approached, everyone offering smiles and hellos to the newcomers.

"Everyone, these are—"

"Cole?" Eli jumped up, obviously surprised to see his godmother's son.

"That's right," Cole said. "And you're Eli. I'm surprised you remember me. It's been a while."

"A while? That's an understatement. How have you been?" Eli pulled the other man in for a bear hug.

"Good, but I hear things aren't as good for my mother. I don't want to steal any joy from the day, and I don't want the meal to be about us, but I wanted you to know, I've thought about what Violet said in her letter. She's right. Life is too precious to waste it on old hurt feelings and grudges. Mom made mistakes, but I did, too. After the meal, I'd like to go see her. If you wouldn't mind taking me."

"*Mind!* I'm going to text and tell her that you're coming. She's going to be overjoyed. Thank you, Cole! You don't know how much this means to her and to me."

"How is she? Violet said she's in hospice." Cole took the seat beside Eli.

"She is, but she's started an experimental treatment, and the tumors have shrunk. The doctor thinks we've bought some time."

"I'm grateful," Cole murmured. "I've been praying that I'd have time to make up for what we missed out on. My family and I are going to get a place close by. As Violet might have already told you, Harrison wants to attend college, and Dana doesn't want to be out off the grid and out of touch anymore. She's a good mom, and I won't make her give up her relationship with our child for my ideologies. Plus, ideologies change, and I've realized we've missed out on a lot."

"Cole, do you mean it," Dana asked, her eyes welling with tears. "We're moving back to town?"

"I mean it, sweetheart. I know you haven't been happy since Violet left, and you're going to be miserable with Harrison gone."

"But what about you? I don't want you to be unhappy," Dana said.

"How can I be if I'm with you?"

"Please, guys. No mushy stuff," Harrison griped, but it was obvious he was touched by his parents' love for one another.

Violet was, too.

How could she not be?

She nibbled on turkey and listened to the conversation swirl around her. A houseful of people who cared so much for each other, and she felt blessed and privileged to be part of their world.

The doorbell rang again as everyone gathered in the hearth room for coffee, tea and dessert.

Violet rose from her spot near the piano, but Gabe put his hand on her arm.

"I'll get it. You look tired."

"I'm content," she corrected, touching his knuckles. "But I'll let you get the door. Thank you."

He walked away, returning moments later with a large box in his hand.

The room went silent, everyone suddenly focused on Gabe.

"What's that?" Violet asked, getting up from her seat, worried that something was wrong. That maybe Lance had managed to send a bomb from prison.

"A surprise the team and I have been working on," he responded.

"Here, let me take the little one," Danielle said, hurrying over and lifting Ava from Violet's arms.

"Were you in on the surprise, too?" she asked.

Danielle grinned. "Of course!"

Gabe set the box on the floor.

It moved. Shimmying to the left and surprising a squeal out of Violet.

"Gabe! What have you done?" she asked, kneeling in front of the box.

"Open it and see," he said with a self-satisfied smile. "Just remember, we did discuss how much room you have here."

"I remember." She lifted the lid off, looked into the box and saw a fuzzy face peering up at her.

Brown and white. Floppy ears. Broad head.

A St. Bernard puppy!

"Gabe!" she cried. "She's perfect!"

"He. Bear wanted a brother," he said with a laugh, leaning down to kiss her head as she lifted the wiggling puppy from the box.

"*He* is perfect!" she said, laughing when the puppy licked her face. "What's his name?"

"Check his tag," he suggested, grinning broadly.

She reached under his soft fur, found the tag and leaned close to read it. "Will?" she asked. "I'd have thought you'd be a little more creative."

"Turn it over," he urged.

She flipped the tag, her heart skipping a beat when she saw the words engraved there: *you marry me?*

"Gabe!" She jumped to her feet, nearly knocking him over as she threw herself into his arms. "You know I will."

"When?" he asked, kissing her gently. Tenderly. As if they were the only two people in the room.

"You pick the day," she said, meaning every word. "I'll be there."

"Then I choose today."

The words hung in the silence, frozen in the beauty of the perfect gift and the perfect proposal given by a man who was absolutely perfect for her.

He was waiting for her response, his body relaxed, his jaw tense. It had taken a lot for him to do this. To put his love out there for everyone to see. He had been hurt as a child, yet somehow, he had still grown into a man who could give of himself. And right now he was putting it all on the line for her, risking the ultimate rejection. Not just in a private setting…but in front of the people he respected most.

She loved him even more for that.

"We need to find a pastor," she said, and she could see tension slide from his face, see joy fill his eyes.

"I have good news for you," Lorenza said. "I just happened to be ordained. I also just happened to have a marriage license with me."

"Just *happened* to, huh?" she said, looking into Gabe's eyes.

"Absolutely," he responded, taking her hands. "So, how about it? Want to get hitched?"

"Absolutely," she responded.

And so they did, standing in front of the people who cared about them both, repeating vows to one another, promising to cherish and to love, to honor and to respect.

The fire crackled in the hearth.

The puppy played at their feet, the canine members of the team watching with interest as Will rolled onto his back and snuffled Violet's shoes.

Snow began to fall, drifting outside the window in fat white flakes that would soon paint the world in wintry light. Danielle stood nearby, Ava in her arms, tears of happiness sliding down her cheeks.

Violet noticed those things, but more than everything else, she noticed the love in Gabe's eyes, the sincerity in his words. His hands were warm as he cupped her cheeks and kissed her to seal their vows.

Their friends cheered and Will howled, startled by

the cacophony of noise. Bear walked over and nudged him, urging him to play.

And Violet had never felt so content.

She had never felt so at home.

This was what she had longed for when she had met Lance. If she could go back and rewrite her story, she wouldn't edit out the chapter that had brought her to this place.

As hard as it had been, as challenging as she had found it, it had brought her Ava and Gabe, Bear and Will. It had brought her a network of friends she could count on for support. It had brought her passion and focus and a desire to help more, do more, contribute more.

It had renewed her faith, it had strengthened her and, most of all, it had brought her home.

To this place in Gabe's arms.

"I love you, sweetheart," he whispered against her lips. "Always and forever."

"I love you, too," she replied, sliding her hands through his hair and kissing him deeply while the fire crackled and the snow fell and the people they loved cheered them on.

\* \* \* \* \*

# Get 3 FREE REWARDS!

## We'll send you 2 FREE Books plus a FREE Mystery Gift.

**FREE** Value Over **$20**

Both the **Love Inspired®** and **Love Inspired® Suspense** series feature compelling novels filled with inspirational romance, faith, forgiveness and hope.

**YES!** Please send me 2 FREE novels from the Love Inspired or Love Inspired Suspense series and my FREE gift (gift is worth about $10 retail). After receiving them, if I don't wish to receive any more books, I can return the shipping statement marked "cancel." If I don't cancel, I will receive 6 brand-new Love Inspired Larger-Print books or Love Inspired Suspense Larger-Print books every month and be billed just $6.49 each in the U.S. or $6.74 each in Canada. That is a savings of at least 16% off the cover price. It's quite a bargain! Shipping and handling is just 50¢ per book in the U.S. and $1.25 per book in Canada.* I understand that accepting the 2 free books and gift places me under no obligation to buy anything. I can always return a shipment and cancel at any time by calling the number below. The free books and gift are mine to keep no matter what I decide.

Choose one:   ☐ **Love Inspired**       ☐ **Love Inspired**        ☐ **Or Try Both!**
                  **Larger-Print**         **Suspense**                (122/322 & 107/307
                  (122/322 BPA GRPA)       **Larger-Print**            BPA GRRP)
                                           (107/307 BPA GRPA)

Name (please print)

Address                                                                                    Apt. #

City                                    State/Province                          Zip/Postal Code

**Email:** Please check this box ☐ if you would like to receive newsletters and promotional emails from Harlequin Enterprises ULC and its affiliates. You can unsubscribe anytime.

### Mail to the **Harlequin Reader Service:**
**IN U.S.A.:** P.O. Box 1341, Buffalo, NY 14240-8531
**IN CANADA:** P.O. Box 603, Fort Erie, Ontario L2A 5X3

Want to try 2 free books from another series! Call 1-800-873-8635 or visit www.ReaderService.com.

*Terms and prices subject to change without notice. Prices do not include sales taxes, which will be charged (if applicable) based on your state or country of residence. Canadian residents will be charged applicable taxes. Offer not valid in Quebec. This offer is limited to one order per household. Books received may not be as shown. Not valid for current subscribers to the Love Inspired or Love Inspired Suspense series. All orders subject to approval. Credit or debit balances in a customer's account(s) may be offset by any other outstanding balance owed by or to the customer. Please allow 4 to 6 weeks for delivery. Offer available while quantities last.

**Your Privacy**—Your information is being collected by Harlequin Enterprises ULC, operating as Harlequin Reader Service. For a complete summary of the information we collect, how we use this information and to whom it is disclosed, please visit our privacy notice located at corporate.harlequin.com/privacy-notice. From time to time we may also exchange your personal information with reputable third parties. If you wish to opt out of this sharing of your personal information, please visit readerservice.com/consumerschoice or call 1-800-873-8635. **Notice to California Residents**—Under California law, you have specific rights to control and access your data. For more information on these rights and how to exercise them, visit corporate.harlequin.com/california-privacy.

LIRLIS23

# Get 3 FREE REWARDS!

## We'll send you 2 FREE Books plus a FREE Mystery Gift.

Both the **Harlequin®  Special Edition** and **Harlequin®  Heartwarming™** series feature compelling novels filled with stories of love and strength where the bonds of friendship, family and community unite.

**YES!** Please send me 2 FREE novels from the Harlequin Special Edition or Harlequin Heartwarming series and my FREE Gift (gift is worth about $10 retail). After receiving them, if I don't wish to receive any more books, I can return the shipping statement marked "cancel." If I don't cancel, I will receive 6 brand-new Harlequin Special Edition books every month and be billed just $5.49 each in the U.S. or $6.24 each in Canada, a savings of at least 12% off the cover price, or 4 brand-new Harlequin Heartwarming Larger-Print books every month and be billed just $6.24 each in the U.S. or $6.74 each in Canada, a savings of at least 19% off the cover price. It's quite a bargain! Shipping and handling is just 50¢ per book in the U.S. and $1.25 per book in Canada.* I understand that accepting the 2 free books and gift places me under no obligation to buy anything. I can always return a shipment and cancel at any time by calling the number below. The free books and gift are mine to keep no matter what I decide.

Choose one:  ☐ **Harlequin Special Edition** (235/335 BPA GRMK)   ☐ **Harlequin Heartwarming Larger-Print** (161/361 BPA GRMK)   ☐ **Or Try Both!** (235/335 & 161/361 BPA GRPZ)

Name (please print)

Address _____ Apt. #

City _____ State/Province _____ Zip/Postal Code

**Email:** Please check this box ☐ if you would like to receive newsletters and promotional emails from Harlequin Enterprises ULC and its affiliates. You can unsubscribe anytime.

### Mail to the Harlequin Reader Service:
**IN U.S.A.:** P.O. Box 1341, Buffalo, NY 14240-8531
**IN CANADA:** P.O. Box 603, Fort Erie, Ontario L2A 5X3

Want to try 2 free books from another series? Call 1-800-873-8635 or visit www.ReaderService.com.

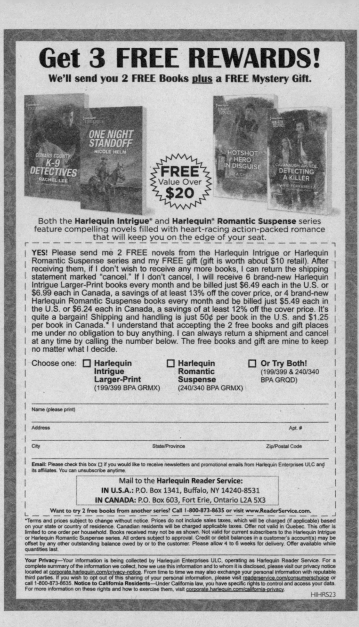